Saving Caravaggio

Neil Griffiths

W F HOWES LTD

This large print edition published in 2007 by
W F Howes Ltd
Unit 4, Rearsby Business Park, Gaddesby Lane,
Rearsby, Leicester LE7 4YH

1 3 5 7 9 10 8 6 4 2

First published in the United Kingdom in 2006
by Penguin Group

Copyright © Neil Griffiths, 2006

The right of Neil Griffiths to be identified as
the author of this work has been asserted by him
in accordance with the Copyright, Designs and
Patents Act, 1988.

A CIP catalogue record for this book is available
from the British Library

ISBN 978 1 40740 690 9

Typeset by Palimpsest Book Production Limited,
Grangemouth, Stirlingshire
Printed and bound in Great Britain
by Antony Rowe Ltd, Chippenham, Wilts.

For Bridget

But he remembered the time when he
    stood alone,
When to be and delight to be seemed
    one,
Before the colors deepened and grew
    small.

Wallace Stevens
(from 'Anglais Mort à Florence')

CONTENTS

PART ONE

CALABRIA AND 'NDRANGHETA

It is produced by way of proof. Rolled out from the old man's lap with a strong snap of the wrists, over his knees and across the ground to my feet. A wave of dust rises up as the last edge flaps flat. I don't move, react. I concentrate on hiding my shock, my disbelief. I look directly at the old man. The two young men to my right, one standing by the door of the small house, one leaning against the new BMW, shift in my peripheral vision. They are restive. It's hot. The sun is at its highest point in the sky. We are sitting in the shade of a tall, still cypress. We have drinks. Whisky. Johnnie Walker Blue Label. The old man is speaking. He's explaining to me that what I want might be like this. He waves an old brown hand over the painting. The image lies over his lap and legs like a vast heavy blanket, splaying out over the ground. The image is dark, cracked. There are webs of cracks and larger fissures. The edges are splitting, frayed and dirty. There is no sheen. Perhaps it has been produced by way of proof many times. But I don't think so – not this.

Every time the old man speaks I have to attune

myself to the dialect, recognize the Italian hidden there; I understand about one-third of what is being said. It has been like this all over Calabria. Everything I say is understood. Even the old man has complimented me on my Italian.

'I am only interested in the Turner,' I say. 'The Turner painting.'

The old man doesn't respond. I see a subtle and swift roll of his eyes. My declaration was too bold; I have been unsettled by the example.

I scan the dark image. I know it very well. I have studied the few reproductions many times: the central light patches are forehead, shoulder, folds of fabric, a face; the darks are the saints; the white section falling over the side of the old man's chair is an angel. I know that the words trailing from the banner in the angel's hand are '*GLORIA IN ECCELSIS DEO*', although only restoration will make them legible again. I also know that if I return with this painting, this image will make the front page of every quality newspaper in the world. I will make the front page. There will be some national coverage if I bring back the Turner, but it will last a day. Speculation over the 'ransom' paid and to whom. There will be little about the painting. There will be nothing about my operation: two and a half months on mainland Europe: Vienna, Budapest, Naples. Now Calabria. Only one week and a single weekend at home.

I press my thumb and forefinger into the bridge of my nose. I am hot, tired. It has been a long

4

morning. An interminable drive through the dry hills in the back seat of the BMW, air con off, windows down. For the last hour I was wearing a blindfold. I need to eat something. I feel my mind slowing down. The mental fatigue induced by heat and the proximity of violent men is particular. It is dangerous. I look across to the younger men. The one by the house smokes; the other is staring down into the shiny black surface of the car. He spots a blemish, rubs at it firmly with his sleeve.

I ask for something to eat. Smile. I explain I can't negotiate on an empty stomach. The old man nods and calls out. A woman appears from the small house. She is much younger than the old man, but could be the mother of the other two. She is dressed in black – black knee-length skirt, black blouse, black shoes. Her bare arms, legs, her face are a deep brown. Food is ordered. The old man then says something to the younger men and clicks his fingers. They move quickly but without haste. A table is found and placed in the shade of the tall, still cypress. Two more chairs are found.

The old man begins to roll up the Caravaggio. Rolling hands, twisting wrists, gently pressing – an automatic, absent movement. I watch as the faded image disappears, the dry paint ground against itself with the rolling movements of the old man's brown hands. When it's done, it is no more than a frayed old rug. He passes it into the arms of one of the younger men, who then takes

5

it into the house. I can tell it has instantly disappeared from the mind of the old man. I help arrange our chairs around the table. The old man pours us all some Blue Label. Nothing is said. I don't sense any hostility from these men. We are like four strangers forced to sit at a small square table in a small hill-village café, content not to talk. We are silent throughout our food. *Spaghetti e melanzane*, with a little chilli. When we are finished the old man calls for another bottle of whisky. It is Blue Label again. Over a hundred pounds a bottle in the UK.

Negotiations begin after *caffè*. The younger men are permitted to stay seated. They push their chairs back from the table, cross their legs and smoke. The old man says he doesn't have the painting but can get it. He'll need the money. I say I don't have the money but can get it. This irritates him. He shouts something I don't understand. The younger men don't react. I have been here before. I fix my eyes on the hazy outline of another small hill village across the valley; it appears identical to the one I've been brought to: twenty or so little white houses, a tiny church. I know that the old man wants the money first and then he will decide whether to hand over the painting. They all want this: to take the money and then to pretend the return of the painting is an act of largesse or a favour. If you're lucky. A million euros ransom is on offer for this painting. Why not just take it? Then sell the painting on. America. Japan.

The old man calms down. He didn't expect me to capitulate easily; he sensed the moment I climbed out of the car that I wasn't an amateur. He smiles.

'When will you have the money?'

'Within twenty-four hours of asking for it.'

He says he'd be happier with two million euros; it is worth ten.

I look across the valley. The hill is dry and rocky. The ground is dry and yellow. The tall cypresses are black and green. A window glints.

I explain that the institution to which the painting belongs will not raise their price. The old man rolls his eyes – the painting belongs to him. It is my turn to smile. Yes. Of course.

The old man, palms pressed on the table, pushes himself to his feet. He says something to one of the younger men, who wearily stands, sleepy from the spaghetti, whisky, heat. I do not understand what is being said; they have returned to deep Calabrian. When they are finished the old man turns and studies me one last time – a final moment for his instinct to make a judgement: does he want to do business with me? I stand, allow myself to be scrutinized. I know I will not meet the old man again. From now on everything will be done by his soldiers – sanctioned by him, based on this last moment, what his instinct is telling him now. I know if I return here tomorrow, the old man will be gone. It has taken almost a month to arrange this meeting and it has lasted two hours.

The BMW is started, the engine revved, the wheels pointlessly spun. A cloud of dust covers the rear of the car. It is time to leave. There will be no handshake or kiss. On this recovery I have made it clear that I am working for the other side. Clear I'm a copper. The institution insisted that I must be seen to be legitimate throughout. No pretence of criminality. There is to be no negotiation. The money is a reward, not a ransom.

I step out from the shade of the tall, still cypress. The old man gives me one last look and then turns and goes into the small house. I climb into the back of the car. I am handed the blindfold. I stretch the elastic over my head, position the eyepatches.

The next couple of days are always the most dangerous. Negotiating the exchange. A location. The money. The handing over of the painting – in this instance a large oil, probably ripped out of its frame, rolled up, maybe even folded. But that's not what must concern me. I need a feel for the internal stability of the organization – is anyone looking to sabotage the deal? Does anyone gain if the deal goes wrong? Because that's when I'm vulnerable: when the emphasis shifts and it's no longer just business. But then, these days it's almost always just business. The wars have dried up. Yet the possibility remains. Especially when the *capo di tutti capi* is as old as this old man.

I don't sense instability. And this is a small deal. There is little to gain by sabotaging it. But the

Caravaggio, that's different. The world's most famous stolen painting. Cut out of its frame from above an altar in a chapel in Palermo in 1969, and for the last thirty years moved around the families of organized crime as a multi-million-dollar marker, a guarantee for anything, from drugs deals to political assassination. Or so the myth goes. Like most policemen in the art world, I was certain it had been destroyed. Like every Caravaggio lover, I hoped it had not.

The car is filled with hot summer air, baked dry, full of sharp fragrances, heavy on the skin. I know that when I get back to the hotel I must call it in. I must call in what is the biggest news in the art world for many years.

FLORENCE AND THE ART MAFIA

1

'It's *my* signature, *my* photo; it's just out of date by a week. Which means it's still valid. You don't even need a passport between here and France.'

'What is the nature of your business here in Italy?'

I pause. I'm here to research a book.

'I'm here to research a book.'

'A writer?'

'Yes.'

The passport officer looks at me, at the photo in the passport, and then seems to mull over whether he believes the combination of this real man before him and the image of him adds up to a writer. I straighten my shoulders – I want to be convincing. I want – my cover aside – to be convincing as a writer.

'In Bologna?'

'Florence.'

The passport officer nods. It is typical. Most travellers flying into Marconi airport go on to Florence.

'How long will you be staying in Florence?'

This is a question I cannot answer. I hope to be in Italy for a week only, but last year my longest unbroken stay was twelve weeks.

'I don't think I need to answer that. EU regulations allow me freedom of movement.'

The question is repeated.

I look past the passport officer into Bologna Airport. It is almost empty. A few backpackers sitting on their rucksacks, businessmen on mobiles, solo holiday types looking like amateur art historians: squarely dressed (more for mountains than museums), *Blue Guides* and Uffizi carrier bags with Botticelli's *Venus* printed on to the white plastic.

I look down at myself. At my wedding clothes. From a marriage not even a year old. Paid for by my wife. My wedding present. A dark-grey wool suit, white Egyptian cotton shirt, dark-blue tie, brown shoes, overcoat. All obscenely expensive. But she insisted. A man in good clothes, she had said enigmatically.

The passport officer should know that few writers can afford to dress so well. But then I try not to cast myself to type, not for this kind of work. Types invite small talk; the ease of being with a type invites it. I prefer to unsettle; it forces people to talk about themselves. Fill the dead space with their fears. It is a trick to human disclosure. So if I am going to be a writer, then wear stylish clothes, devoid of eccentricity, of the bohemian.

11

Within a month of my wedding, two weeks after our honeymoon in Florence, I was given the Turner assignment. I sat in our big house – Sarah's big house – waiting for her to come home, my packed bag the first thing she would see. She said nothing, slipped past me, a vapour to my reaching hands. I was gone for two and a half months.

The passport officer studies me. The quality of my clothes is not lost on him; I am after all in Italy. His gaze lingers on my brown shoes, smooth and sleek – a classic design almost imperceptibly modernized with a longer shape, blunter toe.

On our wedding day Sarah said I looked dashing. On the steps of the Chelsea Register Office on the King's Road we made a handsome couple. Tourists wondered which famous people we might be. My guess is that our marriage will last about as long as the standard famous marriage. Less long. This morning when I kissed her goodbye she didn't stir. Her sleep deflecting love – resisting it. I was gone from her thoughts at midnight when she switched off her bedside light.

'Can you step this way, please?'

I am taken into a small office. There is an Alitalia poster, a 737 banking in the sky. A plain desk. An old computer. Another passport officer sits behind the desk, scrolling through lists of numbers on the computer screen. He is older, forty, a little overweight. There is a packet of cigarettes in the breast pocket of his shirt. He doesn't stand when we enter.

The passport is handed to him and the situation is described by the first officer: it is out of date (by a week, I interject); I am a writer; I am going to Florence; I refuse to say how long I plan to stay in Italy.

The older man looks at me. '*Parla Italiano?*'

'*Si.*'

'How long do you plan to stay in Italy?'

'Two weeks.'

The two officers look at one another. 'Two weeks?' the older one repeats for confirmation.

'Yes. That is all.'

He scrolls through a page on his screen and enters my passport details.

'Where are you staying?' the original officer asks me.

'A *pensione*. In Via Dante.' I have no desire to be obstructive.

'Via Dante' is repeated by the younger officer; the older logs it. He then flicks through my passport. With a second flick, he displays my stamps and visas to his colleague: USA, Russia, India, Japan, Argentina.

'You are a businessman?'

'No, a writer, like he said.'

'Travel writer?'

I calculate agreeing with this might end the interview more swiftly than explaining that I write about art, the history of art, although in Italy this might not be so unusual. Still, I nod. 'Yes, a travel writer.'

My passport is handed back to me.

'You need a new passport.'

The younger officer shows me out and points towards the exit and luggage reclaim.

The bus stop for Bologna Station is directly outside the airport. A bus is waiting. I heave my two bags into the luggage rack, pay the driver and sit down. My mobile rings. I flip it open and look at the caller ID. Work. I press *accept* and say evenly, 'Do we have a name yet? Tell me they've given us a name . . .'

The reception is good, clear – next-room clear. Jim, my boss, tells me: no, Rome is still being difficult, evasive, repeating that the reason they invited in outsiders was because they didn't want anyone local. Or anyone Italian for that matter. I reiterate: a key contact in Florence is the condition of my participation; I don't care who it is. I am not going to be isolated. Not in Italy.

'They say they're working on it.'

'I'll call back at midday. If we don't have a name by then . . .' I pause. I don't know what to say, what to threaten – the ultimatum to give. He doesn't know that I am here for another reason. I should tell him. Confess now. I only agreed to the assignment to be back in Italy, to be closer to the Caravaggio. And therefore if we don't have a name, I am going after it. But I can't. It would involve too much explanation. Why didn't I call it in at the time?

Jim is irritated by my threat of an ultimatum, 'What if we don't have a name by then, Danny?'

14

'I'm coming home.' I flip my mobile closed, stare out of the window at a damp, wide street; spots of rain hit the glass.

I am a Caravaggio expert, but before that a Caravaggio lover. I am a cop third. Or maybe cop isn't that high, although there is little else to compete. Husband, perhaps. Certainly there is little else after that. Narrow interests make me a focused type. Concentrated. Serious. Some would say obsessive. I would say I have passions. I *once* had passions. Meaning I am not what I once was. Despite being the best at what I do.

When I mentioned the Caravaggio it was only to ask what we would do if I saw it. Jim was categorical. 'We inform Rome. A firm-enough sighting and we inform Rome. They've had the same people on it since it was stolen. It's their grail, not ours.'

People have short memories. Forgetting I'm the only Ph.D. in the department. Subject: Caravaggio. So you're wrong. It's my grail as well.

The main drag from the airport to the station is lined with small shops below flat-roofed concrete apartment blocks. Above, the sky is a flat unbroken grey panel. I wrap myself up in my overcoat.

The bus turns right into Bologna Station. The other passengers ready themselves before the bus pulls up. I stay seated, looking out of the window. I wait until I hear the electronic doors open before moving. Last off, after two silent couples – the

15

early flight having dulled their desire for talk – I haul my bags out of the rack and on to the street. Filled with as many books as clothes – the pretence of research? – they seem to be heavier each time I lift them. I drag them into the station. I buy a first-class ticket to Santa Maria Novella Station, Florence. I look up at the arrivals/departures boards. The train will probably be coming from Milan, on its way to Rome or Naples, maybe even Palermo. The next train is due in seventeen minutes. At the station café I order an espresso and croissant. I knock back the espresso and pull apart the croissant; it is both dry and doughy. I can only manage half before it is time to make my slow way to the platform.

Rain drips from the wrought-iron canopy, creating a dark damp skirting along the platform's edge. The train is on time. A guard assists me with my bags. They are tucked in the lower luggage rack by the door. The guard rearranges other suitcases so this can be done. I say many '*grazie mille*'s.

The carriage is full of Italian executives, mostly male, mostly middle-aged, all wearing conservative, beautifully tailored, dark-grey suits, white shirts and dark ties. All their accessories – spectacles, briefcases, wallets, pens – are equally understated. Everyone is unerringly stylish.

I take off my overcoat and sit down at a window seat. I place my ticket on the table in front of me, sit back and close my eyes. The train moves off smoothly, noiselessly. I picture Sarah, herself on her way to work. Taking a bus up Sloane Street, through Knightsbridge, towards Piccadilly, always sitting on the bottom deck, reading in the half-light of a dull January sunrise. I know she's not thinking of me. Even my absence has been forgotten. I am now doubly gone.

2

It is snowing. The sloped lawns of Santa Maria Novella Station are covered in a thick layer of undisturbed white snow; the roof of the church of Santa Maria Novella is white-capped; the snow on the streets is scored by cars and scooters into a complex pattern of circles and arcs. Florence looks more like Moscow or St Petersburg. And it is cold, the sharp wind off the Apennines taking the temperature down to below freezing. The air has a crisp edge, burning my cheeks; it cuts through my suit, my shirt, my skin. I drop my bags to the ground, swing on my over-coat and button it up, flipping the collar around my ears. I pull my gloves from the side pockets and slip them over my cold hands.

The plan was to walk to Via Dante, but I wasn't expecting the icy wind, the snow, the razor cold. At the taxi rank I stand behind chatty businessmen from Torino, Milano, Roma – somewhere. When a cab pulls up I shove my bags on to the back seat and push myself in next to them.

'Via Dante, *per favore.*'

The driver nods and pulls out of the station. He says something about the snow and I nod and say something about the cold. The thought makes me shiver and I nestle down into my buttoned-up coat, chin disappearing.

The cab is instantly in the heart of Florence and I look out of the window and into the sky. I am searching for the *duomo* above the high walls. Sighting the *duomo* signals my real arrival in Florence. To me, Florence, or rather the city understood as *Florence*, only truly exists after the *duomo* has been revealed at its heart. I do not doubt that without the *duomo* Florence would still be beautiful, but it would perhaps not be as wondrous. It would lack splendour.

I am a little shocked when it comes into view in the rear window of the taxi, my neck strained, head back, eyes high in their sockets. The terracotta tiles have vanished, covered with immaculate snow, the dome itself is a seamless curve upward from the white marble of the walls to the white marble of the lantern at its peak. It is a mountain in the centre of the city. Its new beauty almost makes me swoon.

'Wow,' I whisper.

The driver, with keen ears, glances into his mirror.

I explain, 'The *duomo*. It's a mountain.'

The driver looks up out of the windscreen as if searching for an object in the sky. '*Sì, bello.*'

We drive beyond the *duomo* and turn right into Via del Proconsolo. We are making good time due to the lightness of the traffic, which I suspect has something to do with the unexpected weather and the fact that we are not stopping continuously for groups of sightseers to cross the roads. The city seems empty and a little ghostly with none of the stubborn tourist crowds on every corner.

The cab swings tightly into Via Dante Alighieri, squeezing past scaffolding fixed to a small chapel, which with its thick covering of snow looks like the stable in a Nativity scene. We pull up outside number fourteen. I drag my bags on to the pavement. The building is sixteenth century, flat, unornamented, with clean pale walls and dark-green shutters. The ground floor is an American Express office. I am staying in the apartment of Professor Claudio Bramante, arranged for me by a curator at the National Gallery. I open the heavy mahogany doors and haul myself and my bags up the steep stone steps. My footfalls echo. There is a faint smell of disinfectant. I pass a hotel entrance on the second floor, a large wood door with a small grille in the centre. Floors three and four are apartments. My bags seem to gain weight at the bottom of each set of steps. My arms and shoulders ache by the time I reach the top. The big key is weightless in my hand. I push my bags into the apartment with my feet. Before I have the chance to appreciate the place – its vaulted ceilings, exposed wood and stone work, the terracotta floors – I am hit by the ambient temperature, at least five degrees colder than outside. I go straight to the small kitchenette and turn on all the gas rings. The air crackles in the sudden heat. I then check to see if a window has been left open. The view over the rooftops of Florence includes the very top of the *duomo* – the lantern – almost invisible against the white sky. The room itself is divided into two sections. The far end, by the door, is the dining area: a glass table and six chairs. More centrally and adjacent to the kitchenette there are two brown leather armchairs, worn, shiny and cracked from years of use. Between them is a coffee table with a pile of art and fashion magazines. Against one wall is a tall wide glass-fronted bookcase filled mostly with books, some alcohol and one ornament – an award of some kind. Next to the kitchen there is a small bookcase filled with paperbacks. It would be cosy if it wasn't so cold. In the bedroom there is a large double bed, tightly made up, a wardrobe and a dresser with grooming products neatly arranged on top. There is a butane-gas heater in the corner. I wheel the heater into the sitting room, open the back and turn on the valve and press the ignition button until the gas catches alight; I keep it pressed while watching the curtain of flame cross the grille at the front. I leave the cooker's gas rings burning. I drop into one of the armchairs. I am still in my overcoat and gloves. I look at my watch. Ten a.m. Nothing to do until twelve, at which point a decision has to be made. I watch my breath ease out of my mouth like puffs of glitter and then close my eyes. I want to sleep and clear my head, of Sarah, the Caravaggio – obsessive thoughts.

I can't sleep. My eyes refuse to shut, pulling open the moment they close. I push myself against the right side of the chair, dig my hand into the pocket of my overcoat and pull out my phone. I flip open the front, press and hold down *2*. 'SARAH' appears on the screen. I hold the phone to my ear. The air around me is a little warmer but I suspect the rest of the room is still icy cold.

'Sarah Delaney.' Her voice is low, a little husky.

'It's me . . .' I had wanted to sound more upbeat.

'Hello, you . . .'

I can't tell whether this is her attempt at being light, letting me know she doesn't want to argue or prolong the coolness, or whether there are people in the room with her.

'Can you talk?'

'Can you?'

'Florence is freezing; everything's covered in snow . . .' Small talk. Pointless.

'It must be beautiful.' Her delivery is flat, without encouragement.

I don't respond immediately; stare at the orange curtain of flame rustling across the heater grille. 'Look, Sarah, I really didn't want to come – you know that.'

She is silent. It is clear I want forgiveness, understanding, my actions supported. I know she knows. Her unwillingness to help me out maddens me.

'Sarah?'

'Yes . . .'

'I said I didn't want to come . . .'

'But you are there.'

'It's my work. I really think we need to talk.'

'I don't see how we can talk if you're never here.'

'That's unfair. When I am at home you won't talk . . .'

Silence again.

'Sarah?'

'I'm here.'

'Please . . . this is making us both very unhappy.'

'Look, Daniel, I'm at work. We've got an important auction tomorrow.'

It is my turn to be silent. She doesn't intrude on it.

'I don't know what to say . . .' There is no response and I'm forced to say her name for the third time. 'Sarah?'

'I'll call you when I get home tonight.'

'Thank you.'

The line goes dead, and I flip my phone shut. I try to close my eyes again. I do not see darkness, but Sarah, a bright thing, smiling at me, a great catch for the son of a market trader. But before I knew that – the *summa* that makes the catch: position, influence, money – I saw her striding towards me along the entrance hall of Langdon's auction house, long and slender in charcoal-grey and black, with cropped black hair and blue, blue eyes. She could so easily have passed by. Momentum was with her. But she stopped. Stopped and said in that low, husky voice, 'I like the look of you.'

Next we were having dinner, me refusing to talk about my work, thinking she'd never go for a copper; her straight from Oxford into Langdon's, her area of expertise Modern British. 'What's that? Bangers and pesto mash?' It gave a lot away, I assumed. Just isn't the kind of joke anyone but the working class make – not with the long, tight 'a' sounds. But she laughed, and laid her hand over mine and said again, 'I like the look of you,' adding a wry smile to her now wine-rich voice. What did she see, I wonder. The residuum of lost passions?

I wake up sweating, buried in my overcoat, the heater burning the air around me. I push myself up from the chair, turn off the gas rings and shunt the heater into the corner of the room. I look out of the window. A light snow is dusting white all the red terracotta tiles missed by the last fall. It is twelve o'clock. I have been asleep for two hours. I stare across the room at my unpacked bags. No point unpacking until I speak to Jim. I look out

24

of the window again, shove my hands into my pockets, gripping my mobile. I'm not sure what I want to hear when I call. No point of contact and I have threatened to go home. To Sarah. Where I need to be.

On the glass-topped dining table I open the heavier of my two bags and pull wide the sides – a laptop, jeans, T-shirts and three large art books, all with the same name on the cover. The same single name. One in silver, a bold sharp modern font; one in white, at a slant, the signature of easy penmanship; the last – gold – Latinate, grand. The same name spelling so many things: genius, rogue, iconoclast, murderer, psychologist, desperado, enigma. I must accept that he is why I am in Italy. He is my real mission.

I take the books over to the armchair and sit down. But what about my actual assignment? Investigating whether or not there is any truth in the rumour that someone at the Uffizi is being blackmailed to help with a robbery. A rumour! Proving a negative is how Jim sold it. Should be easy. Quick. A political job then – covering Rome if anything should happen. We had Europe's best man on it. Posing as an art writer, an art expert, writing about Michelangelo's *Doni Tondo*. It's not even my area, not really – not in a world of true experts, where glittering careers are made by the interpretation of a single piece of correspondence, a controversial date, proving true or false the claims of other experts. I do have some form; I'm not all cop. Type my name into a search engine and the first entry is always: 'Daniel Wright. Caravaggio: Every World Needs Its Desperado. University of Newcastle. High Resolution Images.' Enough to satisfy the Mafia or some other criminal outfit of my expertise. But the Uffizi, staffed by some of the world's top art historians? I'll need better credentials than a postgraduate thesis if people are to open up to me, discuss the gallery, their colleagues, if they are to confide. For that I will need their trust, which first means respect, which means being regarded as superior to all the other art historians in Florence on research projects looking for largesse from the Uffizi.

I flip up the front of my phone and press *3*: work. It rings ten times before Jim picks up.

'It's Danny. What have you got?'

'They say they're working on it. There's a prosecutor. If they're happy, he's your point of contact. But it won't be today.'

I cast my eyes around the room. 'This could take days.'

'Dan, give it another twenty-four hours. Until this time tomorrow.'

'Why?'

'You know why. Because our work becomes a million times more difficult if we piss off the Italians. They're asking for this favour.'

'It's a waste of my time.' I pause. Another opportunity. Trade: OK, I'll sit around, I'll wait, but in

26

the meantime I want to make some enquiries. Last year . . .

Jim ends the call. 'Relax, Danny. You're wound so tight these days.'

I flick open the top book at a full-page colour plate of *Judith Beheading Holofernes*. One of my favourite paintings. The exquisite brutality. Holofernes' sexually sated weight contorted on the bed. Judith's beauty concentrated in her eyes, the slight squint giving her whole face focus, continued determination midway through the act. I love the wrist of her hand gripping Holofernes' hair – the firm twist of it, turning his head away from his neck, exposing and tightening his flesh so that her sword will slice quickly through. A beheading is more than a killing.

I rest my phone against my cheek. Am I wound tight? I must be. My breathing is shallow, fast; my neck and shoulders ache. Maybe I should relax. Relax and enjoy Florence as tourist, not art cop, or whatever it is that I am, or am pretending to be. Relax as an art lover with time on his hands.

I stand and lay all three books on the glass table and open them at their plates of *The Nativity with Saints Lawrence and Francis*, reading below each picture, '1609, oil on canvas, 105 ½ x 77 ½ in (268 x 197 cm). Oratory of the Campagnia di San Lorenzo (formerly; stolen 1969)'. There is no really acceptable reproduction. Not by modern standards. There is a haze over the pictures, as if its theft is somehow present even in the

27

reproductions, giving it a veil of mystery, an uncertain existence, a hint of its dark life since it was stolen. I focus on the largest version, a full-colour page. A superficial glance will suggest little more than a Nativity scene. Almost by numbers. Heavy on piety, light on inspiration. One of the less exceptional commissions on his flight from Rome, from arrest for murder. There are a couple of recognizable Caravaggio models in there, but otherwise there is little to distinguish it from other devout works by other painters of the time, even of the near past. However, on closer examination there is more. First, the exact moment it is depicting: Mary is cradling her stomach, having just given birth to Christ. There are no precedents for representing the Madonna at this supreme moment. And then there is the dandy in the foreground, the Sower of Doubts, slyly nudging the infant with his shoe: a moment of disrespect, of suspicion. Another radical touch, revealing much about the complexity of Caravaggio's theological thinking. There are the contemporaneous clothes – Italian 1600s, making it more resonant for the contemporary viewer, but perhaps distancing it for the modern audience. Yet for me it is the figure of Joseph which most intrigues. Placed on the periphery of the picture, he leans on a staff, and rather than looking at his child, he is chatting to the dandy. He is on the outside of the supreme moment, patiently waiting to be told when his role as the father of Christ will begin. It seems that up until that point he is content to be just an ordinary old man, talkative, easily distracted – sidelined. The painting may not be representative of Caravaggio's most striking work – the formal austerity, the darkest palette – but his narrative and psychological genius are still present. I am not moved by the painting, yet its existence thrills me beyond any other painting in the world. What if I really did go after it alone? What if I brought it back? Would I become the hero of the art establishment? A world that shunned me fifteen years ago, because, as they made clear: working-class boys just don't 'rise very far' in this world. Of course they didn't actually say 'working-class boys' but 'candidates without the appropriate background' is candid enough. Little has changed. Even now as a policeman and central to the recovery of many great paintings, I am regarded as little more than a bit of muscle needed to make the exchange, a cog in the machine paid for by the British taxpayer. They don't care that I recover and return more paintings per year than any other law-enforcement officer in the world. They are art administrators, keepers of the nation's heritage, a handful of elevated individuals occupying a handful of important posts, not interchangeable coppers just waiting for their pensions at fifty so they can lay a new patio, play some golf or do whatever it is that retired policemen do.

I stare at the painting, remembering the cracks

across it, the peeling and breaking of the surface, the old man's dark hands as he rolled it up. I close each book. Return to the window. The snow is still falling, deepening on the rooftops. I sense its weight, its compact coldness, its brightness, a hundred million silver-white glints revealing its delicate structure. I open the window and draw a finger across the snow on the outside sill. It is inches deep, dry for a moment, and then, after my body heat seeps in, a wrap of moisture adhering to my skin. Then the sudden cold. A freezing moment. Physics at play. My atomic structure, less delicate than snow, but also less extreme, letting the cold in. I shut the window. Feeling numbness at the end of my nose, a patch on each cheek.

I haven't eaten properly since last night. I feel empty rather than hungry. I check the cupboards in the small kitchenette. Only dried pasta, tins of fruit, instant coffee. The small fridge is empty. I mentally map the area beyond Via Dante. There is a small restaurant nearby that Sarah and I used as our regular for lunch on our honeymoon. Slightly irritating young male staff looking to pick up girls – American girls mostly – but the food was good.

The stone stairs still smell faintly of disinfectant. I button up my coat and pull on my gloves. Via Dante is empty. I turn left, then right, thinking I'll recognize the way once I've reached the Palazzo Vecchio, remembering that it's down an alley somewhere off the street behind. I cut across the corner of Piazza della Signoria, keeping the massive Neptune to my right, his shoulders carrying snow like an ermine robe. A small group of tourists are assembled in the centre of the piazza, turning on their toes to get the full three-sixty. A tour guide peers around for stragglers, impatient to start her talk, yet holding out so she doesn't have to repeat herself. Most people visit Florence once in their life, on the school trip, the big culture trip, the long weekend, the honeymoon, part of an Italian or European tour; some visit a few times, for further, deeper exploration; lucky people make it more often, recognizing that few other cities offer so much, at least superficially, as a cultural city-break destination. This is my ninth trip, all but three work-based, and I feel at home. I can still do a double-take now and again: *David* in the Accademia continues to move me like no other single work of art; the serenity of Piazza Santa Croce still enchants me like no other urban space; the small artisan workshops that line the narrow streets continue to make me yearn for something bygone. But it still remains primarily a place of business: streets leading to the offices of museums, cafés as places for meetings not quiet moments with *caffè* and guidebooks. It is also a place of loneliness, of isolation, of deception. On only three of the nine visits have I actually been myself, on only three of the nine have I had company, on only three of

31

the nine have I been able to share my thoughts, feelings, impressions without pressing them through the vector of my cover, the self-editing of myself as another. This is my first time in Florence in the winter but it has seemed a cold place before, with little warmth to be had from its history and its modern wealth particularly chilly.

I pass behind the high brown-brick walls of the Palazzo Vecchio and look out for the narrow street which I think leads to the restaurant. I remember we could see it from the main road – a small sign, a name – Luigi's or something. I peer down one street; there is nothing, just undisturbed snow like a recently unrolled white carpet, narrower than the street, its edges perfectly straight, the contrast with the dark paving giving it extra whiteness, vivid sharpness. The sign is visible from the top of the next street – Luigi's. I can tell it is closed. It's not surprising given the thinness of trade, the only people around clearly native, clad in their expensive overcoats, scarves and gloves. There is the odd tourist wandering around, unprepared for the coldness of the weather, only a cagoule to keep out the wind.

The small café in Piazza di San Firenze is also closed. I decide on Antico Fattore, close to the Uffizi – it's near, the food is passable and it's likely to be free of tourists with the Uffizi closed on Mondays. I head towards the Arno, cross over the road and walk along the river bank. The water below is grey, muddy, quick-running. The tree tops on the hills across the river are snow-capped, the sky above as white. I pass the east wing of the Uffizi and turn into the long *cortile* with its statuary of artists ensconced within the arches of the loggia. The right side houses the most famous: Machiavelli, Dante, da Vinci, Giotto, others. I read their names, glance at their faces, sensing I recognize Michelangelo, Dante – that the strength of their faces is present in the strength of their work.

As expected the restaurant is almost empty. The ageing waiters greet me without warmth and ask, '*Uno solo?*' I nod and point to where I want to sit – a table set for four in the corner of the second room – and head towards it before I can be redirected. As I am handed a menu I order a bowl of *spaghetti genovese* and a half-bottle of Amarone; the menu is withdrawn. Only two other tables are occupied. At the furthest table, four middle-aged men are just finishing giving their orders. They are cultured-looking but could still be bankers. Nearer to me sit two women, more likely to be secretaries than art administrators from the Uffizi. I fold my arms and sit back in my chair. I have been promised a private tour if I go to the gallery today. It's tempting. But it begins my assignment. Something I want to avoid. Yet undisturbed time with the *Doni Tondo* is hard to pass up. On every other occasion I've seen it I've had to muscle in between tour parties crowding around hack art historians bellowing the same story, the same interpretation. How many times have I stood in that small room waiting for just one moment, one silent moment to take in the painting without the presence of idiots with video cameras pressed to their eyes or, worse still, held up a foot away from their faces so they can see the painting nice and clearly in their video screens? And that's what I'd get – longer, I presume – if I stroll over there after lunch.

My cover was arranged by Lucy Stevens, a curator friend at the National Gallery with good personal contacts at the Uffizi. A series of monographs on the world's hundred most influential paintings has been commissioned and Mr Wright has been invited to write about the *Doni Tondo* – might private access be arranged? When I asked for the name of my point of contact Lucy whistled. Francesca Natali. You'll have to be careful. She's very clever. MBA in Milan. Stint with McKinsey's at the Metropolitan. Many people think she runs the show at the Uffizi these days. Lucy then added, with a curious leaping of her eyebrows: she's also very, very beautiful. Adding further: if you like that sort of thing. I wasn't intrigued; I've had quite enough of attractive, well-educated art administrators.

My *genovese* arrives, along with the half-bottle of Amarone. I pour myself a glass of wine and take a sip. I dwell on its slow warmth, starting in my mouth, percolating up into my head, then travelling down into my body, through my heart and into my stomach, relishing red wine as the perfect drug, the subtlest narcotic. I dig into my pasta. The food is OK, rich, with strong flavours, but lacks refinement. More people arrive and are seated. I keep half an eye out for someone who might be Francesca Natali, thinking I'll recognize her – the intelligence and beauty Lucy alluded to being obvious even in Italy.

I finish my pasta and have left enough in the half-bottle of Amarone to enjoy an uninterrupted glass. I push back my chair a little and stretch out my legs under the table, crossing them at the ankles. From this position I can see a small section of the Uffizi out of the far corner of the window. I sip the wine, staring out yet seeing little, my mind empty, just the sensation of the glass against my lips, the wine on my tongue, the softness as I swallow. A waiter passes asking whether I want *caffè*. I nod. My espresso arrives within a minute and I knock it back in a second – a bitter hot viscous jolt. The bill appears moments later, slid on to my table as a waiter delivers dessert to the four bankers.

I leave the restaurant and head back into the long *cortile* of the Uffizi, scanning the doors for the number I've been given. I have nothing else to do. I wait a moment before ringing the buzzer. If I am not here to start the job, why am I here? Does it matter? Undercover cop, undercover tourist – it is all the same. A single layer of deception. I press the buzzer. A security guard appears.

'I'm here to see Francesca Natali. My name is Daniel Wright.'

The door is closed. I rock back on my heels, gloved hands pressed together as fists. The door opens again. A small man in a suit has replaced the security guard. A functionary. Old support staff.

'Do you have an appointment, Signor Wright?'

I think, no, not really. More of an arrangement.

'Yes and no.'

'You're not in her diary and you don't have a pass.'

'I know. Is she here?'

The man shrugs. 'Come with me.'

I follow him up a wide grey stone staircase to the third floor. I am shown into a long corridor with offices giving off to the left. I am taken to the end, to the last office.

'Please.' The old man guides me into a large room with high windows. There is a panoramic view of the south bank of the Arno, the hill beyond, the fir trees crenulated with snow. There is a slim laptop open on the desk, a desktop computer on a small table against the left wall. There is no loose paper, no books anywhere, no printer, fax or photocopier. This is a purely electronic office. There is also no landline. Just a small mobile next to the laptop, next to which is a small espresso cup with a smudge of lipstick, then a pair of tortoiseshell spectacles. It makes a nice row: spectacles, cup, mobile, laptop – spelling efficiency, concentration, intensity. The chair behind the desk is an Eames, its worn leather suggesting an original, or at least one bought long before the recent fad for them. The only other chair, hidden behind the door, is a small light-brown armchair with very square back and arms – classic Italian. There is a blue enamel ashtray perched on the arm containing an extinguished cigarette; there is a similar lipstick smudge. On the other arm there is a book, open face down, spine still unbroken, standing like a little tent. I step back and glance down at the title. *Elvira's Secret*. It appears to be some kind of romance novel. If asked to judge the current reading of the person occupying this office, a novel wouldn't be my first guess; a romance novel wouldn't even get on the list. There is one picture on the walls. A photograph. A Cartier-Bresson. A young man and woman in the sea, taken from above; he is standing, holding her as she floats, her legs wrapped around him. Their faces cannot be seen because of the angle, but she is naked, her breasts visible breaking the surface of the water. It is signed. I walk over to the window, behind the desk, and look down at the Arno.

'Signor Wright.'

I turn. Francesca Natali is at the door; I am behind her desk.

'Come in.' I smile to disguise my embarrassment.

We change places, each moving around a different side of the desk. Francesca folds down the screen of her laptop, slides on her spectacles and looks at me.

Lucy was right – I can see what sort of thing I might like in Francesca Natali's beauty. She is tall for an Italian woman – around 5' 6" – with glowing olive skin, long brown eyes, dark hair falling in perfect spiral curls to her shoulders, each curl bouncing like a soft spring as she moves. She is wearing a long dark-brown linen dress, shapeless in design but tight enough to reveal her shape, and a small black cardigan. On her feet is a pair of Birkenstock sandals over long black socks. The socks force me to imperceptibly double-take. She is older than I expected.

I offer my hand across the desk. Francesca clasps it absently before sitting down. I am not offered a seat. I hesitate, but not wanting to feel like a schoolboy in front of a headmistress I close the door and move the armchair from behind it into the centre of the room. I sit down, push the ashtray on to the desk and pick up the novel, place it next to the ashtray.

'Interesting.'

'I am ashamed.'

'You should be.'

'What are *you* ashamed of?' She picks up her mobile, looking at the screen at arm's length, then replaces it.

'More than I care to admit.' I look beyond her, out of the window to the blue sky breaking behind the hills. She opens her laptop and taps a couple of keys; I hear the soft crunching of the hard drive.

'I like the Cartier-Bresson.'

She looks up at me, over the computer, and then to the photograph. 'Storaro gave it to me.' She shrugs.

'You don't like it?' I vaguely recall the name.

'It's very beautiful.' Her tone is plain, without feeling, for a moment reminding me of Sarah's response to snow falling in Florence.

'But it doesn't move you?' It is a big question – the answer revealing.

Francesca smiles but says nothing. I wait.

'Why are you really here?' she asks eventually.

'To see the Michelangelo.' I am unhurried; it's why I am here today and not back at the apartment in the cold, or sitting in the corona of warmth given off by the gas heater.

'But I imagine you've seen it before.'

'Not undisturbed.'

'I think you are here for another reason.'

'What reason might that be?'

'I don't know. A woman.'

I pause before answering. If I'd been asked to guess the current reading material of this woman based on this conversation, I might have said *Elvira's Secret*.

'I'm not sure I want to know why you think I

am here because of a woman. But I assure you all I want is some time with the *Doni Tondo* and to do some supplementary research. And if possible, maybe do some writing in the peace and quiet of Florence.'

Francesca studies me, then stands. 'Come this way.'

I push myself up from the chair as she passes and follow her out of the office. Waiting for us in the corridor is the old man who showed me in; he holds a pass with my name on it. Francesca takes it from him and clips it on to my breast pocket.

'Silvio will take you there.'

Before I have a chance to respond she disappears back into her office, shutting the door behind her.

Silvio starts up the corridor with an order for me to follow. I am slow to obey, slightly taken aback by Francesca's sudden withdrawal. Silvio calls out to me, waiting at the end of the long corridor, holding open the door.

I am taken up a flight of stairs and shown into the west wing of the Uffizi Gallery. The doors to all the rooms are closed. Silvio pulls out a single key to Room 25 and unlocks the door. Holds his arm out to usher me in. The door is then closed behind me. I hear the faint echo of the turn and crunch of the key in the lock, a precise mechanism. I face the *Doni Tondo*. It is always larger than I remember, bright and imposing – a self-defining masterpiece. Its genius begins here – announcing itself as different from other paintings. I have always felt that genius might be identified by an element of oddness in a work, as if the creator was trying to do something more ordinary, more standard – in this instance a simple depiction of the holy family – but is unable to rein in his originality, thus creating something recognizable yet also unfamiliar, extra. This is certainly true of the young Michelangelo. In this case the oddness is the temporality of the family. Mary and Joseph have lived together, eaten together, talked, discussed, argued; they have looked forward to, welcomed and managed a new child; there is a pre-child past between them, a sexual history; they have differing gender-based, age-based psychologies, perspectives. They are not holy, blessed, divinely elected, or if they are, they do not let it interfere with their lives, the raising of their son. All of these things make the painting the work of a genius – a masterpiece. However, if I am moved by one detail, one indefinable artistic decision, it is the attitude of Mary's right arm. For scholars, the fact that it is clearly copied from a male model seems to be enough, and they ignore what it does in narrative and philosophical terms for the rest of the painting. I love this arm and shoulder and have stared at it endlessly in books. There is form, function *and* feeling in its execution, drawing me into the actual moment that is being depicted: the handing over of the

41

child, a child still light enough, pliable enough to be held, lifted, transferred. It is this detail that reveals the painting as more than a representation, allegory or pious narrative; it is this detail which releases the truth about painting: in the smallest movements between us, humans can display the dignity which makes us the equal of our gods.

I move the stool situated between Rooms 25 and 26 and sit in front of the painting, hands in lap, legs outstretched, ankles crossed. Looking at the painting now, with the privilege of a chair, I begin to wonder what I am doing here. I know what they, the gallery, think I'm doing, but until tomorrow, until I officially agree to the operation – when logically my cover must also officially begin – I am just a man in Florence with a love of art. Yet here I am, alone with one of the world's greatest works of art, locked in with it. There have been many other occasions when I've been alone with great paintings: in hotel rooms, the paintings laid out on the bed, or propped up on chairs, unrolled across dressers. Once I had to move all the bedroom furniture into the bathroom to accommodate the size of a Titian. I needed to be able to see all the damage and relay the information via conference call to the owners, the insurers. I've been in warehouses, cellars, barns, even an abandoned boathouse with great works of art – shorn of their frames, rolled out on floors, over tables, boxes. I have rescued, recovered, saved, chaperoned paintings by Gauguin, Picasso, Renoir, Klimt, Turner, Kandinsky, countless old masters and many, many others. Each recovery – the exquisite moment after rescue, their safety gained by me and now in my hands – offering me a sense of intimacy, attachment, ownership second only to the artist who painted them. There is nothing ever idle about my relationship to a great painting. Even today I want to form sentences for an essay, irrespective of my work, my cover; but I feel ridiculous because the commission doesn't exist, the series to be conveniently abandoned on my return. I know I should consider writing about this picture anyway. But I'm a copper, not an art historian – it would be absurd. Part of me accepts my reluctance is to spite myself, yet I also know that to start writing, and then to like what I write, is asking to be punished all over again. As a copper I am doing a valuable job. And the art world needs a good copper a lot more than it needs another historian.

I stare at the painting, whispering just enjoy it, just enjoy it; you're not working, there's no gangster to see, no deal to be done, no money transfer to organize, no meet to set up, no handover to complete; no plane to catch, train to make, long drive to endure; it's just you and the painting. When was the last time you were in a gallery as a punter, let alone on your own? I sometimes get a little time at Langdon's with Sarah, a sneak preview of a big sale, but she's always on the move, and I'm always on my best behaviour, establishment lackeys trying to intimidate me, the higher echelons unsettling me with their polite questions about my job. Right now I have all the time I need; I don't imagine Silvio will be back any time soon. I drop my arms to my sides, uncross my legs, let my feet splay. I am the picture of relaxation. Physically loose. But my mind is tight, narrow, concentrated elsewhere. Whatever mood state I'm after, it evades me. I stand and turn away from the *Doni Tondo* and scan the other paintings in the room. Albertinelli, Ghirlandaio, Fra Bartolomeo. I now *want* to be disturbed. I go over to the great door and listen. Is Silvio out there? I can't hear anything. I knock gently. Is that the signal required? Surely they can't leave me here without any means of escape. I knock harder. Nothing. Not even an echo. I venture into Room 26, the Raphaels. With every painting so available for scrutiny, I am able to focus. Colour is a haze; composition abstracts itself. I could be looking at late Picassos. I return to Room 25. It doesn't make any sense to lock someone in a set of rooms like this, with one of the world's few genuinely priceless paintings, other masterpieces. What if I destroyed them? I am in the gallery under false pretences after all. Shouldn't a security guard be present, even with my National Gallery credentials? I go back to the door and call out. I look through the keyhole. Just shadow and air. I sit back down. The *Doni Tondo* is the brightest light in the room. I am finally distracted by the painting's lushness, the Holy Family's luxury – their robes are rich bright voluminous; they are not a poor family, an artisan family. I study Joseph, a deeply involved, loving father lifting his son from his wife's offering hands, very different from the old man depicted by Caravaggio.

I hear a key in the door, the door open. I remain focused on the painting, feigning analytical intensity; I don't want Silvio to think I have idle eyes.

'What do you see?'

It is Francesca, her spiral curls gently bouncing. She looks supremely at ease, her small cardigan buttoned up, the hem slightly flared at the middle of her waist, her hips flaring slightly under the linen dress, the dress flaring slightly at her ankles.

I stand. 'Too much to take in.'

'We can arrange more time. In the evening. Next week.'

'That would be very helpful.'

We are standing in the middle of the small room, the stool between us.

'Do you know Florence well?' She pulls off her spectacles.

'Yes and no. I've been here a couple of times. My honeymoon last year.'

Francesca takes this in; smiles. 'You didn't bring your wife with you?'

How nice that would have been, how nice even

as an option: Sarah wanting to come with me. Playful insistences. 'Why *can't* I come? I wouldn't get in the way. *Please.*'

Francesca looks around the room absently. 'This is a small room.' She then adds, 'What are you doing for dinner?'

This surprises me. 'I don't have plans.'

'I'm meeting Storaro and his cronies. They eat at Baldovino's on Mondays. Would you like to join us?'

'Storaro?'

She is surprised I need to ask. 'Immanuel Storaro. Our richest private collector. He has a gallery here, in Oltrarno.'

I try to place the name. 'What does he collect?'

'Everything.'

'I'd like to meet him.'

Francesca replaces her spectacles, pulls up the sleeve of her cardigan and looks at her watch. I roll my wrist. It is five p.m.

'Where are you staying?'

'A friend of a friend's apartment in Via Dante.'

Francesca thinks about this. I suggest that she just gives me a time to meet her at Baldovino's. She smiles. 'Things have to be done Storaro's way.' She rolls her eyes.

'And what way is that?'

'Mondays we meet at seven in the library at Hotel Art, after which we walk across the city to Baldovino's – even in this weather.'

'So I'll meet you there?'

'I think it's best if you arrive with me and I introduce you.' She thinks for a second; I look down at her feet, warm in socks, comfortable in Birkenstocks.

'I'll pick you up. At seven.'

'Won't we be late?'

'He'll forgive me. What number are you?'

'Top floor above American Express. Professore Bramante.'

'I think I know him.'

Francesca ushers me out and locks the big door. Silvio is waiting for us. I anticipate the routine: Silvio will take over from here. I am right. Francesca doesn't even say '*ciao*', disappearing through a side door, with only a slight raising of her hand to let me know she's leaving.

A hard wind pitches through the *cortile*. I button up my coat, raise my eyes to the darkening sky – unbroken slate grey again. The Piazza della Signoria is criss-crossed with the tyre tracks of municipal vehicles. The snow itself feels solid underfoot, the first fall freezing beneath the crisp fresh layer. I am on the corner of Via Dante when my mobile rings. It is Sarah. She interrupts my cheery hello.

'Sorry, can you hang on a second?'

I wait, standing under the scaffolding, water dripping around me.

'Actually, Dan, can I call you back later? Tonight?'

'When tonight?'

'Late. After dinner. I'm out. Sorry, I have to go.'

The phone goes dead. I call her back. 'You fuck me off. I love you, but you fuck me off.'

I hear her laugh. 'Speak later then?'

'Yes, speak later.'

This time I ring off. I drop the phone into my pocket while at the same time searching for my key. The offices of American Express are bright, with queues of people inside.

In the apartment, heater on, gas rings on, I set up my laptop on the coffee table and try to activate the path to the department's network. The name Storaro has been nagging at me since leaving the Uffizi. If he's Italy's richest collector, then he'll have a past – no art collector of pre-modern works is entirely legitimate. You can't be – you'd wait a lifetime for works by the great artists to come up for auction. This is why the art world has often colluded with semi-legitimate suppliers. I was astonished when I joined the department at how flexible those in the trade were when it came to questions of legality. I was more astonished at the number of famous painters' works available on the 'grey market'. But it soon became clear that due to the amount of money and the social and political power of those involved, the trade has been left to govern itself, more often than not operating on the edge of the law.

I wait five minutes, watching the remote-access icon flicker. Nothing. No denial of permission, but no permission either. If I call Jim and ask him to do a search, it'll take hours, days even. I deactivate the path and go to Google – where else? I type in 'Immanuel Storaro'.

Results **1–10** of about **16,670** for 'Immanuel Storaro'. (**0.09** seconds)

The list is a mixture of art sites and newspaper articles. I glance over the first ten results, looking for something to catch my eye. One article asks the question: is this the most powerful man in the art world? I click. Buying power is one factor – his spending outstrips most of his rivals. Obsession is the other – the lengths he will go to to acquire what he desires. So yes, he is, the article concludes, and by some margin. On the next page I find a glitzy site about Italy's rich and famous. There is a short biography of the man. The photos are poor quality – distant paparazzi shots – but he doesn't appear to be the handsome Italian playboy type. I move on to a report about dealers and recovered paintings. Storaro's name appears with expected frequency in connection with recovered artworks. Some deem him a hero – deploying his vast wealth to bring lost works back into the public domain. Others regard him as a menace – perpetuating the criminality of the art world by creating a demand for black marketeers, fences, gangsters to service. Gustav Ballack is mentioned, probably the most powerful man in the art and antiquities black market. It's unclear whether he and Storaro have a connection, but I suspect they have: if you want to buy or sell the best in the world, you go through Gustav Ballack. I scan a couple more articles. Nothing that really suggests Storaro is any different from other rich collectors – happy to bend the law, careful not to break it.

Francesca arrives at five past seven. She buzzes up, announces herself. I make my way down to the street. A black Smart Car is parked snugly to the wall. She waves me over and pulls out so I can climb in. I say hello in English. Francesca leans over so we can greet with a kiss; she is wearing a leather coat, a black crew-neck sweater, jeans, Camper boots. Her driving is quick, precise, fluid. She doesn't sit straight in her seat but slightly to the side, against the door, as if looking at her passenger is as important as looking at the road.

'Have you spoken to your wife?'

'Briefly.'

'Is she missing you?'

'She's not the type of person to miss someone. She's very self-contained.'

'Do you miss her?'

'I don't know.' I am not sure whether all my thoughts about her constitute actually missing her. 'I wish we could spend more time together.'

Francesca nods at this. We drive down Via de' Castellani and turn along the river.

'You don't believe in watching the road, do you?'

She shrugs, takes a cursory look ahead of her, then turns back to me as we shoot below her office.

'Storaro knows you're coming. You should be warned, he collects experts.'

We turn into a small side street and into a tiny piazza. Francesca parks close to the wall.

'You'll have to climb out this side.' She opens her door and unfolds herself into the street, grabbing a wallet from the dashboard and shoving it into the pocket of her jacket. I haul myself over the gear shift into the driver's seat and then out. We are opposite Gallery Hotel Art, Florence's first hip hotel.

The reception is long, with a wide orange bench in the centre. The receptionists smile and welcome us. There are large photographs on the wall. Francesca turns right, leading me past the elevators and down into a big room filled with cream sofas and chairs and low tables. The end wall is a floor-to-ceiling bookcase stocked with big art books. At the far end the sofas have been arranged into a rectangle with single seats at each end. These are taken up by young men in dark suits, white shirts, dark-patterned ties; some are sitting back, imported beers pressed to their chest, others sit forward, elbows on knees, cocktails or long drinks before them on the table. They talk animatedly, calling across to each other with accompanying gestures so prominent that they could be using sign language but for the light breeze of vowel sounds in the air. Which one is Storaro, I wonder. No one is instantly recognizable from the website photographs. However, only one man is taking part in all the conversations, only one man is attuned to everyone around him, and there is only one man to whom everyone is careful to be attuned. The first thing I notice about this man is quite how far from the typical Italian playboy he is; the second, how small. Perched on the edge of his seat – to sit back would risk his feet not touching the floor – he looks no more than five feet tall. Wearing a tailored pinstriped suit and white shirt, his elegance discloses a toughness; he is all hard frame and muscle. Only his face has any excess, with a broad, fleshy nose and lips like overripe figs. There is something atavistic about his hair, made up of recalcitrant, tightly wound black curls; it is the hair of Nero or Caligula. His eyes stand out. They are long like Francesca's – sleekly alert. Also bright blue, and set against his dark olive skin and black hair they shine like marbles lit from within, giving him an uncanny presence, as if their brightness is a signal of raw intelligence, raw energy, a kind of raw divinity. Without these extraordinary eyes, he would be just a face-mashed boxer. With them, there is some-thing of Napoleon about him – a full charismatic, over-brimming, combustible. He also makes me

53

think of Napoleon by the manner in which he is listening and talking to his gang, participating in two, three conversations at once, never losing his train of thought, the rhythm of the talk, the point of each argument; Napoleon could dictate up to a dozen letters at once this way.

Storaro notices Francesca and he is on his feet, round face beaming. He is agile, strong on his toes. The energy in his body at this precise moment is caused by a reflex, to be close to Francesca, to have her near him. She goes to him, weaving between two sofas, the table, deftly avoiding the legs retracting to let her past. I remain outside the rectangle of Team Storaro. She leans down to kiss him; his hand hovers at her hip. Is he also a man in love? Francesca waves me over. I offer Storaro my hand but he chooses to greet me by clasping my elbows, as if shaking my hand might accentuate the difference in our heights, the clasped hand looking more like a hand up, a helping hand. He invites me to take a seat. There is no room. He flicks his eyes at the man on our right, ordering him to shift up. He stands and leaves the library altogether. I lower myself into the vacated corner of the sofa. It is deeply plush, deceptively uncomfortable. Storaro perches forward on the very edge of his chair. Francesca lounges next to him on the arm.

I look at the men sitting around the table. They are like the hot young men of a reinvented political party, all handsome compared to Storaro,

54

dark, strong-boned, every feature defined and prominent. But none have the small man's concentration of aspects. They appear happy as his stooges, his yes-men – content as career sycophants.

A waiter approaches and asks for our drink orders. I order a vodka and tonic; Francesca orders double vodka straight. Storaro continues the conversation our appearance interrupted: his analysis of a scandal involving high-ranking government ministers and Cosa Nostra. He accepts dealing with organized crime is a way of life in the south but he is disapproving of these ministers: they have power, influence, money – their dalliance with Cosa Nostra is nothing more than vanity and greed. And for this they should be imprisoned. But they won't, he says. He has heard – don't ask him how – that these ministers will resign, the witnesses will disappear and the case will be dropped – proving that those who remain in charge must also have access to Cosa Nostra because governments don't lose witnesses. And we accept this, he says incredulously. He turns to me, the stranger, the outsider. 'What do you think?'

I shift in my seat, pull at the creases of my trousers, cast a glance around Team Storaro. 'We deserve the society we permit.'

Storaro nods at this. 'I agree.' He then turns to Francesca. 'Signor Wright is very sensible. This is new for you.' His laugh is forced. Francesca looks at him directly, sternly – a look of censure. Storaro raises his hand, a signal of agreement or dismissal; I cannot tell which. He is clearly happy to reveal the dynamics of their relationship. His love, if indeed that's what it is, has a tough veneer, a public toughness. Francesca's expression is cool, abstracted, opaque.

Our drinks arrive. Thin paper coasters are slipped on to the table, the heavy glasses placed on top. I stir mine before taking a sip.

A couple of Team Storaro talk about Fiorentina's chances against Juventus at the weekend. Storaro is quickly bored. He turns in his seat to look at nothing in particular. He pulls at his collar. He gives the contents of his long drink a small shake. Peers into the glass. He turns to me again, interrupting the others' conversation – stopping it.

'You are here for how long?'

'A week or so. Maybe less. Maybe more. I don't know.'

Storaro takes this in. I glance up at Francesca. Did she know I would be the centre of his attention?

'You are alone?'

'Yes.'

'I do not travel alone.'

I am a little unsettled by the simplicity of the conversation; I could be sitting on a park bench talking to an old man.

'It is depressing,' I offer, out of politeness.

'I find I forget who I am when I travel alone. I

am always surprised by how much we are made up of other people, and therefore to be ignored and not understood, to be misinterpreted . . . it makes us desperate to do things that will define us. Things we might regret.'

What is being said to me? Is he warning me away from Francesca? I look at her. Is she to be warned away from?

'I travel a lot on my own. I think your analysis is right. But maybe – to go back to permission again – our reduced selves permit us to do things our otherwise larger, firmer selves would prohibit.' I sip my drink.

Storaro laughs again, this time more naturally, his long eyes tightening up. 'I think we agree, Signor Wright. On many things. It is good to find new people with whom you share views on such abstract matters.' He remains looking at me but blindly pats Francesca's knee.

Does Storaro think he will seduce me and therefore keep me away from Francesca? Is this his plan: build quick loyalties?

I sit forward. 'It is easy for men to share views on the abstract; not so easy for them to share the concrete.' I smile first at Storaro and then up at Francesca; she is chewing her bottom lip, her empty glass held in her lap.

Storaro cuts his smile. I have made myself clear: I'm not so easily earned.

'You are right, and I am an especially possessive man.'

Team Storaro stiffen a little. My instinct tells me to leave the conversation where it is, yet I hear myself say calmly, firmly, 'I'm sure your possessions feel very secure because of it.'

It is Francesca's turn to laugh. Storaro snaps his head back to glare at her. Being laughed at has caused instant fury. She shrugs and looks away.

I watch his internal decisions flick around his eyes, his thoughts revealed by the tiniest contractions of muscles: he could move into rage mode, wreck the evening, but he decides to allow the joke on him and let the partial humiliation pass. He takes control of himself by asking more questions.

'You are a writer – an expert on Michelangelo, Francesca tells me?' It is a tough question to respond to. I don't need to. He continues, 'Here in Florence we have many experts.'

I can't let this go. 'This is true, but they all say the same thing.'

The Team has relaxed a little, ordered more drinks, lit cigarettes; Storaro permitted this by his decision not to rage only moments ago.

'What do you say that is so different?'

'I am only interested in art that is perpetually modern. Where its delight is not fixed in its time. I am not interested in sources, references, the historical context. I am interested only in the painting's power to move us – move us now. This . . .'

I am cut off. 'So once again we agree. It is imperative that our opinion-formers are not covered in cobwebs, thinking only of their reputations, *their* place in history. Art that survives does not do so because it is clever or perfect, but because it is timeless.' He pauses for a moment, a little flushed. 'Have you visited my gallery?'

Does this give me away? Surely as a scholar, even a radical one, I would have been there. I pause long enough for Storaro to ask another question.

'How many times have you visited Florence?'

'Many times.'

He turns to Francesca. 'Tomorrow, Francesca. Please. Bring him.'

Francesca smiles – it is a faint, bored smile, yet Storaro is satisfied that she has agreed. He then tips himself off his seat and steers his way between the tables and chairs to the door. The man evicted from his seat appears with coats draped over his arm.

Storaro says, 'Thank you, Luca,' picks his coat from the top and swings it on. The action is like that of a diminutive bullfighter – flamboyant but precise. The more I look at this man I realize that his ugliness has its own strength, his height its own dynamism; energy is not wasted on grace, vanity, occupying physical space – it is all at the service of his will, which is extensive, looking to occupy all space.

The others stand and take their coats from Luca, then loiter, waiting for Storaro to lead the way. I look at Francesca, who whispers, 'Napoleon and his Marshals.'

As we leave the hotel, Storaro says 'ciao' to the staff, all of whom address him as Storaro.

'Is he here a lot?' I ask Francesca, holding open the door, Storaro already out in the middle of the little piazza – a lone presence in the darkness.

'He is living here while his house is being built.'

Addressing Storaro, as though for confirmation, I ask, 'So you live here?'

'Yes.' He looks past me to his Team assembling under the awning. For a moment there is straightforward warmth in his eyes, as if these men are in fact his sons and he wants to do a number count before they head off, making sure none is lost. Francesca leans against her car, ignoring anything said to her by Team Storaro. I step away from the group.

Storaro sets off, flipping up the collar of his overcoat, rubbing his small hands together, after which he tugs at his fringe, as if to make sure his curls are distinct and in place. It is clear to me that Storaro's hair is important to him; it is where he directs whatever frustration he might have with his height or looks, regarding it as the only aspect of his appearance over which he can exert some kind of control. I feel a little sorry for him as I watch each curl teased forward tug itself back into its former place the moment it is released. Compared to Francesca's curls, light, bouncy, framing her face with gentle motion, Storaro's are like the hard curlicues of wrought ironwork.

The walk to Baldovino's is led by Storaro, flanked by myself and Francesca, the gang hanging back a few paces. Above us the sky is clearing, the moon is high and full and picks out the remaining snow, the reflected light forcing the shadows to cling to the buildings rather than cast themselves across the street. It feels like Christmas: a gang off to the pub on a cold dark night, the world lit up with the surreal glow of Christmas lights, in this case strings of tiny illuminated beads high above our heads.

Storaro asks me whether I know about the Jackson Pollock paintings that went missing from a French customs house in the 1950s. I say I do, but he doesn't appear to hear me, continuing to outline the details. The ship arrived and no one could remember where they were. He is certain they still exist. He is certain they were not stolen. One day they will be discovered. Someone will just come across them wondering what they are, and then – he clicks his fingers softly, thickly in his dark-brown gloves – imagine: all those Jackson Pollocks on the market! I say, 'Wow,' mostly out of politeness. He talks on about the market, the multi-million-dollar bid he will make. He talks into the cold air, condensation puffed out with a hard plosive force. I am happy not to interrupt. Francesca, between us, is also quiet. I wonder what their true relationship is? She has looked bored from the start of the evening and has hardly said a word, behaving for the most part like the dull trophy girlfriend of a garrulous rich man. I avoided her occasional collusive glance, not wanting to feel my invitation was part of a game. Right now I feel rather like I did when sitting opposite the Michelangelo. What is my role here? Am I working? No. Then why am I here? Is it simply because I was invited and had nothing better to do? Probably. Am I enjoying myself? I look at Storaro setting the pace with big little strides, then at Francesca, hands thrust in pockets, again chewing at her bottom lip. I glance back at the Marshalate following. I have to say yes, of course I am. Because for the moment everyone here thinks I know about art, and not just as a copper. Because right now my ideas count, not my recovery rate. Because my Italian is good, my accent OK and no one cares where I come from, or thinks to care. Because I am in the company of a rising star in the Uffizi and one of Italy's most influential collectors, and tomorrow, when I visit his gallery, my judgement, my expertise will matter. I am enjoying myself because for once I am being allowed to act out a version of myself that fifteen years ago was the real me, or at least the originally intended version of myself before the world asked me to think twice about my abilities, my ambitions, my aspirations. And finally, I am enjoying myself because for the last hour what to do about the Caravaggio has not entered my mind.

We enter the Piazza Santa Croce from the south-eastern corner, with the church at the far end. There is something about this piazza which is heart-stopping. The small dwellings on the left seem to me to be imbued with an essence unchanged from their medieval beginnings. Whenever I read about Renaissance Florence it is these buildings I see in my mind: frescoed, delicately buttressed, their projected upper storeys giving them a fragile majesty. The piazza itself also retains something of its true function, with no cafés, no alfresco tables, no news-stands, no souvenir stalls, just a vast cobbled plain: a place to cross, to meet, to muse, a place to be under the sky in the heart of the city.

Baldovino's is just past the far corner, opposite the public entrance to the church. A modern restaurant, owned by a Scotsman. I have been here before, on my own and with Sarah, discovering on my second visit that I love their cheese plate. The restaurant is an odd choice for a very rich man, but then maybe the lack of old Florence iconography, the tourist Italian chintz, attracts him.

Storaro is greeted effusively – as a friend – and leads the way to a large table at the back, to the right of the kitchen. He informs the waiter they will need an extra place – pointing to me. He doesn't wait for any formal rearrangement, instead pressing the palm of each hand on to two adjacent settings and moving them apart to create the extra place we need. The knock-on effect needs some tidying, which Luca and two waiters set about. Storaro sits down, offering me the newly created space next to him; Francesca sits down on his left.

It seems that while Storaro looks over the menu the others are allowed to lead the conversation. This moment of freedom is taken up by a man sitting opposite me along the right-hand side of the table. He has said little so far. He is asking Team Storaro for their views on the upcoming Venice Biennale. Until this point these young men haven't revealed the quality of their minds, behaving very much like Storaro's yes-men. I am quickly impressed. They speak passionately, intelligently, with the kind of southern European urgency I like when it comes to discussing art, philosophy, ideas. There is an impressive lack of irony, or over-refinement; they allow for interruptions, speak with mouths full, speak with bread in one hand, glass of wine in the other, gesturing to one another to underline a point, impress their judgement, or dismiss, ridicule or insult another's. There is high seriousness, a lot of laughter and a little anger.

Storaro permits the conversation to continue throughout the first course. The Biennale is important, he tells me. I make a show of listening attentively. Francesca is livelier, now butting in whenever something irritates her. She has her favourite artists but is less interested in being an advocate for them than in disabusing the others of their certainties. She is impatient with any over-elaborate theorizing, looking for descriptions of appeal that are plain, simple; she is not interested in the modish, or the flimsy, or the clever.

The second course is Storaro's time – time to make his thoughts clear on all the opinions which have been offered. He points to a member of the Team and recites almost verbatim the member's advocacy of, or objection to, an artist's work, and then explains what he thinks with stronger advocacy, stronger objections. His manner is not bullying or superior; he doesn't ridicule or poke fun. He is happy to give way to further argument, greeting direct contradiction or frustration with energetic shakes of his small head. I notice him gently coax responses from the more diffident and censure the more spirited if they interrupt. He is a fair father. All the while I can sense, and occasionally feel, his little legs fidgeting under the table, his excitement loose.

He deals with Francesca differently; they confer, often whispering between themselves. Sipping my Amarone, chomping on my perfectly *al dente* asparagus, I am content to be entertained. I like this man more and more – art needs people like this: passionate first, intellectual second, yet with fine, quick minds. I sense Storaro requires all egos to be in service to his, but then he has placed his gargantuan ego in service to art – so that is the deal. Maybe we *are* similar. My ego might have taken something of a battering recently – in service to the force, to the criminal, to Sarah – but in terms of its service to art I am arguably his equal. My work puts my life at risk. Places me before loaded guns. To the head. The small of my back. If this man is art's most passionate benefactor, then I am its most passionate protector.

I realize I have tuned out of the conversation. I return my attention to Storaro. He is talking about his latest buying trip to New York. He was there for a number of items: a Carracci, a Rembrandt drawing, a Soutine and a Morandi. He returned with all four. Here he clicks his fingers. It is more to seal the purchases – *got them* – than to demonstrate it having been easy. He then continues, lowering his voice to a dramatic whisper, eyes alert and mischievous. On his last day he was approached to buy Vermeer's *The Concert*. There is a murmur of surprise from the Team, mirroring his whisper. He nods as if to say: all true. He then points to the least stylishly, least smartly dressed of the gang and orders a report: what is known about this masterpiece since it went missing.

Elbows on the table, arms arched over my empty plate, fingers interwined, I am forced to correct him. 'Since it was stolen.'

Storaro turns, curious. 'Stolen?'

I cannot help myself. 'Since it was *stolen*. Stolen along with three Rembrandts, five Degases and a

66

Manet. Estimated value, three hundred million dollars.'

The Team look to Storaro before landing like one eye on me.

'Yes, you are right. Stolen.' I sense his irritability; he has calmed himself once tonight for this stranger, he doesn't want to have to do so again. 'You are well informed. Do you take an interest in this area?'

'Every time a piece of art is stolen we are poorer.' It sounds high-minded, not really the sentiments of a cop.

Storaro sips his wine. 'And if it should be offered to me – to buy?'

I must play this perfectly, remember who I am supposed to be. 'What does your conscience tell you?'

Storaro looks away sharply; he doesn't like the question.

'My conscience is my business, Signor Wright.' I can't see the look he gives Francesca but I sense the brimming rage. He doesn't like to account for himself. When he finally turns back to me he has fixed a look of composure on his face. 'It is academic. I have been offered many stolen paintings. Mostly they do not materialize, no matter how much I want them.'

I should leave it here. This man's favour is worth more than forcing him to confess he will break the law if it is necessary. But I push on.

'I suspect that you own paintings that others

claim as theirs.' Is this why I'm a cop and not a scholar? Was it really the establishment that kept me out or was I destined for this, my will knowing me better than my ego?

'You suspect?'

'Yes. I do not know.'

Storaro looks around the table, to Francesca. He has the flush of exercise. I haven't backed down and he has to deal with it. He addresses the table.

'You say you are a Michelangelo expert, no?'

The Team are his eyes. It is a nice trick. Where do I look – down at my empty plate, off to the side, to the ceiling? That's the point: forcing me to back down to have somewhere to look. It's simple and effective. I am not fazed by such tactics. I have had to make my case to men more dangerous than Storaro and his gang.

'I suppose Caravaggio is where my real expertise lies.'

'Not just Michelangelo, then? I am impressed. I am not an expert. It is not necessary. It is passion that is important. Art has never been loved by cleverness. Not really. It is loved because the heart is opened by it. I buy only what I love. I then display it for others. I do not own a single work of art others don't have access to.'

It is a strong argument. His emotion is strong. We were alike once. A long time ago. I am not his equal. I have nothing left to say.

'I look forward to seeing your collection tomorrow.'

I sense Storaro doesn't want to leave it but Francesca's fingers lightly touch his small hand and he is distracted. How strong are his emotions for her?

A waiter approaches for our dessert orders.

It is half eleven when I receive the cheese plate. Storaro hasn't ordered, choosing instead to lean over my plate and snap a chunk off a thick wedge of pecorino, breaking it into pieces with thumb and forefinger and eating it like chocolate. At twelve exactly he pushes his seat back, says goodnight and is gone. It is so sudden a departure I don't even have time to say goodbye, to thank him. Francesca explains that he gets bored waiting for everyone to finish and likes to walk home alone. I reach inside my jacket for my wallet and throw a credit card on to the table. Francesca slides it back.

Team Storaro quickly disperse. Some shake hands with me, others just disappear. Francesca kisses two, waves at one, ignores the rest. Within ten minutes of Storaro's leaving Francesca and I are alone, just a cheese plate between us. Francesca stares at it for a moment, and then with a long finger pushes the few remaining pieces around the plate to make a flower.

'For you.'

I smile. 'Thank you. How come you didn't just leave?'

'Then you would be alone.'

'I know my way around.'

'Would you like me to go?'

I look at Francesca's face, dark, intelligent, impassive. 'No.'

She messes up her flower pattern. 'Will you speak to your wife tonight?'

'I don't know. It's late. But she's an hour behind. Maybe.'

'You should. She'll be missing you.'

I don't answer. We leave the restaurant and walk diagonally across the piazza to the south-west corner, fresh snow imprinted with our footsteps.

'Do you want to know why Storaro really leaves like that? Girls. He's got a couple more hours to pick up a girl. He likes American girls, tall ones, blonde and tanned. They never know who he is. He doesn't use his money. He gets knocked back and knocked back, but he never goes home alone.'

I laugh. 'What about this time of year?'

'There are always some – rich ones taking classes in painting, sculpture. On New Year vacations.'

'What about you two?'

'Storaro says he loves me.' She shrugs.

'That must be quite something for him: to love something and not get it.'

She shrugs again. I push a little. 'You don't have an opinion?'

She stops and looks at me. 'Storaro is Storaro – you saw how he is. He plays by his own rules. But he is as generous as he is unscrupulous and we make exceptions for our friends.' She slides her arm in through mine; her curls brush my neck.

It begins to snow. The flurries descend lightly, distinctly. A soft tumble. Each snow flake is bright against the darkness of the narrow street, brighter in the haloes of streetlamps and window lights. Flakes flutter on to our clothes, our faces, evaporating instantly on gentle landing. Francesca curls her tongue out of her mouth, capturing the empty taste of its coldness. I dig my free hand deep into my pocket, stilling the vibrating ring of my mobile. Sarah. She promised she'd call.

4

I wake early, a little hungover, in a cold, cold room, condensation breaking into the air above the heavy quilt pulled up to my chin. A crack in the curtains lets the bright sun filter through the shutter slats. Will the snow be gone? Will everything be back to normal?

I roll out of bed, turn on the heater in the sitting room and take a shower. My first thoughts are of Sarah, of not speaking to her last night, ignoring her call, calling her later, the message I left: I want to be home with you; hope to be soon. The words sounding hollow as I said them. I enjoyed the evening too much to want to be home, to the chill of that house, Sarah's chill. And like a child desperate for an outing, I couldn't ignore the excitement I felt about my visit to Storaro's gallery. Once again to feel as though an earlier version of myself was being given new life, free of crime and crooks, of class associations and glass ceilings.

I call Sarah looking out of the sitting-room window

over the rooftops, the only evidence of last night's snow a few inverted drifts secreted in the shadows. I get the answerphone again. Even on her busy days she hasn't left for work by this time. I try her work number. There is no answer there. Her mobile goes straight to voicemail. Is she on the tube? Out of range somewhere? I am a little perturbed.

I leave the apartment. The smell of disinfectant has gone. Warm sunshine hits my face as I step out on to the street, quickly followed by the crisp-cold air. I breathe in; the air is sharp, pricking the back of my throat. I walk over to the small bar on the corner of Via Dante and order an espresso and two pastries. I pick out *La Repubblica* from a newspaper rack on the wall. My mobile rings. I look at the display – work.

'Danny?'

'Jim.'

'This is where we are. They have this prosecutor. They don't like him, but they promise by the weekend he'll be your man. I'm happy for you to come home and go back next week when this guy's in place.'

'Why don't they like him? I need someone I can trust. Someone *they* trust.'

'You know these European lawyers, more interested in politics than crime.'

I turn over a page of the newspaper. 'There's no point coming home now. They know I'm here.'

'Who knows you're there?'

'The Uffizi.'

'So you made contact?'

'I was bored.'

'I told you to relax.'

'That's not your job.' I stare out of the window to the small church covered in scaffolding. Did Dante use it, I wonder. What did he pray for: that Beatrice would love him?

'Danny?'

It is time to be straight. 'Last year. In Calabria, on the Turner job . . .' I pause; how to phrase it – say it quickly? 'What if I told you I really did see the Caravaggio . . . ?'

The interruption is fast. 'You know what! If you saw it, we tell Rome. It ends there.'

My stomach tightens, burns with the bitter heat of the espresso. What do I say?

Jim demands, 'Did you see it or not?'

'I don't know.'

'Danny?'

'What?'

'Tell me.'

'Maybe.'

He doesn't believe me. 'Then you're fantasizing. Only cranks think it hasn't been destroyed.'

Do I doubt it myself sometimes? Yes. Am I a crank? Possibly.

Jim continues, 'And remember, Dan – they're cop-killers down there.'

'I can handle it.'

'There's nothing to handle.'

I change the subject, my heart pounding, realizing

I cannot let the painting go – not to Rome, not even to Jim. 'What do we know about Immanuel Storaro?'

'Why?'

I sense his impatience: is this connected to my fantasy or the operation – which, quick? I go on, 'Is he just some rich boy playing around?'

'What's this connected to, Danny?'

'I met him last night. He has a gallery here. Has some profile in buying stolen art.'

'Don't they all? How did you meet him?'

'Francesca Natali.'

'Is he connected to the Uffizi?'

'He knows her.'

'Do you think he's connected to the Uffizi rumour?'

'The rumour's bullshit, you know that.'

'The rumour is your operation.'

'Storaro interests me.'

'Caravaggio, Storaro. Concentrate, Dan. You're all over the place. You should come home, sort your head out.'

'Make your mind up.'

'Come home, spend some time with Sarah. Go back next week. Relax.'

'You keep saying that.'

'Because I mean it.'

'I don't know what to say to that.'

'Just tell me what you're going to do.'

'I think I'll stick around.'

'And do what?'

'Relax, like you said.'

*　　*　　*

In the apartment – heater on, gas rings on – I boot up the laptop and skim read my emails. There is one from Sarah – sent yesterday. I double-click.

Hi Dan,
We do get up each other's noses, don't we?
Missing you.
Sx

Sent seven-thirty p.m. Doesn't really mean much now, although it does tell me she thinks about me when I'm not there. I have wondered, using Bishop Berkeley's conundrum, what kind of falling tree I am in Sarah's wood. Sometimes I think I make no sound. But then maybe I do. I open a new email.

Francesca,
Thanks for an interesting evening. Are we on for Storaro's gallery?
Do you want to meet there? What time?
Dan

I hit send. Go back to Sarah's email and press reply.

Sarah,
Tried calling. No answer. Everything OK?
DanX

I push the laptop away. The new-mail window pops up. From Francesca.

Signor Wright.
The gallery is open. Piazza Santo Spirito.
Francesca.

Just because Storaro suggested she escort me, I assumed she would; I don't remember her agreement.

Thanks, Francesca.
I will go this morning.
I hope to see you again.
Daniel.

There is nothing to stop me going now. I shut down the computer. On the stairs I pass the cleaner, on her knees with hard brush in hand; the stairwell is high with disinfectant. Outside Via Dante glistens. The mid-morning sunshine has melted away the last traces of snow, leaving only pools of water over the cobbles, mirror-bursts of light. I unbutton my overcoat and jacket; the cold air presses through my shirt and clings to my skin. I dig my hands into my trouser pockets. Walking at a clip, it takes me only ten minutes to reach Piazza Santo Spirito in Oltrarno. The piazza itself is almost as big as the other big public spaces in Florence but without the phalanxes of tourists. It is at the heart of a residential quarter of the city.

There is a small food market set up around the wide circle of trees which borders the pedestrian section of the piazza. At the very centre there is a simple grey stone fountain encrusted with black and white pigeon droppings, municipal cleaning budget going elsewhere. It's the least pristine object I have seen in Florence. To my right there is a church, its façade a flat light-brown stucco as modest, as unadorned, as any Reformation equivalent. The Storaro Gallery is towards the far corner. A new building. Shockingly new for Florence. Shockingly new anywhere. Its design purposefully aggravates the flatness of the adjacent buildings and formally contradicts the church opposite. On first appearance it is little more than a hundred-metre-tall orange egg, half set back into the line of other buildings, half protruding into the public space of the piazza. From a distance, its surface is perfectly smooth, yet as I draw closer, it appears to be made up of thousands of terracotta tiles. From within twenty metres, the surface breaks up even further into arbitrarily arranged half-metre-square planes. The building perfectly echoes and moulds into an organic shape the cubist vista of the rooftops of Florence. There are no windows, just a double door on the far side.

The reception is more like that of an ad agency than an art gallery. The long reception desk is made out of serpentine layers of cedar wood and chrome. Behind it sit two attractive women in uniform (deconstructed grey suits, white shirts, maroon ties with Storaro vertically printed) staring into large widescreen iBooks. The walls are bare. The two receptionists smile at me. A group of young people – tourists, judging from their cagoules, rucksacks, guides – appear from what must be the entrance to the gallery proper. Unusually for Italy there isn't an admission fee. I step up to the reception desk.

'Signor Storaro, please. My name is Daniel Wright.'

One of the receptionists picks up the phone and quietly announces me.

'Sorry, sir. Storaro cannot see you. You are invited to go in.'

I am disappointed. I feel cheated. First Francesca, now Storaro. Was last evening's version of myself not compelling enough even to endure for a single night?

I place my overcoat in the cloakroom. The attendant is as attractive, as smartly dressed as the two receptionists. All recruited from a model agency, I guess. I have seen this before: first in New York hotels in the early 1990s, now in London. This is a first in an art gallery. The security guard posted outside the first room might be from the fashion pages of Italian *Vogue*. Is this part of a campaign to make art more attractive to young people? I give the guard a smile. There is no response. Unlike myself joining the police force, this young man didn't apply for the job to be closer to art. I make my way into the heart of the gallery. The shape of the exterior promised a layout similar to that of New York City's Guggenheim Museum, a spiral adhering to the inside curve; it is more conventional, however. I look at the gallery map. There are six floors, with a central column housing the two elevators. From the map it seems that each room has only four paintings – one per wall. A luxury allowed by a small collection. There is a short paragraph below the map, the gallery's mission statement.

> The first painting you will see was created in 1440, the next within the last twelve months. Some rooms have paintings from four different centuries. It is my belief that if the context and setting are right, everyone can appreciate all art, however distant or difficult it may seem. This is not a museum. Nothing here is old.
>
> Immanuel Storaro

I wander around the collection. There are few other visitors. I find this depressing. I know right at this moment on a cold January morning the sign outside the Uffizi reads: 'Queue time approximately three hours.'

The prizes of the collection are on the third floor. In the centre of the egg. A large, square room. Four paintings. A Rothko, a Cézanne, an El Greco, a Velázquez. My first thought is: where did Storaro get these paintings from? My first feeling, overriding my first thought, is: wow! I spin on my heels to take them in. It is a bold curatorial decision, hanging such strong paintings together. Each painting cannot be looked at for long without the viewer feeling the energy of another exerting itself, a beckoning presence. This is not a 'stop and look at the pretty pictures' room. This room has a centrifugal force that keeps you here. Spinning from one painting to another. There are two tonalities in the room, bisecting it almost. The Cézanne and the El Greco, golden, shimmering, diffuse, yet somehow still sharply present, reach into the room like sunlight; the Rothko and the Velázquez, both recessively dark, shy almost, yet with equal presence, cross the room like moonlight. Each tonality has its beauty, its magnetism. If there is an idea behind this room, it seems to me to be saying art affects the world beyond its details, its emotion, its surface, beyond the intellect and even our emotions. It is saying art fundamentally alters our perception of the world – it has phenomenological sway.

How often does Storaro come and sit in this room? If this luxury was available to me, would I ever leave? I once again spin on my heels. Folded into the modulating light. I stop only when I hear my name being whispered. It is Luca.

'Storaro is ready.'

I hadn't realized I was waiting to be seen. I am pleased. I want to show my appreciation. Right now I don't care whether I'm a dissatisfied policeman or not: I am thrilled that Storaro has reminded me that I can still be shocked, moved, elevated – that my heart isn't blunt.

Luca takes me up to the top of the egg. The domed ceiling is a brightly coloured set of circles – a vast inverted version of a Kenneth Nolan painting. There are a number of partitioned rooms giving off the small central reception. A very lively, attractive American girl greets us. I spot a few members of Team Storaro through open doors, some talking on phones, feet up on desks, fingers fiddling with packets of cigarettes, lighters, staplers; others staring at computer screens, hands poised on mice, gently gliding them around their pads. Luca shows me to a door, knocks, pushes it open and then retreats.

If the design of the gallery indicates Storaro's interest in combining organic shapes and hard lines, his office indicates his interest in the maximum chaos a single space will contain. It is a large room, at least half the top of the egg. To my left there are four tall oak-veneered filing cabi- nets, all leaning forward precariously, top drawers out or half out, clogged to overspilling; to my right there is a table piled high with box files, all open or bulging open, or bulging shut because of the weight of the art books stacked on top. There must be over a hundred exhibition and auction cata- logues scattered on the floor. In the centre of the room there are large wooden crates containing, or once containing I presume, artworks, all surrounded by drifts of tiny white polystyrene packing pieces. Amongst the chaos no technology of any sort is visible. Surprisingly, the walls are bare except for a photograph – the Cartier-Bresson. The Italian lovers in the sea. It hangs at a slight angle.

Storaro is at his desk. On his invitation – another click of his fingers, more from enthusiasm than as a command – I gingerly make my way between the boxes, strewn books and catalogues. Storaro pushes himself off his chair; I notice through the glass desktop that his feet are propped up on a box. He greets me in the same way as the night before, clasping my arms at my elbows. He then turns and goes over to the window, offering a long and curved panoramic view of Florence. One hand tugs at a recalcitrant curl. I join him. He is in an English pinstriped suit. Single button. It is tight just below the ribs. His chest is a little puffed out. We stand in silence for a moment. The hills beyond the city are bright under a translucent blue sky. Storaro is the first to speak.

'Francesca is not with you.' There is a little bounce as he says this. It is very much a statement and not a question.

I now understand the meaning behind the original invitation last night. It had nothing to do with Storaro and myself quickly finding common ground, or his collecting of experts. It was about Francesca. Storaro playing a little power game. In *ordering* Francesca to bring me, he understood that only real keenness on me would have made her obey. The bounce indicates how pleased he is that she has chosen not to obey him. My misunderstanding embarrasses me. I am angry. I try to contain it by staring out over Oltrarno, over the red terracotta roofs echoed by this extraordinary building. Storaro is too full of energy to remain silent for long. I sense us both rock on our heels.

'You like my gallery.' Again, more statement than question.

I want to gush – I love it, I envy him. That room! My dream job once was to work somewhere like this. But I can't say any of these things, not after his first statement, not after discovering the real reason for my being here. Silence is my only strength. Storaro doesn't like silence; he is for enthusiasm and battle, personality and power exerted.

'Who are you?' he asks. Another bounce.

It is the toughest of questions, undercover or not. Explaining oneself, whoever you are, always sounds desperate or somehow excusing. All descriptions of ourselves will be thin. I choose honesty – pithy honesty. 'I am a failure.'

Storaro looks up at me, forcing me to step back so that the angle between us is not so steep. I don't sense any strong dislike, but I do feel scrutinized. There is a slight tremor in his bright blue eyes as he stares at me. I don't sense any vulnerability, however, despite the need for games, the tremor. I also don't sense darkness. Or the requirement for cruelty in games. I refuse to be engaged.

Storaro laughs – he has worked out my game plan. 'The silent type.'

He pats me on the arm and turns into the room. He calls Luca – a kind of absent-minded bellow – and sits back at his desk, unbuttoning his jacket, hoisting himself into his chair and propping up his feet.

Luca appears at the door and waves me over. I hesitate by the window for a moment. I have been dismissed. My little game worked out. His little game played out. There is no reason for my presence. The anger in me is now less well contained. I feel like clipping Storaro on the back of the head. More: smashing the tough little cranium into the glass desk. But instead I lean over him and whisper, 'Hey, Storaro. The stolen Caravaggio, *The Nativity*. Would you like to know where it is?'

I feel him stiffen, a little muscular contraction rising up his back, pulling at his shoulders. He turns slowly. My presence now has intrigue, meaning, possibilities. I do not wait. I cross the room and pass Luca at the door. I hear only quick, machine-gun-fire Italian between the two men.

Emerging from the great egg, my earlier anger has been replaced by a new anger. The aim has shifted from Storaro to myself. I have made the stupidest of mistakes. Why did I tell him? I know why. For childish reasons, with subtler results. I wanted to unsettle him. Take away his control for a moment. Beat the dismissal. Persist in his mind. It didn't matter he was the last person I should tell. Not at that moment. I just wanted to last a little longer amid the chaos of that room, to add to it. Replace his small victory using Francesca with a new, bigger game: the Caravaggio. A stupid, stupid mistake. I should have remained the silent type. Right now he has a member of Team Storaro before him, instructing him to check me out. Check out the insinuation – how could I know where the painting is? How long will that take? With his level of power, influence, money, resources, he could know by the end of the day. But then he might just focus on the painting. It would be the greatest prize of his collection. If it's out there and I know where it is, so too must others – others closer to him, his sway. I picture the Caravaggio on the hilltop, dark and silver under the hottest sun, the darkest tree, hard and crisp and flaking within the grip of dry, dark hands. Its existence is so real to me now it feels vulnerable to others – to others finding it before me. I've just forced my own hand.

5

Back at the apartment I power up the laptop, click Outlook, double-click new mail.

Jim,
Am I owed any leave?

I wait. Standing over the laptop. I am mostly still, only fingers twitching. My eyes are narrowed with strong thoughts, hard internal focus.

Don't do it.

Am I owed any leave?

No.

I think for a second, less –

I'm taking some personal time.

I email Sarah.

> Want to come home – really. But I can't.
> Out of radio contact for a while now. Don't
> worry.
> Speak to you in a few days.
> DanX

I pack what I need, no more. Change into jeans, white T-shirt, black crewneck. Back in the sitting room I open up my wallet and dump everything on to the table. The cash is pressed back. I shuffle through the credit cards, discarding work's, the joint account, my own, sliding the remaining one back into the wallet. Name on it: David White, my pseudonym – close enough to my own name to get my attention if called out. I hunt for my mobile in the right-hand pocket of my overcoat, find it in the left. I place it on the table, give it a spin, leave it spinning.

Wednesday, Thursday, Friday, the weekend. Back Sunday night. What will I learn in that time? Something. How close will I get? If I can find Italo Nenni, maybe something, maybe close.

I walk quickly towards the station. Nothing can stop me now; there is no way to contact me, no one knows where I am going. Jim will suspect, but what can he do? Send in the troops? Personal time is allowed; the job proper now starts Monday. He'll just be fucked off – won't want the hassle of me out in the field with no brief. Can't just turn up with a Caravaggio and claim all the glory. But why not – if I find it? Say it was a personal mission? Funded by myself. On my own time.

At the station I buy a ticket for Naples – due in fifteen minutes from Milan, going all the way to Palermo, loaded on to a boat at Reggio, sailing across the Messina Straits. I know there is no point going straight to Calabria. It might be closer to the Caravaggio but I don't have a contact there, and if there is one region in Italy where the people are in full denial about their organized crime, it is Calabria. It has to be worked through Naples, through Nenni. It was only six months ago I got to the old man via this *camorrista*. But then in six months the *'ndrangheta* could have switched allegiance and now be working with Cosa Nostra. If this is the case, the Sicilians will have taken out anyone they deem a liability – and that means Italo Nenni. This is law enforcement's real problem: every organized crime syndicate knows every other organized crime syndicate's informants, so when new allegiances are forged these men become the first victims, often within hours. Three murdered men – car bomb, a restaurant killing, a drowning – doesn't mean the start of a war; it usually means the end of one. Italo Nenni must be alive, because without him I'll have to cultivate a new contact, and that takes longer than four days.

I buy a *Guardian Europe* from a news-stand and take my place on the platform, leaning against an iron column. The train pulls in. Exactly on time. I read the newspaper during the slow disembarkation and then climb on myself, choosing a forward-facing seat with no one opposite.

Just under four hours to Naples. Time to think – think my way into this. Two big problems to solve. How to be shown the Caravaggio a second time? And then what to do? My job as a copper is to recover stolen works of art on mainly semi-legitimate terms: buy back (pay the ransom), trade back (do a deal), occasionally take back (make an arrest). But this is different: I don't have the money to buy it back, no one is offering a deal and I've no powers of arrest. It is unlikely the department will supply any money; a deal requires complicity from both parties; arrest needs the involvement of local law enforcement, which means being kicked to the sidelines. That leaves . . . stealing it back myself.

NAPLES AND CAMPANIA

1

I check into a hotel close to the station. My room is modestly corporate – all blond laminate and beige. The bed is hard, the two pillows shapeless, as if full of cotton wool. I am happy to be back in Naples – Western Europe's last great pre-twenty-first-century city, visibly free from globalization, e-modernity, brand essences.

I dump my bag on the bed and head out. Naples is warmer than Florence. Busier. The traffic, as always, is clogged and stalled. The Vespa riders, legs splayed to the street, guide their scooters around the cars to find clearer passage. The pavements overflow with makeshift stalls selling fake goods, pirated CDs, DVDs. The air is full of conversation and argument. Even with the low cloud and the expectation of rain the city feels like a North African outpost.

The Forcella district, the heart of the Camorra in central Naples, is just off Piazza Garibaldi, close to the station, close to my hotel. If Nenni is still alive, this is where I will find him. Making contact, however, will not be easy. I'll need to sight Nenni and be sighted by him, after which we will need to manoeuvre ourselves to a place of proximity, a café, a street-crossing, where a few words exchanged will not be noticed, where '*scusi*' or '*grazie*' or '*prego*' can be changed into a location, a time – the old-time cop/grass pas de deux. My only concern is that for whatever reason, Nenni will decide not to follow my lead, will need coaxing, or worse, will choose to announce to Naples what only he knows – I am a cop, a *sbirro*.

I've already decided on the location. Chosen by Nenni last year. Up on the hill, in Vomero. An ice-cream parlour. Because, as he explained in his high split-octave voice, the Camorra doesn't frequent ice-cream parlours on the hill – too bourgeois. On that occasion I paid him five thousand euros for a name, the name that eventually led me to the old man. I groomed him over a week: three meets for trust, the next for the deal, last one for the exchange: name, money.

Italo Nenni is hard to miss, whether you're looking for him or not. He is bone thin, tall for a southern Italian. He has big, red-rimmed and bloodshot eyes, olive-sallow cheeks, a wide mobile mouth. Always short of breath, he is endocrinologically hyper: words come quickly, spillingly. He is stupid, also. You don't become a gangster if you talk too much. But then clearly other people are more stupid; they talk around him. What Nenni does inside the organization, I don't know. Not very much – why else would he be on the take? But that isn't always how it works; I've met informants with plenty of money who do it just for the thrill, the power. They like playing both sides, dictating terms, having influence – private sway. Don't care that it will never bring them prestige, fame, glory. Just like having other people's fate in their hands. I don't know what Nenni's motivation is but the power surge when the exchange of information took place was visible. He knew every word was a potential death sentence.

Forcella is dirty, poor, cramped, the buildings a mix of medieval and modern, every one in need of renovation, investment, cleaning. There is no charm. There is something about these streets which is excited. The air vibrates; the atmosphere feels combustible. It is always busy with human anger: the men agitated, the women bickering hard. Despite being so central – close to the station, to Spaccanapoli, to the port – it is like a prison – a prison of dark bonds, psychological bondage. You sense deep atavistic reasons for people being unable to break out, to leave. There is a kind of claustrophobia exuding from its walls. Tourists accidentally finding themselves lost here feel unsettled, quickly desperate – core fear, danger is experienced. Even in high summer, with bright blue sky above, the sunlight has its own quality: heavy, hard, adding another transparent wall for its people.

It starts to rain. Warm soft rain. I look up to the

sky – the cloud cover is low, thick, complete. Bad weather is no good for tracking down people in Naples, the streets quickly empty, the *bassi* doors close, the gangs of *camorristi* hanging around the tiny piazzas, the street corners, the cafés disperse. I must persevere. Time is short. I walk for an hour, stopping now and again to shelter from the rain under archways, doorways, the porticos of chapels. I know that if I find Nenni this afternoon it will be a miracle. But what can I do? I think about Storaro: what is *he* doing? How many of his team are on it? Will he go straight to Goldini – the one Italian investigator who still believes it's out there? I doubt it. Like me, he wants it for himself. At least I want to find it myself, beyond that I haven't planned. How close can Storaro get – in real terms? I can't know. Somewhere, nowhere. Nearer than me? Unlikely by now, only hours into desk research. I try to relax; I am in Naples looking for a man who got me closer than any other person outside of organized crime in over thirty years. I am ahead in this game.

I return to the hotel, shower, change into dry clothes and go to the bar. It is evening. I order a drink – whisky – and slump into an armchair. Rain smacks against the window. My last chance to run into Nenni today is at a *trattoria* at the end of Spaccanapoli, on the edge of the Spanish Quarter. If he's alone, which is almost certain, and the place is busy, which is probable, I might be able to work a seat at his table.

I look at my watch: 8.10 p.m. Still too early to catch a Neapolitan at dinner. I order another drink. My first concern is how to persuade Nenni to give up what he knows with no real cash on offer. I need to convince him a skim off the profits will be more worthwhile, which means I'll need to convince him there'll be a profit, and given that Nenni knows I'm a copper – a straight copper – that's going to be tough. I watch the wind blow the rain against the window. The night sky is dark, cracked by black cloud. The streetlights are dull, diffuse, weak bursts of orange, yellow, white.

The rain eases up at nine and I leave. The night air is damp, close. The pavements and roads are pooled with water. The speed of the Neapolitan driver means a permanent spray rises over the pavement. I have never known Naples so dark; every wall casts a shadow so wide the streets are thick with darkness – it is double dark. Some streets are so narrow they can be spanned with open arms, both hands disappearing completely into black shadow.

The *trattoria* is open; a smoky glow gives on to the street. From across the road I search the diners for a thin, agitated presence, conspicuous from even this distance. He is there. Sitting at the back. Alone. A bowl of pasta is placed before him. The restaurant isn't busy enough for me to be offered an occupied table, and to insist on Nenni's will raise the suspicions of anyone happy to have them. I take a quick walk around the block and into the backstreets, side-stepping the junkies perched on the steps of Salita Pontecorvo, stopping to look down at an array of used needles and syringes spread over the stone steps like a conceptual installation. The junkies don't look up at me or speak; they are all slumped in a post-hit euphoria, vomit loosely falling from their chins.

The restaurant is busier when I return and I can't see an empty table. I push through the door. A waiter asks, '*Uno solo?*' a hand ready to apologetically show me how full they are, that I will have to share. I smile and explain that I'm hungry, happy to share, all the while making my way to the back.

Nenni looks up, his body performing a sequence of jerks: surprise, apprehension, confusion. I say, '*Ciao*,' and sit down. There is a reflexive movement backwards from his head to the centre of his chest as if he's avoiding a punch. It's the reaction of someone wound tightly; the same thing would have happened if I had really been just a hungry tourist moving into his space. I smile, my expression telling him: take it easy. He returns to his food. The aggressive twist of his fork in the spaghetti makes the *ragu* sauce arc into the air and across the table. He chews with his mouth open, preventing food falling out by constantly adding bread. I suspect Nenni doesn't regard the contents of his mouth so much as food but as fuel, carbo-energy to keep his overdriving body from going into a slump, a slump which might signal the end. For the first time I realize that it is probably Nenni's hyperactivity which keeps him alive; there is a kind of alertness about him that computes danger fast. He doesn't sense I am there to hurt him.

I look up at the menu on the wall. I order the *spaghetti alla puttanesca,* followed by sausages and *friarielli* – my Neapolitan favourite. And a bottle of cheap Taurasi, the only kind available. I am going to wait until my *primo piatti* arrives before I speak. Then it will only be tourist stuff: what can I see in Naples? Where do I get the boat to Capri? Is Sorrento as nice as they say?

Nenni doesn't wait. 'What are you doing here?'

I smile. 'Do you know where I get the boat to Capri?'

Nenni shakes his head; his left shoulder spasms. 'I know you. What are you doing here?'

'Is Sorrento as nice as they say?'

'Forget it, *sbirro.* What do you want?'

I look around the restaurant; no one looks interested in our conversation. My pasta arrives.

'I want to know about a man.'

'Don't know him. I work for myself now.'

'That's a coincidence, so do I.'

Nenni looks up, curious. Two things intrigue him. First, as a Neapolitan, he is superstitious, and therefore coincidence must be recognized as meaningful. Second, if he's not sitting opposite a cop, who is he sitting opposite? He wipes his bowl with bread, chews on it.

'I make good money. I pay Savarese, but still it's good.'

'That's a coincidence. I make good money. I don't pay Savarese anything.'

'You are not *camorrista*.'

I shrug. 'I need a name.'

Nenni looks up as the waiter brings his *secondo piatti*; hands always needing to be busy, Nenni offers up his pasta bowl while at the same time taking the large plate of *fritto misto* from the waiter before he has a chance to place it on the table. There is a moment of confusion.

I gently turn my fork into my pasta.

Nenni is defiant. 'No names. I work for myself now.'

I read pride here, and a need to explain.

'What are you doing?'

Nenni shakes his head wildly. 'No. No.'

I take a mouthful of food. 'You don't want to tell me?'

'What do you do now, *sbirro*?'

'Same thing but for different people.'

Nenni's eyes bulge, threatening to pop out of their sockets and into my pasta – mozzarella balls in tomato sauce.

We both eat. I let Nenni talk – gabble. He's married now. A beautiful woman. And again: plenty of money. Nice car. Moved out of Forcella. Too dirty. The waiters, he says, call him Don Italo now. I'm not sure I've heard this, but I nod my head pretending to understand, to be impressed.

For my next question I add a little mocking deference.

'Tell me, Don Italo, how do you make all this money?'

'You steal my business, *Inglese*, I have to kill you.'

A fork is pointed at me. I laugh. 'You don't kill people, Nenni.'

'I pay. It's cheap in Napoli.'

'Don't threaten me. I can still talk to Savarese. Your secrets are not safe with me.'

Nenni wipes his mouth, chin, cheek with a tomato-sauce-stained napkin. 'Tell me, who are your customers?'

For a second I don't understand the question; but then I realize Nenni is taking it for granted that if I am no longer a cop, I must therefore be a crook, and if I am a crook, I have either victims or customers, and he's judging I haven't moved such a moral distance in six months that I now have victims.

'Their tastes are too expensive for you, Nenni.'

There is a moment of calm, followed by a smile. 'Maybe. Maybe not.'

I sense certainty in Nenni, which is something new. His body is still as uncontrolled, but his conversation is more measured. I let him think I am intrigued. 'I don't know what you deal in.'

He grins; he is satisfied he can manipulate me now – things have changed.

'You have Japanese, Americans? They have the money.'

'A name first.'

He tries to still his arms by laying them flat on the table, either side of his plate.

I wait. Nenni's metabolism means he lacks patience. Like Storaro, he is unsettled by silence – his mind needs stimulus to work over.

'How long are you in Napoli?'

'As long as it takes me to get a name.'

'What is it worth?'

'To me or to you?'

He smiles widely. He has a large mouth, full, mobile lips. His teeth are unexpectedly regular, clean.

'Do you need money?'

There is a darkening of his eyes; an assessment is being made. 'I am a businessman,' he says quickly, hiding something.

It is my turn to smile.

Nenni thinks for a moment, blinks; I feel his legs bouncing nervously under the table. He leans forward, whispering. 'We make easy money together. Forget Savarese.'

I sit back. 'Now I know you're not serious.'

'I am serious.' His eyes dart around the restaurant. 'I need a new partner.' This is dangerous talk however far we are from Forcella. He nods to my chest. It has just occurred to him I might be wired. I open my jacket, rub my shirt – no recording equipment. I want to know where this is going.

'What do you want, Nenni?'

'Meet me tomorrow night.'

'Let's talk now.'

Nenni thinks about this; his thoughts are visible, physicalized: his hands clench, his thin skin tightens over his thick, hard, protruding cheekbones. He cannot decide what to give away.

'What do your people buy?'

I think of Storaro – deep pockets for art. I think of Gustav Ballack – the biggest man, in all senses, in the art underworld, always searching for ever more precious objects. I decide for the purposes of this transaction I am an agent for these people, people like these – big dealers, fences, collectors: the biggest.

'I have people who will buy art. Important people. Deep pockets.'

'Other things?' Nenni leans over the table; he wants more flexibility over my customers' needs. Waiters look at us. I take another mouthful of pasta, a sip of wine – the gesture is saying I am unperturbed by this man.

He shifts the subject. 'Tell me what the name is for?'

It is my turn to stiffen, tense up. I don't want to be told he doesn't know, he can't find out – for the conversation to end here tonight. I need Nenni to be more deeply entwined than this, to have reason, motivation, to want to give up this name. And not to lie.

'You want a name but you won't tell me what for?' I sense Nenni's irritation is getting beyond his control; his neck is twitching, the veins pulsing, pushed out through his skin.

'You need to be careful, Nenni.'

He is angered by this. The red rims of his eyes look watery, pinkish, sad for a moment; his thick, mobile lips tremble. His anger is sublimated fear. There has been a lot of posturing tonight, I realize. His confidence has been an act of will. There is something desperate beneath his display of relative composure.

'I'm Italo Nenni – a fool, they think. You think. But you are here. You want something from me. Then tomorrow night: Piazza del Plebiscito. Ten p.m. Remember, I will want something from you.' He stands, knocking against the table, rattling glasses, plates, cutlery.

Money is dealt out on the table, over the batter and bone remnants of his *fritto misto*. I want to tidy it, shuffle it into an orderly pile and place it neatly in the centre of the table for the waiter, but it will seem odd, doing this for someone I don't know.

He stands by the table, a jittery presence beside me. He wants confirmation I will be where he has ordered. I sip my wine and stare ahead at a big framed photograph of Vesuvius before its last eruption, its plume of smoke rising slinkily to the sky.

Nenni refuses to wait any longer and leaves, a difficult manoeuvre in a busy restaurant for someone so much lacking in control over his limbs. The regular diners pull their chairs in for him and watch him through the door with sympathetic looks. A waiter comes over and apologizes to me while removing my pasta bowl, replacing it with a small plate with two thick sausages tied together and a portion of *friarielli*, its deep green colour bleeding into the olive oil pooling across the plate. I eat, asking myself: what can Nenni be into? What would generate so much enthusiasm and could also make him think I would be interested? Stolen antiques, artworks? It doesn't seem likely. The bigger question, however, is whether to meet him tomorrow night. I accept that if I want to get close to the Caravaggio in the next couple of days, I don't have much choice.

2

I am on the corner of the Piazza del Plebiscito at ten p.m. The wind, coming up from the bay, is light, cold, salty. I expect to wait at least an hour for Nenni, if he turns up at all. Yet within five minutes a brand-new Alfa Romeo Sportwagon pulls alongside me and the passenger-side window glides down. Nenni leans over, looks up at me and around the empty piazza. He then pushes open the door.

I back away, shaking my head. 'If you think I'm going anywhere with you, you're crazy.'

Nenni stiffens, his back arching across the car. 'You will be safe.' He slumps back into the driver's seat.

I lean in. 'Forget it.'

His fingers in dark-brown driving gloves tense and splay, drum the steering wheel. He looks into the rear-view mirror, the side mirror.

'I am not waiting, *sbirro*.'

'Goodbye.' I slam the door and step back. The gears crunch and the car shunts forward a metre into the empty piazza. I do not move. Nenni's skills don't include this kind of brinkmanship. The gears crunch again and he reverses back; the window is still open. He stays where he is, focused forward, ready.

'If I am going to get into this car with you, Nenni, I need to know what we are doing.'

He shakes his head; he has regained a little of his initial confidence. 'You have to ask yourself, *sbirro*: is the name you want worth the risk?'

I think of Sarah first, then Jim; neither knows where I am, both would say: don't get in the car.

I stand up straight, pull my shoulders back, try to focus. Heat is coming off the car, the high-powered engine turning over with a low hum.

I lean back in. 'Tell me how you knew where the Turner was last year?'

Nenni smiles, lips wide, loose. His fingers are still. 'The man you met in Cosenza. My cousin. Did you not notice the resemblance?' He laughs. He knows the man I met was hard, tough-looking – a pile-driver of a man. Nenni continues. 'If it's something he might know, we can do business.' He motions with his head for me to climb in.

I am assessing the risk. Nenni offers the only quick route to the Caravaggio; I cannot find one good reason why he would want to harm me. Plus, I overhear myself thinking, if you don't take the risk, it really all ends here.

I climb in. 'I guess you're not going to tell me where we are going?'

Nenni holds a finger to his lips, as if the car is bugged, and presses down on the gas. The three-point turn is poorly executed; gears aren't found, pedals mistimed. This is going to be fun, I think. However, the moment we are moving forward I notice a reduction in Nenni's tics: his neck stops twisting, arching; his breathing seems more regular; his knees, always bouncing against the rhythm of the incessant tapping of his feet, are now perfectly still.

We head out of the city and along the port, following the signs for the A3. The bay is a black wall rising from the shore to the sky, without distance, a horizon; Capri, the Sorrentine penin-sula are invisible. The Sportwagon snakes easily between the beat-up compact Fiats, Smart Cars and Vespa hordes.

I rephrase my question. 'Are you going to tell me where we're going?'

Nenni looks at me quickly, eyes flashing. 'It's an expedition.'

'Just tell me. I can still call the *carabinieri* and have them pick you up. Do you want to spend a week in jail worried what Savarese is thinking you're telling them?'

Nenni laughs. 'Call them. This is my car.' It is half-joke, half statement of fact. I laugh.

Nenni concentrates on the road. 'Who are your people – your buyers?' A shudder passes along his shoulders and then down his body; there is a slight shake of the car as his hands roll the steering wheel left then right. I ignore the question. We leave the last vestiges of the city itself and pass through derelict industrial land, poor suburbs. The sky above us is high and dark, cloudless, star-specked. Traffic is beginning to thin. Within ten minutes, having rounded a dark Vesuvius – a relief of night against night – we are on a long open road, straight, level, tree-lined. Nenni presses down on the gas and with smooth gear changes the car builds speed. A sign displays a fork in the road, east or south. Nenni moves left, and eases the car on to a slip road which takes us on to the *autostrada* heading south. I am surprised by this. Not surprised we have left Naples – the only business Nenni was going to have to himself would be outside the city, but for some reason, I'm not sure why, the south was unexpected. Maybe because the south is other people's territory.

Nenni's hands grip the steering wheel firmly, his arms are straight, foot on the gas, head locked forward; he is either a man with a mission to get somewhere fast or a man directing his concentration down into his body in the knowledge that one tic and the car will spin out of control.

'Do you like driving?'

Nenni presses the accelerator to the floor, the needle of the speedometer pressing on to 185 . . . 190 . . . 200 kmph. With few cars on the *autostrada*, he takes the racing line as the road sweeps through the southern countryside. Far off to my right I can make out a range of mountains, a low, jagged, black edge against the horizon. Below them, a dark stretching plain, with only the occasional nest of lights. This is sparsely populated country – hard country.

Nenni slows down slightly as he takes his left hand off the steering wheel and turns on the radio; it is tuned to a classical music station. I don't recognize the music – it's richly orchestrated, colour more important than development: Berlioz or Resphighi or something.

'You like this music?'

Nenni nods, quick, certain.

'You're chatty tonight.'

'Who are your buyers?'

I decide answering will open up the conversation. Plus I want to know what he knows.

'Immanuel Storaro,' I say flatly. 'Right now I'm buying for Immanuel Storaro.'

Nenni's eyes narrow, the thick, loose lips purse.

'Do you know him?' I ask.

He laughs. 'He is very famous in Italy.'

I am certain there is more. I wait.

'He is very ugly, no?' He laughs again.

Nenni doesn't seem very impressed that he is my client. 'What else do you know about him?'

'He owns Fiorentina – they never win.'

'That's it?'

'He likes women.'

'He's Italian.'

'This is true.'

Nenni lacks Neapolitan inscrutability so I decide

he really doesn't recognize Storaro as an important underworld buyer. Somehow I am both pleased and unsettled. It limits his chances of moving quickly on the Caravaggio. It may mean, however, he is forced to go through legitimate channels – channels which leak this kind of news and will drive the painting underground. Plus a legitimate recovery would certainly mean the painting returned to the San Lorenzo Oratory, and Storaro knows this.

'Your turn, Nenni. Where are we going?'

After a pause Nenni flicks his head against the headrest. 'Look in the back.'

I turn to the back seat. It's empty.

'In the back!' Nenni is impatient and takes one hand off the steering wheel, thumbs towards the rear of the car. The car swerves in the road. I am forced to steady the steering wheel like a driving instructor. I wait until the car is under control before pushing myself between passenger seat and driver seat and extending my body over the back seat to peer into the boot. There is a large Nike sports bag, unzipped and bloated. Inside there is a set of long chrome rods, two spades, a pickaxe and two heavy-duty torches. There is also the dark shape of a handgun – a Glock 9mm. I ease myself back into my seat.

'Well, we're either burying something, digging something up or we're doing a bit of landscape gardening. Why the gun?'

Nenni looks over. 'I am *camorrista*.'

I accept this. 'It stays there, Nenni, unless I instruct otherwise.'

Nenni shrugs. 'No one knows where we're going.'

A series of signs appear – south, east, smaller towns – signalling an interchange. Nenni guides the car across to the slip road, following the directions east. I only know two things about this area: it is very poor and it is famous for the quantity and quality of its Greek vases. Every year increasing numbers of vases are illegally excavated, illegally exported. It's becoming a mini industry. I met Sarah while investigating Langdon's for offering the sale of ten vases found to be without international registration numbers – the scandal almost closed the house. And so it clicks: the destination, the tools, the objective. Nenni is a *tombarolo* – a tomb raider.

I laugh. 'You're a *tombarolo*, Nenni.'

'I am *the tombarolo*.' There is obvious pride.

'Business good?'

I have some sympathy for the collectors who create the demand, who tend to be obsessive classicists desperate to have and to hold something, anything, from their beloved era. I am also aware that they are scrupulous with any new historical information which may come to light, disseminating even the smallest detail via symposiums and monographs, often donating the vases to public institutions on death. But like so much in the world of art and antiques, the demand creates supply, and supply creates people like Nenni, people worse than him. And in the search for their merchandise, other precious artefacts are destroyed. The world loses important pieces every time these people smash their way into a new tomb. And not only artefacts but the tomb itself: its design, layout, all disturbed or trashed in search of the vases – the one commodity they know moves quickly. The *tombarolo* is as much a vandal as a thief.

'Will Storaro buy these?'

For the first time this evening the desperation I noticed towards the end of last night returns.

'They're not for Storaro – he doesn't go back that far. He starts with Giotto. But there are others.' I am thinking of Gustav Ballack, but Nenni doesn't push me. I sense his mind at work. The car is quicker than all the others on the road. I turn down the radio.

'How do you sell them on?'

Nenni laughs nervously. 'Savarese. He is the salesman. I find them.' Here he quickly taps his forehead. 'It is my gift.'

I look at the clock on the dashboard: 10.55 p.m.

Nenni continues, 'I think Savarese makes too much money. I want to sell straight.' He looks at me.

Hubris from a man like Nenni. He wants to bypass his boss and start up on his own. Wants me to provide the clients. What kind of mind thinks like this? Savarese is a killer, and as far as he knows I am an ex-cop. If I didn't know Nenni better, I'd think I was being set up.

'Nenni, don't double-cross Savarese. He'll kill you.'

Nenni glares across at me. 'Savarese is a salesman.' And then he taps the centre of his forehead again. 'I can locate them.'

Nenni is making a classic mistake. In his world a gift has no value when it's not in the service of the strong. Lorenzo Savarese is perfectly happy living in a world without Nenni's gift, whatever that might be. He is perfectly happy in a world without Nenni.

We leave the *autostrada*, cross an intersection, and within a minute we turn on to a narrow road, single lane. Nenni moves down gears at the last possible moment; I could be next to a professional driver, such is the smoothness and patience of the change. We pass through a series of small villages, the white stucco walls flashing in our headlights. The few people we see are old-world Italian: faces hard, rugged, dirty; clothes made of thick, heavy, earth-dark material. They stare at the Alfa Romeo as if it's the first car they've seen in a long time. The road is the most modern construction around; there is not a single transnational brand banner, no neon. The only sign of industry is a rusty Fiat badge hanging above a small garage. The terrain is flat, dark. A black plain. The dipped headlights are the only bright point, our forward motion the only movement.

The world feels wide, vast, and at the same time tiny, compact. The car comes to halt. The lights die with the engine. There is nothing. I can't see anything. Nothing at all.

I hear Nenni's breathing, quick and shallow.

'Why no light? There's no one around here.'

Nenni climbs out of the car, trudges to the boot, opens it. He roots around impatiently; I turn in my seat and look into blackness. Two beams of light suddenly appear, hard and bright, shining directly at me. I am momentarily blinded.

'For fuck's sake,' I cry out in English.

Nenni points the torches down at the ground and trudges around to my side of the car; he knocks the door with the head of one of the torches. I climb out and grab one from Nenni's hand.

'Now what?'

Nenni has returned to his jittery self, the circle of light from his torch juddering over the ground, revealing a wet surface of mud and small rocks. He has the bag of tools in his hand; it almost tips him over. I hear myself offering to take them, but Nenni ignores me and slings them across his shoulder. I shine my torchbeam around arbitrarily. I am looking for something, anything, which might tell me where I am, something which will be easy to recall and locate if I return in daylight. There is nothing, only hedgerows, fences, a ploughed field stretching as far as the light will reach. The place is so nondescript we could be anywhere in

Europe, north or south. I aim the torchlight into my face, like a kid wanting to look scary; I watch my breath floating out of my mouth. I repeat, 'Now what?'

'Now we walk. You follow. Nenni – he will locate.'

I picture Nenni tapping the centre of his forehead, and just to confirm this I shine the light into his face. The condensation from Nenni's breath bursts out in small puffs. He's not tapping his forehead. He turns and sets out over the ploughed field. I follow ten paces behind with the light of the torch pointed at the centre of Nenni's back – a target. I then jog to join him, miscalculating the peaks and troughs of the earth and almost turning my ankle. I call for Nenni to stop. To wait.

'We go slowly. It's not far.'

From an imaginary vantage point above us and a little behind, I can see myself and Nenni, two men walking across a wide field, boundlessly wide, flat and dark, thinly ridged, heading nowhere.

'Tell me about your wife, Nenni.'

It is Nenni's turn to stop. He pauses before answering. 'She is beautiful. She cooks beautiful food.'

I hear Nenni kiss the ends of his fingers to signal the beauty of the food. There is something very poignant in his pause in motion, his pause in thought and then the old-fashioned gesture of quality, perfection. It is so unexpected I think it must be true – her beauty and the beauty of her food. This startles me for a moment – the shock of the truth here.

'You are very lucky, Nenni.' I say this softly, thoughtfully, and hope Nenni understands I mean it. I then ask, 'Does she know what you do?'

There is no answer this time. It was a cruel question and I regret it. I say, 'My wife is also beautiful. Her food is dreadful.'

I hear Nenni laugh. I aim my torch into his face. He tries to bat the light away. I keep the beam of light where it is. 'She works for Langdon's.' I watch Nenni compute this information, every thought visible on his face: he's heard the name before; he's heard it in connection with the vases.

'You can sell through there?'

I am not sure why I am offering Nenni this information, this false hope. None of this is fair on this half-crazed *camorrista* with a beautiful wife who makes beautiful food. It's not fair because despite years of criminality and betrayal he doesn't seem to understand what he's doing is wrong. It's as though he thinks that this new venture, or rather trying to channel this new venture away from Lorenzo Savarese and the Camorra, is akin to going straight. That's it – Nenni thinks he's going straight. There's no killing, no drugs, no threats, no blackmail, just the trade of incredibly old and fragile objects that real people, non-criminals, desperately covet. I suspect that it's something about the honest desire of the end-user which is giving Nenni this false impression, even justifying

115

his right to take the business away from Savarese, a high-end criminal. I take the torchlight away from Nenni's face and drop the end point of the beam to my feet; I can feel my socks becoming damp through my shoes. I hate that, and think for a moment: what am I doing here?

Nenni halts. I reposition the torchlight on his face. The movement itself asks the question: why have we stopped?

Nenni is silent. Still. He turns forty-five degrees and starts off again. The tools crunch and twang in the bag.

I wonder whether I've just witnessed the Nenni gift, the locating gift. I follow, pointing the torch-beam into the night sky – a hard vanishing light.

We walk for another ten minutes. The field seems endless – interminable ground. Then the tool bag is dropped. I pick it out with my torch, the open zip glinting. Nenni pulls out a long metal spike. With two sharp rolls of his wrist it is two metres long. Nenni presses it into the earth. It sinks in easily, the earth grateful. When it's almost disappeared, Nenni grabs another section from the bag, screws it into the first and continues to push down while extending the second section upward – it is a smooth and dextrous manoeuvre. He repeats this one more time. The spike must be almost six metres deep into the earth before Nenni runs out of extensions.

'It is here,' he says to himself. 'I know.'

He pulls out the spike, breaking the rods apart

as he goes. He then moves slowly, laterally across the field.

'How do you know it's here?' I am certain he can't have discovered its location from an ancient text; he can't have outdone the scholars, the archaeologists.

'I've been here before. There is one here. I know.'

I nod absently, choosing to ignore the implication of reincarnation in the statement, possibly his only way of knowing.

Nenni presses the spike into the ground, adding and extending the poles without looking. My feet are cold, wet. I hear Nenni muttering to himself.

What are we going to do if we find a tomb? Dig our way down? Raid it? It seems so, no point in bringing axes, spades otherwise.

'Let's make this clear, Nenni. If we find something, I'm not helping you.' I shine the light on Nenni's face for emphasis. 'Understand?'

Nenni looks up from his task, the final extension in his hands.

'We are not workmen, *sbirro*. I pay others. I locate.'

'Who do you pay? *Cammoristi?*'

Nenni laughs – a big laugh. 'No. *Cammoristi* are barbarians. I pay students. Poor students.' He laughs again, and repeats, 'Poor students.'

I am shocked by this, more shocked than by Nenni's earlier display of uxoriousness and honesty. I am shocked at the audacity and the genius in persuading poor students to do his excavations. In

Naples, the south of Italy, many of the university students come from one-room *bassi* or one-pig farms – whatever he pays them will subsidize both their long education and their family.

Nenni continues, 'They are very careful. Good workers. Intelligent.'

I nod in the darkness – yes, I can imagine.

Nenni has pulled out his spike for the second time, repositioned himself ten metres away and is beginning all over again. I stay where I am, looking up at the sky, wondering whether I would have taken the work when I was a student if it was going to pay for a better life. Probably.

I hear Nenni chuckle and call out.

I trudge over. Nenni grabs my hand and places it around the handle of the fully extended spike. 'Listen. Feel.'

Nenni flicks the spike with his finger as though it was a tiny tuning fork. I hear the ringing travel down the inside of the spike, ending in a very faint echo. I look to where I sense Nenni is standing.

'The echo means there is a space, a cavity?'

'Just feel.' He flicks at the spike again.

I loosen my grip, ready to pick up a vibration as subtle as the echo was quiet. I feel nothing.

'Nothing.'

Nenni flicks again, this time harder. I feel the vibration descend the spike and into the ground where suddenly it lessens through the tightness of the earth but remains faintly present. I am about to admit defeat when I feel the vibration increase, the oscillations widen. It has left the hug of the earth and expanded. More proof of the gap.

'What now?'

'I measure its size and we go back to Naples.'

'Then what?'

'Tomorrow my team come here and we have vases for Americans, Japanese. Your wife. It is easy.'

I ignore this. 'How will you remember where it is?'

'I will remember. Don't worry, *sbirro*.'

I trudge around while Nenni repeats the exercise four times, only calling me over once when the sonic evidence is indisputable – a big tomb down there.

It takes us thirty minutes to find the car, by which point my shoes are waterlogged and the damp has risen up my jeans to my knees. Nenni throws the tools in the rear and climbs in. I sit in the passenger seat, feet outside the car, and take off my shoes and socks, wrest the clinging denim from my legs. As soon as the engine is started I turn on the heating and direct it down at my feet.

'I'm not sitting here for hours with cold feet.'

Nenni doesn't respond, and spends the next five minutes trying to turn the car around, the tyres spinning in the mud. He keeps turning the rear wheels against the direction he wants, forcing me to lean over and pull or push the steering wheel to help out.

Once we're on the road Nenni settles down and takes control. We do not pass a single person on our way back to the *autostrada*. All the lights are out. It is an old night.

I wait for Nenni to offer me the promised name. I don't want to appear desperate, especially with Nenni now knowing my most useful contact is my wife, and figuring, in the good old Italian way, a family contact is the best you can have. We listen to a whole performance of Brahms's third symphony conducted by Ricardo Muti. Nenni is visibly excited by the mention of the maestro's name.

'Muti is the best,' he says confidently, proudly, after I ask him what is so great about the Italian conductor, apart from him being Italian.

As we glide into Naples I have the sensation that Nenni and I have made a connection in some way, that we have found a level of communication which isn't purely about dark things: gain, greed, manipulation, threats, fear. It also involves wives, food, music – bright things. It might be the casual way Nenni asks me where I am staying and the easy way he takes a quick left in order to drop me there – it's late after all, three in the morning. Or then it might be the awkward way, once we've actually stopped outside the hotel, Nenni remains where he is, unable to begin the conversation about the name he owes me, as if we have become too friendly over the last five hours to exchange such ugly information sitting in a car on a dark street in the middle of the night. I wonder whether I should invite him into the hotel, to the bar, and we should discuss it over a drink. I remain where I am.

Nenni cuts the engine and begins to fidget. Eventually he turns to me. 'What name do you want?'

I have waited a long time for this. I look ahead. The inside of the car is dark, the night is grey. I look beyond this to Sarah sleeping. A deep sleep, a long time before dawn, before the alarm and her no-nonsense attitude to the cold in the bedroom, the bathroom.

'I want to know who has the Caravaggio.'

I hear Nenni laugh at the simplicity of the request, the impossibility of its surrender.

'Forget it, *sbirro*.'

'I just want to know who's got it.'

There is silence between us for a moment. I listen to the tapping of Nenni's feet on the pedals.

'Do you know who has it?'

'Why do you want it?'

Good question. I think about my answer. I need my reason to make sense to Nenni. I decide to tell him the truth. 'For the same reason you don't want Savarese taking all your money. I want something for myself, purely for myself.'

'The Caravaggio?' Nenni is surprised.

I laugh. 'No. I've loved Caravaggio for more than half my life, but that's only part of it. I confess I want a little glory in my life.' I say this evenly, plainly, coldly. I even understand as I say it that, as an objective, it has something of the hubris with which Nenni has decided his 'gift' entitles him to freedom to operate outside of the world that's supported him for the whole of his life. It is the same for me. Despite the despondency in my job, the police have allowed me access to the things I love in a way others have not.

'You want the name?'

I turn my head and look out of the passenger window and across the piazza. Pools of rainwater are specked with dull lights. Coaches stand dark, empty. The occasional small car appears from a side street, careens on to the piazza and then disappears. We have no fear of being watched or followed. No one is interested in us, sitting in this car, outside this hotel, in this city, despite the subject of our conversation, the deals and deaths connected to it. No one is interested because we are both inconsequential in this city and, I sense, inconsequential when it comes to the business of art. We are safe having this conversation.

'Yes, Nenni. Give me the name.' I am not willing to be inconsequential – it wasn't the plan.

There is an almost imperceptible pause before Nenni, with a jerk of his shoulder, says, 'Ruffelle. Massimo Ruffelle.' This is followed by another pause before he adds, jerk-free, 'But he's dead.'

For a moment I don't know whether Nenni is laughing at me, whether or not tonight has just been some kind of display of power: getting me to go with him, trudge across a field, respect his gift – a stupid display of his new station in life so changed from last year when he was just a pathetic informant. I slam the steering wheel.

'Fuck you, Nenni.'

Nenni shudders in the seat, his body turning like a screw, his breathing quick and shallow. He tries to speak but shortness of breath prevents him.

Nenni was not laughing at me. He was offering me honesty again. I turn to him. His desperation is now unfirmly rooted in his body, it is shaking him in his seat. It is obvious to me that Nenni needs a deal.

'What is it, Nenni?'

He needs to calm down before he speaks. It takes an act of concentration, of controlled breathing, a slow nodding of his head, an internal dialogue.

'I am sorry. He was the last man with the Caravaggio. I don't know who has it now. But if you get the vases out, I will get you a name. I promise. But it must be soon. I must start a new life with my wife.' He nods. He has made it as clear as is possible. He is telling me that his desire for independence has reached Savarese.

I hold out my hand to him. It is not meant to be a shake to seal the deal, it is offered for other reasons – reasons I can't quite fathom because I know straightforward warmth and kindness in this world is a short cut to betrayal and I'm not that foolish. But there it is – a hand offered.

It takes Nenni a second to position his hand correctly before we can shake.

'I find you.' It is said in English and with a smile.

My return smile is wry rather than reciprocal. I climb out of the car. I want to lean in and wish him luck and warn him to be careful. But instead I just say without emotion, 'The name, Nenni, tomorrow. OK? Otherwise I return to Florence and I can't help you.'

He nods rapidly, accompanied by a single jerk of the shoulder. 'We have a deal.'

I turn and walk up the steps of the hotel. I hear the Alfa Romeo's engine turn over and the car pull away. I push my way through the heavy hotel doors into the bright, brassy light of the lobby.

In my room, lying on the bed, drinking a vodka miniature, in clean T-shirt and shorts after a hot shower, I think about my next move. If Nenni comes up with a name, what do I do? Help him get the vases out, pay for a new life? There is no way I could involve Sarah and Langdon's. It will have to be Gustav. But then I'm really stepping over the line, selling illegally excavated vases to the art world's most influential fence. Am I prepared to do that for Nenni, for the Caravaggio?

But then what if Nenni doesn't get a name? Is this little adventure all over? It can't be. I will be. It could take months, years possibly, to work a route via the *'ndrangheta*. Nenni is my only real hope. My only hope. I shake my head, snap the lid off a second vodka. If Savarese really suspects

Nenni of taking business away from the clan, he might be dead by tomorrow. Lorenzo Savarese has an impressive sense of urgency when it comes to killing.

I look across to the time display on the TV. Four-twenty a.m. I look out of the window and wonder whether the orange glow above the city is the beginning of the sunrise. I am instantly sleepy. I turn on to my side, away from the window, and punch the pillow to get comfortable. How many other people are dreaming of the Caravaggio tonight?

3

I wake at eight into bright morning light. I roll over and bury my face in the pillow. The light reaches round into my eyes. I roll back, push myself off the bed and close the blinds. The room is now black, except for a thin strip of yellow under the door. I climb back into bed; four hours' sleep is not enough. I clasp my genitals – a comfort zone. My mind is heavy and I need a light mind, a nimble mind. My legs ache from the cold and damp of last night. My chest heaves. I am troubled – long-term troubles. Sarah. I know a heavy mind will muster melodramatic thoughts: I am unloved, which means splitting up, which means divorce, which means failure. More failure. I must relax. I concentrate on my breathing: in through the nose – slow, full – out through a loose mouth. Sleep approaches. Glides away. I turn on to my back, my eyes open; my body knows that it is day. I go to the bathroom and stare into the mirror. I am not surprised by the tiredness visible on my face. I get back into bed, recalling a sleep trick taught to me by an old girlfriend. Relax every muscle in your body, starting at your toes, and then work upwards. Tense, relax, move on. Toes, feet, calves, thighs – every muscle in every part of your body. It begins to work. The darkness around me is quickly heavy, invading me, meeting my own dark need for sleep, my own dark need for oblivion.

I awake at twelve-thirty, cleanly, brightly. I am in and out of the shower within minutes, my mind light, fresh, energetic. Waiting for Nenni is a thing to do. Part of a greater thing to do. Saving the Caravaggio.

At the front desk I tell the receptionist I'll be gone for a couple of hours if anyone wants me.

The sun is out. The sky is white-blue. It is warm. On Spaccanapoli the Christmas lights that have lasted past Epiphany are being taken down. Men standing high on ladders at sheer angles to the walls argue as they untie the thin electric cables and lower the heavy lines of coloured bulbs. Everyone on the street has an opinion. Much of the shouting is harsh, angry; a few people crack jokes and laugh. I watch the hands of the onlookers: every unwanted piece of advice is accompanied by a gesture dismissing the previous instruction or invoking a higher power to follow theirs. The men on the ladders shout back and gesture – leave us alone. There are lights the length of Spaccanapoli, if they carry on like this, it will be Christmas again before they complete the work.

I find a small restaurant and order *spaghetti vongole* and water. I feel optimistic that Nenni will come through. That by the end of the day I will have a name. Then it will be about the deal. How will I tease the painting away? Gangsters are competitive and image-conscious. The former makes them open to risky deals, the latter blinds them, makes them vulnerable. Both make them volatile. It must always be remembered they are not ordinary businessmen. They don't understand fairness. Everything must be stacked in their favour. They like their partners to start in an unfair position and then to negotiate better terms *for themselves*, using their favourite negotiation tactic – violence. Violence and its many representations: intimidation, threats, blackmail, torture, beatings. In all my experience with these people, their world always begins and ends with this irreducible first essence. Violence is the existential fact of the gangster.

I leave the restaurant with my earlier energy ebbing away. The Christmas lights argument is still going on, moved just a few metres down the street. Different set of onlookers, same instructions, same gestures. There are no messages waiting for me at the hotel. I ask the receptionist whether she has noticed anyone lurking – you can't miss this guy, is all I say. There has been no one. I sit in the bar with a bottle of water and *La Repubblica*. I read the paper absently. Little interests me. I even doze. Every now and then I look out of the doors of the bar and into the lobby, sensing Nenni is nearby; but there is nothing, just bright, shiny tiles, the glint of gold leaf, terrible paintings of pre-war Naples. I finish my water, toss the paper into the armchair next to me and go to my room. It is four o'clock. I lie down on the bed, wrap my arm over my eyes. This is madness. Madness. Even with a name, what am I going to do? What's the deal? The deal that will make them offer it to me? There isn't one. Recovering the Caravaggio is an impossibility. There are good reasons for it not having been recovered before. I stand and look out of the window. Despite the high sky, the obstinate sun, Naples is so much darker than Florence. My stomach keeps contracting, spasming, taking my breath away. Why is that? Is it because I shouldn't be in Naples? Is my body trying to tell me something? No. This always happens. Waiting is difficult. Waiting is dark. The world is always in shadow when you wait. I stare across the still rooftops of Naples and overhear myself asking, where are you, Nenni? Where are you?

4

At nine p.m. I set out for the *trattoria*. I go on the assumption, my last assumption, that if Nenni has got me a name, he might be waiting for me there, and that if he hasn't got me a name, he's unlikely to be at the only place where I know where to look for him – so either way I'll know where I stand.

Nenni is not there. I decide to stay and eat, just in case he turns up later. I order the *fritto misto* and steak, the strongest Taurasi. I drink more than I eat and feel quickly drunk. I push the bottle away when the steak arrives. It is rare, sinewy, tasting of blood and olive oil. I eat half, then pull the bottle back and fill my glass. I order another bottle. What is Sarah doing now, I wonder. What day is it? Thursday. If she's not out, she'll be sitting in the basement kitchen, ready meal turned into a bowl, fork in hand, radio on, flipping over the pages of a magazine. Maybe it is time to go home. Give this up. Put all my energies into my marriage. I shake my head. It's not my marriage that needs my help, it's me. I need to recover my former self – a fuller self. Right now I feel made up of only drifting parts, desperate parts, with no force of coherence to bind them together. Love of Sarah. Love of Caravaggio. Resentments, hungers, sensibilities. All scattered. Scattered and drifting. I pour myself a full glass of wine and drain it.

I am given a limoncello with the bill. It is ice-cold, very alcoholic, sweet; it breaks the thirst created by the one and a half bottles of red wine. I leave the restaurant as unsteadily as Nenni two nights ago.

The night air is warm and heavy, with the promise of more rain. I feel a rush of dizziness. It must be the adrenalin, or the depletion of it, mixing with the alcohol. I head for Spaccanapoli, the straightest line to the hotel. I'll need to pass through Forcella. Where the fuck is Nenni? I was certain when we parted last night I'd know by now who had the Caravaggio, and my biggest problem, in the short term, would be helping him. But all I am certain of now is that it's not going to happen tonight. I lose my footing and stumble forward. I am slow to react. My knees crack on the hard stone, the balls of my hands slide forward; I just manage to stop my face from smashing on the ground. There is a sharp pain in my knees; my hands sting and burn. I struggle up, feeling pathetic, ridiculous. I brush myself down and pick grit from my palms. I look around me. Naples is empty.

There is no sign of Nenni at the hotel, no message. I head straight for my room, the mini bar. I lie on the bed and drink two beers with whisky chasers. It's over. Time to go home. What was I really going to do with the name anyway? Wasn't it just something to add to the fantasy? To permit me to dream up ever more perfect ways to recover the painting while never really having the means to go after it? To imagine and bathe in the post-recovery glory? The post-recovery transformation. From art cop . . . to what? What, precisely? Art celeb? For fifteen minutes. Ridiculous. Pathetic. Motives for failure, I know that. There is only one motive which guarantees success. It's the only motive in life. Do it for love, and because only I will dare do it. Only I will take the risk. Me, Danny Wright – art's desperado. I hear myself laughing – laughing deeply, loudly; what's left of my residual self scattered and drifting, laughing, laughing, laughing.

I sleep fitfully. I sleep fitfully, knowing Sarah cannot contact me, knowing Nenni should have turned up by now, knowing I feel numb from drink but also numb generally, although pain still darts through. I sleep fitfully because the dark has weight. And the room feels like Naples feels at dusk – forbidding, unsettling, threatening. It suggests anything might happen in this room, at this time, in this dark. I sleep fitfully because I am scared. I am not usually scared. Not of the

132

dark in Naples anyway. Not of being alone in a hotel room. Or being involved with the elements I am involved with here. Or even of all of these things combined. I am scared because my sense of self is way off-kilter, and I am ignoring this. Or it is off-kilter because I am ignoring it, and now I don't know what I'm thinking, or what I'm supposed to be thinking – the central thoughts, the abiding stuff, the processes that make me good at what I do, that make me safe. And these are reasons to be scared. I sleep fitfully because I am listening to my body and my body knows it shouldn't be in this bed, in this room, in this city, not even in this country, yet at the same time it doesn't know where it should be. I sleep fitfully because my mind is brown and will not still itself – it is turning to keep the world flat and my passage through it straight.

PART TWO

FLORENCE, THE ART MAFIA AND THE CAMORRA

1

I am back in Florence by ten a.m. It is still cold – colder than when I left. The breeze has extra bite. The sky is pale blue and high. There is no sign of the snow – no slush, pools or puddles in the road. Everything is dry. The air is silver-blue bright.

The train journey was a dreamless sleep. No Nenni, Caravaggio, Sarah. Just an unfilled darkness. Yet the moment I awoke I knew immediately I wasn't going home.

I stop on the north side of the *duomo*, my favourite spot from which to look up at the cathedral. It is here in its shadow, tight between its smooth hard marble walls and the dry textured stucco of the buildings opposite, that I experience its metaphysical properties at play. It is from here that the *duomo* transforms the city, from this dark aspect that everything is disclosed. Without it the world is just a drawing on paper, at best an architect's model, flimsy and inconsequential. Whereas standing in this spot, the dome itself invisible, an extraordinary alchemy is at work and the sky above is more truly the sky – a dome itself: today, bright blue and celestially high – and the buildings opposite more fully themselves, every cornice, shutter, balcony rich with reality. The walls are not merely divisions in space but objects in relation to other objects: walls, high ceilings, vast floors, together creating corners, which create rooms, which contain furniture, under which objects – adored, lost, abandoned – are at rest. I picture with tactile distinctness a shoe, an earring, a coin.

I move on. I have been here enough times to know I will not be transformed by the experience. I know that I will not be a witness to the transubstantiation of ordinary matter into poetic matter, into spiritual matter – a metropolitan metaphysics that will move me to new convictions – and I know, straightforwardly, that this is just another way in which the world can be apprehended, that now and again the world must be apprehended this way if we're to remain sane.

I walk down Via del Proconsolo and into Via Dante. American Express is busy. The stone stairs are dry, the disinfectant faint. The apartment is again colder than the rest of Florence. I turn on the gas rings, the heater. I check my mobile for messages. Jim, Sarah, an old friend. Only one from Sarah. Telling me to be safe, that she loves me and wants me to be safe. My safety is her key concern. To not be loved and be in danger – she doesn't want that for me. This is what I get from her message. Her guilt modified into worry and sentimentality – the imaginings of a tragedy. She doesn't love me, then? I can't know this. I am being paranoid.

Jim says Rome is ready. Ready with the name. Contact them directly. I write down the name, the number.

I power up the laptop and log on. Email floods in – spam, friends, Sarah, Jim, Francesca. I know what Sarah will say: it will be word for word exactly the same as the message left on my mobile; she always does this. I click anyway. It is the same. Ending 'Sarahx'. Which is also the same. The mobile message ended in a kiss.

I click on Francesca's email.

Where are you, mystery man?

Sent Thursday. Should I respond? Probably not. I move on to Jim's emails. Mostly irrelevant stuff I've been cc'd on. No orders to return to London. Nothing that suggests he knows where I went, the purpose of my visit. Should I tell him now? It was the Caravaggio. It's in Calabria somewhere. In the hands of an old man. I open new mail.

Jim,
Back in Florence. Look, last year . . . I did see The Nativity. I'm sorry, I should have told you . . . look, do whatever . . . It's in Calabria. East of . . .

I stop. Do I want to do this now? It will mean press coverage within twenty-four hours. Goldini and his men seconded to Reggio di Calabria. The painting . . . probably gone. Rolled up and hidden somewhere, somewhere likely to cause further damage. A basement, a garage, an outhouse. Is it safer left alone? I ignore what I overhear myself thinking. There is also Storaro to consider. How close will he get? I realize I care less about Storaro discovering it than law enforcement. But then, he'll never do it without them. So unless I send this to Jim, the painting is safe. From others. I backspace and delete, rewrite.

Jim,
Back in Florence. Got the details. Will make contact.
Cheers,
Danny

I pull my mobile out of my overcoat pocket and call Sarah at work. She answers with her name, late-night huskiness in her voice.
'It's me.'
'Hello, Dan.' It is self-consciously flat – playfully flat.
'What have you been up to?'
'All I do is work when you're not here. My success will be entirely due to your absence.'
'You sound tired.'
'A little. What about you? Where have you been?

140

Jim called me. He wanted to know whether you've talked to me about Caravaggio's *Nativity*.'

'What did you say?'

'I told him you've never mentioned it. Why's he asking?'

For a moment I think I'm going mad: Jim's suspicion; Sarah's ignorance; my secrecy. Right now it's as though the painting isn't in Calabria but inside of me; its existence is a part of me.

'Dan?'

I shake my head wearily. 'I might have seen it last summer. I just wanted to check it out.'

'Why didn't you say anything?'

'I don't know. I didn't tell anyone.'

'What's got into you, Dan?' She is weary of guessing, of further evidence something is wrong.

I don't know. What happens when passion turns to dissatisfaction? I want to say I'm lost, but I know Sarah doesn't do weakness, not in herself or others.

'It's just work.'

'Jim also said I should expect you home.'

Fucking Jim. 'He shouldn't have said that.'

'Why not?'

'Because he doesn't know what's happening here.'

'What *is* happening there, Dan?'

What did Storaro say about travelling alone? We forget who we are and do desperate things to define ourselves?

'I promise I'll be home as soon as I can.'

'Are you sure?'

'Yes. And when I am we need to talk.'

There is a pause.

'Sarah?'

I sense a shift in the tone even before she's spoken; her voice remains husky, still almost a whisper, but now the sound is pushed through her teeth, looking to contain her frustration. 'What's left to talk about, Dan? We've been over it all.'

I have no response. Her frustration is final.

'Dan?'

'What?'

'I don't understand you. You say you want to talk and then you just go quiet.' We both know this is unfair – this is what she does.

'Just tell me one thing: are you happy with the way things are?'

'No, of course not. But I don't think it needs another pointless conversation about your dissatisfactions, my privileges and all the other stuff you go on about. Why can't you just come to terms with this stuff and we can get on with our lives.'

I wish she'd said 'our life' – everything solved.

'Is this how posh people stay married?'

'I don't know, darling. You seem to know everything there is to know about posh people.'

'Sarah, I love you and I want to do whatever I can to make this work.'

'If that's true, why aren't you here now when you could be?'

I don't have an answer. Our goodbyes are flat, unresolved.

I drop into the armchair and open Francesca's message again: 'Where are you, mystery man?'

No fucking idea. I hit reply.

> Back in Florence. The snow is gone. Alone
> for the weekend.

These things are true. I hit send. Wait. Will there be a quick response? No. I look at the contact details in Rome to set up a meet with the prosecutor. I call. I am told firmly how it is expected to work. Establish contact today or Monday, after that nothing, unless it's absolutely necessary, and at no point must I give anything away. All this man knows is that I am working for them in Florence and it was decided that I should have an independent and local point of contact should any issues arise. I nod my way through this, thinking they're not expecting any issues to arise, they're not expecting much of anything to arise. As I've suspected all along: this is about someone with power covering themselves. 'OK,' is all I say before hanging up. I call Sarah.

'It's me again.'

'Hello, you again.'

'This is a bullshit operation. I promise I'll be home soon.'

'Dan, don't make promises.'

'Really. By next weekend. I promise.'

She understands that now is the time to be generous. 'I look forward to it.'

Midday. I am sitting outside a café with coffee and a sandwich, a Caravaggio book open. I don't read. I am hunched up, collar up, cold. Gloved hands dully turning the pages. I am not thinking much. Just staring at the pictures. I am waiting for my contact to appear. I look at my watch. I turn a page, hunch myself up further; stillness allows the cold to dwell. I concentrate on *The Taking of Christ*. One of my favourites. It is a Christ I recognize, as intellectually certain as he is spiritually unyielding. A mirror to hypocrisy. A charismatic through sheer good looks. I understand the submission to martyrdom in this painting.

The prosecutor sits down opposite me, ordering an espresso from the waitress as she passes. He is younger than I expected: early forties. He is unusually scruffy for an Italian professional: brown suit, grey shirt, knitted brown tie. We shake hands over the table.

'Signor Comanini.'

'What are you really doing here?' He is irritated; it is a cold, cold day and he knows like I know that this is all a waste of time.

'I don't know what you've been told.'

'That you're here to learn about Uffizi security, the police.'

I nod.

'Then why am I involved?'

Gloved hand slides over a page. Two paintings of the *Supper at Emmaus* – did Caravaggio need to paint a second painting because his perspective had darkened, deepened? Did he need to reimagine Christ as a man of wisdom and fate as much as faith? I prefer the second Christ – he is beyond glory, the miracle of resurrection; he is instructing contemplation of its meaning; he has become a metaphor.

'I'm here to learn about Uffizi security, the police. I don't know why you're involved. Maybe they don't trust me.'

The prosecutor knocks back his espresso. 'Maybe they don't. But I don't trust them.' He pauses. 'So maybe we are on the same side.'

'Why did they pick you?'

'I don't know. My father was Giovanni Comanini. They say Cosa Nostra killed him. Ha! More important is who pulls the strings than pulls the trigger.'

I have to study this man's face. What's the deal here: conspiracy theorist or genuine crusader?

'I'm here a week. I should be in London saving my marriage.'

'Then go back. There is nothing to learn here. It's a joke.'

'I have your number.'

The prosecutor stands. 'You have my number, but I don't work for these people. If you get into trouble, just go home. Florence is a holiday camp. Nothing happens here any more.'

'Then why are you here?'

'It is my home.'

I watch him walk away. What do I think? Can he be trusted? I close the book, drop a couple of euro notes on the table and leave. A day's work: one conversation, badly handled, at an outside table between two men who don't want to meet again.

I remember Giovanni Comanini's assassination. A car bomb outside his home. He was on his way to sentence two high- ranking Mafiosi. There was talk at the time that it was a convenient moment to take out a man who was as anti-government as he was anti-Mafia.

At the apartment there is an email from Francesca. I open it.

I'll see you at 7 p.m.

I reply:

Where?

Her reply is instant:

Here.

Let's hope she's not a honey trap, I think to myself wryly. Then, how could she be? She thinks I'm a writer. No one here is interested in me.

I go over to the window. How many hours have I spent staring out of strange windows? Usually hotels, often apartments. Rarely is the view much at all. The other side of the street. An alley. A car park. Another part of the hotel. Dark windows. I yawn. I hate this part of the job. The soft wait. Nothing to do. Not knowing what will happen next. Knowing it always does: a call; a conversation; seeing two people together, or the expression on a face; or a sudden thought even, in the shower, falling asleep, just prior to waking fully. But then I am certain nothing's going to happen here. I ask myself: why am I in Florence? This isn't even what I do. I recover paintings – make deals with hard men. I don't infiltrate. I don't really do undercover. So why was I assigned this? Credibility. I don't look like a copper. Don't comport myself like a copper. Perfect to get inside the Uffizi. I have to ask myself: is my presence in Florence linked to being shown the Caravaggio? I can't think how. It was my first time in Calabria, my first time with the *'ndrangheta*, my first time with that *cosca*. It was a simple deal. I was transparent. Working for the other side. Clear on that. There just isn't a reason, or a motive. And even if there is the slimmest possibility that I pissed someone off enough for them to want me killed, why bring me here to do it? Things like that don't happen in Florence. Like the prosecutor said, it's a holiday camp.

I dump myself into the armchair, rest my head

and close my eyes and think back to the one attempt on my life. In a shack, in a wood, thirty miles outside of Vienna. Some big-muscle Eastern European decided to take out all the witnesses. I was there to broker the exchange. Independent of both parties. The Swiss government and a band of Yugoslavs – Serbians. What happened happened fast. One man went down, shot twice in the chest, and I was next, the barrel of a gun pointing at me. My face. It looked like some giant cone – a dark, disappearing hollow. I stared at it. I thought I saw the bullet appear, slink out of the end of the barrel. Death coming in slow motion. I heard myself take a deep breath, registering the end of myself with a signal of life. But the bullet didn't make it; it really did just slink out of the end of the barrel. Drop to the ground. I grabbed a plank of wood close by, tore into the side of the shooter's head and kept beating. Went at it deliberately – destroying him. I reasoned, between hits, I'd seen the killing of a man by this man and I was next, natural justice was mine to mete out. So I beat him for those reasons. So he'd understand: you don't fucking kill people. You don't fucking kill me. I left him next to the man he killed, figuring he'd die if someone didn't find him soon, and there was little chance of that in a shack in a wood on the shore of the Danube.

When I got back to the hotel the receptionist asked me whether I'd spent the day at a health club, I looked so bright, fresh, invigorated. In my room I looked at myself in the mirror. It was how I looked.

I didn't tell anyone. The department was notified when the bodies were found. I said when I left the two dead men were still alive, joking around, talking about Viennese hookers. How one was shot and the other beaten to death, I couldn't explain. Said there were loads of people involved – it was a messy deal. You know these fucking Eastern Europeans. What were the two guys waiting for, Jim asked. I didn't stick around to find out.

It was a headache for Jim. I was undisturbed. I didn't feel changed by it. The original brightness was adrenal – a metabolic aftershock. I wasn't scared by this. It was natural. And all I cared about was being alive. I was getting married in a week.

A couple of nights before the marriage I asked Sarah: do you sense anything different in me? She was lying next to me, head on my chest, fingers of one hand resting in my pubic hair, damp from her. You're always lovely, she'd said, believing it back then. And I believed it – I was a good guy: straightforward, trustworthy, honest, loyal. So I let it go – whatever it was that allowed me to beat a man to death like that.

I wake, the image of that forest floor imprinted on my mind. Two dead men. Leaves already gathering around the stillness of their bodies. The light fading. The light was brown, full of trees and leaves and the brown sound of the river. These days the memory seems more like a scene from a film. I

149

am not even in the picture. Just the two prone men, heavy in their pretend death in brown light, under airborne leaves. But then I remember something of the lightness in their bodies when death wasn't being pretended. I can't picture that now. I can't withdraw from them, in my mind, what was withdrawn from them in death, making them seem light.

I wake again; this time fully – sweating, aching. I feel light, death light. Empty, brown. Leaf light.

I sit forward. Focus on the computer screen. I lean further forward and push at the pad to kick it out of sleep mode. One email. Jim. I delete it. The clock in the corner of the screen says 17.15. Time to get ready.

I shower, brush my teeth, trim my nails. I clean my shoes. I sniff my absent host's various after-shaves and select one. I dress. I call Sarah at home, leaving a message, reiterating my promise to be back by the end of the following week. I drop the phone on to the bed and leave the apartment. The fragrance from the aftershave mixes with the smell of the disinfectant on the stairs; it is not unpleasant.

The street is dark, empty. Only the American Express office glows; there is a balloon of light reaching beyond its windows to the centre of the road. The biting breeze has gone, leaving a static chill in the air. I walk briskly to the Uffizi. A different, older man takes me up to Francesca's office. The door is open. She is behind her desk, talking on her mobile, laptop closed, absently pushing her spectacles around. No ashtray, no romance novel. She is whispering firmly, as though to a child. She is impatient, cross with whoever is on the other end. She doesn't notice me in the doorway. She is wearing the same linen dress, this time with a thin cream V-neck sweater. There is a long loop of luminous green beads around her neck. Her curls bounce as she speaks. Do they never not move? Are they ever totally at rest? I sense even her breathing inspires their spring.

Francesca finishes her conversation, flaps the phone down, rocks back in her chair. It is only now she notices me. She rocks forward and puts on her spectacles, regards me without saying anything. I raise my hand, belatedly signalling my arrival. Francesca looks up at the Cartier-Bresson, pursing her lips thoughtfully.

'Storaro called me. Wanted to know whether I still had this up.' She pauses. 'He asked me what I thought of you. He never asks me things like that.'

'He has the same photograph on his wall.'

I suspect she knows this and doesn't care. She stands and walks around to the front of her desk, pushes herself up on to it, and sits forward, hands clutching the rim, heels gently knocking the oak panelling.

'Why do men give these kinds of gifts to women?'

'What gifts?'

151

'Expressions of other men.'

'We hope you will be moved like we are, and that the emotion this produces will somehow be transferred to us, and that you will think we have inspired them, and that you will then be in love with us.'

Francesca takes this in. 'Men don't really think that, do they?'

I remain standing in the doorway. 'Not think it, no. But that is the idea behind it. Interestingly, the less likely it is to work, the more likely the man is to employ it as a strategy. I'm not sure why that is.'

'How do you know all this?'

'I have done it. I have made the mistake. I am a subtle reader of the male mind.'

'What about the female mind?'

I smile. 'It is not for reading.'

'What is it for?'

I pause, thinking. 'Multi-tasking, or so we are told.'

Francesca laughs and pushes herself off the table.

'Do you want to have dinner with me tonight?'

'I would love to, but you must have better things to do . . .'

'Why must I have better things to do?'

'I don't know.'

'No, you don't.'

Francesca squeezes past me, forcing me to pull myself in. She then instructs Silvio, who has appeared from nowhere, in something I don't catch and hands him some keys.

'I need to go home first. There is a little place nearby where we can eat.'

The Smart Car is parked near Antico Fattore, pressed up against the wall. This time Francesca has to climb over the seats. We drive south, across the Arno and along Lungarno Serristori; again Francesca sits sideways in her seat.

'You'll kill us both.'

'I am thirty-seven. I have never had an accident.'

We pull into a little nexus of streets, turn right and under the high arch of the city's medieval gates. A hundred metres on, Francesca pulls in and stops the car.

'You stay here. I'll be two minutes.' She climbs out and disappears through a doorway opposite, leaving the car door open. I stare out of the windscreen into the darkness. I am looking forward to dinner. A drink. A few drinks. A few drinks with a woman where the talk isn't all about ourselves – the catastrophe of ourselves.

Francesca reappears, climbs in, slams the door shut. She is wearing fresh lipstick. She isn't wearing her spectacles. Replaced by contacts, I presume.

'That's better.' She turns the car around in the narrow street. We drive back through the city gates and stop. We are both able to climb out of our respective doors this time. The bar is a little further down and to the right. Francesca opens the door with familiarity – no pause or imperceptible test of the push/pull options, just a quick pull open. It is a typical local bar, dark, warm, smelling of baking and sweet things – almonds. There is a large drawing of Dante's profile in poster-form above a door at the back. Two couples sit at the tables. Two businessmen, with espresso cups between their fingers and thumbs, stand at the bar.

Francesca says hi to the bartender and orders a bottle of Pinot Grigio – specifying the producer. She clasps the two glasses placed on the bar between the fingers of one hand and grabs the bottle with the other.

'Start light – it's the Italian way.'

She sits down at a window table, reaches into her pocket and tosses her cigarettes and lighter next to the bottle and glasses. I pour the wine. We clink and drink.

'It's nice to have company on a Friday night. The worst thing about being single is filling your weekends.'

I am not sure I believe a woman of Francesca's abilities, looks, position can be so socially hard up.

'I'm not sure I believe you.'

'Really? Why not? There are no eligible men in Florence. I won't do a long-distance relationship. I've been on my own for over a year now.' She pauses. 'Of course, there's Storaro. But he's not for me.'

'Why not?'

'He likes me too much to himself.'

'I can see that.'

'How so?'

'Certain men like to make it hard for a woman in that way, usually insecure men, who are nonetheless aware they have a lot to offer and therefore can get away with it.'

'Are you like that?'

'I have been.'

'What do you have to offer that lets you get away with it?'

'In Storaro's case it seems to be charisma.'

'I didn't ask you about Storaro. I want to know about you.'

I don't respond.

'It's an easy enough question. Just be honest.'

'You want to know what I have that means I can get away with behaving badly?'

'Yes.'

I smile at her insistence. 'I'm not sure.'

'Yes, you are.'

'As with everything, it's a number of factors.'

'What are those factors?' Francesca smiles playfully – a straightforward fun smile. Her long eyes are serious, thoughtful. I have the sensation I am looking at two people.

'Why are you so interested?'

'It might help me to understand more about men, and then I won't need to have dinner with mysterious Englishmen on Friday nights.'

I wait for her face to break into a single expression. But the smile remains fun, the long eyes remain serious.

'So I lose out?'

'You are here now.'

'OK. But I still can't answer your question.'

Her expression changes finally; the smile is less playful, her eyes brighten.

'I think you are a little charismatic yourself. But not like Storaro.'

'Thank you. I think.'

Francesca shrugs, clearly also not convinced that charisma is a compliment – she gets quite enough of that elsewhere. I change the line of conversation. 'Anyway, I'd like to thank you for asking me to join you for dinner.'

Francesca takes a sip of wine. 'You seem nice. Englishmen always seem nice. They are not usually handsome or pretty. Which makes a change. You are quite handsome, I think.'

I expect a smile of one sort or another.

She continues, 'It is nice to talk about how a man looks, rather than a woman. Italian men are vain, but they always want to tell you how beautiful you are – they think it makes them charming, sensitive. Artists!' She pauses, then says, 'Tell me about your wife.'

I'm not sure I like the way I'm being handled here. 'My wife is very beautiful. Very smart. I am very lucky.'

'What is your wife's name?'

'Sarah.'

Francesca ponders this. 'How long have you been married?'

'Not long. Just under a year.'

'Are you happy?'

I look away; I don't want to have this conversation.

'Does that mean no?'

'Yes, no. We are happy after a fashion, or whatever it is that Tolstoy wrote.' I sip my wine; Francesca tops up both glasses.

'And you live in London?'

'Yes.'

'I don't like London. Too big. Too dirty. For a city . . . it has no *bella figura*.'

I am acutely aware that the conversation has moved from playful flirtation to vague nothings about a city neither of us is interested in discussing. I pull across Francesca's packet of Pall Mall, draw out a cigarette.

'May I?'

'Do you smoke?'

'I used to.'

'What will your wife say?'

'She's not here.'

Francesca leans forward with the lighter, ignites it with a roll of her thumb, scorches the end of the cigarette. She leaves the flame present between us, staring at it, while I take a long, first drag. The smoke hits the back of my throat and is pulled down into my lungs. I feel a mixture of

157

sickness and warmth; every muscle in my body loses tension. Six months' not smoking – six reasonably OK months compared to the giving-up horror stories I'd heard. I take another couple of drags and stub it out. 'It's making me light-headed.'

'Come on. Let's go.' Francesca is up, counting out euros on to the table. 'I'm hungry.'

She has drunk two glasses of wine to my one. I stand, the light-headedness more striking on my feet. 'Dinner's on me.'

'I invited you.'

'We'll split it then.'

Francesca shrugs one shoulder. I lead us out into the cold evening and take in a deep breath of icy air; my lungs feel small, tight, dry. 'Where are we going?'

'Over there.' Francesca points to a small restaurant across the street. The windows are tinted. There is only a soft, diffuse glow inside. We walk across quickly, the cold hastening us. I open the door for Francesca. The diners are couples and businessmen – the same clientele as the bar. Francesca gets us a corner table by the dark window; outside is blank. We are handed menus. Francesca disappears behind hers; I lay mine on the table and read it that way. The usual *primo piatti, secondo piatti* options – fabulous food, so tiresome to choose from.

'What do you recommend?'

'It's all good.' The voice is disembodied from

behind the menu. 'I'm having risotto and then the veal chop.'

I choose the Florentine onion soup followed by devilled rabbit.

Francesca discusses the wine choice with the waiter. She is looking for a balance across the four dishes; she thinks it can be achieved. She is eventually persuaded by his description of a young Barolo. She looks across the table at me and raises her eyebrows. I read: we have made an interesting choice! She seems happy; both her smile and her eyes reveal it.

We discuss Storaro. I tell her about my visit to the gallery – some of it. All the while Francesca looks amused, having, I assume, heard this all before. She says despite the money, the power, the notoriety, he's no different from all men: has to prove himself. Any man that walks into a room, especially with her, will have to endure something of Storaro's competitiveness. She repeats that she thinks I did rather well; most men fall into line more quickly. She then adds, 'Right now, he's being even more insufferable because he's losing so much money.'

I want to know more.

'There's no dark secret. He's a terrible businessman. He only spends money on things he loves. He doesn't invest. Or if he does, it is in mad schemes he falls for. The house he's building is costing him . . . I have no idea. It's been going on now for two years and it's not even half finished.

He's still got hundreds of millions but when you lose a million a day, it doesn't last long.'

'It's that serious?'

'He says it is, but you never know with Storaro.'

Our first course is removed along with the first bottle of wine. Francesca orders a second. She lights up, offers me the packet. I decline.

'Do you know what I do at the Uffizi?' she asks – all brightness disappearing from her face.

'No.'

'Everything; nothing. It is all politics, politics, politics. I think the grander the building, the more trivial the business being conducted inside.'

'The Uffizi is hardly trivial.'

'Not the gallery, no. But the business. I don't know. A girl needs a little glamour.'

'Then work in Gucci.'

She laughs.

'Are you from Florence?'

'Rome. But if I worked there, I'd have to see my parents all the time. I couldn't stand that. They are both lawyers. One is a prosecutor, the other defence. They are celebrities. They are on TV all the time talking about big trials – it's so stupid.'

'I don't have celebrity parents,' I say in English.

Francesca immediately, deftly moves into English. 'What do your parents do?'

'You don't see yours. I don't talk about mine.' What would she think of me if she knew they were market traders like those in the Mercato Centrale?

There is a pause. A quizzical look on Francesca's face.

'You don't look to me like a writer.'

I smile, watch her eyes narrow, squint. I think maybe she isn't wearing contacts and her serious eyes are simply the expression of hard focusing.

'Why do you say that?'

'When you came into my office on Monday I thought, this man is not a writer – why's he here?'

'Do you think I'm pretending to be a writer because having seen you somewhere it's the only way I might get to meet you?'

'Maybe I have thought that, but you've seen the novels I read.'

'So why do you think I'm here?'

'To write about the *Doni Tondo* for your National Gallery.'

'Boring, but true.'

Our second course arrives and Francesca picks at it, preferring to nurse her glass of wine with both hands and study me. I dig into my rabbit. I don't have a strong sense of being seduced by this woman, but she is intrigued by me for some reason. I remain fairly certain she is not a honey trap.

Back into Italian, Francesca asks, 'What will you be writing about the *Doni Tondo*?'

This is my chance to lay any suspicions to rest. I explain my thesis will be simple. It is not a religious painting. It is not devotional. It is the first humanist painting and way before its time. The

161

first painting about human dignity unmediated by faith. For me, it's a work which presages the great painter/psychologist – Caravaggio. The first humanist painter.

When I have finished she says, 'Sounds good,' and knocks back her wine. She then says, 'I wish I could write. My talents are charm and efficiency.' She holds up her hand to silence any argument. 'It's actually quite a rare combination. Charm is more useful than we admit. Efficiency is always in demand. But still, you wouldn't put them high on a list of desirable attributes.'

'Are you not also quite clever?'

'Charming and efficient, that's all.'

I sense the wine is making her maudlin. We have shared and almost finished three bottles, and the conversation is taking on the eager vagueness of drunkenness.

'If we're talking gifts, mine are, well we've discussed my charisma and handsomeness . . .'

'You can write.'

'Perhaps.'

'You're a writer.'

'We can't all write.'

Francesca empties the last drops of the wine into her glass. 'Time for a *digestivo*.'

She stops a waiter passing our table. 'Two *grappa*.' And then looks back to me, big brown eyes now wide, her curls swishing with the quick turn. 'I drink far too much to be an Italian. I'm like your women.'

I laugh. 'Fifteen Bacardi Breezers and a shag – I don't think so.'

'You'd be surprised.'

The *grappa* arrives and Francesca asks the waiter to clear the table. Another cigarette is lit and the packet offered to me. I shake my head.

Nothing is said while we sip our *digestivo*. Francesca occasionally sighs and squints through the tinted glass to the empty street. I think of nothing, the *grappa* releasing all thoughts from my mind into somewhere that is not my mind, but a dark nowhere inside me – a pleasant elsewhere. I feel beatifically drunk. Sarah is gone, the job is gone, the Caravaggio is gone, even Francesca is fading away.

'Are you ready to go?' A credit card sits on a small metal dish across the bill. I recover myself with a sharp shake of my head. Francesca is smiling, leaning on the palm of her hand, cigarette burning precariously near her curls.

'Thank you very much.'

'I haven't finished with you yet.'

Outside our drunkenness keeps the cold out. We walk slowly towards her car. Francesca points. 'That can be left there if you'll walk me home.'

I give an exaggerated nod. The street is dark, the moon the only light. Francesca stumbles on a loose stone; curls spring about her neck.

A hundred metres along the street, Francesca turns into her doorway, disappearing into a complete darkness. For a moment I think that is the last I'll see of her tonight, but she quickly re-appears, lit up by the yellow flame of her lighter. She looks directly at me.

'I'll be straight with you. You can come up and we can make love or you can go – I don't mind.'

I can find no immediate response. She continues, 'It is up to you. We make love and I go to sleep or I masturbate and I go to sleep.'

I laugh – my nerves, her candour. I have to accept the choice is genuine – she really will go with either. I guess that I am her preference, but I am not certain. My response, when it comes, is a meaningless, 'Well . . .' I want to add to this that I am married but refuse to be so corny. Yet I am married and I know to fuck Francesca at this point would be to end it.

'I want to, really. Right now, I really want to. But I can't, can't . . .'

Francesca takes my hand. 'Don't panic. You can't; you're married and you love your wife. Go.'

I stay where I am.

'Go. Masturbate. And after' – she makes a little explosion with her fingertips around her lighter – 'you will sleep and not care that you didn't . . .' She stops; we both understand.

I lean around the lighter and kiss her on the lips. Francesca takes her thumb off the lighter gas and is gone. I sense she is still there, an arm's length away.

I turn and head down the street, saying to myself: you have until the city gates to turn back. She'll wait that long but not longer . . .

164

I pass beneath the high arch and don't stop. I am at the Ponte Vecchio before I allow myself to slow down. I am in the apartment before I allow myself to think about what has just happened. I open one of the three Caravaggio books and flick through, a shudder of darkest browns, darkest reds, darkest gold, of palest flesh, freshest flesh, dirtiest flesh, of shadow, of light, of desperate human action, the dignity of human action. The first humanist painter? Yes. Recognizing the sway of the body, of desire, indulgence, weakness, corruptibility. Painting its transcendence. Why didn't I give in tonight, maestro? It is because I have drawn up different battle lines and I must reserve my strength. I flick to *The Nativity*. Is this where my fidelity actually resides? Why I am here and not at home? Listen, if you want me to recover your painting, maestro, it will take more than strength, more than fidelity – it will take more than love.

2

I wake, turn into the pillow. Although events towards the end of last night are vague, I know instantly nothing bad occurred. There is reason for guilt, however, and some embarrassment. I lean over to the bedside table, grab my mobile and call Sarah. A quiet voice answers, a husk of a voice.

'It's me.'

'What time is it?'

'Ten a.m.'

'That's not early, is it?'

'Not really. Not for grown-ups.'

'Are we grown-ups?'

I have caught her sleep-filled, not battle-ready; she hasn't yet wrapped herself in toughness. 'Yes.'

'I suppose we are. We've been getting at each other like children though, haven't we?'

'Maybe not like children, but like something.'

'I miss you being here, Dan.'

'Do you?'

'It's hard for me. I'm not used to talking

about this stuff. I was a tough girl before I met you.'

'We have to talk about this stuff, and we have to keep talking until we work out what's going wrong.'

She is silent for a moment before she says, 'Something is wrong, isn't it?'

'At least we're agreed on that.'

'I'm scared it's me. I can't face it being me.'

'It's partly you, it's partly me.'

'How do you feel?'

I don't know how to answer this. I blame her. Her unwillingness to understand. Her wrap of toughness.

'I'm certain of my love but that certainty needs something from you if it's going to last.'

'So it *is* me?' There is nothing defensive in this – the question is genuine and heartfelt.

'Feeling like you don't love me may be just as much to do with me . . .'

'But you don't think that do you? You think it is to do with me.'

'*Do* you love me?' She doesn't immediately respond. 'Sarah?'

'I think I do, Dan.' It is said hopefully, as if looking for reassurance: if you think you do, then you do, right?

For a moment there is only white noise, the world scaled away to nothing, only sound, hard rushing sound filling my head. I feel sick. I realize now I didn't really question her love, it was her emotional generosity that I doubted.

167

'Dan?'

'I'm here.'

'I'm trying to be honest with you. I'm saying I think I love you, but I have no way of knowing. I miss you when you're not here; I get cross when you say you're off somewhere. I think you're lovely-looking. But it doesn't feel like it did. At the beginning. I *can* stop thinking about you; I do. I get on with my life and I sometimes wonder whether you really exist. I keep saying to myself: we love each other, we're married – now get on with it. But something else keeps – I don't know – you're the expert, you're the psychologist in this relationship. What do you think is happening to us?' There is still nothing sharp in her voice; it is as if now that we're finally talking she has decided that this is the morning to get things sorted out, and she is doing so as straightforwardly as she knows how.

'I don't know. We probably got married too quickly. The marriage is in the way of our feelings, or us listening to them clearly. We're both worried that if we weren't married we wouldn't still be together.' I pause; does she think this? She is quiet – waiting for more. 'Look, Sarah, relationships go through difficult stages. We're just panicking because we're going through a difficult stage within a year of getting married. We're thinking: isn't this the time when we should be blissfully happy? Therefore something fundamental must be wrong. But things aren't that simple. If we were going out, it wouldn't seem so bad. Would we be calling it a day? I don't think so. We'd be calling it a stage.'

'That makes sense to me.' Sarah is pleased by this – keen on it as an answer.

I am irritated by her quick acceptance of my analysis, but I recognize she's trying. 'Do you want to go with that for now? We're just going through a stage? It might give us a little time off. Allow us to start enjoying being with each other again.'

'That's right. You're back next Friday, aren't you?'

'Yes. Definitely.'

'Then let's do something special. Have the weekend to ourselves. You choose something to do and I'll choose something.' Her enthusiasm is high for practicalities now, the talking having yielded such sense.

'That sounds great, Sarah.'

'I do love you, Dan. But . . . it's . . .'

'You don't need to explain. I knew you were high-maintenance from the off.'

'Well, I always knew you were big trouble.'

'Me?'

'Dan – you threaten to beat up my friends.'

'Not to their faces.'

'Dan!'

'What can I say – I used to fight my way home from school. I'm hard.'

There is a little laugh. 'I feel so much better.'

'I'll call you later.'

I drop the mobile into my lap and close my eyes. She wants to love me, but she doesn't. I force myself out of bed and before the bathroom mirror, opening my eyes wide. I stare in. I don't know what I'm looking for – maybe traces of inner darkness, inner light, something signalling how I might be feeling right at this moment, beyond the paranoia, the desperation, the scattered and drifting yearning. I check my tongue, also without knowing what I'm looking for.

I wrap a towel around my waist and go into the sitting room, turn on the gas heater and the gas rings. I stare out of the window to the lantern of the *duomo*. It's probably time to decide how I'm going to approach my work on Monday. First, I'll need to get hold of a list of Uffizi employees. Second, I'll need some way to isolate those for whom blackmail might be an option. Third, get them to talk. I know the procedure, the process, but again, it's not my thing. I hate having to ingratiate myself. I don't do charm – not like this. It's why I deal with gangsters; they don't do charm. Not really. They do toughness. And I don't scare easily. Other men don't frighten me. That's my thing.

The apartment now has pockets of warmth; heat glows in the kitchenette and there is about a metre of warmth in front of the heater. I go back into the bedroom, shower and dress, after which I boot up the laptop. I'm not expecting any important emails; Jim should leave me alone over the weekend, believing a copper has enough problems to deal with without being bothered at the weekend by other coppers. I am certain Sarah is fully enjoying the start of her weekend now we've settled things, and I doubt I'll hear from Francesca. Spam streams in – porn, Viagra, mortgage deals, pyramid selling. No Jim, no Sarah; I was wrong about Francesca.

Storaro has asked me to invite you to his new house today. We are going to see the 'work in progress'. I'll pick you up at 12.

I look at my watch – it's eleven-forty. Do I need to reply? Am I too late? Why is Storaro inviting me? What does Francesca think, being ordered to invite me after last night? She's agreed to pick me up, but she has changed her mind before. Taking her at her word, I decide she really was happy either way. I finish dressing and head out.

The Smart Car is parked across the road. It's not quite twelve. I tap on the window. Francesca looks up at me, spectacles on, and gestures for me to move aside. She pulls the car away from the kerb to let me in. We kiss quickly, warmly on each cheek.

'It's not far. Just on the hill. Below Fiesole. Did you get back all right last night?'

'Yes, thank you.'

I am not sure whether she's expertly not referring to what happened as a way of saying don't

you refer to it or whether she is perfectly comfortable with her invitation and my decision to refuse.

'Thanks for a wonderful evening.' I say this
looking directly at her sitting sideways in her
seat, looking directly at me as we drive around
the *duomo*.

'I enjoyed it very much. Have you spoken to
your wife today?'

'Yes.'

'Did you feel very proud of yourself?'

I laugh. 'No.'

'I suspect one of Storaro's spies saw us. He
insisted we come today.'

I can think of another reason. I am not sure how
to play this. What has Storaro got planned? What
does he know? Is he finally going to take me on
as a competitor for his love-object, looking to
destroy me publicly before her: 'By the way,
Francesca, did you know this guy's a cop! Not a
writer. Not an expert. Just a cop pretending. What
do we think of that?' I guess it all depends on
what he's discovered about the Caravaggio.

There is little traffic in the centre of Florence,
only slightly more as we circle Piazza della Libertà
and head up towards Fiesole. I turn to Francesca,
still nestled into the corner of her seat. 'How was
he when he invited us?'

'Funny. Chatty. Insistent. You know.'

I don't know.

Close to the top of the hill, Francesca whips the
car right and into a small lane marked out by

needle-sharp cypress trees. All around us, built on small plateaus dug out of the hill, pastel-coloured villas overlook the city.

We arrive at a building site, a plot of about three acres. Half a building stands at the far end, the rest is just a foundation and the beginnings of a frame. There are a few workmen. Storaro is in the centre of the plot talking to a man in blue overalls. He is wearing a long expensive-looking black overcoat and a white safety helmet; the helmet is slightly too big for him so he has to keep tipping it up off his face while he follows the other man's hand, drawing an invisible building for him across the sky.

Francesca parks close to the edge of the plot. The hillside falls away sharply; there is nothing obscuring the view across Florence below.

'Who's the architect?' I ask as we climb out of the car.

'Raphael Goldberg.'

'Did he design the gallery?'

'Yes.'

'Is he here?'

'I doubt it.'

I look out over Florence resting neatly in the Arno basin – a gentle city. The *duomo* lies in amongst the other buildings like a red lion at rest in russet grass.

Storaro turns and stares at us as we make our way towards him, weaving around the puddles, patches of mud, building materials and machinery.

His helmet falls forward; he shoves it back. When we reach him he displays his small muddy paws, excusing himself from his usual greeting. Francesca bends down to kiss him. I don't sense he has plans for me. But I do understand we are meeting on different terms this time. Francesca is not our sole connection, our sole fight.

I look around for members of Team Storaro but none are present, not even Luca; but then the heavy sound of a big car is heard and a monumental black and chrome Range Rover Vogue appears from the lane, Luca driving, cronies back and front.

I lean over to Francesca and whisper, 'Are these guys always around?'

Francesca whispers back, 'There's always someone.'

Storaro watches this exchange.

'So why are we here?' Francesca asks, perfectly aware we are being scrutinized because we've been caught whispering.

Storaro looks around at his unfinished house.

'I wanted Daniel to see my house. Do you want to see my house, Daniel? It has been designed by Raphael Goldberg. They say his buildings are "too beautiful". What does that mean?'

I walk over to the only section of the house that is completed. The external walls are long horizontal serpentine lines of terracotta brick and dark cedar wood, held together by chromed bracing about ten centimetres thick, protruding from the surface like a kind of exoskeleton. I imagine under the white hot Tuscan sun the chrome will glisten and shimmer and it will seem as though the house is held together with water.

I describe what I see and what I think about it, adding that I've just noticed that the lines – tile, brick, steel – run parallel to the flow of the Arno miles below. Storaro nods. 'But, please, tell me: what is too beautiful?'

I look over at Francesca, standing with her back to us, arms folded, dark-brown curls rustling. 'In my experience it is the criticism used when you can't find a fault aesthetically, but still somehow the thing doesn't feel right or you're not moved by it.'

Storaro shrugs. 'But it is not the case here.'

'No, Storaro. It is not the case here. This is simply beautiful. When will it be finished?'

Storaro throws his hands in the air. Who knows! I am then led away, a mud-encrusted hand hovering at my elbow. 'Follow me. I want to show you another fascinating aspect of the design.'

We walk across the front of the finished section of the house and over the edge of the plot, down a muddy bank made up of rudimentary timber steps to a flat promontory looking over the city. I wave to Francesca as we disappear; she waves back. Storaro tells me this area is going to form part of the basement extending out beyond the hill – the perfect place to look over the city. I peer over the edge. There is a sheer drop of about thirty metres. Storaro directs me to his partially finished house, looming above us. From this angle neither the brick nor the cedar wood is visible, just the chrome ribbing. Somehow the structure gives the illusion of being no more than a cage.

Storaro explains this is what he loved about the design. From the city the house will look like a massive steel sculpture, yet the house itself is in perfect accord with the city. It's a great example of organic subversion. He wants me to comment, to appreciate, to understand. I do. But I know I've been brought down here for other reasons. I make myself clear.

'Why have you brought me here, Storaro?'

He laughs. 'To look at my house.'

I take a deep breath; the air is damp, cold – I can taste the mud, dirt, dust, wood within it.

Storaro continues, 'Do not worry, this is not like the last time.'

'If it is, I'll push you over the edge.' I do not smile. But it is not a real threat. He laughs again.

'You know why you are here.'

'Because I chose to be.' He is not a gangster and I am not interested in flattering him.

He gives me this with a bounce; he wants to get on, move on to the important things – his core interest. Storaro has no conversational fat. His passions are lean; he is hard in his desire. It is a dangerous monomania: obsessive, aggressive, blind, ruthless. If he hadn't been born rich, he'd have been a self-made man, his maximal attention focused on the gaining of wealth rather than the displaying of art. I indicate he will need to start if he wants me to talk.

'We are here to talk about the Caravaggio. You cannot know where it is. I have checked. I have checked personally. It was destroyed. In Campania. Over twenty years ago.'

I do not say anything. This is old news. A story still believed by some. The painting ruined or lost in an earthquake near Naples. I know of at least two confirmed sightings since then. And countless testimony to its existence, its uses, including a trip to Johannesburg where it was used as a guarantee for a consignment of diamonds. Storaro must also know this. He is irritated by my silence.

'Do you believe it still exists?'

I am a little moved by the manner of his question, modulated by hope, fascination, a desire for collusion: he wants me to believe it still exists so he can then believe it, because believing gives him a thrill and he wants to feel the thrill. He could be an eight-year-old child being told about some legendary trump card, never seen but known to beat all others.

I envy him his undiluted enthusiasm, the simplicity of his desire; I resent him because it is an eccentricity allowed only by extravagant wealth. I look over Florence, sensing Storaro looking up at me. For this one moment I have all the power. He wants something specific and he wants it irrationally, almost irrespective of the truth. He is resisting bouncing on his toes because he knows it is a display of uncontrolled need. His need is greedy, desperate, fat.

I decide that there is no point in dragging it out. 'No. I just wanted to get underneath your skin.'

I do not know whether he believes me. As usual, he laughs. He looks up at Francesca. She is standing on the ridge now, with her back to us. He contemplates her, the strong wind wrapping her clothes tightly across her body, her curls lifted, shifted, jostled about her shoulders. Which would he choose, I wonder, Francesca or the Caravaggio? I see no reason not to put the question to him, our two moments alone have each been about one of them. But then there is no need. Without taking his eyes off Francesca he says, 'If you know where the Caravaggio is, you should tell me. Don't play with me for *her*.'

I now realize Storaro's great strength is that he makes things around him seem vulnerable. Announcing the limitation of his desire for Francesca, he has made her appear vulnerable for the first time. Her body, tugged at by the wind, now seems less certain of withstanding it, and her hair, lifted and jostled, now seems to contain more than a hint of loneliness.

He also makes me feel vulnerable. I lack his certainties. His will. When he goes out in search of tall blonde American women he is exercising his will. He surrounds himself with tall handsome

178

clever men, to exercise his will. He is taking me on because I am tough and have taken on tough men, and his will recognizes this. There is something half child, half emperor about him – an unstable mix. This is the first time I think he is as dangerous as he is passionate.

He doesn't let go. His long eyes are bright. His hard curls resist the wind. 'If you know anything about the Caravaggio, tell me. I want the painting. Do you understand?'

I am doubly driven to continue the game: my will also recognizes exercise and I am foolish enough to want to get further underneath his skin since his dismissal of Francesca. I lean down to his ear; I sense him stiffen. 'It would look great in your gallery, Storaro. Really put it on the map.' I pause and lay my hand on his shoulder. 'I'm surprised you haven't got closer to it in the last few days.'

I feel him bristle with excitement; finally, he has a reason to believe. I imagine his mind suddenly whitewashed, becoming a high wide wall – a wall prepared and ready for the giant altarpiece. And there it is in his mind: an umber and gold emanation. I can see on his face he now knows it's out there. No matter what he is told.

I look up at his house, the exposed ribs, the serpentine lines, picturing the terracotta and cedar between. Part of me thinks: so what? If I can't get it, then maybe Storaro should be given the

179

opportunity. After all, he will cherish it, spend money on it, display it with reverence and feeling. But then part of me thinks: fuck the rich kid with his extravagant hobby and voracious will. This is about a poor kid looking to reawaken his passion before it's too late.

Storaro is gracious, nodding his thank you humbly. I pat him on the back. The two gestures are the most significant exchange between us. Storaro then turns and clambers up the bank. I follow him with big strides. We arrive at the top together. Luca is there to meet Storaro, a hand out to help. Francesca is there, arms folded. She wants to know what we've been talking about. Storaro gives her a cold smile. 'Signor Wright has been entertaining me.'

Francesca is irritated. 'Why did you invite us up here, Storaro?'

He doesn't want to be cross-examined. She doesn't want to be ignored. 'Why, Storaro?'

The rest of us might as well not be present. But Storaro refuses to engage. His mind is not free for this kind of debate or distraction. His jawbone clenches. His stare ranges inward. To the white wall. To the painting. Francesca turns away; her hair caught in a gust of wind is a parabola of curls. Storaro calls over the foreman and disappears around the back of the unfinished portion of the house.

Team Storaro return to the car, light cigarettes and lean on the doors.

Francesca walks over to the window of the finished portion of the house, tiptoes up to look inside.

'What did he say?'

'Nothing – he just pointed out the effect of his house from the city, or at least as seen from below.'

'You unsettle him, I can tell.'

'I don't think so.'

She ignores me. 'Then why are we here? So he can take a look at us? Decide whether we've fucked or not?' She shakes her head, her curls afloat for a moment. 'Don't be taken in by him. He's not your friend.'

I know this. For a moment the connection was deeper.

'Did he ask you about me?' She pulls hair from her mouth, whipped in by the wind.

I am not used to being in the middle of things like this. My job is always to enter, negotiate, leave. I like to be on the periphery, only a small part of my circle within the larger circle.

'We talked about his house.'

Francesca is not impressed by my lack of candour. 'What do you want to do now?'

'What do *you* want to do?'

'We came here together, that doesn't mean we have to leave together.'

'I was being polite.'

'Sorry. I don't care what we do. He'll expect us to have lunch with him.'

I don't want this. I want to get away from this

man now that I have given him what he wants. He can go after the Caravaggio if he dares.

Storaro appears, tipping up his hat, rubbing his muddy hands together and then on to his expensive overcoat, leaving streaks of mud on both lapels. He looks over at us standing on the ridge.

Francesca slides her arm into mine. 'We're not coming for lunch,' she calls.

Storaro is unmoved. He looks at me. He wants to know whether I have in fact chosen Francesca over the Caravaggio. Part of him considers me as a potential ally.

'Daniel?'

I shake my head. 'Sorry.'

He laughs but I can tell he is irritated, disappointed. He is used to being magnetic. With powers beyond Francesca's beauty, intelligence, hidden vulnerabilities.

It begins to rain. Storaro looks up; his helmet falls forward over his eyes. His patience runs out and he tugs the thing off and throws it to the ground. 'Why am I wearing this? There's no building going on here!'

Without being directed or ordered, Team Storaro bundle into the Range Rover and Luca drives it over to his boss. At this point Luca climbs out and, with his fingers intertwined, his palms together, he helps Storaro up into the high car. Storaro then directs Luca to circle the plot and pull up alongside us. The window is lowered. Heavier rain begins to fall. Storaro looks across the city, suddenly under heavy grey cloud. The hills opposite have disappeared completely.

'It is like England,' he says under his breath and to no one in particular. He then looks at me. 'My house is not too beautiful, you are right. Francesca, however, is. This kind of beauty is not good. It causes only pain. Beauty that causes pain is not real beauty.'

I sense Francesca's anger building. Storaro leans a little further out of the window. 'Only men really appreciate the kinds of beauty which will destroy us, isn't that right?'

'It is only men that are attracted to it.'

Storaro looks at Francesca. 'Daniel is a complicated man, Francesca. He is more like me than you imagine. But he is poor, he is married and he is foolish.'

I do not respond. The window slides silently shut. The car eases forward, rocking heavily over the dips and ridges of its previous tracks.

We are alone, the rain heavy, the mud under our feet softening. We don't say anything for a moment. Storaro may have priorities, but he also has big appetites. He is not content with one battle. Francesca remains between us. The only thing I can think to say on the subject is to ask, 'How tall *is* he?'

Francesca laughs. 'One-point-six metres.'

I try to convert metric into imperial. Around five-two, five-three. I am momentarily sympathetic, moved. 'It must be tough.'

'Poor Storaro,' Francesca says sarcastically.

'On the other hand,' I add, 'he's clearly a monster and must be stopped.'

Francesca laughs again. We head back to the Smart Car, arm in arm, awkwardly hanging on to one another as we avoid the mud, puddles, material and equipment in our way.

Francesca reverses out of the plot, down the lane and out into the road; I watch her for the first time concentrating on her driving.

'What do you want to do this afternoon?' she asks without looking at me.

I want to relax, enjoy my time in Florence, happy to be rid of Storaro, happy to have let the Caravaggio go. Move on. Maybe even think about my assignment, pick Francesca's brains about her colleagues. I have promised Sarah I will be home soon, a promise I can't break. So that's what I want to do: relax, work and go home soon.

'What do you suggest?'

'Lunch and then a film? It's my usual Saturday afternoon.'

Francesca steers the car down the hill and into the city. We say little. I stare idly out of the window. We park across from the Odeon. *A Touch of Evil* in English.

'Have you seen it?' Francesca asks.

'A long time ago.'

'OK then. There's a good restaurant around the corner; we've got an hour.'

The restaurant is busy, yet we are quickly seated

and orders taken and food served. We share a bottle of wine. The film we watch alone. I check from time to time, scanning the rows of dark empty seats for darker forms, but we are alone throughout. We sit in the middle of the stalls, Francesca low in her seat, head resting against my shoulder. We remain where we are during the intermission; the wine at lunch has made us dozy. Francesca says this is not the first time she's been alone in here, especially in January watching an original-language film.

It is still raining when we leave; there is a cold wet wind. Francesca tucks her arm into the folds of my sleeve and pulls herself closer to me.

'Cocktail? They make a great martini at the Savoy.'

The hotel is directly across the Piazza della Repubblica. The entrance glows warmly, richly. We stroll over, huddled together. Seen from above the grand arch, I imagine we must make a romantic picture, pressed together, heading for a drink, a single silhouette of love moving across an empty Italian square.

The bar is dark, lit from delicate spots refracted in the glasses and bottles displayed behind the bar. The bartender welcomes Francesca by name, leans over for a kiss and says, 'Martini?' Francesca nods, asks for two. She suggests we stay at the bar rather than take a table by the window, describing the vista as gloomy Florence. Nothing is said for a moment. Francesca lights a cigarette with a book of Savoy matches, which she balances tent-like on the bar; she pulls an ashtray, next to my elbow, towards her with an index finger. I watch Francesca take a drag, blow the smoke away, drop the match in the ashtray.

'Am I being unfaithful?'

Francesca picks up my hand, spreads out my fingers and places hers against it. She looks directly into my eyes. 'In the books I read, this would be unfaithful.'

'Our hands like this, or this whole thing?'

'It depends how you feel right now.'

'Why do you read those books?'

She shrugs, takes her hand away, presses out her unfinished cigarette and picks up the martini that's been placed before her.

'Do *you* think you're being unfaithful?'

'Nothing's happened. That's how it's measured these days, isn't it?'

'And you're not in love with me, so what are you doing wrong?'

I pick up my martini. 'I have to ask myself how Sarah would react if she saw us.'

'I think she would be very angry.'

We both eat the olive before taking the first sip of our martinis. My first sip confirms my suspicion: they are almost pure gin. I watched them being made: shaker and two glasses placed on the bar, ice added to all three to cool them down, ice tipped out; gin poured into shaker, followed by two tiny drops of vermouth, followed by a cursory shake, shaker back on the bar; zest of lemon circled around rim of glasses, mixture poured, followed by the zest of lemon being waved over glasses, not a single drop falling into the martini – a kind of homeopathic addition to the recipe, the spirit of lemon.

Francesca takes a second sip. 'Good, aren't they?'

I knock over the matchbook. However much I try to separate myself from the painting, I know it's out there, and being out there is as good as being inside of me. But do I want it more than Storaro? Is this where he beats me again – the depth of his desire?

Francesca nudges me. 'What are you thinking about?'

I force a smile. 'Nothing. I'm sorry.'

'You're not doing anything wrong.'

'I know.'

I feel like confessing everything in the hope of being rid of it all, cleansed of it all. The strain of pretence – cop as writer as date; the strain of being unhappily married and not willing to give up; the Caravaggio, a dark, frayed and cracked presence pulling at me – the scattered and drifting pieces of my self.

We sip our martinis.

'You are a mysterious man.'

I laugh. 'Not really.'

Francesca wants to play, to flirt, to use our time together well. I am moved by her insistence; the vulnerability revealed by Storaro remains in the trembling of her curls as she beseeches me to tell her what I like in a woman. I refuse to answer. But my vulnerability, also revealed by Storaro, means I will give in soon; flirtation is easier than denial, a perfect state for temporary forgetfulness.

'Tell me why you're so unhappy?' The smile is mobile, tempting me: tell her, don't tell her, she doesn't care, but she wants me to feel excited by this.

I try to explain. 'It's complicated. I'm in the middle of a lot of things. I am here for reasons that I cannot explain. It was a mistake. It was a mistake to come here. To Florence.' I shake my head wearily; giving up the Caravaggio required almost all my strength.

Francesca knocks back the last of her martini and orders two more. I roll the last of mine in my mouth and push the glass towards the bartender.

'Don't worry. You are safe with me. But I think we need to get drunk.'

There is warmth in her curls, warmth in the brown eyes flickering behind her spectacles, warmth in her hands patting my knees to show getting drunk is a good decision, well made.

Our second martini is sipped in silence but with open smiles and penetrating looks – looks that are conscious of our good behaviour.

Our third martini is drunk more quickly, resisting laughter, our good behaviour tipping into a staring competition. Francesca leans forward, a hand splayed on my knee, arm propping her up; her face is close. She is happy to cheat. She mouths words that mock her earlier good behaviour. I use more traditional methods: no expression, still eyes, just the subtlest of movements when she is on the brink.

I win. Of course. It's what I do. Francesca strokes my hand as she turns to the bar to order our fourth martini.

What happens next happens in my peripheral vision. Outside in the gloom. A presence passing by. A shadow against darkness. A transparency against the night air. I act swiftly. Whisper to Francesca that I'll be back in a moment. She remains where she is, stomach to the bar, talking to the bartender.

He is thirty metres away by the time I get outside, walking away from the piazza towards the Arno, a thin form, hesitant and nervous, a shape out of focus in the mist. It has stopped raining. I look up to the sky; it is clear, starlit, with only a few heavy black clouds passing over.

Can he really be looking for me? Of course he is. I peer through the dark window of the Savoy bar. Francesca is still chatting to the bartender. She is expecting me back within minutes. My fourth martini is delicately placed next to where I was sitting. I have to make a decision: stay, go. I am on my way before I have an answer. I need to catch him up and then head away from the centre of the city, away from the few tourists, natives, cops. It takes only a minute to get level with him. He sees me, and then the next moment we're off the main drag, ten metres apart, walking at pace. I can hear his breathing, shallow, irregular; he is unused to exercise.

He calls, 'Wait.' Takes a deep breath and adds, '*Sbirro*,' weakly. I ignore him. I am taking us somewhere specific. A place I have passed a couple of times, a tight break between two buildings, barely an alley. Two more streets away now. I turn. Nenni follows. To anyone watching, it's obvious I am leading him somewhere.

The alley is less than a metre wide. The walls are high, black. We enter, first me, then five seconds and Nenni is in. We are both hidden by strong shadow. It is like Naples. The sky above appears little higher than the buildings.

Nenni walks further in, disappearing into total blackness. Drains drip around us. I am the first to speak; I want to control the conversation. 'What are you doing here?'

There is no response. The only sound I hear is his high tight irregular breathing. He is waiting to speak. Concentrating on being firm, convincing. Making his case.

'Nenni?'

'I have a name.'

I don't believe for a moment he's come this far north just to give me a name.

'Forget it. What are you doing here?' Even in this dark I am able to sense Nenni's jerks and spasms.

I reach out and grab at him, pull him forward into the half-light. My hand is tugged away.

'Do not touch me.'

'Then step forward. I'm not talking to you if I can't see you.'

Nenni appears, eyes blinking, body tense, movement held fast.

'Tell me: why are you here?'

'I have a name. I promised you.'

Nenni tries a smile, but it looks more like he's been struck in the face and is reeling from the pain. His thick lips cling to his straight teeth; his mouth is dry, sticky. I lower my voice, soften my tone. 'You don't come all the way to Florence to give me a name. What do you want? If you don't tell me now, I'm walking away. And if you follow me, I'm going straight to the police. I'm sure they'll be very interested in what a *camorrista* is doing in Florence.'

'I'll say you invited me. You asked me to supply you with vases.' Nenni thinks this is smart, quick thinking.

'Forget it. I'll just tell them I'm working on a case.'

'I have a name. For the Caravaggio. It's what you wanted.'

I am suddenly aware of Nenni's desperation, present in the oscillations of his voice under his short breath. I want the name. I am like Storaro only hours ago, waiting for an utterance which will convince me not to give up.

I lean forward, whisper, 'Give me the name.'

Nenni laughs. 'Not for nothing. We had a deal.'

'We didn't have a deal.'

'Yes. You help me get out the vases and you get the name.'

I realize that for some reason Nenni really believes we did make a deal – a good, simple deal which we are both bound to honour.

'There was no deal, Nenni. I said I might be able to help you. I waited. You didn't show.'

'I was trying. It is hard.' He is plaintive, looking to stress how committed he has been, the pounding of the streets, the favours traded, the risks involved.

'Why should I believe you? You were going to give me the name of a dead man. Whatever reason you're here for is a good enough reason to make up any name. Sorry, Nenni.'

He steps closer to me; his face is only inches away and miraculously still. 'Savarese says he will kill my wife.'

I grab him and drive him backwards into the alley, into the dark, until we hit a hard surface. I smash my forearm into his neck.

'Nenni. Don't fucking play with me. Don't fucking play with me, OK? Why should I care what happens to your wife? I just wanted a name; you didn't have it. End of story.'

Nenni is wriggling under the force of my arm pressing him to the wall. He is feather-light, fragile – a bird; his bones would break with any further push; any extra pressure and his ribcage would cave in. I can feel he is completely without fat, muscle, without protection. I drop him. He groans weakly.

I'm not sure why I reacted like that. I cast my mind back to our little adventure, trudging across that endless dark field, and our little joke about our wives. Nenni continues to groan. I straighten him up. 'Tell me the truth, Nenni.'

He tries to speak but only manages a cough, his body buckling into me. I have to hold him up. There is a spluttering. I feel something hit my shoes.

'Nenni?'

'It's my lip, *sbirro*. It's split.'

'I want you to tell me the truth.' I pull him up again; thin skin inside thin clothes slides off loose bones.

'Savarese says I have been stealing from him.'

'Have you?'

'No.'

'But he just says that. He found out I wanted to work for myself. With you.'

Nenni has just added the last detail to implicate me, to tie me into his nightmare.

'Bullshit.'

He perseveres. 'Really. We were seen together, at the restaurant.'

I push him against the wall, slap him – it is not hard, but I need to force compliance, the truth.

The crying is honest. 'OK, OK. I don't know what he knows. He just wants money.'

'How much?'

'Fifty thousand, otherwise . . .'

'Otherwise what?'

I feel Nenni brace himself for more punishment. I hear his weak, quiet sobs and realize there is nowhere inside of him for the desperation to resonate more loudly.

'Tell me, Nenni.'

'He will kill my wife.'

This doesn't make sense. 'Why doesn't he just kill *you*?'

Nenni's laugh is sharp, angry, ironic. 'Look at me. Look at me.'

There is no need for light. I know what he means, what the man standing before me looks like. I can imagine Savarese making the threat, watching Nenni's nerves go to pieces, everything disconnecting in this barely connected man.

'OK. Let's go.'

'Where?'

'To my apartment. We can't stay here all night.'

I release my grip on Nenni's arm and lead him out of the alley. In the streetlight I see his torn lip, open, swelling. His chin and shirt are streaked with blood. I look down at myself; the cuffs of my trousers and my shoes are splattered. Evidence enough that all this has been a mistake.

We are only two streets away from Via Dante. There are few people around. I make sure no one sees us enter the building, instructing Nenni to turn his face away from anyone we meet coming down the stairs. In the apartment I show Nenni to the bathroom and tell him to get cleaned up. I turn on the gas rings and the heater, rub my face. My hands hurt. What is Francesca thinking? How am I going to explain?

Nenni – face clean, lower lip turned out like a ripped fig – reappears. I order him to sit down, to relax; I point to the armchair. Nenni lowers himself down gently, his bones bruised, hurting. I feel bad. It never occurred to me that this man could be so fragile. I reckoned he would have the toughness of the lean, the wiry, the toughness of the wired.

'Who knows you are here?'

'No one.'

'How did you think you would find me?'

'*You* found *me*.'

'It's a six-hundred-mile round trip – you couldn't have known that.'

'Firenze is a small place. Not many people.'

I pull out a dining chair and sit down, facing him. 'I don't have the kind of money you need.'

'*Sbirro*, I don't want your money. I have vases. From the tomb. The one we found.' He nods – remember? 'I knew it was good. Your wife buys them. One hundred thousand euros. They are worth more.'

'You said Savarese wants fifty thousand.'

'Yes. Fifty for Savarese. I want fifty for me – to take my wife and leave.'

Nenni has convinced himself of a new simplicity

in the deal – the transaction, the numbers, the plan. It all adds up – it is certain to work.

He is being naive. Fear can do that: it breeds hope, denial, mistaken certainty. Things that get you killed. I don't know what to say. Nenni is here without a hope of selling on his vases.

'How long have you got?'

'Next week. Three, four days. I don't know.'

'Even if I wanted to, I couldn't get anything set up in that time.'

'But your wife. I have the name.' He hopes the proximal uttering of these two factors will make the deal more attractive to me – clear, simple.

I want to say I don't care about the name, but every time Nenni offers it I want to hear who it is. I want to know how I feel when I hear it. I know finding seventy-five grand is easy if I can promise the recovery of the world's most famous stolen painting; the problem is the time – no bureaucracy works that fast. I also know I could get the name for half that – Nenni having little choice but to take what he's offered. As far as I'm concerned, he can dream up another way to extort the money he needs for a new life.

'Do I have your word that you know who's got the Caravaggio?'

Nenni nods. So it starts again. I think of Storaro, Sarah, Jim.

'OK. I can try to get the money. But if I can't – I promise you I will have tried.'

Nenni isn't interested in uncertainties. 'It's your wife. She will buy. Tell her you trust me.' Nenni is hoping for a ring of trust – husband, wife and him.

'I told you it was a mistake to take on Savarese.'

Nenni shrugs, feels his lips – his long fingers dancing across the rich red split.

'Nenni?' I want some admission of stupidity.

He understands he has made a mistake. 'I was a fool. You cannot escape what you are – not in Naples.'

'Not only in Naples.'

Nenni makes to push himself out of the armchair.

'Wait. Before you go I want to see a picture of your wife.'

Nenni spasms; his eyes dart. 'Why?'

'I want to see her. You've talked so much about her.'

Nenni's hands go to his knees and he tries to hold them steady against the sudden bouncing rhythm of his legs.

'Don't you have one? A man who loves his wife as much as you do would have a photograph.'

Nenni nods – this is true.

'Do you have one?'

He nods again.

'Then show me.'

Nenni places his hand inside his jacket.

'Slowly.'

He produces a wallet, an Armani eagle in the

corner. He opens it with shaking hands and pulls out a photograph.

I take it gently between thumb and forefinger. I'm not sure what I expect. Nenni described her as beautiful. What I see is a middle-aged woman, older than Nenni, thin, hard-looking, with deep-set eyes, straight black hair, only a faint smile. I suppose she must be quite a catch for this casualty before me.

'She is pretty.' I hand the photo back and Nenni slots it into his wallet. 'Maria,' he says under his breath.

'Now you need to leave. How are you going to get back to Naples?'

'I have my car.' It is said as if I couldn't possibly have forgotten the Alfa Romeo Sportwagon.

I show him to the door, thrust a piece of paper into his hand. 'Call me at seven o'clock, Monday evening. I will tell you then whether I can help you or not. If I can't, I can't. Do you understand?'

Nenni grabs at the paper, shoves it into his jacket. 'It will work. It is a good deal.'

I study him one last time. 'No promises. OK?' I push him out of the door and shut it, not wanting to see or hear any expression of misplaced certainty. Not wanting to see or hear any misplaced hope.

I remain at the door listening to him walk down the stone steps. It is nine-forty-seven p.m. The martinis have been subsumed by the adrenalin. I need another drink. I open the glass doors of the bookcase and squat down. There are a number of bottles in the corner of the bottom shelf. Some decent Scotch, *grappa*, vodka, a one-third-full bottle of dark rum – Havana Club. I take the rum over to the kitchenette and wash up a glass. I pour myself an inch. The hit is instant – sharp to my brain, warm to my stomach; my heart beats a little faster. I pour myself two inches more. It's time to think and think fast. I need to act now. I sit down at the laptop, placing the bottle of rum on the floor, the glass on the arm of the chair. I brush my thumb over the mouse pad. The screen lights up.

First decision: in order to help Nenni, do I go public with the Caravaggio information? I'll need an explanation. What will it be? I have plenty to choose from. Midlife crisis. Delusions of grandeur. Glory desperation. Failing marriage. A working-class hero was always something I wanted to be and this was my chance. And then play it straight: I need a hundred thousand euros for a name; I am certain the source is reliable. Or do I continue to go it alone? Find the money myself and run with the name – see how far I get? My first thought is why give up the chance – the slimmest of chances – of recovering it myself? I've always worked alone. There is less chance of a bureau-cratic fuck-up. Of Rome, Interpol muscling in. Driving it back underground. I take a sip of the rum, tasting brown sugar, molasses, lemon. Alone then. It is difficult, risky. No back-up, no support.

None of the security of representing a legitimate force – the dimension which will always give me a little extra time and space to manoeuvre if things go wrong, with only Cosa Nostra quick to kill cops. I take another hit of rum. Some of the surface alcohol has dissipated and the cane-sugar taste is even sweeter. The central question remains: how do I raise the money? I lean forward and type:

The job?
Sarah?

Nothing happening on this job would need that kind of money; Jim would suspect something immediately. Sarah has the money. But can I ask her? What do I tell her? Can she be trusted? What if I lose the money?

Francesca??
Storaro????

Has Francesca got the money? Why would she give it to me? The easiest thing would be to go to Storaro. Tell him who I am, the contact will only work with me, I've done this a hundred times before – let me make the recovery, take the glory, then it's yours to fight over.

I knock back more of the rum – rich, viscous, hot. High risk, Storaro. Do I really know how he'd react? Would he go into overdrive – fuck it up within hours through sheer exhilaration and the need to control, to be involved, wanting some or all of the glory himself? A fundamental force, he may be impossible to predict. Least-worst-case scenario: his indiscretion alerts Italian law enforcement. Worst-case scenario: he thinks money will out and he goes straight to the underworld looking to buy it, not understanding the one thing that it's not is for sale. We'd have had it back years ago if that was the case. Forget Storaro for the time being. With the easiest access to money, he can be a last resort. I hit the return key a number of times and type:

Gustav Ballack

Big Gustav. The key if I can put the first half together. If he'll bite. Five names. One from the top to supply the money, then Ballack to bite. At its simplest it's two countries, three nationalities, three to four days. It's not possible. Not possible. I sit back. Sorry, Nenni. It can't be done. For a moment I think of him in his Alfa Romeo, jerk- and spasm-free, taking the racing line through the Italian countryside. Maybe Maria fell in love with his driving.

My thoughts are disturbed by the apartment buzzer. I am out of my seat; Nenni back – why? There is no reason. A friend of the *professore*? At this time? It must be Francesca. What am I going to say? Can I ignore it? The buzzer is pressed again, this time more urgently, a staccato rhythm – insistent. I place my glass on the counter, and go to the door. Bz Bz Bz. My finger hovers over the intercom button. Bz Bz Bz. I push it, to kill the noise as much as anything.

'Daniel? Daniel?'

It is Francesca. I experience a sensation of delight and irritation: delighted by her urgent presence, irritated by her bad timing amid other urgencies.

'Top floor.'

I buzz open the street door, then flick up the latch of the apartment door. Half in, half out, I listen to the tap and echo of her quick footsteps. The moment she reaches the top of the stairs, breathless, curls vibrating, I realize I don't have an answer to her obvious first question: where did I go? She passes me in the doorway, dipping under my arched arm and walks into the centre of the room where she turns, her hands firmly in the side pockets of her leather jacket, two bulges telling me they are balled into fists.

'Who was that man?'

'What man?' She can't have seen him; she was turned to the bar.

'You know.'

She is a little drunk, agitated, unfocused. I go to the kitchen, wash a glass, collect the bottle of rum from the floor and pour us both a drink. She slumps down into the armchair. 'Thanks for abandoning me.'

I place the glass on the arm of the chair. 'I am sorry.'

Francesca drinks; a quick shudder passes through her. 'So are you going to explain?'

'What?'

'That man. Who was he?'

I sit down on the dining chair. 'What man?'

'The man you ran out to see.'

'How would you feel if I said I can't tell you?'

Francesca sits forward, presses her forefinger on the mouse pad of the computer, lighting up the screen. Before I can cross the room and shut the top, she sees the list, scans down and reads her name. Her eyes fix on me. 'Why is my name here? What's going on?'

I press down the lid. 'Nothing is going on. It's very boring.'

For a moment her face is sarcastic, disbelieving, hard. 'I don't think it's boring. You suddenly disappear, you don't come back, and my name is on your computer. I want to know why.'

I am still, eyes shunted sideways, trying to catch a thought sitting just outside myself – how to play this.

She continues, '*And* Storaro's name is there.'

I nod confirming this. 'Yes. And my wife's. And others.'

'Why?'

I say nothing, remaining where I am, glass hanging from my fingertips. I sense Francesca relax a little as she takes her second sip of rum, the alcohol warming her, softening her, providing a little continuity to her mood – her mood before I fled the bar, the mood disturbed by having to come here in the cold, disturbed by seeing her name on the computer. I also think she likes to operate at a certain level of drunkenness and the rum has added back a little of that edge the cold and her name being on the computer had taken off. I watch her squint, blink, concentrate. She wants focused thoughts. She looks up at me. She has for the moment forgotten about her name on the computer.

'Storaro called.'

I do not respond. What is being added up in her mind: my disappearance, a strange man, Storaro calling with information about me?

'What did he say?'

'He wanted to know whether I thought I was in love with you.'

Whatever game Storaro is playing, he is not letting Francesca in on it. Maybe this is her game? She looks up at me – fun smile, serious eyes. 'What do you think?'

'The possibility has not occurred to me.'

'Why not?'

'Don't play with me, Francesca.'

'How am I playing with you? You're the one disappearing mysteriously, typing up lists.'

'You're the one talking about love.'

She shrugs. 'Love is very ordinary. Everyone falls in love.'

'Please, Francesca. I can't have this conversation right now.'

'Why not?'

'Because I have things on my mind. And I'm married.'

'I merely said Storaro thinks I might be in love with you and I wanted to know what you think about that.'

I add more rum to Francesca's glass. 'I think Storaro is . . . Actually I don't care what Storaro is. As I've said: the possibility hasn't occurred to me.'

'I want to know what you think about me.' It is boldly said, with a starry smile; her drunkenness is still playful. But we are no longer playing.

'I don't know what I think. But if it's important, then I think you're almost irresistibly sexy and irresistibly sweet. Which means I can probably resist the sexiness, but I'm not sure about the sweetness . . .' I break off, adding after a moment, 'Maybe you're a honey trap after all.'

'What's that?'

'A beautiful woman sent to seduce a man.'

'You were sent to me. Maybe you're a honey trap.'

I laugh at this. 'Yes, maybe.'

Francesca stares up at me; I can see her thinking, amassing thoughts and then picking through them. She stands, passes me, places her glass on the dining table, opens the Caravaggio book and flicks through the pages absently. 'Who was the man, Daniel? And why is my name on the list?' She doesn't look up from the book.

My response is firm, the beginning of a story. 'If you must know, the man was a policeman. Your name is on the list because he asked me to write down the name of the people I've spoken to this week.'

Francesca closes the book. 'What do the police want with you? Why didn't he just come into the bar?' She looks around the room, her mind casually focused – as drunk as she is, she is confident she can catch me out if she wants to.

'All good questions. My wife's company – she works for Langdon's – got mixed up in a scandal last year. Trading in unregistered antiquities. Greek vases, mainly. A consignment has turned up here. I'm here. They wanted to talk to me. That's it.'

Francesca takes this in; something's not right. 'I don't understand what it's got to do with you.'

'It doesn't really.'

'Then I don't understand what you're telling me.'

'Please, can we forget it? It really doesn't matter.'

'It matters if you want to be straight with me.'

Can I be straight with her? No. She works for the Uffizi. What would they do to get the painting? My options are only to say nothing or to continue to invent. 'I need to know how much of this is simply because you're intrigued or because you genuinely think you should be told?'

'I might not be so insistent if I hadn't read my name on your computer. I have a very important job here.'

I nod, acknowledging her right. 'OK. But don't judge me.'

Francesca holds out her glass to be filled; I pour her the last of the bottle. She moves from the table, the pages of the book open, I notice, at *Doubting Thomas*, and sits back down in the armchair and lights a cigarette. I locate an ashtray in a cupboard above the sink and place it next to the computer. I lean against the kitchen counter, arms crossed, glass of rum lodged in the crook of my elbow.

'It's embarrassing. A while ago I helped a dealer in London bring in an old master from here, in Florence. Nothing famous or special, just something he wanted desperately. Writers don't make much money. It was a favour. And this stuff goes on all the time. Anyway, it got out. I was interviewed. Nothing came of it. Then the whole thing at Langdon's kicked off. It was a really big deal. It was in all the newspapers. I'm married to one of its senior members of staff; I've done freelance stuff for them. So when they saw my name again . . . As I said, it was very embarrassing.'

'Where were you all this week? You weren't in Florence.'

'How do you know?'

'Were you?'

'No.'

'Then where were you?'

'Seeing a friend. Perfectly innocent.'

She looks sceptical.

'I promise. Really, it's nothing. The interview lasted ten minutes; I was just too embarrassed to come back to the bar.'

Francesca looks away. 'I don't believe you. But then, what does it matter? When are you leaving?'

'Next week. Friday.'

Francesca presses out her cigarette, knocks back the last of her rum. 'Are you going to let me stay tonight?'

I push myself off the kitchen counter, arms still crossed, laughing at the audacity. 'You *should* be a honey trap.'

'You know what I think?'

'What?'

She stands in front of me, her fingertips on my bare forearms. 'I think we're very alike. People decide what they want us to be. And then that's how we act.'

'And what do you want me to be?'

'Right now, just how you are.'

Her fingertips vibrate against my skin.

'Don't play with me, Francesca Natali.'

'Don't play with me.'

'I'm trying not to.'

Francesca looks down. 'Then why is there blood on your shoes?'

I step back and push her arms away. 'This is mad. We can't get into this.'

'Into what?'

'Any of this. I'm married, for God's sake.'

'And you have blood on your shoes.'

'Right. I have blood on my shoes. That should tell you not to get into this.'

She shrugs. 'Maybe.'

'Then what are you doing?'

Francesca turns on her heels, goes to the window and closes the shutters. 'I don't know. I like you. My life isn't very exciting.'

'Your life isn't very exciting!'

Another shrug. 'Is yours? Don't answer that.' She gestures at my shoes. 'Look, I don't really know why you're here, and I don't really care. I'll go home if you want; I'll stay if you want. I'd prefer to stay, but I really don't mind.'

'I want you to stay. I want to take you to bed right now, but I can't.'

'OK. That's fine. Thank you for being straight with me.' She looks at me directly. 'Will I be seeing you on Monday?'

'Monday?'

'You wanted more time with the *Doni Tondo*.'

Gallery business – good to sort it out now, while we have the chance. I don't want this to be about gallery business.

'Daniel?'

I affirm wearily, 'Yes. That's right.'

She passes me. 'Because you are a writer, aren't you? This is why you came to Florence.' Her smile is quick, sarcastic, disbelieving.

She opens the front door. The game must be played. I nod. 'All true, I'm afraid.'

'Good.' She rises up to kiss me. She aims for my cheek but I make my lips her target. Our mouths open. Francesca moves herself closer to me. The shape of her body pushing against me – hips first, then chest – invites me to press against her. There is a command from my chest, from my heart, to hold her. I slide one hand around her waist, the other to the back of her neck, the back of her head. My grip stills her. I want our bodies to be firm, our kisses to be firm. To be locked like that. Suddenly her confession 'my life isn't very exciting' makes sense and I ask myself: where's the real excitement in my life? An excitement that isn't desperate or impossible? There is none. And certainly none that makes my body shudder and press, my chest heave and my heart command. Nenni and the Caravaggio? The plan to help one, recover the other – just business, vanity, madness. Saving my marriage? Nothing more than shame, embarrassment, a pointless battle against failure. All nonsense, a fantasy. Whereas right now, Francesca is a body of promise, insistent, emotional, honest, real.

Even so, I cannot succumb. I drop my hands, pull myself away; for a moment our lips stick together, open and dry, resisting our separation. Francesca looks up at me and smiles. I want to say something, but I cannot find anything meaningful to say, nothing that is not absurd knowing she is about to leave and I am unlikely to see her again, not even on Monday under the pretence of being a writer, the first absurdity in all this. She turns with a barely audible '*ciao*'. I do not stop her. All I can manage is to listen to the tap and echo on the stone steps, as quick and as light as her arrival only fifteen minutes earlier.

3

The following morning, the sky blue, the sun high, the air dry and glistening, I make two phone calls. I make them walking down Via Dante, head down, concentrating, crossing the street back and forth, stopping suddenly every now and again, then back on the move. At one point I gaze in the window of American Express at my reflection, the talking face, hand and mobile at my ear, the conversation in my eyes, then with a slight shift I am facing nothing, just the dark mirror-swim of the window. I am lying. Which is the reason I am making these calls on the street. I want a sharp breeze to break them up and blow them away. I sound breathless, and the adrenalin it takes to make my story believable makes each word boom in my head. I am persuaded that what I am doing is right, the right thing to do; I am helping someone after all. 'In dire need.' This is the phrase that my mind finds, uses, lets loose inside my head, becoming almost a chant. I know for the most part it's looking to drown out other things, beyond the veneer of altruism. I am going to have to let four classical Greek vases disappear into the black market. I will have to do business with two ends of the criminal spectrum: a poor desperate informant and a rich sophisticated fence. And then there is the Caravaggio. I reason that the recovery of the Caravaggio puts me at considerable risk. So the lies are small and necessary, and inconsequential in comparison. If I work it well, no one loses. No one loses and organized crime gets dealt a symbolic blow. Ending all the taunting from the witness box, sending art detectives and art historians into a spin with just a mention of the painting's existence. In succeeding in this, I remove one of their subtler torture techniques, while at the same time destroying a myth that gives them extra strength. Someone once said the taking of *The Nativity* was the Mafia saying: nothing's safe. Well, I'm saying: you're right, nothing is, not even in your hands. You take it; I'll take it back. It'll become a symbol for *us*. For art – its endurance. Everything you are, you have, you do is temporary. Because once it's been replaced above the altar in Palermo this thirty-five-year absence will be no more than a footnote; every *mafiosi*, *camorristi* who laid their venal hands on it will be nothing compared to its timeless majesty.

Sarah is the first call. She is uncertain what it is that I am asking for. A loan? Who will pay her back? I say the department, Rome; she will get it

213

back. She must trust me. I am on to something. But it needs to happen quickly. Will she think about it? That's all I'm asking. And just one more thing: don't call Jim.

The second call is tougher, transgressing more boundaries. Breaking precise rules. This one has to be perfectly paced – firm, exact, clear, convincing.

I walk towards Piazza della Signoria, scrolling for the number. I must trust myself – this is the right thing to do, ethically within the outer circle. The outsider's circle.

'Gustav, please. Daniel Wright.'

I wait. I hear nothing. I know the house is big. That the pure mountain air carries sound clearly, with dizzying precision. I don't hear Gustav shifting to take the call, to bring the phone to his ear. Yet I know Gustav is there.

'Thank you for taking my call.'

I hear a deep, deep breath – a big body bringing in air, to concentrate. It is Gustav's permission for me to start, to explain. Why am I calling him? I know I have about as much time as the big man will take to expel the big breath.

'OK. You're not being set up. Trust me. I promise you're not being set up. There are reasons for this. Reasons I'm coming to you. There can be no questions. No movement on times, money. I've got four vases from a new tomb in Campania. Perfect condition. The most exquisite I've seen. I want one hundred thousand euros for them. You know that's less than they're worth. I will be at the

Central Station in Florence, Wednesday morning – nine a.m. I'll wait thirty minutes. Just one condition: if you sell them on, they don't go to the UK. Do we have a deal?'

The breath ends. The call ends. I shove the phone deep into my pocket. I have to trust Gustav will be there. I am sweating, my back, neck, hairline. My heart is jumping against my ribs – a separate force wanting out. The actual exchange with Gustav in three days' time – that is when I cross the line; any moment before that I can pull out, give Nenni and Savarese up, hand over the vases and it all goes away.

I take a table inside at Caffé Rivoire, order an espresso, reach over for a newspaper on another table. Concentration is difficult. I read too quickly, skipping lines, whole paragraphs. Nothing interests me. This is the hardest time: the hard wait. The plan a small series of blocks that need to fall into place. First, Sarah needs to say yes. Then the money transfer needs to happen. Then Nenni – the first exchange. And then Gustav.

I leave the café and head back to the apartment, buy on my way dried spaghetti, fresh tomatoes, basil, garlic and anchovies and two bottles of Amarone. In the apartment I turn the gas rings on for cooking, pour myself a glass of wine, chop the tomatoes, basil, garlic and anchovies, simmer them in a copper frying pan – a circle of lava, rippling, popping. In the sitting room I point the heater towards the dining table. I open the three

Caravaggio books, sit down and eat. I have left my mobile in my overcoat pocket. It will ring when it rings. I have learned this is how to deal with the hard wait. Ease the frustration with simple things. Be comfortable. Be warm.

The food is good, the wine good. I read for an hour, immersed, concentrated, fingers propping up my head, a semicircle around my left temple. I am looking not for clues but for the heart of my love for this painter. What made me fall in love with him? It is the faces, simply. I am not interested in whether they were friends of Caravaggio, whether they are rogues, whores, rent boys, etc. It is that the human condition – that old-fashioned term – is disclosed by every one of them. Each face displays a set, a range of feelings which I think help us understand what it is to be human – the varieties of pain, conflict, joy, bravery, submission, responsibility. Caravaggio paints the recognitions – ours in others and therefore ourselves. Caravaggio is us.

Warm, comfortable. I am soon sleepy. I close my eyes and drift. My mobile rings. The sound is distant. No movement is possible. Too warm, too comfortable. Anything important can wait. I am waiting. Everything can wait – even the Caravaggio. It will happen. It will happen. Rolled out under the hottest sun. The burn-white, scar-white sun. Rolled out. Under the shadows of a shifting cypress, shimmying in the breeze, its fine point still. The old man is there and the BMW and a pistol. In my side. Organ deep – kidney kissed. Then slung around my neck, a dark arm, hard against my throat: arm pulling me back, gun – dug deep – forcing me forward. I am being marched like this, the dry dust dispersing around me with my slipping, struggling, sailing steps across the flat hard ground. To the BMW. The tinted glass. And the slam of my face into the mirror-swim.

I wake. That's the risk. Being rushed towards death. A rushing that will not be escaped. Human agency too firm – committed, tough, muscle strong. Experienced. In a business killing. A business death. And quick. I am not one of them, won't have betrayed anyone, broken any code. Just stupid hubris. Misreading my abilities: courage, intuition, strength, hardness. A mistake they need to deal with. Another copper, ex-copper, bent copper – dead. So that's the plain risk: being killed. Playing on the inside, where there is no tacit understanding not to kill the middleman, the honest foreigner cop. In this deal the rules of business will include killing me. If I get close. And then falter.

I need to wake up fully. I rub my eyes, two fingers in each – a hard caress. I go to my overcoat, pull out the mobile, press voicemail – Sarah. She says she feels uncomfortable about this. Doesn't understand. If it's my job, then why aren't *they* giving me the money?

I call her. I am calm. They are good questions.

'This is not straightforward, Sarah. I need you to trust me. The department takes so long to process this kind of thing. If I was in danger, maybe. But not a tip-off. Not a hunch. Not when it's not what I'm really here for. Please. Just trust me.'

If she agrees, she asks, what should she do? I take her through the process. The horrors of a large bank transfer across Europe. I tell her: every time they say they can't do it right away, it will take twenty-four hours, she must insist. I will set it up at this end. I will call first thing tomorrow with the details. My confidence affects her – the mode I am in: doing my job. She has never really experienced this.

'Will you do this for me, Sarah?'

'I don't know, Dan. I don't understand why I can't speak to Jim.'

'Because he'll tell you not to do it. He'll say I'm up to something. He thinks I'm obsessed with the Caravaggio.'

'Are you?'

'I'm not the obsessive type.'

'Dan – you are completely the obsessive type. You told me you didn't think it really was the Caravaggio.'

'Please, Sarah. How many times can I ask you: trust me.' I decide to change tack. Take a risk. 'Look. Think of it this way: you have the money. You have the money spare. You can afford to lose it, even though you won't . . .'

'Yes, but . . .'

'Wait, I haven't finished. So we're spending all this time chatting on about money. Just tell me: when were you ever so concerned about my safety?'

She hangs up. That was the risk. I call back. Straight to answerphone.

Mobile back in overcoat pocket, myself back to the armchair – feet up, book, wine. Early evening drifts past. The rest of the evening is the same. Same food, wine, book and dozing. I call Sarah at eleven p.m.

'I'll do it. But not because of what you said, which was mean. And you know it was. You'll get the money, but you spoiled . . . I was feeling really positive about everything.'

I stare across the room, beyond the silver-black window to the terracotta rooftops and the *duomo*'s lantern concealed by night.

'I'm sorry,' is all I say.

NAPLES, NENNI AND MARIA

The arch is narrow – a single coach wide – and high; its grey marble blocks are large, square, unadorned, severe. It is set back from the street. The cheap fluorescence of the shoe shops, electrical shops and butcher shops distract most passers-by. A small workshop is situated between the street and the arch. Two small Fiats, fit for scrap, are being cut in two; they will soon be melded into one. The hard fire of the blow-torch carves through the soft metal, its flaccid fireworks illuminating the arch. They announce me, my appearance from the street. The building beyond the arch was once very grand – a smart Naples residence, ambassadorial perhaps. It is now run-down apartments, too close to the cheap goods on Via Roma and the hub of street noise on the Piazza della Carità ever to be gentrified. All the ground-floor windows have bars. Above me, laundry is strung from the wrought-iron balustrades of the small balconies and passage-ways. Warm light seeps from the shuttered windows. The noise from TVs, radios and families at dinner mixes above my head.

The staircase is imposing with broad, shallow steps, designed to accommodate the languor of the aristocratic stride, its lack of effort. I have agreed to meet Nenni here, in his home, because when it was suggested I couldn't think of any objection. And Nenni was firm: he didn't want to leave his wife.

I knock on the first door of the first floor.

Nenni is quick to call, 'Who is it?'

I shake my head, thinking this is wrong, something about this is wrong. We should have done this somewhere neutral. I feel an adrenalin rush working through my body. I need to be calm.

'Who is it?'

'*Sbirro.*' I say this impatiently – I am not here as a cop and therefore referring to myself in the slang just doubles the absurdity of what I'm doing; it mocks me.

The door is unlocked, three heavy clunks, repeated three times, top to bottom. It is a slow event. The door opens. Nenni standing there in an old brown suit, dirty vest. He has a thin white scarf wrapped around his neck.

'I have a cold. She makes me wear it.'

Nenni invites me in with a wave of his long hand. The door is relocked, bottom to top. Nenni's hands fidget and slip across the bolts and catches; they disobey him and he is irritated by the simplicity of the task revealing his weaknesses.

'It is not easy when you are unwell.' He looks flushed, sweaty. And scared.

Behind him, behind the door, against the wall, there is a shoe rack – mainly women's shoes. Between a pair of gaudy but still dainty patent leather pink and green slingbacks, the black handle of a gun protrudes – an easy draw when you're thrown back, the door pushed in.

Nenni finishes with the locks. We stand silently in the hallway. He looks down at the bag I have with me – a cheap holdall I bought from the Mercato Nuovo in Florence. He cannot control a spasm of relief – it is more a shiver: if that is the money, then they will get through this. He leads me into a sitting room, where he unwraps his scarf. There is a raised rash on his neck, red, purple, a livid patch in the centre. It looks horribly painful.

I survey the room, its contents. I had expected something like this: a world of loot, jammed in, piled high. But I'd expected a fabulous array of classical antiques, items raided from tombs – vases, sculptures, other artefacts. However, the first thing I see is a set of modern musical instruments: a bright-white electric violin, a bright-red electric guitar, a tall bongo with a fringe of beads dropping from the rim of the skin. Standing together in the corner they promise a horrendous nightclub act. Directly next to them are boxes of Napoleon brandy, stacked to the ceiling – twenty, thirty cases. Against the bottom rows lean a number of paintings, three, four deep. Nothing of quality. Nothing stolen. Just cheap and dreadful renderings of famous Neapolitan vistas: the bay, the shoreline, the iconic marine pine. There is an impossibly dark copy of Caravaggio's *Flagellation of Christ* from Capodimonte. In other parts of the room, wherever there is a little space, there are open boxes of fashion accessories, branding visible beneath the plastic wraps: Gucci, Louis Vuitton, Balenciaga. On a sideboard there are watches – Rolexes mainly – in crunchy piles. There is other jewellery – indistinguishable as separate items – all woven together like handfuls of treasure, ready to slide and drip off the sideboard. Stacks of bootleg CDs, DVDs are piled on stacks of their players. There are no antiquities. Nothing of value. Just junk.

In the centre of the room a white leather sofa and a glass coffee table face a widescreen TV. The TV is on with the sound down. A game show.

I look back to Nenni. The raised rash is thickly fleshy in contrast to his thin dark throat skin.

I lift up the holdall. 'I only have fifty thousand, Nenni.'

Nenni jerks, blinks hard. 'One hundred. We said one hundred. We said one hundred for the vases. It was the deal.' He stutters, dry-mouthed, trying to be businesslike. I hear below the stutter a new tremor, new oscillations. I sense fresh threats have been made. Times and places have been set.

'It was fifty or nothing. You only need fifty.'

Nenni looks around the room, eyes landing on

the white electric violin; the ridiculousness of such a thing in this room at this time is visible on his face.

'Nenni? You only need fifty. Fifty is all I could get in that time. Focus.' Directing him through this will be exhausting; I only have enough energy to get me through it.

Nenni switches his stare back to me. 'Can I see?'

I place the holdall on the white sofa, unzip it, tip out the packs of notes – fat, chunky, sharp-edged. Nenni snatches up a bundle, and with suddenly nimble fingers fans the bills. It is a thing to do. He is not counting or assessing. Or checking. He believes me. One thousand euros per bundle. Fifty of them.

There is a knock at the sitting-room door, a single-knuckle knock, light – a signal: I am here, outside. Nenni drops the pack. He looks at me.

'My wife. She would like to meet you.'

I ignore this. 'Where are the vases, Nenni?'

'I have them. But not with this junk.' His hand judders in the air as it follows his gaze, scanning the watches, the jewellery, the CDs, DVDs, their players.

'My wife?' Nenni looks to the door.

I am irritated; this is taking too long. 'What?'

'Would you meet her?'

I want to make the exchange quickly, leave Naples, meet Gustav, make *that* exchange and be done with this part. I want to be left with the name, the fifty K I will make on the deal and myself. Meet Nenni's wife: why? I look directly at Nenni. 'I want the vases.'

'*Sbirro*, please. You can have your vases.'

Nenni opens the door, feeling his neck, the rash; he winces.

The first thing I realize on seeing Nenni's plain, stern wife is that she doesn't know she's the one at risk, and this is why she is here, standing in the door of this room, insisting on meeting the man who is helping her husband, the one at risk. I see myself in their eyes: a welcome stranger, trustworthy foreigner, a man they've talked about, decided will come and sort things out. Nenni has sold this story to them both. It is believed. In their fear – hers for him, his for her – they have lost any fix on reality and have cast me in a greater role than middleman. This irritates me further. I want to be less not more. A nameless, faceless courier.

Nenni introduces us; I correct him. 'Daniel not *sbirro*.' Maria's hand is cold, bony. Her grip light, but firm. She offers to take my coat. Below the window a Vespa shoots past. We all shunt our attention to it. We wait for the high whine to disappear into the night.

'The vases, Nenni.'

Nenni places his long hand on Maria's thin shoulder. They are very alike, except for the metabolic racing of Nenni's circuitry; he jars his head back, instructing Maria to fetch them.

She is gone only a moment. The four vases are

brought in on a large silver-plated tray, edges scalloped. Bending at the knees, she lowers the tray on to the glass table, as though placing down a full tray of tall drinks. They are red-figure vases. The condition perfect as promised. Exquisite as promised. The scenes are very active – battles, games, abduction and flight, music-making. The black background is smooth, unchipped; the orange-red decoration is simple, bold, clear. As much design as storytelling.

Maria stands by the table. I am invited to inspect them. Nenni looks at his wife as she picks up the largest of the four and presents it to me. I look it over, knowing my eyes admire only the artistry of such a distant age, the superficial beauty, its delicacy. An expert would appreciate much more.

'It's fine. We need to pack them securely.'

It is Nenni's turn to leave the room. Maria remains next to the display, stiff backed. We are forced into conversation by our proximity, the hardness of the silence. I ask how long she and Nenni have been married. Only six months, I am told. Where did they meet? Through her sister. He liked my cooking. I know all this, but pretend the information is new, interesting. And do not tell her my marriage is not much older and almost as desperate. Maria points to the money sprawled out on the leather sofa and asks if this is it – the payment? I nod. It doesn't look like one hundred thousand euros. It is an idle observation, a moment of simple curiosity, probing an expert.

But I also sense something about the volume of paper tumbled there doesn't seem right to her, feel right. I decide her husband can explain.

Nenni returns with a roll of bubble wrap, news-papers, tape, scissors, and unloads them into his wife's arms. She says again, to him: the money – it doesn't look like one hundred thousand euros. Her curiosity is now a question. Nenni answers with instructions to wrap the vases; he will break them. The question has unnerved him; he clasps his neck, the rash. I watch the pain induce a shudder across his shoulders. Maria orders him to be careful: where is his scarf? She is impatient. Nenni ignores her, adding friction between his hand and rash for more pain. It's helping him focus – it doesn't matter that it is not one hundred thousand euros.

Maria takes down two brandy boxes, decants the bottles, flattens the cardboard dividers. She unfolds the newspapers into single sheets and crushes them into various-sized tight balls. She lines the bottom of both boxes. She moves on to the vases. She uses the bubble wrap. Her fingers are light, nimble, trembling with soft touches, the vases manoeuvred through the process like a liquid form. It doesn't take long; she has done this many times. When she is finished each vase is little more than a big ball of bubble wrap and tape – a ghetto football. She places two in each brandy box. She then adds more newspaper balls as buffers between vase and box. She tapes the boxes shut, after which she fashions a handle on each box by twisting lengths of tape and creating a thin twine with it. She tests their strength and purchase on the boxes. She is satisfied. Nenni and I have been watching her, Nenni by the door, nodding during each stage of the process, forming silent words. I have been merely staring in at the activity, hands in my pockets, looking at Nenni from time to time, remembering the first things I learned about this woman: her beauty, her cooking. I can see her beauty through Nenni's eyes – she is like him but stiff and still and in control and this must register as beautiful to him. And if the precision and deftness she has showed in wrapping the vases is applied to her cooking, her food must be good.

Kneeling between the two boxes she looks up and pats the tops. They are ready. I imagine that Nenni has told her that I am buying them for myself, simplifying the deal, my motivation, giving her less to worry about.

'Thank you.' I turn to Nenni. 'What is the name?'

Nenni stills himself and then leans into me and whispers a name. He settles back. I know instantly that Nenni believes this man has the Caravaggio. The deal will be lucky if he is honest. No dead man this time, no rumour.

'I don't know him,' I say with only slightly lowered volume.

Nenni shrugs, and then adds by way of explanation, 'You will need a gun.'

'How did he get it?'

'He has it because the old man gave it to him. He killed the men who wanted to take over the *cosca*. He couldn't ask for money – it is not honourable in this circumstance. But the painting . . . it is a symbol of prestige. It is a badge. It was a great honour to be given it.'

I haven't heard anything of the internecine murders he's referring to. What I understand, however, is that if Nenni is right, the man who now has the painting is an ambitious killer operating under the pretence of honour – hence the offer of a gun.

'I believe you, Nenni.'

I watch as the rash on Nenni's neck disappears, the colour darkening, the thick edges smoothing back into his thin skin. For Nenni the deal is now done – everything is complete and his wife is safe. My trust has absolved him: he was right about the straightforwardness of the deal, he was right to have come to me, he was right to be insistent, honest in his desperation, in his trust. This is why the deal is complete and his wife safe and his rash gone – the good faith will now certainly carry over to the deal with Savarese.

Maria is crying, tears dropping from her eyes easily, without visible emotion. They circle her smile. Her husband is safe now. For her, the rash was caused from direct fear of his own death, and in death, leaving her. That fear has left him.

'We must celebrate.' Nenni looks nervously at

his wife; he is not sure it's appropriate but is emboldened into wanting to make a gesture of some kind.

'This is business, Nenni, not a party.'

Maria unfolds her long body up from the floor. 'Italo says you are his friend. That you do not treat him like all the others – a buffoon to be . . .' She snaps her long fingers from the tip of her chin towards him. I read 'to be insulted'. She continues, 'You understand he cannot help how he is. That is a friend.'

What is there to say? I think: this man is not my friend. I am doing this for myself. For a name. For money. For a painting. For a new life. For love. I know if I'd gone directly to Gustav I could have raised the hundred thousand euros he's going to pay for the vases, and Nenni could then pay off Savarese and get a new life, just like he wanted. But I chose this way instead. A deal leaving me with fifty thousand – enough to move a step closer to what I want. I see Nenni and Maria exchange glances. He is a husband proud of his wife. I am still here. Her small speech has had an impact.

Nenni leaves the room and returns with a gun. He slides out the cartridge, shows me the full complement of bullets, locks it back in. He offers it to me, handle first. He doesn't let go of the barrel, his long fingers gripping it tightly.

'You will need this, *sbirro*. But do not have a need for it. Please. Leave the Caravaggio where it is. It is in a dangerous place for you. Go home to your wife. I understand now what is important. It is not honour, or glory, or money. It is being loved for who you are.'

Nenni regards this as an original insight. And good strong honest advice. He wants us all to have a new beginning. If I drop my idea, he will have done me an extra favour. He is after more good luck.

I pull the gun free of Nenni, look at it in my hand. What does it really mean that a *camorrista* is telling me I'll need a gun? It's not something I can think about. I slide it into my pocket.

Maria looks into my face. 'Does your wife know what you are doing?'

'No.'

'Are you protecting her?'

I don't respond; I can feel the weight of the gun, low in the side pocket of my overcoat, pulling at me. I feel suddenly exhausted. Maria bringing Sarah into this room requires extra concentration from me to keep her out, to remain focused.

'Italo is right. Your wife loves you because you are good. You have helped us. No one else would. In one day we were . . .' she passes her hand in front of her face. 'It is wrong what Savarese says, but who will say so. You helped us. Because you are good.' She shakes her head. 'Go home to your wife.'

Nenni has his hand on his wife's shoulder – they are unified in their advice.

Maria pulls away, picks up the silver tray and

leaves the room. Nenni invites me to sit down, packing away the money into the holdall, making space for me on the sofa. I reluctantly sit down. Nenni perches on the arm, holdall clutched in his lap. The game show is still on. Nenni chuckles now and again. I find myself trying to work out the rules, yet for all the activity, the enormous set, it seems to be just hot-looking Italian women in various states of undress walking on and kissing contestants.

Maria is back with the tray, this time loaded with bottles and glasses. She sets it down on the glass table. Nenni and I stand. There is white wine, champagne, whisky. I say I'll have a small whisky. Maria is directed to have champagne by her husband, but she says she prefers whisky. Nenni explains that he cannot drink; he will have Coke. I expect a toast, but neither husband nor wife says anything. I am forced to break the silence as we clink glasses.

'What will you do?'

Nenni shivers, clutches his neck. He has temporarily set aside the fact that whatever his hopes – new honesty, building luck in his favour – it doesn't end here, with this drink, this celebration – he will soon have to face Savarese.

Maria answers for him. 'I have family in the country. We must go there. Italo will be a farmer.' She laughs at this. I feel obliged to laugh. Nenni then joins us. He knows it is funny, this picture of him as a farmer. For a moment the seriousness of the situation has been forgotten.

I settle my glass on the tray. 'I must go.'

Maria places her glass, untouched, on the table. She then picks up the two boxes and gives the handles one last firm controlled test. Nenni shows me to the front door where she carefully hands the boxes over to me; the handles feel strong, the tape thin, tight, sharp across my palms. I know this is how it's done all over the world. The trade in priceless, beautiful objects. Madly simple: brandy boxes, bubble wrap, tape.

Maria unlocks the door, long deft fingers flicking at the dead locks from top to bottom. The door is not opened. I notice the gun I saw earlier, nestled between her green and pink slingbacks, is still there. Nenni hasn't given up his only defence to help me. Maria insists on kissing me. She leans in, careful of the boxes.

I wish them both luck; it's a reflexive statement – not really about Savarese, the next final important part of the deal, but the next part of their lives, hoping they will cope.

'Maybe you come and see us on the farm,' Nenni says as the door is opened.

No one laughs and Nenni understands that we won't see each other again. We have been playing at friendship because we are in his home and his wife is there. Something about this pretence forces Nenni, with long arms outstretched, to embrace me.

'Thank you, *sbirro*.'

I pull away; I don't deserve thanks. There was

a better deal for them, but I chose a compromise – something for them, something for me.

I step out on to the landing. I feel that under normal circumstances, as a couple, they would watch their guests leave, wait for them to appear in the courtyard below and follow them from the balcony through the arch, at which point they would give a last wave. But they quickly retreat. I hear the dull catching of the three locks and a shake of the door to check all have caught.

Passing the garage – both white Fiats are now sliced in two, ends tipped up, like giant eggs cracked open, birds flown – I notice the mechanic, visor pushed up, watching me. Savarese will soon know Nenni's visitor has left.

I cross to the taxi rank on Piazza della Carità. The driver of the first car, leaning against his taxi, smoking and talking to a man holding a small kitten, nods me into the back, not bothering to offer the boot for my boxes. I slide in one box, then curl in myself, the other box pulled in next to me. I rest my elbows and forearms across the tops, fingers tapping the sides. I want to sleep. My body feels on the brink of collapse. I only realize now how draining the last hour has been.

The traffic is slow-moving, cramped. I use my arms to brace the boxes against the rise and fall of the taxi dropping in and crunching out of potholes. The cab driver is unusually patient for Naples, happy to wait for gaps to open up, doesn't block side roads or cut off smaller cars; his wing mirrors are safe. It takes twenty minutes to get to Piazza Garibaldi, a further five to reach the station. It's almost eleven p.m. The train to Florence is waiting at the platform. There is no one following me.

FLORENCE AND FRANCESCA

Gustav is fat – conspicuously fat. But he's handsome also, with a strong head. His teeth are good – straight and bright. His eyes are bright. He has chosen criminality because other criminals don't care that he's so fat, just that he knows what he's doing, that he knows what he knows. He likes international travel. This is his euphemism for international boys. And girls. Gustav is a tonne of the polymorphously perverse – *his* description. Legal but under twenty, he'd added, with a shrug of his large, round shoulders, hefty under sheer silk with motifs of archly drawn men and women at patterned sex.

I met Gustav three years ago. Interviewed him at his home overlooking Lake Geneva. A fat man in a fat house – abundant in riches: mainly antiquities, eastern art, ornate European art and design of the late nineteenth and early twentieth centuries. His home, its contents, were a testament to his abilities because, as I discovered, there was no record of him ever having worked or having received any kind of inheritance. We liked each other instantly. I was seduced by his

236

manner – languid at rest, lumbering on the move, always mentally swift, always debonair. Gustav was straightforward in his appreciation of me: he liked having this serious handsome policeman in his house, he said.

If he turns up this morning, it will be because of the connection we made over those two days of interviews – interviews in various rooms, fresh food always to hand; glasses of grapefruit juice made by an ebony spike twisted into the flesh by Gustav's massive hand; the coffee made by me to Gustav's detailed instructions; the biscuits displayed in hand-folded boxes tied with fine ribbons, scissor-curled. Lunch was made by a man as small as Gustav is big. A man of unplaceable European origins. Three languages, more cuisines, Gustav said. This was how the big man liked to live. Surrounded by the best, quantumly better compared to the standard best – the metropolitan best. He sought objects, people, produce which transcended star ratings. Gustav is interested in the scale-free – talent and taste liberated from the measure by their proximity to perfection. I live outside Plato's Cave, is how he explained it.

I position myself in the middle of the concourse, boxes on the floor between my feet; it is nine a.m. If he is coming, he will be here soon. When he appears I will feel his presence, his bigness affecting the environment, his mass sending out molecular messages. I turn to my left. He approaches with heavy strides, wearing a big tweed overcoat, belted up; hard leather boots, stiff to the rim; a wide-brimmed fedora, worn at an unexpectedly jaunty angle for the time of day. He is carrying a light-brown suede-leather attaché case.

We shake hands. Gustav reads my internal distress with his big clear eyes. This is the toughest part of the plan for me. This is where I break out of the one circle which includes me – being a good copper and what that stands for in the wider world. Gustav is saddened that I am distressed but recognizes it as private. He hands over the case, bought at great expense, adding a thousand euros to the cost of the deal. He regards this as an acceptable loss. What's the alternative? Carrying cash in a canvas holdall? I am a little ashamed of the brandy boxes with tape handles. I have to pull at the handles to make room for Gustav's big gloved fingers.

'You may or may not read about the reason for this in the near future. If not, I hope to tell you about it one day.'

'You are still a policeman?'

'I don't know.'

Gustav gives me a rueful smile. A policeman suits me, he is saying.

'Thank you.'

Gustav nods in appreciation but knows gratitude is irrelevant – it implies something less straightforward, less well balanced. And everything about this deal is clear. We both know that to double-cross the other means an end to something for each of us; for me it will mean an end to my career – Gustav is well connected and ruthless. And for him it will mean the end to something of his marvellous lifestyle. If the money is not in the case, he knows the police will be waiting for him on his return home and will find four uncatalogued vases in brandy boxes in his possession.

So nothing else is said. We each turn away; Gustav in the direction from which he approached, to a car, I suspect, even modern European trains not offering anywhere near the acceptable first-class service or big-enough seats that he requires. I head out of the main entrance.

The day is bright, breezy, clouds moving quickly across the sun, their shadows visible as grey shapes passing over the buildings, the streets; the sun's presence, when it is revealed, gives everything a golden wrap, a bright and palpable lustre.

I cross Piazza Stazione, ignoring the horns, the swerving cars. I am too tired to be nimble, alert to others' intentions. I feel light, hollowed out, hot. My metabolism is on reserve. Too much coffee, displaced anxiety, adrenalin rush. I didn't sleep on the train back from Naples – my eyes were dry, sore, too keen to focus; I was overly alert. I was alone at a table for four. There were a few others in the carriage, elsewhere, unseen. The lights were low, glowing, a little burst in the window. The vases were next to me, secure, pressed between seat back and table. My thoughts were a simple recording of things, spoken to myself silently, as if to a stenographer, precise, clear, measured. I can't remember now what I said, so I can't have been recording things, not for immediate recall anyway. In Rome I knew I should have been tempted to get off and stop this, but I just stayed in my seat, fingers curled around the curtain, pulling it back, and stared on to the bright platform saying 'Rome', and nodding to myself, trying to think what I liked about the city, the memories I had, to record them efficiently. Coffee was brought every thirty minutes – espresso – and I'd knock it back regardless of desire. It was thick, tasteless – a sensation more than a flavour. It coated my tongue first, then my throat, then my stomach, making me want to vomit. I felt like Nenni, or how I imagine he feels trying to control the world, the stimulus coming in, the onslaught of it – needing to pare it down to cope, letting in only essential information and allowing out only vital responses. I was feeling something similar: that I must try to pare it all down from now on, gather only essential information and concentrate only on vital responses. Even with a few hours' sleep – in my clothes, on top of the bed – my skin feels brittle, my blood thin. Like Nenni again, or how I imagine Nenni must feel, encased in his body, his metabolism so overstretched, life's attrition working from the inside out. I feel my neck – I sense a rash. A cloud passes over me, followed by the sudden glare of the sun. I am too fragile for such transformations. I need a steady predictable world. I stop where I am. I need more sleep. To end this episode fully. Focus forward. I roll my fingers around the handle of the attaché case. The money is an impressive dead weight, grossly heavy. The case suggests subtlety, that the contents will be precious, expensive – light.

My mobile rings. I dig into my pocket and flip it open. It's Sarah. I turn away from the sun, stare at the attenuated shadow of myself. She is cold, matter of fact. Little inflection. Bored even. 'I've spoken to Jim. He is furious. What was the money for, Dan?'

I don't respond.

'Dan?'

I feel that the moisture in my eyes has become granulated. 'I asked you not to speak to Jim.'

'I was worried.'

'About me or the money?'

'You. You. Why do you always think the worst of me?' I don't know. She continues, 'I don't care about the money. I just want to know what's going on. Are you in trouble?'

'I have the money here. I don't need it now.'

'So what did you need it for?'

'It doesn't matter. As I said, I don't need it now. So you can relax. Call Jim. Tell him.'

'Dan, why are you being like this?'

'Like what?'

'So cold.'

'I'm tired. I'll be home soon.'

'Friday?'

'Maybe not Friday.'

'But you promised.' It is not plaintive, disappointed. My promise must be exposed as a lie.

'I'm sorry. I just have to finish up here.'

'I don't know what to say.'

I think: it's complicated. Say it.

'It always is with you.'

'I promise I'll be home soon.'

'You'd better call Jim.'

I can't think of an argument against it though I know I won't call him, so I just say I will. I want to end the call with an honest 'I love you' but I am too low on energy to find the words, too low on strength to send them meaningfully out of my mouth and for them not to sound like a weak request for reassurance. I end the call with a flip of the phone.

I reach the apartment just as Francesca is tucking the Smart Car neatly against the kerb outside American Express. I roll my fingers under the handle of the attaché case again. She climbs out; there is no smile, no greeting. She follows me up to the apartment in silence. The smell of disinfectant is strong. I am as useless with the keys and locks as Nenni last night. Beads of sweat build up on my forehead. When I open the door I sense for a second the place has been visited since I left yesterday, but then I realize it has been, by me earlier this morning – my exhaustion is playing with my memory, making me paranoid.

I place the attaché case on the glass dining table, turn on the gas rings, the heater. Francesca's eyes follow me around the room. She pulls out a packet of cigarettes from her pocket, lights one and tosses the packet on to the table. She takes a long drag.

'You lied to me.'

The games, flirtations, evasions, longings are distant feelings. 'I'm tired. Really tired.'

'You lied to me.'

My body is hot, feverish. My pores are open, but there is little sweat. I am dehydrated. I go to the kitchen and drink some water. Francesca stands behind me.

'That man. That man on Saturday wasn't a policeman.'

I wasn't expecting this. If anything, I had expected her to have found out somehow that *I* was a policeman – to be mad about that. I don't respond. I slip past her and sit down on one of the dining chairs. She continues.

'I saw him leave, you see. I gave you a chance to explain but you refused. Maybe you had your reasons. I decided to let it go.'

I look at her wearily. 'That doesn't mean he's not a policeman.' I try to sound calm, but I know she's building to something – something I don't want to hear.

Francesca shakes her head firmly, the curls whipping around her neck and throat. Her certainty is physical. 'He's a gangster. And do you want to know how I know?'

I look away, plant my elbows on the glass top of the table and press my face into my hands. I don't want to hear. Hear it said.

'Because he's dead. Him and his wife. In Naples. It was on the news. What is going on?'

My stomach, chest, throat contract, breathing cut off, caught in my lungs – I feel like I am suffocating, paralysed and suffocating, my blood hardening, muscles hardening, eyes hardening. For a moment I am blank. Just a staring thing in a room, mapping things as they are on to the still white flatness of my mind.

Slowly my body releases itself from the paralysis and begins to breathe. I hear my voice, whispering, vibrating with anger, 'Fucking Savarese. I should have known, I should have known.' Maybe I did. He would never have been satisfied with just killing Maria. His mind is too pure for that – for straightforward revenge, punishment. He would have factored in the psychological and economical implications. A man, even Nenni, ridiculous Nenni, thinking he can walk away with a slice of the business because he thought he had an ability (a gift!) which somehow entitled him to go it alone. It gives the wrong impression. The worst impression: that working for the Savarese clan is an option, a starting point. So he needed to deal with it. But first he wanted Nenni to understand the level of his betrayal. So he threatened to kill his wife. Make him understand his power that way. Embed it in true felt fear, not just anecdotal or mythological. Fear that raises rashes and sends the fearful to do pointless deals with flexible coppers in the hope of mercy, understanding, a breath of country air – new beginnings. It was never going to be. I know how it happened. Maria was killed first so that the power was not only felt to be real, it was visible and true and irreversibly displayed – doubly real. Followed by Nenni himself: the essential death. So others would understand. Psychology and economics. What other way was there?

I look up. 'How was he killed?'

'I don't know. It was on the news. They were lying on the street. It was horrible. Those poor people.'

I drop my head, roll it from side to side. I can see it all. From the first confrontation: Savarese accusing Nenni. A handsome young man seated while the older man stood, fidgeted, bit into his lip. An offer would have been made, a way to redeem himself, and Nenni would have taken it, believed it. Savarese would have been warm in his entreaties that Nenni understand what he had done wrong. His explanation to Nenni of the necessity of such hardness would have been full of special pleading. He would have asked for Nenni's forgiveness. Even beseeched him: I'm sorry, Italo, please understand I don't want to do this – really, I don't. And Nenni would have left thinking: as long as I pay him, this is not a man who really wants to harm my wife, he just needs to be seen doing the right thing.

I should have known this – foreseen it and lied to Nenni. Told him the moment that I was through the door: I've heard – don't ask me how – that Savarese is planning to kill you. *I* should have beseeched them: leave. With entreaties: don't you know who you are dealing with? But I wasn't thinking, wasn't listening to myself that way. I didn't bother to examine the situation fully for all involved. The risk assessment was limited to myself only.

I hear Francesca moving around the room; I look up, my eyes tight, pulled long by the concocting of the action I should have taken.

I am asked, 'Who are you?'

I stare at her, with no interest in answering, unsure what the answer should be now – now everything's changed. She repeats the question.

'Daniel!'

I look directly at Francesca, the room fading from view, Francesca somehow moving forward, perfectly clear. She wants an answer, an explanation. Possibly comfort.

I hear myself saying, but the words do not sound like my own – they are light, faintly echoing, with too much melody for such a moment, 'You are very beautiful. But you know that. No one would argue, would they? It's objective. Whatever we say about nothing being objective, some things are, and one is you. And that's all before knowing you. And you're lovely, aren't you? There is something so lovely about you. And that's objective too. Your loveliness. Being close to you is lovely. I feel it. I feel I might be able to rely on it. Do you know where I was last night?'

Francesca withdraws fractionally, the room reappearing, mostly straight lines and dark patches, not entirely in focus. She shakes her head. She doesn't want to be told.

'I was with them. That man and his wife. In their home.'

Francesca's hand is instantly at her mouth.

'Don't worry. I didn't kill them. I was there to help them. He needed money. That's why he was here Saturday.' I rub my face. 'This wasn't supposed to happen.'

Francesca stays where she is, curls still, perfectly still, as if stillness is equal to silence as a display of respect.

'How do you know him? The news said he was a notorious informant – a *mafiosi* . . .'

'There was nothing notorious about Italo Nenni. Hopeless maybe – sad, pathetic, ridiculous. Only these kinds of things.'

'Was he a friend?'

I shake my head wearily. 'No.'

'Then why were you helping him?'

I wonder at this, eyes staring past Francesca, past the kitchenette, Florence, the world and into a white mist, drifting snow. 'Because we shared a joke once.' I know this is only half true; there were other reasons – other darker motives.

'I don't understand.'

'There's nothing to understand.'

Francesca scratches her head, fingers lost in the curls. 'I need a drink.'

I gesture to the bottom shelf of the bookcase.

Francesca pulls out the bottle of Stolichnaya, goes to the kitchen, places two tall glasses on the sideboard and pours a generous amount of vodka into both of them. I close the book, push it away, and with elbows back on the glass top of the table, head in hands, hair fanned out between my fingers, I stare down into the reflection of my face. My skin is pale, hair black – a face equal to anything painted by Caravaggio at his most morbid.

'The reason your name was on my computer at the weekend was that I was listing people I might get the money from to help him. You're in no danger.'

Francesca stops, one of the glasses in her hand, looks over at me. 'Thank you. What about you? Are you in any danger?'

I emerge from my hands for a moment. 'Me? No.'

Francesca picks up the second glass, places it before me; there is the dull rattle of glass on glass. She is shaking. I watch her sit down next to me, my head turned awkwardly in my hands.

'Who are you?'

I sit up, rub my left eye. 'Does it really matter? I'll be gone soon.'

'Is Daniel your real name?'

'Yes.'

'What are your true feelings towards me?'

'I think I've said.'

'I mean, really?'

'I could be crazy about you. Mad about you. In love with you. But I can't be. You know that.'

Francesca stands her cigarette packet up, presses firmly on the shorter edge, flipping it over.

'Please tell me who you are.' It is now an emotional request, no longer stemming from fear or even a sense of right.

I take a deep breath. 'I'm a policeman.' I wait for a reaction, but there is nothing: it is not such a big deal after so many lies and two deaths. I continue, 'I was asked to come here – to Florence – by the police department in Rome which is similar to mine in London, to investigate a rumour that there was going to be a major theft from the Uffizi and it is – was – my job to find out whether anyone on the inside was involved.'

Francesca's reaction to this is a tiny shake of her head, a double-take. 'You mean . . .' She can hardly believe it. 'Me? You were investigating me?'

I manage a short wry laugh. 'No. You were just a point of contact.'

Francesca looks visibly relieved; however, her long eyes continue to search for the sense in all this.

'What have you found out?'

'Nothing. I haven't even tried. I've been too preoccupied with you, Storaro and this other thing.'

'With the dead man?'

'Yes, with the dead man.'

'So you know him as an informer?'

'Yes. But recently he's been illegally excavating ancient tombs and exporting the loot.'

'Not any more.' It is a solemn statement of fact while also searching for a moment of lightness.

I manage another laugh. 'No. Not any more. Neither is his wife going to cook beautiful food.'

'Was she a good cook?'

'I don't know. He said so. I believed him.'

Francesca leans over the table, places her hand over mine. 'I'm sorry.'

'What for?'

'Your friend is dead.'

'I only met him a few times.'

Francesca's grip increases until I look up at her and acknowledge with a rueful smile that I am feeling it more deeply than I am letting on.

'What happens now?'

'Nothing. No one knows I'm involved. Except you. It's over.'

Francesca sits back, flicks her cigarette packet again – a double spin this time.

'Do you need me to help with your investigation? I don't mind. I can't think who it could be. They're all a fairly straight honest bunch.'

There is only one thing I need from her right now – I want her to take me to bed, invite me to disappear inside her arms, help me forget what has happened and force sleep on me. Annihilating sleep.

'Daniel?'

'Thank you, but it's too late.'

'Why?'

'I don't know. It just is.'

'What are you going to do?'

There is nothing to do. 'Go home. Fix my marriage.'

Francesca looks down into her glass of vodka, then knocks it back. I haven't touched mine; she switches glasses. The rattle again. I look at her; is she trembling? I cannot tell. All I see is warmth: her skin, her hair, her eyes – gradations of brown, like autumn.

'You're like autumn. The colours of autumn.'

She places my glass back down on the table without drinking from it and without sound.

'When I first saw you I thought there was something quite special about you. Exciting. Have I said that?' She doesn't wait for a response. 'Look. I don't know about your wife, or your marriage. I don't even really know who you are. But none of that means I can't see clearly you're very unhappy. You say you could be crazy about me. Well, *I am* crazy about you.' She curls her top lip into her bottom lip, smiles and shrugs – there, it is said. She looks at me, elbows on the table, fingers resting around the edge of the glass of vodka.

'I don't know what to say.'

Another shrug. There is nothing to say. I move the attaché case under the table.

'What's in there?'

What indeed?

'Something for my wife.'

'A present?'

'No.'

Francesca flicks her cigarette packet – a single spin – before slotting it in her pocket and standing. 'I should be at work.'

I don't want her to leave. I don't want to be alone. But I push myself up from the table. This is mine to face alone. To reconcile. 'Thank you for understanding.'

I sense Francesca has decided not to understand. Her reply is cool. 'I hope everything works out with your wife.'

'Thank you.'

I lead her to the door. 'Are you sure you're going to be OK?'

She smiles – yes. She wanted a little excitement and she got it.

At the door there is no kiss this time. However, as she passes me, she gives my arm a quick rub. Reassurance, regret, comfort, contact. It makes me want to hold her back. I even feel my hands open and my arms begin to reach. But I realize to stop her now would be to invite straightforward comparison between her and Sarah, and I know Sarah would never have rubbed my arm like that, that she isn't capable of such a simple gesture signifying such a complex of emotions, at least half of which concern me, my well-being, my troubles. Sarah would lose against the measure of that rub. But I also know I can't stop Francesca because against that other measure – the one that counts – she would lose, despite her beauty, loveliness, sweetness – her aura of autumn – and the simple rub of my arm. So I let her go and close the door behind her, shutting out the sound of her slow steps down the stairs, shutting out the lack of stopping, the silence of her turn and the tap and echo of her rushing back up to me. I close the door behind her and shut all this out because I realize I desperately want her to come back, and keeping the door open and listening out for the stopping, the silence of her turn and the tap and echo of her rushing back to me, will make certain she leaves. I close the door to invite fate to send her back; it does not.

LONDON, SARAH AND MORE ART MAFIA

1

The immaculate whitewash of the walls; the glistening darks of the doors; the empty trees, branches cross-hatched; the new Jaguars, compact VWs, Saab Diesels; the nannies with three-wheeler buggies; the discreetly hidden wheelie bins; the sepia interiors just visible through the silver-clean windows; the two blue plaques; the hard wind; a McDonald's wrapper around my shins; two neighbours, ancient Chelsea residents in manner if not years, one also in years; my blue Audi 80; and our house – Sarah's house – a basement and four storeys of Georgian simplicity and townhouse homeliness. I search for my keys, deep in my overcoat pocket, rattling underneath my phone. I open the door and call out. A big call, a four-storey call, perfected, no shout, just the right level of projection to scale the walls and stairs. There is no response. No soft footfalls resonating down, creaks resonating through the house – no human sound. I hang up my coat and walk down to the basement, to the kitchen. I lay the attaché case flat on the table. I drink some water, rinse the glass and upturn it on the drainer. In the ground-floor sitting room, standing by the tall window, rocking on my heels, I stare out over the crescent to the spare trees and beyond. Without a cloud break it is a permanent dusk out there. I know I need to call Jim and make it clear: it was either come home or quit. I am a liability. I'm making all the wrong decisions out there. Maybe I should just request a transfer? I was good at being a regular copper. So what if it's not what I wanted from life? I'll be at home more often. Not looking to right old wrongs, to compete with Sarah's crowd. They'll be in art; I'll be in straightforward public service. No overlap. They certainly aren't in public service. At least not all the public. So maybe that's the answer. Just be a good, regular copper.

Sarah appears at the end of the street, bulky Waitrose bag bumping against her leg, door keys ready within ten metres, held firmly as if already in a lock. I back away from the window, position myself in the sitting-room doorway, leaning against the door frame. I listen to the keys in the lock, watch the heavy front door swing open, my existence a thousand miles from her thoughts. I watch her lower the Waitrose bag to the floor, dump her handbag and keys on to the hall table; she doesn't notice my overcoat, a stiff billow over all her jackets and coats.

In a whisper. 'Hello, darling.'

Sarah looks up startled, surprised. 'Dan! What are you doing here?' There is no brimming joy on her face.

'I came back early.'

Her expression shows suspicion; she doesn't know what she thinks about my unexpected appearance. I watch her search for the correct response. She forces a smile while searching for the happiness within herself that she thinks must be there.

'You should have called.'

I attempt to kiss her as she passes, but it isn't quick enough, obvious enough, confident enough. I follow her down into the kitchen, where she opens the fridge, pulls out a two-litre bottle of Evian and pours herself a tall glass of water.

'So what happened? This morning you didn't know when you were going to be back.'

'I don't really want to talk about it.' I point to the table, the slim attaché case. 'Your money is there.'

Sarah's eyes stay focused on me. 'You look terrible.'

'I'm unhappy. What can I say?'

She takes a sip from her glass of water.

I continue, 'I'm going to request a desk job, or even a different department.'

She assesses this. 'Why's that? I thought you loved what you do.'

'Is that what you think?'

She ignores this. 'So does that mean you're going to become a proper policeman?'

'I don't know. Maybe. Does that bother you?'

'I want you to be happy.'

I step towards her, take the glass from her hand, place it on the sideboard and lean in for a kiss. This time our lips touch; I feel her respond for a moment. She then shakes herself free and slips away.

'Not now, Dan. I've got to go out tonight. I need a bath.'

'Where are you going?'

'Marcus's. For dinner. Naturally you were invited, but I said you were out of town.'

'Can I still come?'

She hesitates, pursing her lips, knowing how difficult an evening of easy fun will now be. 'You hate him.'

'He's a pompous dick-brain. Too clever by far, even richer, and he sees through me, which is really irritating.'

'Then why do you want to come?'

'Because I want to be with you and I don't want to hang around here on my own.'

'Are you sure you wouldn't prefer to go out with one of your friends?'

'Is that what you would prefer?'

'I've told you, you can come if you like. Marcus will be thrilled – you know he finds you fascinating.'

'Marcus finds everyone fascinating – it's one of

his strategies. He makes up for a lack of integrity with boundless enthusiasm.'

'Why are you like this? If you want to come, come. But please: try and enjoy yourself. Even if it's just for my sake.'

'I'll try,' I say mock-wearily.

'Why do you find it so hard?'

'Because no matter what we talk about, everyone will be super-ironic; he'll be super-oily; I'll drink too much; then something will be said which will make me mad and I'll do my best to bite my tongue, and then slowly resentment will build up until I get either angry or depressed or both.'

'Try not to be so sensitive. How do you expect us to have any kind of relationship if we have to go through this every time we're invited out? Marcus is lovely. You used to love him. Every time he was on TV you'd say, "I love that guy."'

'Actually I don't mind Marcus. It's his gang. They're so disdainful, contemptuous. Don't you remember last time we were there? We were talking about the Tate's initiative to attract more less-art-inclined people. Someone said: don't they have snooker halls for these people. It was a joke, of course. But it wasn't – not really. Then when I said: I love snooker halls, that's where I spent most of my youth, they all laughed because they thought it was a joke, but it wasn't. I wanted to beat them all to death with a snooker cue.'

'Dan. What are we going to do? You're so angry all the time. These are perfectly nice people. So they're a bit – I don't know – like everyone else like them. You are like how you are. No one's judging you. In fact, everyone thinks you're great. They're always asking me what you're up to.'

'OK. I'll come.' I smile but immediately notice Sarah stiffen; I lose my smile.

'I'll have to call and tell them.'

'Fine. Call and tell them.'

'But I want you to promise you'll behave.'

'ABC, Sarah, ABC.'

'What's that?'

'It's a lesson I learned from you lot.'

She is suspicious. 'And what's that?'

'Always Be Charming.'

She leaves the kitchen with a shake of her head. 'I don't understand you, Dan, I really don't.'

I call out, 'I'm the handsome man you couldn't wait to marry.'

She shouts back, 'You're a dickhead is what you are.'

I raise my voice, knowing she is now almost two floors up. 'Can I get in the bath with you?'

Sarah, I can tell leaning over the banisters, answers, 'Only if you wear your policeman's hat.'

I lie back in the bath. Sarah sits up, long back curved, shoulders gently rounded. Between us is my erection. Sarah holds it.

'We don't have time for sex. Can it wait until later?'

'You won't want to do it when we get home.'

259

'Who says?'

'I do, because I know you and you won't.'

She increases the pressure of her grip. 'Maybe you don't know me as well as you think.'

'Don't do that or I'll be required to take you by force.'

'Will you read me my rights?'

'That's the law.'

'What if I still resist?'

'I'll have to call for back-up.'

'Does that mean more policemen will then come to take me by force?'

'Would you like that?'

Sarah gives me an extra, final squeeze and then, gripping the sides of the bath, heaves herself out. 'Come on then – but it'll have to be quick.'

2

Marcus appears thrilled to see me – grand gestures, exclamations, an insistence on being regaled by my exploits. His charm is slippery and I am able to glide past him, take a corner seat and withdraw into myself. The other guests are old friends. Two couples. All with prominent positions – semi-creative – at liberal establishments, establishments they seem to wholly disapprove of. They all want to work for *other* liberal establishments. I suggest they all just swap jobs. My delivery is edged with my own brand of disdain, contempt; it is not deemed a funny or useful suggestion. Sarah tries to make the best of it: how would they get on in each other's jobs? They decide it is, in fact, a good dinner-party conversation. Clever Dan.

The food is good, the wine excellent. Marcus and his wife, Lucy, are relaxed, generous hosts. The Blacks' supper is always a four-couple affair when they eat at home. Various kids nip in with things to fix, for arbitration, scavenging snacks, eventually disappearing and falling asleep on the sofas.

The conversation moves on to Marcus and Lucy's proposed move to the country. Will they do it? How long will it last? Will Marcus be able to cut down on attending every private view, opening, party in town? He says he will. He has an idea to breed pigs. To write and to breed pigs. A book on Titian. Husband big fat pink pigs. He is happy not to be believed. Happy to be examined, analysed, interrogated – a little ridiculed even. It's an appealing kind of vanity. I don't contribute much to the conversation, not knowing anything about country life, although the idea of strolling outdoors into wet grass and soft ground appeals.

The main course is simple: four chickens, roasted peppers, rice. Marcus dextrously carves us all a breast; elbows in, big hands together, he looks as if he's performing keyhole surgery as he cuts the meat away from the bone while trying to retain the dark crisp skin intact. Inevitably the conversation finds its way to the late-Caravaggio exhibition currently running at the National Gallery. So inevitable is it, I introduce it. Ask Marcus his opinion.

He is super-enthusiastic. It was a great show. His decanting of appreciation is a kind of plainsong of art criticism, with precise rhythms, thought lines clear. He likes to retain an aristocratic distance from his passions, finding the emotive, the personal, muddling and muddy. His rhetoric is deceptive: subtle, insightful, forswearing irony, yet not without humour. He talks mainly about two late paintings not included in the exhibition: the *Beheading of Saint John the Baptist* and *Saint Jerome Writing*. He is interested in the formal expression of the subject's interiority – how we are drawn into what they must be thinking. In both works the torsos are bright, guiding the viewer to the physical activity. Yet somehow we don't linger there. Caravaggio forces us to contemplate the darker faces, their thoughts illuminated by highlights on their brows, their temples. What is it that St Jerome wants to express on his small piece of paper, gently laid out and held firm? What is the executioner thinking as he holds St John firmly to the ground, blood pooling out from his neck? Marcus is exercised by these questions. Caravaggio's genius is that he gives his subjects true interiority – real thoughts. It is our responsibility to think them.

I am impressed. It is an original idea. Storaro would be ecstatic, I imagine. The other guests are not as generous, regarding any subject of conversation as an excuse for their wit and erudition to conflate into self-aggrandizing pronouncements. They want to talk about *Sick Bacchus* as a representation of the exquisite depravity Caravaggio must have indulged in. Within minutes they have turned his life into *Carry On, Caravaggio*. Marcus tries to bring the conversation back to the seriousness of the work, but even he has adopted a flippant tone. There is something post-ironic on both sides.

I yawn. I don't cover my mouth and, avoiding shoulders and backs left and right, I stretch out my arms. I am happy to announce my state of mind, happy to take on their flippancy with a more aggressive boredom. Sarah jumps in, refusing to look at me and give me the satisfaction of a glare. She reminds them my Ph.D. was on Caravaggio. She says this to include me before it's too late; she knows my battle-cry yawns.

Marcus hears (perfect social antennae) that I am to be included in the conversation, but refuses to allow (imperfect ego) the true objective of Sarah's aim. He turns to me. 'How did you find the security at the show? Any chance of anything going missing? Wouldn't that be terrible? On your watch.'

I don't know what to say to this. I am furious. In his eyes my job discounts my having any other perspective. Once again I want to shock with the news of the existence of *The Nativity*. But I understand in this company what I know doesn't give me an extra dimension, it keeps me narrow; whatever their response to the news, it is news from an art cop, my knowledge procedural, operational, part of a parallel universe of cops and robbers. I don't answer.

Marcus pushes, 'Daniel?'

Sarah gets it in for me, her blue eyes flashing

coldly at me, brightly at the rest of the table. 'Last year, Daniel thought he saw *The Nativity* . . .'

Lucy bursts into the vacuum, 'My God. I thought it had been destroyed.'

Does it matter what I tell them now? Before I tell Jim, before Jim tells Rome? Should it include the deaths, the name? I don't have time to decide. Marcus leans back and pulls a newspaper from a pile on a sideboard.

'Old news, I'm afraid. *Herald Tribune* yesterday.'

He flaps us a look of the front page, 'Firm Sighting of Missing Masterpiece', before flapping it back to read. He paraphrases. 'Italian police believe it still exists. It's in southern Italy. Condition unknown. Special task force. Big reward. Closing in. Etc.' He is not displeased that he is the bearer of such details, usurping my coup.

The others recognize this. For a moment no one around the table says anything; cigarettes are drawn, wine poured and sipped, napkins folded, shaken free of crumbs on to plates.

My secret is out then. Am I relieved? I should be. I want to let go of the painting: let go because two people have died already; let go because it involves deceit and dishonesty; let go because my grasp was always a fantasy. I ask Marcus to pass me the newspaper. Where did the story come from? There are only two possible sources: Storaro and Savarese. It is unlikely to have been Savarese. He would have known, I am sure. He would have learned it all from Nenni on the rooftop. Who was

265

I? What did I want? But there would be no reason to release it unless he had a particular grudge against the current holders of the Caravaggio. It must be Storaro, either accidentally in search of more information, his team hitting the phones for any clue, or because going via legitimate channels is his only option. I have to accept it is for the best. I feel like crying, however, maudlin self-pitying tears. I feel deeply that something special has been taken from me. There is nothing new in the piece. Renewed confidence in its existence is the heart of the story.

'Will you be involved, Daniel?' I shrug. He pushes again, wanting to have some fun. 'Aren't you supposed to be the best? Sarah says . . .'

I interrupt, not feeling fun. 'I think the Italians will want this for themselves.'

He continues, 'But just imagine. What a hero you'd be!' His sarcasm is subtle, his exuberance impressive. Half of him wants me to be a hero; half of him finds heroism vulgar, vain. His sarcasm relies on me being a simpler soul and wholly believing in the hero. Perhaps he's right.

Sarah is looking at me. Gone is the alarm, fear, embarrassment, shame. Marcus has made sense of me for a moment. She is asking me: was that what the money was for? So you could go after the Caravaggio? Were you looking to be a hero? She understands that my presence at this table means I must have failed.

I do not know where to look. Marcus is challenging

me; Sarah pitying me; the others wondering where the fun has gone.

Marcus is exercised by my disinclination to talk, to play the role assigned to me. He performed earlier at my request, and it is now my turn – not to do so would be rude. He is also suspicious. He is a perceptive reader of faces, of expressions, of interiority disclosed.

'Daniel!' he exclaims with a faux glare and a little campness, adding extra delight to his suspicions. 'Don't tell me you know something they don't?'

The table is intrigued. Sarah is the only one who doesn't want more mystery from me: I am home; we have made love; it's now time for a period of calm, normalcy, happiness.

'Daniel?' Marcus smiles, open eyes provoking me.

What do I know? A region, a name, why it is where it is. Yes, things they don't know. But I also know I have not seen the bigger picture – people's lives.

'What could I possibly know, Marcus?'

'What possibly . . . ?' The sarcasm is less well hidden.

I think: fuck you. I say it.

'Daniel!' Sarah is furious.

Marcus is unperturbed. He adopts an attitude I have seen on TV. He hunches his shoulders, screws up his eyes and scratches his head. It is his reaction to bad taste, stupidity, vulgarity. It doesn't offend because it seems reflexive, eccentric. In this instance he is feigning shock, pain: he is mortified that he has offended me. But I know it's actually a kind of preparation; he's summoning up a line of attack.

I invite it. 'Marcus?'

'Sorry?' He looks up surprised, as if I have interrupted him from a reverie.

It is my turn to repeat his name, for disinclination to be engaged. 'Marcus – your thoughts?'

Like Storaro, he laughs before he speaks. 'Really, Daniel – you certainly are value for money.' His chin bobs a little, pointed in my direction. The other guests might be forgiven for thinking he wants to end it here, declaring no offence has been taken, that he is happy to glance away my bad manners with oily flattery. But I know it's not over. He grabs another bottle of white burgundy from the sideboard. Sarah is still looking at me, but I can't bear to see her disappointment. Marcus drills in the corkscrew; a strong arm draws out the cork; he concentrates on filling everyone's glasses. When he reaches me he stops, his face passive, his delivery casual and inquisitive, and not in any way modulated by condescension or disdain. 'Tell me, Danny, why don't you like us? I am intrigued. What about us – precisely – do you find so disagreeable?'

Lucy lays her hand over Marcus's arm, shakes her head. Sarah stares ahead, beyond me, the table, the humiliation.

I wait for my wine glass to be filled, and then lean forward on the table, arms crossed. 'It's very simple, Marcus. I don't like you because you have the privilege to not care about anything. I don't like you because you abuse that privilege and really don't care about anything. And that fucks me off. None of you is moved by anything. Everything is a game, everything is fun. All you ever do is look for new ways to finesse the negative. It's ridiculous. It's hell.'

There is a brief silence. 'I like that, Dan. New ways to finesse the negative. There is an element of truth in that. May I now tell you why I don't like you?'

Both wives interject. 'Daniel, Marcus. Enough.'

'Go on, Marcus.'

'I don't like you because you have a chip on your shoulder. And that's ugly. And not fun.' The smile is neither mocking nor unkind, but it has something of the eternal about it. Tonight hasn't left a scratch on him.

I laugh. 'You will never be beaten, Marcus. Thank you for making that plain.'

Sarah is standing, eyes red, a tear resting on her left cheekbone. 'I think it's time to go.'

I have let her down again. I instruct the table not to get up and slide out. 'I'll be seeing you all soon, I'm sure.'

In the hallway I ask Sarah to wait – I've forgotten something. At my reappearance Marcus stands, the eternal smile irritated: he doesn't want to deal with me again, not tonight. 'Have you lost something?'

'Just a word, Marcus.'

I lean in, grip his arm and whisper, a temporary smile on my face. 'Speak to me like that again, or ever speak of this, and I will fucking break you apart. Understand?' I underline my point with a tightening of my grip, my entire arm behind it – it is more than the promise of pain. I feel a sharp compliance from my host. 'Good.'

Sarah and I do not speak on the street; we wait at opposite junctions, arms poised to hail the first free cab. Nothing is said until we are close to home, until Sarah has mustered the strength not to cry if she speaks. I feel cold, shivery – my threat has emptied me. Going back in was the real defeat. Letting Marcus's atavistic confidence reveal my atavistic aggression. I do not feel fury, regret, rage, hatred. Just emptiness. My eyes are dry, my vision glassy. I look only to the darkness of sleep. I try not to hear Sarah.

'You ruin everything. Everything. Why? Why? I want to know. You say it's me, but it's you. It's you. Tell me why?'

It is all she says. I have no response.

3

I remain in a half-sleep while Sarah dresses. I turn into the pillow, pulling the duvet high across my face. I listen to her, her routine – the order of dressing and the sounds. She will not speak unless I make it clear I am awake. Even then I doubt she will respond. I should apologize. The weekend might be saved that way. Our special weekend. To spend time together, that was the deal. I'd decided on a drive to Bray and lunch at the Fat Duck. I should tell her. Offer it up in the bargaining for forgiveness. I feel her perch on the end of the bed to slip on her shoes. I only have seconds left; it is the last thing she does before she descends two floors to tea and toast. Her weight shifts on the bed for the second shoe; the mattress refreshing itself as she stands.

'Sarah?' She is by the door, her hand holding it – half gone. 'I'm sorry.' She is fully gone. I am not sure whether she actually stopped, whether or not I imagined her pause when I called her name. Is she even willing to listen to what I have to say?

I lie still for a minute or two before I swipe away the duvet, pull on my bathrobe and go downstairs. Sarah is sitting at the kitchen table eating toast, a mug of tea next to her. She is staring into space listening to *The Today Programme*.

'I don't have time to discuss any of this now, Dan.'

'I know. I just wanted to say that tomorrow I thought we'd drive down to Bray and have lunch at the Fat Duck.'

Sarah picks up her tea and drinks; the mug is kept airborne between further sips.

'Sarah?'

'We'll never get a table.'

I know she's right. 'Please, you're going to have to find a way to forgive me.'

'Why? Why should I? You humiliated me.'

'I humiliated myself.'

'I don't care about that.'

'I've said I'm sorry.'

'Tell me: what are you sorry for? Are you sorry because you embarrassed me? Are you sorry because you lost control? Or are you sorry for the things you said? How do you think it makes me feel – hearing those things. I'm one of those people. One of those people you hate. You say you love me, but you can't. You can't.' Her tone is hard, plain, uncompromising.

'You're not one of those people, Sarah. I didn't mean to include you. You might share the same privileges as Marcus but that's where the similarity ends. If I thought you'd think what I said included you, I'd never have said it.'

'But you've said this kind of thing before. To me. About me. About my family. My friends.'

'It's different.'

'You think it is, but it's not.'

'Please, Sarah, let's do what we said and have a weekend just to ourselves. No intrusions, just you and me, whatever we want to do.'

Sarah brushes toast crumbs from her fingers on to her plate, takes the plate and mug to the sink.

'I have to go to work. I don't know what time I'll be home tonight.'

'Can we have dinner?'

'I don't know.'

'Let me come and meet you.'

'Daniel, don't come and meet me. I'll be home at some point tonight, probably not late.'

I listen to her leave. I know the order of this too: jacket on, handbag opened – contents checked, keys dropped in – handbag closed; a pause at the mirror, lips rolled in, rolled out; then out into the street with a firm slam shut of the door.

I turn on the portable TV – the only TV in the house – next to the radio, next to the cereal boxes. BBC *Breakfast*. I watch, elbows on the table, knuckles pressed into my cheek. I should go into work but I know I won't – can't. Some internal messages are clear. I must call, though. But I can't think why. What is happening to me? My sensations are like polished silver spikes, sharp and gleaming, but my mind is like mud, thick mud. Is this what people mean when they talk about a mental breakdown, a nervous breakdown, those old-fashioned terms? Is that what's happening to me? It's not how it feels. Or how I imagine it would feel. What does Sarah think is happening to me? Is she thinking about it right now, sitting on the bus, staring out of the window, the morning opaque with the dawn's last darkness? Or is her gaze inward? Examining the regret. That would be my guess. Regret is keeping her from her book, the window, the morning darkness. I experience a deeper regret – a double regret: marrying her, then hurting her. But at the time I was so sure she was my prize, the reward for accepting my failures equally. And still working hard, trying to be the best. The prize for acceptance and effort: Sarah Delaney, beautiful, intelligent, rich, with a great job at Langdon's specializing in Pesto Mash.

I go upstairs and drop on to the sofa, flip open my mobile.

'Jim. It's Danny.'

Jim is immediately, dynamically furious. 'Where the fuck are you?'

'I'm at home.'

'Jesus – have you seen the papers?'

'It depends . . .'

'Rome thinks you know where the Caravaggio is – do you? They're going insane.'

'What are they saying exactly?'

'What have you been doing over there? You've been linked to the painting from two sources, they say. One involving the murder of some fucking lowlife called Italo Nenni – do you know him?'

'Things got out of hand.'

'Telling me they did. You're suspended.'

To thank him would sound sarcastic.

'Danny?'

'I'm still here.'

'Do you know where the painting is?'

'No.'

'Why didn't you tell me you were certain it was the Caravaggio?'

'Don't know.'

'What the fuck am I going to do with you?'

'Right now, I really don't care.'

'Danny, just tell me what you know. The more I can give Rome . . . Jesus – do you know you've just fucked up one of our most important relationships. You're a fucking menace. I should have seen it coming.'

'What?'

'You – doing something stupid. You going off. I always knew you were a liability. You've got that fucking look.'

'And what's that?'

'That look. Too much fucking – I don't know – hunger. Caring too much. You should have joined the security services – they're all like that.'

Am I like that? Again, maybe once.

'Danny?'

'What?'

'Tell me, what do you know?'

I slip on to the floor, sit cross-legged, staring into the dark intricate pattern of the Persian rug.

'I saw the painting in Calabria last year. I don't know where. Two hours east of Catanzaro is the best I can give you. An old man had it. He showed it to me. Like a fucking blanket to keep his knees warm. Its condition is bad, but not so bad it can't be restored. That's it.'

'Fuck you, Danny. What else?'

'The old man doesn't have it any more.'

'Who does have it?'

Do I give up the name that easily? A name that cost two lives? A name which means within twenty-four, forty-eight hours the painting is sure to be recovered, and my part in the operation will be little more than as the bad guy, the selfish guy, who wanted all the glory for himself, and who was responsible for the murder of a lowlife couple from the Naples slums. Is that what I want?

I watch myself from above, a huddled boy, phone pressed to his ear. My stomach is tight, all muscle contracted. I cannot let go of the name. I cannot let go of the painting. Not yet. I know that to let go even of the fantasy is to be left stranded at the edge of myself with nothing left to hang on to while I'm out there. To have nothing to pull myself back with. And I don't want that. I want to pull myself back. And soon. Yet I realize it will be this pulling, the sharpness of effort that will be required, which will finally release me into a spin, and right now I cannot be sure that I will spin surely, upright and on the spot, and not wobble and skid and in an instant become just another of the world's crashing things.

I give Jim a name. It is the name of a dead man.

It is midnight when Sarah returns home, very drunk and angry – and with complicated things to say, things she's thought about all day, decisions she's made about us, about me, the way I am. 'Oh God,' she screams through gritted teeth, arms pressed to her sides, hands aimed at the earth, frustrated and furious.

I sit on the end of the bed, just jeans on, sit awkwardly, abjectly, watching her slam down her bracelets, her earrings, kick off her shoes.

She says she hates me, hates me. All that nastiness inside me. She didn't marry me for that.

As she undresses in the bathroom I want to call out: it's not nastiness, it's anger, fear, disappointment. What *Marcus* said was nasty. So she's got it wrong!

Back in the bedroom, in her dressing gown, tightly wrapped. 'I don't understand you. You've got so much. Or maybe you don't think so. Maybe you don't think I'm up to much. Well, do you? Don't answer that. I've had a long think, Dan. I couldn't concentrate all day. All I could think about was . . . those things you said. I know I'm different, but imagine if you really did think all

277

those horrible things about me and I didn't know.' A shudder shimmies down her body. She sits at the dressing table and smears her face with make-up remover. 'That scares me, Dan, not knowing why you are with me. That it might be for some horrible reason. Why would someone be with someone like that?'

I place a hand on her shoulder; she immediately shrugs it off. She looks at me briefly via the mirror while padding around her eyes with a cotton ball.

'I think I've always been emotionally honest, Sarah. But that doesn't mean what I feel is straightforward.'

'That doesn't make any sense to me. It's one or the other.'

'Don't be so naive. You know things are more complicated than that. Just please don't doubt that I love you, however complicated the reasons.'

Sarah replaces the top on the bottle, screws it on. 'So you admit it then?'

'Admit what?'

'That you're with me for the wrong reasons?'

'No, I don't.'

'I want to know why you think you're with me.'

'I don't want to talk about it.'

She dumps the cotton ball into the little bin under the dresser. 'Suit yourself. I'm going to bed.'

We both climb into bed, yanking at the duvet for adequate cover. We both lie on our backs. Neither is ready for sleep, yet sitting up, reading, is not an option.

'What are we going to do, Dan?'

'I don't know.'

I turn over, burrow my hand under my pillow and cup my head; I dig my other hand between my thighs. I can hear Sarah crying, staring at the ceiling; it is quiet and soft. The tears are temporary, however, quickly replaced by soft, quiet snoring, her drunkenness disregarding her anger and sadness.

4

Sarah is awake and up before me, dressed, with coffee in hand, and standing at the bedroom window, staring out over the crescent. I sit up in bed, hands limply, meekly in my lap.

'I'm going out for the day. I'm seeing my sisters in Portobello.'

The plan we'd made has been replaced by a new plan. I want to remind her of the old plan, but I don't see the point.

'What are you going to do?' she asks.

'Do you care?'

She turns from the window. 'Not really.'

'Then why ask?'

'Politeness.'

'Bullshit.'

She turns to me. 'Are you saying I'm lying, or that politeness is bullshit?'

'I'm using it as a catch-all. Right now it means whatever you want it to mean. Including fuck off and see your sisters.'

'Charming.'

'You know me.'

Sarah leaves the room. I swing out of bed and go to the landing. I watch her head disappear down the first flight of stairs. 'We were supposed to be spending the weekend together, if you remember.'

I hear Sarah stop. I hear the silence of her stopping halfway down, hand on the banister. I see the mid-step she's in – one foot airborne. I see, hear the moment of thought – whether to answer me. I see, hear her decision: no – ignore it, ignore him. I see, hear the order of her leaving; it remains the same.

I go out for breakfast. I have to walk a mile to the nearest greasy spoon. The other end of the Fulham Road. I buy a newspaper. The story is on the second page: 'Caravaggio's Masterpiece Missing for 35 Years'. For the briefest moment I think it's been found. I almost vomit. My body is instantly hard and full of aching; bones, limbs, blood shine with pain. I try to calm myself, to focus. Read the piece. The details are similar to those of the story in the *Herald Tribune*, but with new additions: a British policeman is involved. Me, I presume. The painting is believed to have moved from the Sicilian Mafia into the hands of a small southern Italian crime family. Italian police say they have the strongest leads to its whereabouts since its theft. The accompanying photo is of the altar from which it was stolen, the huge blank space reaching to the ceiling oddly moving in its emptiness.

I stare out of the window, hardly aware of the food placed before me, my chin resting on the heel of one hand. It is raining hard. The velocity of each raindrop is impressive, the impact on the pavement visible as a bounce and spray, a thousand tiny fountains.

I accept the Italians are closer than they ever have been, but what does that mean? They know it's on the mainland. Anything more? Whatever they know, the information is likely to dry up the closer they get. Unless they're lucky. And sooner or later they will get lucky.

I can't eat. I stare at the altar, stare beyond the image and into the gradations of grey which build the image on the page and then further beyond to the white of the paper. I am looking at Storaro's white wall, his imagined place for the painting. His desire is so simple: he wants to hang the painting in his gallery. What do I want? To stand in front of a multitude of flashes, holding the painting unrolled to my feet, to take deep breaths of glory, knowing . . . knowing what? Things will have changed?

I leave money on the table, fold the newspaper and slot it inside my coat. The Fulham Road, usually rammed on a Saturday morning, is clear, the rain so strong the pavements are like liquid silver. The rain soaks my hair, my eyebrows; it runs down my forehead, temples, the back of my neck. I walk for an hour before jumping on a bus. It's only when I am sitting on the bus I realize where I am heading: the National Gallery.

The gallery is busy. An old couple stand before the work I am here to see. Caravaggio's *Salome Receives the Head of Saint John the Baptist*. The man directs the woman to the space between John's severed neck and the gold plate. The woman winces. He says of John's open mouth, slack, black, desperate, it is either in mid-groan or mid-prayer. But it was a life taken midway through something. Isn't it wonderful? Such . . . he searches for the word. He finds: honesty. They move on across the room directed by him. They are not shuffling through the gallery giving every painting a cursory glance. It is a bespoke tour. I am touched by this.

I have come here because I want to understand from this painting in what way I might be guilty of Nenni's and Maria's deaths. Certainly I wasn't obeying orders like the man who killed them, which is the traditional excuse of the executioner. I accept most of the guilt lies with Savarese. But is there a portion of guilt shared by all three of us? The painting consists of a group of four: Salome, an old woman, John, an executioner; its story is the execution of John the Baptist. Its theme is responsibility. The executioner hands over John's head in a confident gesture that declares he is not culpable for the death, he was obeying orders and was expedient and professional in the carrying out of his duties – a gesture declaring that now it is time for those who ordered the execution to confront their actions. The executioner suspects their motives lack honour. This is all articulated by the distancing arm, John's head suspended by hand-gripped hair. I suspect that the executioner is pausing before placing the head on the charger held out by Salome, a pause in which Salome confronts her motives, forcing her to look away.

Did Nenni jerk in death? How long did his body take to calm and still? Did he find some strength in his weak, fragile body to protect his wife for a brief moment? Or was it Maria who tried to protect her husband? I cannot know, just like I cannot know whether warning them to leave Naples immediately would have made any difference. Yet I still feel some responsibility. Is that responsibility in this painting? I look for myself. I am not there. Not even in the shadows. Not even within a fraction of one of its subjects. I am not an executioner; I did not order their deaths. I am not the old woman, I did not look on. Did Caravaggio paint my part somewhere else? I don't think so. There is little drama to be found in my actions. Little which might reveal essentials. It was a plain act of selfishness. Banal. How much of the human condition can be expressed like this?

I am dizzy and need to sit down. I make room for myself on the bench in the middle of the room. My actions were banal yet I feel they have pushed me beyond the edge of myself now, beyond normal life. When I close my eyes all I see is a thousand circles, each circle containing a crowd, happily cramped together. No one is pushing their way out. There must be a thousand circles, a hundred thousand people cramped and cosy. There is singing. Not a single song, but various tunes, all cheery and merry and inviting all voices to let rip. I want in. I really want in. I understand that being outside only allows for further distancing. Further aloneness. I blink back to the gallery, but it has gone. With eyes open all I see is a man who looks very like me thinned out to a rim on the edge of some centrifugal force. I watch this thinning rim spinning around me. This is what it feels like to be on the outside. It is something you watch. You are witness to it. Beyond yourself. Forgive me, maestro, but am I right in thinking this is something even you would have found impossible to paint?

I cannot rid myself of the feeling of being only the rim of me. I feel it on my way to Harvey Nick's food hall. I feel it as I buy the food that I am going to cook for Sarah. I feel it sitting in the kitchen watching the final football scores come in, shopping bags on the counter. It persists while I watch the clock, cooking without knowing whether she'll show up. The feeling is so strong it sends me to the mirror to prove to myself I have extension, that I exist in three dimensions. Every now and again fear overcomes me and I have to stop and catch my breath, lean on the table, steady myself.

I have prepared Sarah's favourite food, wine, pudding. A laid table.

She is back at nine-thirty p.m. Paul and Joe, Orla Kiely bags. I notice the double-take at the kitchen door. Then the hardness. She is not late – this wasn't arranged.

For a moment I feel pulled into full relief. I want to be back in Italy, with Francesca, drinking martinis and playing staring games. I want to be without this thinness and lack of breath and not to be confronted with my stupidity, asking myself why I've cooked this meal for this woman standing by the door, looking to tough out the ambush – her favourite things. Because the result of her day is that she has gone cold, partly from a decision to, and partly because it is the case inside her and she can no longer deny it.

I have nothing worth saying. Offering her some wine is the most I can manage. She insists on changing. I wait. I have moved back from the rim. I am aware of being in the kitchen, at this moment, hovering around this table, knowing I have pushed her to the brink of something. It is her turn to be thinned out. She has chosen to be a hard wire in my presence. All her warmth, volume, slender soft-ness is elsewhere.

Back, in her pyjamas, she takes the glass, sips, turns the bottle on the table and reads the label.

I think to say, 'It's a Saint Emilion – your favourite.' But I know she knows what it is, her regard for it, and only love cares for the surprise of the familiar. I serve myself some of the cold food and eat. I can tell she wants to get away, go straight to bed. So I say, 'I met a woman in Florence.' And watch her. She smiles grimly, almost pleased – looking to build up her case.

'Did you have sex with her?'

'No.'

'Then what are you telling me for?'

'We kissed.'

'I don't see how this is going to help.'

I shake my head. 'What about you? Do you have anything to tell me?'

She is surprised at this and looks directly at me. 'Me? Like what?'

'I was just wondering.'

Sarah sets down her wine, smoothes her pyjamas over her chest and thighs. 'Actually I do have something to say. I think you're right that our class makes us different. I love my job; I love the world I work in. I've done well because I worked hard. And I worked hard because I love what I do. I'm not ashamed to be highly qualified and successful. And neither should Marcus. Those people at his house? They are also very good at what they do. So they're all from privileged backgrounds with good educations. Great. It means we have good critics, film-makers, curators. That's a good thing. And that's not about class.

'And then there's you. What do you bring to the table: passion, enthusiasm, reverence? And we're all supposed to bow down to that, as if somehow you're better than us. Somehow your opinions, your responses are untainted. Why's that? Because you're working class? Is that what you think? Really, you can't believe that in this day and age. You're not an artist, so it can't be about that. And it can't be that you're better, less tainted, because you *didn't* get a job at Sotheby's, you *didn't* get a job at the Royal Academy, you *didn't* get a job at the Courtauld? So what is it? What makes you so special then? I've racked my brains. And the only thing I can come up with is that you just *think* you're special. It's got nothing to do with class, with education, with bad luck; it's got nothing to do with our lack of passion, enthusiasm, reverence – not that I even agree with that. It's got nothing to do with any real virtues at all.' She stops abruptly, as if she expected to go on but has realized suddenly that she has said all that needs to be said. She pulls at the V of her pyjama top. I look at her for more, wanting a complete demolition.

Sarah stands. 'I'm sorry, Dan. I can't be with someone like you. You're too complicated for me.'

I watch her as she leaves the room. I hear her fast footsteps up the stairs. I hear the escape. I hear in her footsteps, in their flight and lightness, that she feels free of me, she has said her piece and I am owed nothing. I see her slipping into bed. Content enough to open a book.

I take the bottle and wine glass upstairs and into the sitting room. I then return for the TV. I locate a metal coat hanger. All I want is a decent picture on BBC ONE and to watch *Match of the Day* in comfort – for the first time in this fucking house. No slouching goes on here. Not even for a film. Me and Sarah sit up straight like schoolchildren, arching backs, rolling shoulders to stay comfortable for ninety minutes. Watching a romantic comedy.

I concentrate on finding an acceptable picture. I skewer the coat hanger into the socket, bend it into a Y-shape, crush the socket tight with pliers. I do not care how long it takes me, I will succeed. I do it silently. I stop every now and then to think things through. Do I unwind the hook of the coat hanger, straighten it? Do I shift operations near the window? And then I set to it again. Eventually there is a reasonable picture; it has taken almost half an hour. I lie on the sofa and pull the alpaca blanket, draped over the back, across me. If Sarah is still awake, she'll be able to hear the TV. Unlikely to come down to complain, though. She'll let me have this. More proof.

There are three dull games, so I mainly stare at the ceiling, cradling my wine. Sarah has pulled me back into shape. Her assessment has filled me up, pushed out my sides. I am not special. If I have thought that, I am mistaken. Have I? Again, possibly once, a long time ago. I drink more wine.

I watch the chiaroscuro shadow patterns of the

spare trees on the walls. I hear cars pull up, doors opening and closing, the reverberating thunks rattle the windows. There is low talk. The traffic on the King's Road is constant.

There is an argument at the end of the crescent, a girl and boy – drunk. The words are indistinct but he is pleading with her; she is being as understanding as she can manage without giving in. A Saturday-night break-up. Be merciful, girl. And don't plead, son. I listen to my breathing: it is slow, heavy, fearful. My chest is still full and pressed out with my new banality. I drink some more wine, head pushed up, lips out to avoid a spill. Chewing it in. The taste is acute – medicinal. The heating, timed to go off late in this cold house, clunks and bangs. I hear echoes that I know end in our bedroom, where Sarah is lying, reading or asleep. I feel a tear tip from the corner of my right eye and run down my temple and into my hair. I am not crying: it is just an escape of sadness. But it proves I am not numb enough, not closed down nearly enough. I drink again. Big gulps. I try to avoid any movement so my muscles, nerves, bones take on the heaviness of prolonged stillness, the heaviness of paralysis. I can feel the cold track of my tear down my temple. My mouth is dry. The wine is too young, the tannins sticky. The heat between myself and the alpaca blanket is soft and enfolding. I turn off the TV. The noise from the King's Road is suddenly closer. The pubs are letting out. Groups of friends assembling, stumbling about, making plans to extend the evening. The sound is mostly joyous. Joyous and trilling. Some people are singing – girls' voices. Beatles songs, of all things. Easy melodies. Easily shared. I can hear in their voices the full weight of their will to express themselves as fun, a little mad, and free. I am not yet numb enough to forgive them for their lack of originality, their easy happiness, their freedom and certainties. But I am numb enough to ignore them.

Sarah shuffles in next to me, whispering, 'Dan, Dan. Hold me.'

I turn over in the limited space, pull her into me, her back nestling into my stomach. I think she just wants cuddles in the cold. To be sad and cold is too much, even for Sarah. But she pulls free and twists round, her hands bracing my face to kiss me. I place a hand on her waist, between the bunched-up pyjama top and the loose band of her pyjama bottoms – her skin is hot. I slide my hand around to her back, to hold her. She pulls away, unbuttons her pyjama top, turning it off her shoulders and her arms. I yank and twist off my T-shirt. We return to kissing, Sarah manoeuvring herself on top of me. I slide my hand into her pyjama bottoms, over her behind and between her legs. I then move my other hand down her stomach and between her legs – both my hands pressed into her. She rocks forward, whispering something I can't make out. I stop her moving, cutting out the white noise to listen. All I hear is 'more' repeated. It is not an instruction to either of us; it is an incantation to be taken somewhere beyond herself. I move out from beneath her, steadying her as she falls awkwardly off me and on to the sofa. I pull off my socks, my jeans, my shorts. I stand before her, naked. She sits up, taking me quickly in her mouth. I dip my fingers into her hair; her spine is concave, her behind arching out. Her skin is delicately cross-hatched by the shadows of the branches of the trees. I lean over, stroking her back as if to feel the pattern. I pull myself free and kneel, pull her pyjama bottoms off. Part of this is routine, an established order we follow: me in her mouth; my mouth to her. I push her back on the sofa, pull her legs forward. My cheeks feel the smoothness and the heat of her thighs. I am only there momentarily, for the taste of her and to feel her body react to me – to tighten, then yield, then melt. Routine, established? Yes. But I know tonight is a last fuck and therefore it is none of these things. I lead Sarah to the floor. Sitting back on my knees I watch her lie down, get comfortable on the thick hard rug, pull her legs up, widen her hips. I climb over her knowing that at the point my collarbone is parallel with her shoulders our genitals meet and I should push in, a long thrust, so the sensation is long, full. Her arms drop back, to a dive shape, a white diamond shape. She is brightly visible in the moonlight. From hips to waist to chest, high arms, clear contours against the dark rug, a shape almost suspended in darkness, a shape hovering over nothingness. Only my hands pressed to the floor tell me there is something beneath us. Her face is shadowed by my head; I pull away to see her, the woman I love for the last time taking me in. She doesn't want this intimacy; she pushes me away, sits over me, pushes my face to the side, to look elsewhere, to the edge of the room, the window and the silver glass, the night, the grey bark of the trees. I feel her impatience as she shunts back and forth quickly, jerkily. It doesn't feel right. She rolls off. The empty wine bottle is knocked over, falls and rolls away. I move the wine glass. A stretch away. We lie side by side. Her breathing is quick, short, shallow. The whispering has stopped.

'What do you want to do?' I ask.

'I don't know.' She says this straightforwardly, loudly, without the breathlessness of desire, erotic entrancement.

'Turn over.'

'You do it. You turn me over.'

She has made her decision – the marriage is over and she now wants whatever gave her that strength, that certainty, taken away, so she doesn't feel hard, heartless, cold. She doesn't want to be correct about herself.

Hands on her hips, I twist her over, her hips halfway round before her upper body and legs follow. She is flat on her stomach, arms by her sides. I then pick her up by the hips – a satisfying hold; her shoulders stay firmly on the floor, only her knees, thighs, bottom cranked up. The perfect fuck position. Desiring, enticing. I press myself in. The first thrust is as slow and as deep as I can make it. My grip on her hips is tight; she cannot move. I pull out slowly, as slowly as possible and then push back, listening to her moans. I want these few minutes to have something of the eternal about them. A fuck in boundless time. I push in, ease out – no change in speed, rhythm, thrust. I have worked out what she wants: it's not the activity of the fuck but the tension of it, a fuck at its physically most keen. I keep hold of her – easing in, easing out – feeling my cock ever-hardening: the tension working equally on me. Sarah moans deeply, her chest resonating on the floor. I continue, pressing a little harder this time, looking for the moan at the end of my long push. I watch my cock slip in, the length disappear, and then watch the moment of confused, vague conjoining, hair, skin, darkness. Then out: the pattern of the rug below us. I take one hand off her hips and place it under her. My cock keeps its motion. She works herself on my fingers. There is now something almost contrapuntal – her circular movements over my fingers, my straight thrusts. She begins to come. I feel it; it is achingly slow for her. I know the sensation is beyond pleasure and will be momentarily obliterating – a white light rushing through her limbs and surging upwards. I wait until her momentum is unstoppable and let go myself. I sense the double rush she feels – her orgasm filled with mine. We both moan through it, and then slam on to one another to prolong it. All steadiness is lost and we topple over. Sarah rolls away – a long, glistening body in the moonlight. I kneel up. Legs trembling, cock trembling with short spasms. Sarah is silent and still, staring at the ceiling, hands by her sides, palms up, flat. I lie down next to her. I look up at the ceiling where I can see us lying there next to each other. It is as clear as a mirror image in a bright room. We are both flat, without volume. Sarah doesn't stir. I hear her breathing lengthen, deepen. She will soon be asleep, wanting to escape again. I reach for the alpaca blanket on the sofa and float it over her. I remain still, silent, until I am sure she is fully asleep, beyond the twitching, the soft mutterings. I slide away. The clock says 3.47 a.m. I collect up my clothes. I leave the room on weak legs. I shower quickly and pack silently. In the kitchen I divide the contents of Gustav's attaché case, building a block of bundles on the table – a square, sharp monolith of notes. Within thirty minutes I am out the door, once again in my wedding clothes. I drop my house keys through the letter box, careful not to let the brass plate slap. It is cold; condensation from my breath is thick, lingering. I hesitate on the front step. The inside of my mind is the inside of the sitting room: Sarah asleep under the blanket, a dark form, the contours of a sleeping woman visible as a relief of a long body wrapped and draped; her pale shoulders are hidden; only her face is visible in the grey light shimmering above her body like a mist. The sitting room is my entire mind, and Sarah is like a scar across it.

FLORENCE AND FRANCESCA

1

I t's the same passport guy, recognizing me but not caring to recall why, barely looking at my photo, not noticing the date, just handing the thing back with a gesture to move on, which I do, with bag and attaché case, to the exit, to the bus stop for the railway station. I experience a feeling of lightness, the lightness of a mission, an inwardness extended out towards a thing to do.

It became clear on the plane, at take-off, over the thrust and vacuum, stomach pressed into the back of the seat, that there is little difference between what I am planning to do and the many ways other men and women go in search of themselves, the strong tests they take. There will be an element of danger, death will be a possibility; but neither is definite, and death is unlikely – man in fact being more predictable than nature – so what I am doing might be assessed, in terms of mortal risk, as less dangerous, less foolhardy than, say, climbing Everest, crossing the Sahara or sailing wherever it is that sailors sail. And then following on from that, I determined that the glory and public awe I will receive will be in direct proportion to the risk. The glory will be limited, the public awe light. But then these are now not my motivations. I am doing it because I have nothing else with which to define me. Only action will add bulk and layers to my self. Only action will undo the vanity which has undone me. Only through work, risk, sacrifice will I be able to redeem myself. It is only through these things that I will restore earlier passions to the heart of myself. And become something Caravaggio might want to paint.

And Sarah? What will she think? How long was it before she awoke in the grey light and transferred herself back to her big bed? Did she wonder where I was? Did she call out? Look for me? What were her thoughts between the sitting room and the bedroom? Did she manage more sleep easily? I cannot know. What am I feeling now the numbness is gone, the yearning for numbness has gone? I remain in love, I am certain of that. I am aware of pain, a layer of keen hurt, thickishly sore beneath my skin. But the sadness, the desperation, they have been set aside. It is important for my mission to be emotionally narrow. These things closed out.

I try not to think about Francesca. Yet I know that she is where I am heading first. Someone needs to understand what I am doing. Whether she will care, or even care enough to listen, I can't be sure. But I don't dwell. My doubts must also be narrow. All uncertainty is closed out.

Florence again, two weeks on from when this first started. But this time no snow, just a warm breeze beneath a powder-blue sky and small sun. I walk briskly down Via Panzani, my overcoat flapping behind me. I don't stop beneath the *duomo*, yet I am instantly aware of its work at the heart of the city, at the heart of the world, at the heart of myself. It's one of the reasons I am undertaking the mission. If the *duomo* reveals things as they are, I want to be content with the things of myself which might be revealed when I pass beneath it. What's the point of being less than fully human, *four* dimensions full?

At the apartment I stand the attaché case on the table, open the bookcase, remove the Caravaggio and Raphael books and pull out Nenni's gun. How long, I wonder, until Bramante found it? What would he think: a gun hidden in his bookcase? I set it down next to the attaché case; it rattles densely on the glass. I check the contents of my wallet. It doesn't really matter who I am now; the story of myself will have to be made up as I go along. There are enough credit cards and enough loose notes for a few days' high spending without dipping into the real money, which I want to preserve as a pure fifty K – giving it an 'at first glance' credibility to anyone used to looking at that sort of dough bundled up.

I unpack my laptop, plug it in and boot up. First things. I email Francesca.

I am back. Will explain. Can we meet?
Daniel X

I hit send. Wait perched on the edge of the chair. What does she do on Sundays? There is no immediate response..

I check the battery bar on my mobile – high. Swap batteries; reserve battery is low. I search in my bag for the charger and plug that in, connect the phone. I check my email again – nothing. What am I expecting? Francesca at her computer, waiting for me? I go to the window, open the shutters and stare out beyond the top of the *duomo* into the lazy blue sky beyond. I stare deeply, without thought, without focus, without narrowness. It's an open stare which is somehow reflected back by the sky, encompassing me, entering me. For a moment I feel airborne, held high by the blue breeze, my mind blue to its edges.

The ping of an arriving email whips me back. Spam. I delete it, sit down and double-click Internet Explorer, type in a name, the name given to me by Nenni, and hit return.

Results **1–10** of about **1,830** for **'Pasquale Lomazzo'**. (**0.19** seconds)

Most of the sites listed are online versions of newsletters and newspapers, with a few 'Mafia' sites purporting to be serious but nevertheless focusing gratuitously on the violence and glamour. All but two are in Italian. All I want is enough for a basic profile. So I know who I am after. Age, family, history. A photo. Something about his attitudes. I also need somewhere to start. I might be the only one who knows that the painting is with Lomazzo, but where he is, even I don't know.

I read through the first ten entries. Lomazzo is thirty-one or thirty-two. The nephew of the old man. A rising star. Police suspect he has his own micro-gang within the family. Four or five loyal soldiers. There are no photos. For all I know he could have been one of the young men in the BMW last year. There are two accounts of how he dealt with the power struggle within the *cosca*. Hearsay via journalists, testimony from a trial. Three hits within one hour – all carried out by Lomazzo. When it came to the third, the target knew Lomazzo was coming for him so he holed up in his house. Lomazzo called him. Offered to meet and discuss a truce. Watched the guy leave his house, get into his car; the explosion echoed quickly around the hills. So he's clever, then, when it comes to killing. But what turns him on outside of murder? What differentiates him from the other middle-ranking soldiers? Nothing worth mentioning, it seems. Which means, then, he must be content with the basic business of heroin, extortion, art-napping, and the income these bring. I keep scrolling, keep clicking, keep reading. I find one photo: five men around a table, only one occluded by a raised glass – Lomazzo. He doesn't appear to have ever been arrested or even made a court appearance. This tells me something important – Lomazzo is secretive and smart.

It is late afternoon. I check my email again. Nothing. I send myself a test email. Instantly receiving. My mobile has been silent. I check it's working. Should Sarah have tried to contact me by now? At least to find out where I am? Should I call, tell her? Text her even? Indecision sends me back to the list of webpages on Lomazzo. I need to read everything, no matter how repetitive – every new reference, every variation of detail, every fresh perspective adds something, and if it doesn't quite equal a man, *I* will gain from it, *I* will grow, and that makes me stronger, safer. I don't make a single note. The information must take root inside of me; synapses must form containing it all. Only then will its recall be quick enough to help me, to give me an edge.

Six o'clock. No message from Francesca. I wanted to see Francesca first. First. Before the other person I am here to see. Who I am sure is expecting me.

A beautiful tall sweet-faced Scandinavian girl is at the hotel reception desk. She smiles engagingly – she wants to help, but Storaro doesn't take calls from the reception, and the elevator has to be called from the penthouse suite.

'Is he expecting you?'

I explain it's a surprise visit. And ask whether she has any way of knowing if he's up there.

She tells me her shift has just started and she doesn't know. She asks a colleague but is answered with a shrug. We speak in English; her accent has an attractive drawl.

I take a seat in the library, open a book on Giotto and order a beer. I had wanted to leave tonight, hit the south, the true south, beyond Naples, by the morning. But two encounters must take place first.

I wait an hour. Drink another beer. My presence will reach him. I swap the Giotto for a book on Raphael Goldberg – there are photos of the Storaro Gallery. Another hour passes. I order food. A bowl of noodles. They are fragrant.

I am called at nine p.m. The Scandinavian girl escorts me to the elevator. At the top I am met by Luca. The penthouse sitting room is large, square, one side leading out on to a terrace. The furniture is all classic Italian – clean, perfectly moulded lines, single-colour fabrics, thin darks and heavy lights – designs hardly changed from the 1960s but somehow futuristic-seeming. Most surfaces are covered with books, magazines, catalogues, papers. But there is none of the chaos of his office. A housekeeper must keep the place tidy.

Storaro is sitting on a low chair, wearing a pinstriped suit, buttoned up, his white shirt ruffled up between the lapels. A finger is entwined in a curl which he pulls forward, lets spring back, pulls forward again. He is daydreaming. Relaxed. Bored even. I take my place opposite him. Has he been expecting me? What does he think I am here for? I look beyond him to a lamp: a tall thin flat column of burnt orange. More glow than light.

He understands I am not here to talk. There is no deal on offer. I am here to make it clear that I am going after the Caravaggio and he must make his decisions based on that knowledge. Being here in front of him tells him I know more than anyone else so he must think carefully.

He regards me amiably, with deep breaths, his chest heaving contentedly. He is not discomfited by my silence this time. He crosses his small strong legs; he has to pull on his shin and hold on to it to keep the position. His body is a tight mass, unsupple in tight positions. I sit back, legs crossed, arms across the back of the sofa.

He lets go of his wrought-iron curl. 'A policeman?'

'Yes.'

It is for confirmation only, and complete silence is not for him for long. In his collection of experts I'd be quite an addition. His expression is honest. I am finally worthy of some respect.

Luca places a glass of water beside me, Coca-Cola for Storaro.

The night beyond the window is a landscape of dark roofs, the looming mass of the *duomo*, further a distant endless black, and a rim, the horizon, a hard jagged shape of the earth. His house is up there, unfinished, a beautiful idea.

'I liked your house.'

He pulls hard on his shin to keep his legs crossed. His blue eyes are interested in me. This is an interesting encounter. The thrill and excitement he experienced at his house has been replaced with something more subtle – mental activity which will make possession of the painting a reality. The appealing tremor in his eyes isn't visible from where I am sitting. What do I look like to him? Tired, certainly. But he is concerned with my deeper resources, my mission-confidence. I am a different man from the one he first met two weeks ago. New dimensions have been revealed. Which is why I'm here. So we are both clear. Trust me to go for it alone. Permit it. Retract your reach for a few days. Let me bring it back from the underworld – then we talk.

'How is the painting?'

How is it? Frayed. Cracked. Webs of cracks. Larger fissures. A mess.

'It will live.'

Storaro drinks. Strong hand around the glass, elbow high. He empties the glass. I sip my water. It is lime-scented. Not flavoured. There is no lime.

'Good.'

We have agreed it is worth saving. Worth our inner desperation for it. Permission is often granted this way. I do not need to respond. It is time to go. Prepare.

Before I stand Storaro says, 'Francesca . . . she is yours.'

I smile. Of course. Too much power. Mistaking it as generosity, largesse, goodwill – an incentive even. People, objects – same circle. He doesn't register his mistake. Of course not. He pulls at his shin. His chest is a little puffed under his ruffled-up shirt, squashed between the lapels of his tight pinstriped suit. He doesn't stand. As I leave he has the same daydreaming look as when I entered. Relaxed. Bored even.

2

I wake late. It takes me a few moments to remember where I am, why I am here, the decisions I have made. My first thought – an image lying across my mind, a gossamer photograph – is of Sarah's body offered up to me: her way of finishing it, finalizing the decision she made. The classic closure. Shut down, then give back – making sure you don't want to give indefinitely – then close down completely. I was right to leave immediately. Seeing me – a hollow crashing thing in her big house – would have quickly disgusted her. Only one thing will make it good.

I check my email, mobile. There is no response from Francesca, nothing from Sarah – the cyber and satellite world is quiet and still. I leave the apartment. The stairs are stone bright and odourless. I head straight to the Uffizi under a low grey sky.

Even though this is our third meeting, Silvio doesn't appear to recognize me, asking for my name and whether I am expected. I lie. I am led up to Francesca's office and left by the open door. She is sitting back in her Eames chair, reading, her laptop open, a cigarette stubbed out in the ashtray, spectacles resting above her eyebrows.

'Hi.'

She looks up, not displaying surprise. She places the book on the desk and rocks forward in her chair. She taps her spectacles on to her nose and, with a little wrinkle and a gentle right-to-left shove with her finger, settles them into the correct position.

'I didn't expect to see you again.'

'Didn't you get my email?'

The side-to-side tremble of her curls indicates no.

'May I come in?' I don't wait for permission. I shift the armchair to the centre of the room.

'So why are you here, mystery man?' There is no warmth in this, little sign of her earlier interest in me.

I glance up at the Cartier-Bresson.

'How is Storaro?' More deception.

Francesca jerks one shoulder – doesn't know, doesn't care. 'Why are you here?'

'I wanted to see you.'

'Why?'

'There are things . . .'

'What things? Are you not a policeman?'

'No, I'm a policeman. I was a policeman.'

'You haven't come to confess to the murder of that man and his wife, have you?'

'No.'

Another shrug, a question asked to herself.
'Maybe I should go.'
'It's up to you. You're lucky you caught me.'
'Can I ask why you're being like this?'
'I can't think of any good reason for you being here. I'm busy.'
'I wanted to see you. My marriage is probably over.'
'I don't understand how the two things are connected.'
'Yes, you do. And there are other things. Things I'm not going to talk about here.'
Francesca pulls off her spectacles and places them on her laptop. 'Where then?'
'I don't know.'
She lights a cigarette, rocks back. 'I was honest with you last week because I didn't think I was going to see you again. Now you've turned up you embarrass me. You should have stayed away.'
'I'm sorry.'
'How long are you in Florence this time?'
'I'm leaving later today. Tonight.'
'Will you be coming back?'
'I don't know. I doubt it.'
'So I'm going to have to get over not seeing you again – again? Why did you come here? Did you think about its effect on me?'
'No.'
Francesca stubs out her cigarette, stands and walks around the desk and perches on the edge

facing me. A position of interrogation, seduction. 'Have you left your wife?'

I shake my head.

'Then why are you here?'

'You're right. I should go.'

'Maybe.'

I stare up at her. 'You are quite extraordinary.'

Again, the one-shoulder shrug – yes, possibly, but she doesn't care.

I stand, my hands stretched tensely, palms taut, fingers sharply splayed out.

'You seem anxious.'

'Will you meet me later? It won't take much time. Please.'

My desperation is sudden. It transmits forcefully. Francesca stares into my eyes. I let her look into me, read me. After a moment she returns to her chair, replaces her spectacles to the ridge of her brow and picks up her novel.

'Come to my home. Eight o'clock.'

'Thank you.'

'Do you want to have a last look round while you're here?'

I am not sure. There are things to do. To prepare. But I am full of white light and white noise – bursting with it; I need to calm down.

'Thank you.'

Francesca calls Silvio. He is instructed to give 'this man' an hour in the main gallery. Then in a whisper to me, 'You know, if you steal anything, we'll have to run away together.'

'You need to read other books.'

Francesca closes the book, a long finger keeping her place. 'I know. But look around you – I'm thirty-seven and I'm surrounded by dust and old things. A girl's got to find her excitement somewhere.'

'Excitement is overrated.'

She opens the book again. 'I'll see you tonight.'

I am escorted to the gallery floor. Silvio tells me he will be back at three p.m. to escort me out. When I am alone I stare down at the *cortile* for a full five minutes until my head clears, my mind ceasing to be a cubist rendering of Francesca's office with Francesca still beautiful, but angular, tough, lacking her sweetness. I then sit down on a bench, lean back against the wall. I can still hear Francesca asking me: why are you here? I imagined the answer to be straightforward, so straightforward, I now realize, I didn't bother fixing it inside myself. In the taxi to the airport, at the airport, on the plane, I told myself I was going for the gun and to make good the story I told her, and to tell her about the Caravaggio. But isn't it more simple than that? Sarah has rejected me and Francesca only days ago declared . . . what? The possibility of a new beginning, and right now that's what I need – the correct context: not an end of things but something to give me impetus, to head south full of energy, full of desire, full of adventure. Am I looking to Francesca to supplant the mad tragic reasons for doing what I am doing with honest heroic ones? Am I looking for a reason beyond myself?

Francesca – beautiful, sexy, playful, sweet. Eros' honey trap. The worst kind. The first kind. The purest kind. The truly intoxicating kind. Is *this* why I am here? I need intoxication? That extra madness? Certainly Sarah's sanity would mean doing this for her would have failure in-built; she'd never go for the romance of it, the delirium of it – these things not easily ignited in her. I sit forward, head in my hands. I picture Francesca sitting back in her chair, the romance novel in her hand. Has she ever read one about the recapture of a missing masterpiece? I guess there must be one; there have certainly been films, with handsome action heroes doing similar things with romantic inclinations. There is little originality, then, in what I am doing. Is that why I am here? Francesca will fall for it. *She* will be ignited by the romance, the delirium of it. She will look at me and see a romantic lead, an impossibility in Sarah. I laugh into my hands. Has it come to this? Shopping around for someone to believe in me.

I stand, feeling weary, weak and pathetic, and not someone heroic, romantic, to be believed in.

I stroll along the two great corridors, hands in pockets, stopping occasionally to peer into a room. I feel like a head of security.

Silvio is waiting for me at three and I am silently shown out, left by the door with an enigmatic smile. Does he know who I am? Had I come here and done my job properly, would I have discovered it was Silvio planning to help the Mafia break in?

From the Uffizi, I walk to the station to hire a car. I choose an Audi A3. Compact and powerful. Silver. A mirror beneath the southern sun. I drive back to the apartment through empty streets. I park close to the wall and climb out of the passenger-side door.

Before I leave for Francesca's, I make sure everything is prepared; I will leave directly from there. I take the money out of the attaché case and carefully replace it, leaving a space for the gun; I spend time making the gun snug, no rattle. Two-thirds of the space is a hard block of cash, the other third – jammed in – the hard shape of the gun. I pack away my laptop, its cabling, the mobile charger. I then give the apartment a quick tidy: cups washed, sinks and bath wiped down, bed ordered, furniture back in place. It is seven o'clock when I am finished.

On the street I open the boot of the car, drop in my bag, shut the boot – the catch is soft. I place the attaché case on the passenger seat. My overcoat, folded with the lining out, is draped along the back seat. I slide my mobile into the small tray by the handbrake. I start the engine, switch on the lights, check the settings against the rear of a car parked in front. The radio takes time to tune: World Service, an Italian news station, a music station. I stay on the music station: *Il trovatore* – a little muscular Italian opera just right for my short journey.

The drive to Francesca's takes longer than I expect, my route confounded by one-way systems, the heavier traffic of Florence out for dinner. However, I am still early when I park behind the Smart Car. I listen to the end of the opera. I take the attaché case in with me; I leave the mobile in the car.

Just like it was ten days ago, the archway is a complete dark. It is only when I have passed through a few steps of darkness that sensors switch on the lights – two high spots crossing me. There are three doors. The nameplate on the right – Rovezzano. In the centre – Harrison. I press the bell to the door on the left.

Francesca answers quickly, smiling, ushering me into a long hallway. She is wearing jeans, a black roll-neck sweater, Birkenstocks. She points to the attaché case.

'What's in there?'

'I didn't want to leave it in the car.'

'The car?'

'Hire car. I'm leaving tonight.'

She nods at this as if assessing what it means; she didn't expect me to be leaving by car.

'South,' I say by way of explanation.

'You are free to go wherever you want.'

She leads me down the hallway into a large split-level sitting room. The ceiling is vaulted, with exposed beams and brickwork. The room is lit by two tall lamps standing next to the two shuttered windows, shutters closed. The walls are hung with artwork: a Peter Halley (from Storaro, I presume), a Persian rug, a medieval tapestry – everything dark, a long or square shadow. In the lower section of the room – three white-painted stone steps lower – there is a small log fire inside a big open stone hearth. Opposite the fire are a long low table and a long low sofa. Francesca leads me down, offering the sofa; she sits on the floor, cross-legged, elbows on the table, hands cradling her face. She is relaxed and expectant, looking for me to talk, explain. There is no intimacy in her manner, apart from the girlishness of her position looking up at me.

I try to get comfortable, sunk deeply into the sofa. I sit forward, push myself back, try leaning left, then right. All the while Francesca watches. I give up and slide on to the floor, crossing my legs, folding my arms flat on the table. Francesca is up.

'Wine?'

I stare into the fire, searching for small talk, something to call out: a question, an observation – the natural thing to do.

'Your house is very nice.'

Francesca, with a bottle of white wine in one hand, two glasses in the other, says, 'I'm very happy here.'

She rejoins me around the coffee table, slides a glass over to me and pours. I notice a slight shake

315

in her hand. I pick up my glass and sip. I can't think of a follow-up question. Francesca doesn't seem impatient to talk. I notice two small speakers either side of the fireplace.

'If you were to put on some music, what would it be?'

Francesca shakes her head; her curls swing vigorously – she doesn't like the question. 'That's a boy thing.'

'What – music?'

'Thinking about music like that.'

'Like what?'

'People think music is romantic, but it's not – it's distracting. If we were lovers and had the same taste, and the moment was right, then maybe.'

I look around the room. 'I suppose I imagined your place to be very modern. Hard lines. Light.'

'Like my office?'

'Yes.'

'This is my home.'

'Which is most you?'

'They are both me. Why shouldn't they be?'

'I don't know. Most people are consistent – without surprise.'

'I'm cooking us some food. I don't want to go out. What time do you have to leave?'

'No fixed time.'

'Are you going to tell me where you're going?'

'Probably. But I need to know I can trust you.'

'How will you know that?'

'I have to decide.'

'How do you know I haven't already gone to the police and told them I think you had something to do with that man and his wife?'

'Have you?'

'What do you think?' She stares directly at me, eyes wide. She wants me to judge her – to judge her correctly by reading her, by making the effort to look into her. She likes overt collusion.

I pause before answering, delighting in her big brown eyes, stopping at them. 'It hadn't occurred to me you would. I don't think you've thought about doing that for a moment.'

'You'll never know.'

'Which is how it works.'

Francesca sips her wine for the first time. 'Maybe.'

We are silent. The fire spits, hisses, crackles – rearranges itself.

'I keep asking myself why I'm here.'

'You should.'

'What do you think?'

'I think you are back because you say your marriage is over.'

'What do you think about that?'

'It is predictable.'

'Did you predict it?'

'I didn't know your marriage was over. I thought you were gone. Am I surprised you are back? Maybe you have other reasons.'

Has Storaro talked to her? It's the first time this has occurred to me. Would he be foolish enough to tell someone in Francesca's position, someone at the centre of the art establishment, that the painting was definitely still out there? Maybe it just slipped out. Enjoying an old battle, he realized he might romance her with the idea of going after it, enjoying something of the gangster glamour, the glory of a recovery on himself.

'What other reasons?'

'You're a mysterious man.'

'Not really.'

'Where are you going when you leave here?'

'It's difficult.'

Her point is well made.

'As I said, I'll have to get over you again.'

'Yes, you did say that – it's very honest, but I'm not sure what it means.'

'It means what it says. I think I said right at the beginning I'm not interested in long-distance relationships. I have a lot of rules. Maybe that's why I'm still alone.'

'What other rules do you have?'

'I discover them as I go along.'

'Aren't we all like that?'

'Maybe I like you, maybe I don't. I'm not sure myself. But it's irrelevant. You're leaving. And even if you came back, you'd be off again. I don't fall in love that way any more.'

'How do you fall in love these days?'

'I try not to.'

'Just read romances instead.'

'I did that before.'

Her expression from our first night at dinner returns: playful smile, serious eyes.

'I don't get you.'

'Is that why you're here? I intrigue you. That would be boring.'

I look away. 'Why boring?'

'Because that's what all men think and I'm not that interesting. I've told you, I'm charming and efficient.'

'That's at work.'

'Maybe that's all I am.'

'People are less straightforward.'

'I don't care to analyse.'

'Clearly you do.'

'No, I think about things; there's a difference.'

Francesca tops up my glass; I notice how little she is drinking.

I think for a moment: Sarah's charming and efficient. That's not what I get from Francesca. Underneath the playfulness there's too much raw unhappiness, which is not the product of charm and efficiency – that just produces toughness, smooth discontent.

'I'm not sure love in its purest sense – its break-your-heart sense – is available to us much past thirty.'

Francesca picks up her glass, then replaces it without drinking. She lights a cigarette, locating an ashtray from under the table. 'That would be sad.'

'I think we only get one killer heartbreak and by

our age the chances are that's already happened. And by our age we know too much about ourselves. We become professionals and professionals don't get hurt, don't allow it; they don't get emotionally involved.'

'Are you saying past thirty we don't get emotionally involved, even in relationships? That would be quite something. What about you and your wife?'

'All I'm saying . . .' I glance around the room, my hand following. 'How many times have you done this? This – exactly. You sitting there, man here, wine, a conversation not dissimilar to this? More than once, I'm sure. A few aspects will always differ but much of it will have been the same.'

'Is this how you were with your wife?'

'Basically.'

'In what ways are you being different – you said a few aspects will always differ?'

'I'm speaking Italian.'

'That doesn't count.'

'I think it does, but it's not important.'

'Do you want to know how I am being different?'

'You're not drinking so much?'

'Listen to me!' Her anger is a flare, a brown light in her face – sharply bright, quickly gone.

'Ever since I met you I've let myself be carried along by my feelings. It doesn't sound like much, especially to a man – that's what they do every time – but for a woman, it's very difficult. For me it's very difficult. In the romances I read it is always this way, but not in life – women are more controlled.'

I know what is being said, but I want to be sure, to draw her out, to hear her say it. 'Why?'

Francesca pauses, sips her wine, draws on her cigarette.

'The snow.' A plume of smoke follows.

'The snow?'

'Yes. I thought it would be romantic to fall in love in the snow.'

She looks directly at me, wanting to be believed. She wants her reason, however flippant it might sound, to be accepted as legitimate, credible, and not just a product of the books she reads. I keep my eyes on her open, warm face. I want to believe her, believe that I am lovable so soon after being unloved. However, I don't want to be played with, so my response is cool.

'It does make a difference.'

Francesca throws this off with a little jerk of her shoulder. 'But it's all gone now. And as you say, we've done this all before.'

'Do you want to know why this is different for me? I'm in love with someone else but I'd rather be here, in love with you.'

She doesn't like this: it feels cheap, too easy. 'Maybe you should go back to your wife.'

'I don't think she'd take me back. Besides, I have something I need to do.'

'What is that?'

'As I said, I need to trust you.'

A small log shifts in the fire. There is a burst of flames.

Francesca shifts up from sitting cross-legged to kneeling. 'The food should be ready.'

I watch her as she stands. She pulls at the hem of her pullover, pushes at the hips of her jeans with the heels of her hands, shakes her curls with one quick, tiny right-to-left tremor of her head – movements to reassemble herself from potential lover to no-nonsense hostess.

'Let me help.'

'No, I'll only be a couple of minutes.'

I lean back on the sofa, for the second time today anchoring myself with arms wide. I am looking to take up space, to be firmly present, to feel justified in being where I am. It doesn't work. I am fighting lightness, expectation, momentum. The situation doesn't feel real; too many of the fundamentals of fantasy are present. Only the end of my marriage can be real at the moment.

But why? Why can't Sarah, our marriage, be the fantasy? Certainly she was a fantasy catch. And I am certain that what I feel now has sensations which cannot be dismissed. The aliveness of desire in my hands, desire as a physical impulse to reach through space to Francesca and press that space away, has a vibrating energy which must come from bodies in space reacting to one another, rather than a dreamlike yearning to possess, to overcome oneself in the possession. And if there is one thing I am most certain about, it is that

Francesca, overflowing in beauty, honesty, sweet-ness, is not a fantasy. She has vibrated as fully human from the moment I first saw her.

Francesca stands above me with big white bowls. 'Can you take these?'

I kneel across the sofa and take them from her lowered hands. 'Now pass me the wine and glasses.'

I do as instructed. Francesca leaves and quickly returns with a bottle of red wine, open, and fresh glasses, and cutlery bundled together.

I stare into my bowl – couscous and lamb.

'I hope you like it. It's North African.'

I pour the wine; we clink, drink. The subject of conversation turns to gallery business – a Titian exhibition to be held in the summer. The Uffizi's plans over the next ten years, her role in that as part of the strategy team. She shakes her head at the prospect. Doesn't bear thinking about. We then move on to Storaro. He's been a nightmare, she says. Calls her up, makes an arrangement, cancels.

'I'm surprised he hasn't called. I don't usually miss Monday nights with him.'

'Have you told him the truth about me?'

'No. You must understand, in Storaro's world you were an interference for a week or so. Finding you interesting was incidental. I'm sorry.'

'Fuck him,' I say in English.

'Yes, fuck him,' Francesca echoes, laughing. Then with a mock wince, she says, 'Let's hope he hasn't had my apartment bugged. Otherwise we're all in big trouble.'

I laugh. Francesca looks up to the ceiling. 'Hello, Storaro, if you're there – don't worry, nothing's happened. We're eating, we've got our clothes on – it's all perfectly innocent.'

Her ignorance over his limited love moves me. But then Storaro's limits are vast compared to others', his desire for her is still a battle that needs strenuous effort on her part.

I push my bowl to one side. Rub my face. The world would be a weary place even without war, famine, pestilence. Francesca yawns. Apologizes.

I look at my watch. I need to go soon. I don't imagine that convoys of squad cars are heading south, lights spiralling in the darkness, but I do know the south is now the focus of good minds, with knowledge, contacts, deep resources, with a determination based on the dynamics of professional pride, moral outrage, public service. Healthy motivators. However, I also know that they will be slow-moving, risk-averse, bureaucratically impeded.

And there will also be Storaro. He will not rely on me. I will not be his only line of attack. He will have released money – the promise of money. Rumour will be travelling south – millions will be pledged for its rescue. Outstripping the government reward by some margin.

I might know more than all of them, have a straighter, clearer course to get close, but I know I am not alone in this.

'This thing I'm going to do . . .'

'Wait.' Her hand is raised.

'What?'

She looks at me, chews her top lip, shunts her eyes left. Her breathing is on hold. 'I want to come with you.'

It takes a few seconds to make sense to me. She repeats it, quietly, a whisper, but with greater emphasis, meaning it.

My answer is firm, with an ironic laugh. 'Forget it. No way.'

'Why?'

'Because you can't. That's all. Forget it. You don't even know what I'm going to do. Why take that risk?'

'I've told you: I'm letting myself be carried along by my feelings.'

'But that was when it was snowing.'

'Maybe the memory of snow is enough.'

'It's not. Believe me.'

'That's not for you to decide.'

'What if it gets dangerous?'

'Will it?'

'Possibly.'

Francesca picks up my bowl and places it in hers and stands. 'Wait.' She leaves the room. I don't know quite what to think and shake my head in disbelief. I should go now.

I hear her re-enter the room. 'You think it's mad, don't you? Maybe it is. I don't know what you're doing. You've already lied to me once. Then there's that man and his poor wife. And then letting myself be carried along by my feelings, that's just a thing you say – a thing you say in this game we're playing. But it doesn't have to be a game. What you're doing isn't a game, is it? You're trying to escape something. I've worked that much out. Maybe I am, too. Being charming and efficient – I'm tired of it. I'm tired of my life. What does it consist of? My work. Dust and old things, as I've said. And pandering to Storaro. That's it. And I drink too much, if you haven't noticed.' She pauses, takes a breath. 'And then it snowed and you showed up. I don't think I'm in love with you. And anyway, you love your wife. But whatever it is you're going to do, as long as it's not going to get me killed – I want to come along.'

I stand, turn, look up at her: she's holding two small plates with a single dome of ice cream on each, small spoons pointing over the sides.

It is my turn to say, 'Wait.'

I leave the room and return with the attaché case. 'Look in here.' I flip open the latches, open the lid and display the sharp packs of money, the sharp shape of the gun. Francesca parts the plates and looks in.

I try to make it as clear as I can. 'You're right, it's not a game – it's very serious. And it's not official, either. It's just me. Me. OK?' I shut the lid of the case, press down the latches and place it on the floor.

'I understand.'

'What do you understand?'

'That it's serious. And it's just you. But I still want to come.'

'What about your work?'

'I'll call in sick.'

'Forget it.'

'No.'

'Francesca, you can't come.'

'You need me to approve of this – that's why you're here.'

'I'm not sure it's approval I'm after. But whatever it is, it still doesn't mean I have to let you come.'

'You're right.'

Francesca steps around me, the ice cream melting on the plates, and sits down by the coffee table. She gestures for me to join her. 'Eat.'

I sit down. 'Look at me.'

Francesca glances up, small spoon upside down in her mouth. She pulls it out. 'What?'

'That money.' I gesture with a flick of my head. 'I got that money by selling illegally excavated Greek vases, bought from the dead man, to Gustav Ballack. Have you heard of him?' Francesca shakes her head. 'He's a very powerful man in the art black market. I sold them to him for twice the amount I paid for them. I borrowed the initial money from my wife. The gun is, was, Nenni's. I want you to know what I had to do to get to where I am tonight – to be able to do the thing I'm going to try to do. Do you understand?' Francesca nods.

'If I hadn't been solely concerned with myself, I would have realized the person that killed them didn't want the money and I could have told him to get himself and his wife as far from Naples as possible. I didn't do that. Do you understand?' She nods again. 'OK.' I pause. 'Now, if you are sure you understand that, I am going to give you one opportunity to come with me. One only. But you must agree that if I make you this offer and you refuse, that's it – we forget this whole conversation, you let me go on my way and you don't speak to anyone about this.'

Francesca leans over and digs her spoon into my ice cream. 'OK.'

She is listening – expression serious but for the eating of ice cream. She'll back out when it comes to it, I am sure.

I don't say anything until the plan formulating in my head is clear to me. It's then a list and set of instructions that I give her. 'I need Uffizi stationery. Something no one from the outside could have. I need your personnel file. And I need a painting – something from the archive. Doesn't have to be anything valuable, but it must look impressive.' I then open my arms, hands in profile to illustrate a large square – sides first, then top and bottom. 'About that big. To fit into a hatchback.'

'Why?'

I look directly at Francesca. 'You're going to be my honey trap.'

Francesca lays her spoon across the plate. 'Does this make what you're doing easier?'

'Possibly. But you cannot think about that.'

'Maybe if I say yes, you'll arrest me right now – how do I know you're not recording this?'

I laugh. 'Of course. My original assignment. You'll just have to trust me.'

'How do I do that?'

'I don't know.'

'What you're asking isn't that difficult. My personnel file is probably harder to get than the painting.'

'Are you agreeing?'

'It changes things.'

'I know. You're not coming along for the ride.'

She taps her spoon on the side of the plate and takes off her spectacles. Her eyes appear smaller, narrower, too small for her face, giving her an intense, youthful look. Vulnerable again. Lonely. I watch her think through the proposition. Once again her eyes shunt to the left, rest in thought, and then dart back. For a moment she stares into the middle distance, beyond me, before staring down, her gaze in her lap. Her lips are pursed. She then looks up and glances quickly to the right and back again to the left – a circular thought needing chasing. It all ends with a still stare inward, eyes ever so slightly to the left, ever so slightly narrowed, gaze now fully trained on the central question.

'Francesca?'

'What would you prefer – me or to go alone?'

I pause. The right answer is easy, but she does make it simpler: she gives me a plan. 'To go alone.'

'Really?'

'Of course.'

'I'll get you what you want.' It is said matter of factly.

I reach across the table and take hold of Francesca's wrist, pulling her slightly towards me; she has to shift position to accommodate me.

'What is it?'

'What you are doing is foolish. Foolish and dangerous. The only reason I'm even considering this is because most people would think that what I'm doing is foolish and dangerous. We have no support, no back-up. As I said, it's just me.'

'And me.' This is said with equal matter of factness, but contained within is her wish that I accept her now as my partner in this, whatever it is I am doing.

I add, 'And let's add, just to make it all the more clear: it is not illegal.'

For a second, I think I notice a faint look of disappointment on Francesca's face.

'I understand,' she says with a little mock seriousness, as if she is taking orders from a superior. The playfulness is returning; she cannot resist it.

'I should never have come here.'

'Why?'

'Because this is mad.'

'But you're doing it.'

She's missed my point. 'I *have* to.'

'At our age we don't *have* to do anything.' She lights a cigarette, offers the packet to me.

'I don't smoke,' I say irritably, adding impatiently, 'and we have to leave tonight. Soon.'

'Fine.'

'Can you get into the gallery tonight without making anyone suspicious?'

Francesca replaces her spectacles. 'I should go alone. In my car.'

I drop my head into my hands. 'I should leave right now.'

'But you're not going to.'

I look up. 'I'm waiting for you to come to your senses.'

'I'm not a sensible woman.'

'Then let's go.'

'Really?'

She offers the perfect deal. 'Yes.'

Her smile is wide – she is super-pleased, breathing on hold for the second time tonight. My response – my smile – is wry, uncertain, tired.

Francesca is on her feet. 'I'll call Silvio on my mobile, from the car. I'll tell him I'm going away for a few days. I need some papers. We'll just have to hope no one sees me leave with the painting. Does it need to be framed?'

'Definitely.'

'And why my personnel file?'

'To prove who you are.' I stand. 'OK. You need to go. Any later and it will look suspicious. If anyone stops you, you've been out to dinner and you're on your way home and remembered something you need. If you're not back within one hour, I'll be gone.'

'I need to pack some things.'

'I'll do that.'

'Give me five minutes.'

'No. I'll pack for you. You'll have everything you need.'

At the front door she turns, presses a foot on my foot, looks up into my face. 'How do I know you're not just going to leave?'

'You don't.'

'Are you?'

'One hour.'

The complete dark of the courtyard is only marginally dented by the soft light of the hallway. Francesca steps out and waves her arms out in front of her to activate the light sensor. 'Wish me luck.'

I watch her pass through the arch and turn left to her car. The lights go out.

Francesca's bedroom is through the sitting room at the back of the apartment; it has the same fireplace. It is a large room: white walls, darkly varnished floorboards. The bed is high with a white duvet and large white square pillows. Above the bed is another Peter Halley. To the right of the bed is a small table with a phone, a lamp and a small twist of books – romances. I sit down and take the one from the top. 'Can a woman love two men? Men who are enemies? Both great lovers, both killers.' I replace it asking myself: can a man love two women? Opposite the bed are two large mahogany chests of drawers. Between two exposed beams there is a packed clothes pole with some items in dry-cleaning bags. Underneath there is an uneven line of shoes sitting on their boxes. The door of an en suite bathroom is ajar. The bathroom is small, compact; no bath, just a shower. I find an empty washbag. I choose a shampoo from a selection of three, all open; a conditioner from a choice of two; shaving foam and two razors. I open a small cabinet above the basin, drop in a small packet of tampons, a packet of aspirin. Her toothbrush is electric and charging; I decide to pick up a manual or travel-electric on our way. I flip closed the lid of the toothpaste and drop that into the bag. I pull a tube of cotton pads from around the handle of the cabinet and collect together make-up remover, moisturizer, cleanser. The cosmetics I leave for her to pack. I zip up the bag and go back into the bedroom. I find a medium-sized suitcase under the bed. I open the first drawer of the bigger of the two chests: photographs, jewellery, her passport (I flick to the photo, look for date of issue – five years ago; she looks a little younger, otherwise she is unchanged). I quickly shuffle through the photos – places, sights: New York, Paris, Russia, somewhere in South-East Asia. Her and a guy. Buddhist temples below grey skies. Smiles and kisses in the foreground. I close the drawer. Next one down: T-shirts, light sweaters – boutique brands, well cared for. I pick out the cardigan she had on the first time I met her, two sweaters, three T-shirts, one from the Tate Modern – a surprise. I find chunkier sweaters in the deep bottom drawer; they expand as I pull the drawer out – I have to press them down to shut it. I step sideways to the chest's smaller neighbour. First of the two top drawers: bras. I pull out a black one – sheer, no lace – and lay it across the top of the chest, then a white one made of sturdy lace, followed by a pale-green one. Next drawer along: pants – twenty, thirty pairs. I search for those that match the bras, knowing this might be something to get right, and then pick out a few more, without prejudice. I do my best to fold them carefully and pack them away with the sweaters. In the lower drawers I find some DKNY combat trousers, some Levis; I throw them on to the bed. The clothes on the pole seem to be mostly for work. I unhook the long linen dress she was wearing when we first met, a black fitted shirt, a green shirt almost the same colour as the bra. I lay these all out on the bed before folding everything neatly and packing them away. She can decide on shoes. I zip up the case and return to the sitting room, drop it next to the attaché case.

I go into the kitchen and open the fridge. I pour myself a glass of San Pellegrino. I feel focused despite the change of plan – or rather because of the plan Francesca's coming has offered me. In deal terms it's perfect. Beautiful woman, central to the Uffizi, access all areas – the promises I can now make to Lomazzo. Along with a great story: ex-cop and lover on the make. Be as transparent as possible. We're looking for a big payday. Want to go and live . . . where? . . . South-East Asia. Become Buddhists. I go back into the bedroom, open the drawer with the photographs in and skim through them. I need a couple of the location. A couple of Francesca looking happy. One with me. Or rather the presence of me – an expression on her face, a point, laughter at the camera. I select six, dump the rest. They go into a pocket of the attaché case. I listen at the front door. Dark silence. She's been gone just over twenty minutes. I have little doubt she'll be back. But do I wait longer than the hour? Yes – the limit was primarily to focus her.

I sit down on the floor, my back to the door, staring down the hallway at the uppermost glow of the fire. So why's she doing this? Is it really to escape dust and old things? To escape her charm and efficiency? For a bit of excitement? Or is it like she said, she has decided she must follow her feelings? I cannot blame her for that. Maybe she is in love with me, or at least thinks she is due to the snow and has taken the decision that that is somehow enough for an adventure. But why take the specific risk of coming with me? She knows what she's getting involved in. She's seen the blood on my shoes, the blood of a man who only days later was murdered. Perhaps she doesn't remember that you don't have to take this kind of risk. Maybe after a year or two without love you forget this. Desperation is forgetful. Or maybe she has been persuaded by the novels she reads that adventure is the only path to true love? Maybe it is. Maybe you do need to submit yourself, offer yourself up. And not so much to the straightforward emotional risk-taking stuff, but the life-changing, shifting from singleton to – I laugh – partners-in-crime stuff. Maybe. Either way, right now she feels it is worth taking the risk because something in her fears that if she doesn't all the love talk, all the sex talk, and the emotional leaps and swells that inspire it – stuff she *does* remember – will become as ossified as all the art talk that she hears interminably at the gallery, everywhere in the city, endlessly from Storaro and his cronies. She is taking this risk because deep down she hopes it will revitalize something in her – her internal vista – a place she has got bored staring at, living alone, wandering Florence's 'too beautiful' streets, surrounded by dust and old things at work. The question she was asking herself earlier that required such a strong focus once she'd caught the answer was: what's the alternative? She is taking the risk for the same reason as me.

I look at my watch. She's been gone exactly an hour. I mentally trace the route. This time of night: ten minutes each way maximum, giving her thirty–forty minutes inside the Uffizi. Surely enough time. I open the door. If I concentrate, I can hear cars speeding along the Arno embankment. I shut the door. Perhaps she's gone to the police. Explaining there's a man with money and a gun in her apartment, says he's a policeman, but he's also said he was a writer, and he knows that man, the man killed in Naples with his wife.

How much longer to give her? Five, ten minutes? I need to set a limit. I look at my watch: 11.36 p.m. Until midnight? I go back into the sitting room and take a sip of red wine. A car door – something like a car door. I listen, wait – nothing. I go back to the front door and open it. Silence and darkness. I step out – two steps – into the realm of the light sensor and into brightness. I pass under the arch and into the street. I assume she'll be coming from the right. The light behind me switches off. I stare down to the end of the street, through the ancient city gates, to the grey, misty light of the small piazza. Light rain hits my forehead. I can't wait any longer. I go back inside, shut the door. I collect the attaché case. What about the fire? It is dying – a single short flame occasionally twisting from beneath a concave husk of black wood. I go out to the car, lay the attaché case on the front seat and climb in. I start the engine, turn on the lights and sit there, engine warming up, and peer into the rear-view mirror. Where *is* she? I cut the engine in frustration. A car passes the end of the road. For a moment my heart races, hand going to the door handle. It's not her. I slam a palm against the steering wheel. I want her with me. I don't want to do this alone – to be alone. Without her the whole enterprise now seems ridiculous – foolish, childish. I feel like I did on Saturday night: sitting at the table, food cooked, wine opened and no Sarah. The planning, energy, application wasted.

I start the car again, release the handbrake, clutch, turn the car around and roll down the hill. Maybe it's better this way. I take a deep breath and expel the air slowly. At the bottom of the hill I shift the car into gear and pull out on to the small piazza, turn right, then left and right again, heading east along the Arno. After three hundred metres I pull up sharply and double back on myself, cross the river and drive along the embankment to the Uffizi. I park up on the pavement, cut the lights, the engine. Everything around is quiet and dark and still. I don't know why I am here, what I am looking for. Her car? I suppose that if something has happened, if she'd got caught leaving with a painting, there would be activity. There is nothing. No one is about. Maybe she's gone to find Storaro, prowling the city for tall, blonde American girls. Between the apartment and gallery she finally saw sense and needed his devotion to make her act sensibly. What will he say? Will his devotion see the weakness in her, her fervent vulnerability – coming to him after pleading with me? Of course, instantly. His big little chest will heave with the opportunity. What

338

can she tell him? That I am leaving to go somewhere; nothing he doesn't know, although my not
having left yet will irritate him, my willingness to
take her will frustrate him. He will not gain. The
clock on the dash says 12.15 p.m. This is what I
feared: the straightforward distraction, driving
around Florence looking for her when I should
be on my way. This was meant to be done alone,
for me – to change myself, *my* internal vista. I do
a U-turn and head back to her home; I cannot
stop myself. I know my way out of the city, but
can't take it. Last chance, I say to myself: if she's
not there . . .

I turn into her street and stop, click the lights
on to full beam: a white blaze coats the cobbles
and walls of the narrow street and reaches into
the night. The Smart Car is not there. She *must*
be with Storaro. My mobile rings, vibrating in the
plastic tray. Does she have my number? I flip it
open: 'HOME'. I hesitate, picturing Sarah asleep
on the floor in the grey light. Once again my mind
is filled with the room, the tall room, the heavy
drapes, the darkness, the scar of Sarah underneath
the alpaca blanket. How long has it been since I
left? Two days. I press *accept*, but she's gone. Will
she leave a message? I wait for the beeps. No
message. My thumb hovers over the *1*: home. What
will I say? There is nothing to say, not yet, even
if she wants me back, which I doubt. I ignore the
sharp contraction of my stomach. I close the
mobile, toss it on to the passenger seat and reverse

sharply into the piazza. No more madness. Go – drive. There is still the idea behind the plan, if not the material to back it up. I pull out of the piazza just as the Smart Car appears from the other side. I skid to a halt, yank up the handbrake. I cross to her hurriedly. A large flat square object covered in a black cloth is on the back seat. She opens her door.

'Sorry.'

'Drive back to the house. Go inside. I've packed your bag. You just need shoes – shoes you can walk in – and make-up.'

She pulls the door shut and swings the car into her street. I reverse into the piazza and all the way up until my car is parallel with hers. I transfer the painting into the boot of the Audi, taking a cursory look – bright Madonna and child, big gilt frame. I lock the car and go into the house, the court-yard lights still on from Francesca passing through. I find her in the bedroom, packing cosmetics; on the chest is a pair of Camper boots, drooping like rabbit's ears.

'Thank you for waiting.'

'I didn't wait.'

'It's twelve-thirty – you waited.'

'What happened?'

'I'll tell you later. I have everything.'

'Then let's go.'

In the sitting room Francesca stokes down the fire, brushing all the embers and ash into a pile at the back. I pick up her suitcase and head down the hallway. Francesca follows with boots in one hand and cosmetics bag in the other.

Outside, both car boots open, I take the Campers and cosmetics bag from Francesca, arrange my bag, her stuff and the painting. She opens the passenger door of her car, then the glove compartment, and pulls out a file. I climb into the Audi, shove the attaché case over on to the back seat, replace my mobile in the tray next to the handbrake. Francesca gets in, opens the glove compartment and slides the file on top of the maps. I pause, thinking, listing. I know what I have packed for myself, for her, the attaché case is in the back, the painting in the boot and the other stuff I wanted, I assume, is in the glove compartment. Everything. I start the engine, switch on the lights. I hear, feel, sense Francesca drag over her seat belt and lock it in. I do the same. OK, I say to myself, Remember: this is just a little adventure. Just a little adventure. Isn't that right, maestro?

PART THREE

CALABRIA, FRANCESCA AND 'NDRANGHETA

1

The night is gloss black. The sky above the night is a thinner black. The stars have perfect centres. Pluckable. The countryside beyond the *autostrada* is ridged with heavy folds of different darks – forest dark, olive dark, mountain dark. The car is quick, powerful, pulling ahead of the trucks from Milano, Torino. Francesca adjusts her seat – sliding it back, pushing her headrest lower – settling in for the long drive, as always angled towards the centre of the car, the other occupant. I adjust the air conditioner, the fan, the vents, roll my shoulders, looking to relax, preparing for the concentration needed on a long straight road, to keep a high speed steady, directed.

We have said little since leaving the centre of Florence. Francesca said she will get us to Rome, past Rome without referring to maps. I said we will stop at dawn wherever we are, we won't make it all the way to Calabria. She doesn't display any surprise this is where we are heading. She's never been to Calabria – that's bad, isn't it? I shrug – there's not much down there. Rugged, harsh sun; burnt land in the summer. In the winter, I don't know. Ancient Greece is everywhere, a few feet under the ground. It's temple land: Apollo, Venus, Persephone. Francesca nods, enthused about the trip, the unknown. She hasn't asked what we are doing, not even in a roundabout way. As we left Florence and joined the *autostrada* she did place her hand on my thigh for a moment. I didn't respond outwardly; inwardly I felt warmth, excitement, and looked across at her as she withdrew her hand. I only had a second to watch her without her noticing; she was smiling, eyes wide, staring out into the night ahead of us. Her face had lost some of its sophistication, its northern stylishness, and had become a little more open and starry, whatever had kept her so long at the gallery seemingly forgotten.

I look into the rear-view mirror. How open and starry is my face now? I squint, muscles tight and tense. I take a hand off the steering wheel and rub my eyes, wanting them to adopt a new gaze. All this is to be enjoyed: being with Francesca, the road trip, the plan, the recovery, the escape. I want there to be photos like those with the Buddhist-temple guy, evidence of a good time, of romance, laughter, smiles, kisses in the foreground. We'll need a camera, I think. But that's not the point – the point is that my mission has changed. It is about something more fundamental now, offering so much more than glory. I yawn. Shunt my eyes back to the mirror. I am tired. I doubt I'll make it to daybreak. Signs for Roma, the south flash past. I turn to Francesca. 'How are you feeling?'

'Fine. Great. What about you?'

'Good. Tired.'

'Do you want to stop?'

I shake my head. 'I'll be OK.'

'Do you want to talk?'

'What about?'

'Anything.'

I pause. 'My wife called earlier. When I was waiting for you. I didn't answer it. She didn't leave a message.'

'How did it make you feel?'

'Not sure. I'm trying to pretend . . . to blank her out.'

I turn back to the road, knowing Francesca is looking directly at me from the far corner of her seat, her thumb tucked under the seat belt, pushed out for a little slack, to allow for her position.

'Shouldn't you call her?'

'You are here, she isn't and never would be. I'm concentrating on you.'

'I like that.'

I think back to my trip with Nenni and our talk of wives. We were both so proud of our marriages, being married. The reasons must have been very different. I loved the fact of Sarah – present in the heart of London, busy and beautiful with a dynamism I could feel a thousand miles away. Not needing me. It compelled me to think of her. The fact of her so different from the look of me as a thing to like, to be compelled by. Perhaps she also liked the idea of me for a while: working-class hero. Working-class desperado. I snort at this. Is this the final act of a desperado, the real definition: heading into the night, a beautiful woman by his side, a case of black-market money and a gun from a dead *camorrista*, with one thing to do, which will be done, no matter what the risk?

Probably. I laugh. Francesca looks at me; I continue to laugh. 'Do you know what I do?'

'You're a policeman.' And then adding with a little mock-drama, 'An undercover cop.'

'Yes. But my dream was to have a job like yours. And to write. Write on art. But maybe that wasn't for me. I've been a policeman for over ten years, most of that time I've been in arts and antiques. I've been all over the world. I've met men who have just walked into galleries and taken pictures off the walls – some of the world's most famous and prized paintings. Not hardened criminals, not dangerous in the slightest; just opportunists, chancers, looking for a big pay-out. But I've also met killers, from Eastern Europe, South America, here. People who have carried out or ordered the most savage acts. And I've done bad things myself in this job. Bad things. But it's all been with one aim – get these artworks back. Didn't really care who for. Didn't like them usually – aristocrats mainly, looking down their noses at what I was doing for them. But that didn't matter, not really. I was just enraged that these people could do it. When an artwork is stolen there is a fifty per cent chance it will be destroyed. They're the odds. Sometimes it's by accident, but mostly it's through basic disregard or – can you believe this? – because something within the recovery plan – the ransom, the location, I don't know – pisses someone off. Destroyed because somehow a roll of canvas becomes a hindrance to them if we aren't jumping through enough hoops to make them feel powerful. Jesus, I've been moaning on and on about what I do for so long – I don't know, maybe I couldn't have done anything different. That's why I am one of the best. It's right for me.'

'You're like the men in the books I read.'

I laugh loudly. 'What do you think of that?'

Francesca pushes her thumb forward extending the seat belt, then releases it back across her chest. 'I suspected as much.'

'Yeah, right.' I pause. 'Do you want to know what we're doing?'

'If you want to tell me.'

'Do you know?'

'What do you mean?'

'Because Storaro already knows.'

She looks surprised, confused – suspicious. 'I don't understand.'

'Has Storaro talked to you about me?'

'I told you.' She is now irritated. She was promised information not an interrogation, a game.

'OK. I just wanted to know.' I pull out into the fast lane, overtake a truck. There is nothing before us, just swift darkness.

'Last year I was shown Caravaggio's *Nativity*.' My glance to her is quick. What I see is the information being processed in bold form: painter, painting, what is being implied. I help her out. 'And we're going to rescue it.'

Her expression is disbelief with the traces of her earlier suspicion still present.

'Of course. Everyone's been talking about it. Everyone but you and Storaro. All that time and you two knew one another.'

'No. I met him with you at the hotel. It's a long, stupid story. But we have come to an understanding now.'

'What understanding?'

'If he does what he can to clear the way for me and I recover it, he'll get the painting.'

'And what do you get?'

What do I say? You. I get you. Storaro offered you as an incentive. It's quite flattering after all – in his mind you are desirable enough to warrant such an offer.

'The glory, I guess.'

'Don't trust him.' She is firm.

'I don't. But I understand his passion. And passion is fifty per cent desire, fifty per cent fear.

350

He knows I have the best chance and he doesn't want to jeopardize that.'

Francesca is not impressed.

I press further down on the accelerator; the speed of the car is now a sensation in our bodies rather than purely visual, the elision of *autostrada* lights passing us. 'I saw it in Calabria. It was with a boss of a small *cosca*. He showed it to me. I don't know why. Maybe he didn't realize what it was; maybe he was old and wanted me to know he still had power, prestige.'

Francesca turns her face to the passenger-side window, mirror black. She looks at her reflection, her eyes, curls framing her face. 'How dangerous is it?'

'It's hard to say.'

She looks around, demands, 'How dangerous?'

'Do you regret coming along now?'

Francesca shakes her head sharply. 'No. The details make it seem more real. I just wanted to know. Please, don't think I'm scared.'

'We're ten miles from Rome – there's nothing to be scared about.'

There is a pause. 'I admit the thought of these people does frighten me. They killed your friends.'

'They weren't my friends.'

'You're very hard. I think he was your friend.'

I am not sure why I want to make this point; I can't think of any reason to deny it further.

Francesca continues, almost to herself, '*The Nativity* . . . wow.' She finishes her thought with a single, small shake of her head, curls vibrating. She turns to the window, much to think about.

We pass a sign showing the intersection which will take us directly into Rome. I change lane, preparing to follow the continuation of the A1 to Naples, circling the capital.

'If you want to stop off and see your parents – say now.' It is meant as a joke.

Francesca doesn't respond, focused inward through the eyes looking back at her in the window. I understand her silence; whatever she's said about her readiness for this, now she knows the details she needs time to assess the danger for herself. Whatever she thought we were going to do, she must reconcile herself to the fact she is now playing a part in a big story, a story she assumed was a myth.

We circle Rome; little of the city is visible. We could be on any urban orbital – a world of bursting fluorescence, lights glowing in the dark like paint dropped in water: red, orange, yellow, green. The night is a miasma of colour, breaking apart, melding, igniting, diffuse and electric. It is like a kaleidoscopic pattern seen through a distorting lens, stretching and circling. The boundary of the road – a black line of absence, a drop to nothingness – is made distinct by a landscape of warehouses, sudden high-rises, derelict factories and vast wasteground. The road slopes, banks, flattens. I concentrate; the new traffic, the Roman traffic, is agile, volatile, reckless. I will be able to relax a little when we are south of the capital, the north behind us.

Francesca is still quiet.

'Do you want to smoke?'

She shifts round in her seat, to her preferred position, with thumb pulling at the seat belt. 'No. Thank you.'

'Are you sure? I don't mind.'

She runs her thumb up the inside of the seat belt. 'Do you know why I applied for the job at the Uffizi? I used to be taken there as a child and I thought it was a place for old people, and all these lovely paintings shouldn't be just for them. I thought somehow I could change that. Not that I think it will ever be a place for children, but that doesn't mean it can't be a little more vibrant, feel a little – I don't know – fresher. Do you know what people say when they leave the Uffizi? I hear them, in English, French as well. It's boring, that's what they say. Isn't that terrible? It means it's really only interesting to scholars. And people like you.'

'*I* think it's boring.'

'See. One of the world's greatest – if not *the* world's greatest – collection of pre-modern-era paintings and it's boring. It's not to do with the art. It's not to do with the building.'

'Then what is it?'

'It's an atmosphere thing. And the reverence you're supposed to take in there with you. I don't know what can be done about it. Funky lighting isn't the answer.'

'Better lighting would help.'

'True. But I also think it needs fewer paintings. I suppose my radical solution would be to have two collections – the greatest hits surrounded by a number of the best but less famous works, and then the other stuff elsewhere, for the truly engaged.'

'The greatest hits would be packed. You'd never see anything.'

'You give them something else, to thin the crowds out. Films, talks – away from the paintings. Then there has to be an interactive element. I even suggested we give away CD-ROMs of the collection, so people could take the entire gallery away with them.'

'How was that idea received?'

'It takes so long to do anything.'

'Do you want to stay there?'

There is no answer for a moment. I give her a quick look. She is chewing on her top lip.

'What is it?'

'I'm here, aren't I?'

'This will last a few days. You haven't quit your job.'

She lights a cigarette. Lowers the window. 'I don't know.'

I don't push her; she wants to be in transition while we're on the move, nothing fixed. This is the deal she made with herself.

We are now past Rome. Beyond the high-rises, the sprawl, and into the country.

'Caravaggio spent his last years in the south. Did he ever go to Calabria?' Francesca's question is light, interested, chatty.

'I don't think so. After he killed Tomassoni he fled to Naples, then when that didn't work out he went to Sicily, and after that didn't work out he tried to become a knight in Malta, *and* after that didn't work out it was back to Naples. So, no, he missed Calabria.'

'It would be nice if we were travelling in his footsteps – you know – to get the painting back.'

'Things don't work out like that. Anyway, if the painting was still with Cosa Nostra, if it was still in Sicily, we wouldn't be going at all. They kill people for fun down there.'

'And these people don't?' It is a straightforward question.

'Not for fun, although they do kill people. They like to lose people in the forests and let the wolves do the rest.'

'So you have a chance?' Is she imagining herself in the darkest wood, pursued by wolves? How she would escape?

'They probably shoot you first. Both knees. That would be after a beating. The odds aren't good.'

Her imagination has limits, and although I sense she tries to picture the scene, she doesn't enliven it with the despair, the fear, the horror.

'But don't worry. I'll look after you.'

I turn to her to make sure she understands, believes me. She smiles, open, bright, starry; not the smile I'd expect after such a gruesome description.

'I trust you.' She isn't looking for reassurances. She adds, 'It's very exciting, isn't it?'

I turn back to the road. 'Just because we're not going to get killed, doesn't mean it won't be dangerous. Don't forget that.'

'I won't, I promise.'

I look across to her once more. She has closed her eyes, her head resting against the side of the seat. She wriggles a little so her shoulders aren't hunched up; one hand rests in her lap, the thumb of the other hand still pressed behind the seat belt. I drive on. The traffic is thinning. Now it's mostly trucks, with stretches of nothing. Abundant nothing raced through. I accelerate, feeling the speed, the power of the car, and the road slipping away beneath me, both faster than my thoughts, now ebbing a little. I don't survey the darkness around me, any outcrop of deeper black or constellation of light. I pass through phases of acute wakefulness – eyes wide, fully focused, agile – and moments when I am hardly able to fend off sleep – sudden sleep, eyelids sinking shut, rolling down like heavy shop shutters. I play with the air conditioner, recalling that changes in temperature increase alertness. It's three-forty-seven a.m. The exterior temperature is five degrees. I look over at my passenger. She looks content. A sign says: motel, thirty kilometres. We are close to Naples. We have been driving for almost three hours. I want to be past Naples before the first stop, but I am not sure I can make it. I accelerate. Suddenly the desire to sleep is desperate. To be lying down, stretched out – my body wants it now, pushes for it. The kilometres click up, filed away behind us. Ten minutes and the exit is approaching. I glance the car into the nearside lane and ease it off the *autostrada*. I pass a petrol station and turn into the car park of a small motel, a square block of brick with dark-green shutters and a white awning. I park by the entrance and whisper to Francesca that we've stopped; I am going to get us rooms. Without opening her eyes fully, she whispers, 'I want to be in with you.'

I register using my personal credit card. Francesca is waiting by the car, stretching. Up on her toes, arms high, fingers splayed; she wobbles as she relaxes down. I grab all the handles of our bags with one hand and take them in. Francesca follows with the painting.

The room is basic, with two narrow single beds, a desk and chair. I drop the bags and shut the blinds. Francesca leans the painting against the desk, ducks her head into the bathroom, searches for the light cord, pulls it. 'I'm going to have a shower.'

'I need sleep.'

Francesca moves over to me, slots her arms around my waist and presses her hips into me saying: you sleep. She then pushes herself away and goes into the bathroom. I turn off the lights, strip down and climb into the far bed. There is a glow from the half-open bathroom door. I can hear the white noise of the shower, Francesca's body moving around underneath it altering the pitch of the water as she interrupts its velocity, sounding light and fresh as it hits her, hard and heavy as it hits the enamel of the bathtub. I imagine her standing there, swivelling – 180 degrees at the shoulders. I want to stay awake but know sleep is only moments away. I turn from the bathroom to the grey wall, my whole body aching for deep, obliterating sleep. The last thing I hear is the sudden silence of the stopped shower.

2

When I wake Francesca is asleep in the other bed, facing me, hands together under her cheek. The room is warm and she is naked under the pale-yellow sheet, pulled as high as her hip. Her body is a deep olive dark. Her curls have been pushed away from her face and are completely still. Naked, close to me, asleep, beautiful, dark, and with an undulation of hip to waist to shoulders, Francesca's body creates within me the overwhelming desire for an early-morning fuck, semi-sleepy, unadventurous, yet full of subtly precise sensations. I could climb in next to her; I have reason to be sure she'd respond.

What is Sarah doing now? What time is it? Eight? In England? Seven? I've been gone three days. A single call and no message. What must she be feeling? What would she think seeing me now, a naked woman a bed away, my desire evident, and my lack of sexual opportunism? I have no idea. I suspect right now she must feel at least a little sad, a little confused, and regretful. But this is a guess. I haven't ever seen her cope with ineluctable emotional issues – no death or dying, no reasons for desperate feelings in the lives of her friends. Only stress and demands from work, and me. I turn on to my back; I hear Francesca stir, moving under the sheet, her body sliding, repositioning itself.

'Good morning.'

Her response is a long murmur, followed by a big yawn and the rustle of a stretch. I move on to my side, to look at her: she is arching her back, arms out wide, the sheet, pulled up above her chest, lightly billowing from the air beneath her body.

'Sleep well?'

She breaks out of her stretch, turns to face me, propping her head up on her hand, elbow jammed between pillow and mattress. 'Great, thank you. How are you feeling?'

'Good. Good. I'm going to have a shower.'

I yank my sheet free from the mattress and wrap it around my waist and trail off to the bathroom. I lock the door.

Francesca is still in bed when I've finished. I sit on the desk chair, towel wrapped around my waist. She pulls herself up, wrapping her arms around her knees. We look at one another with awkward smiles.

'Don't be annoyed if I keep thanking you.'

'What for?'

'Letting me come.'

'I want you here.'

She slides herself to the end of the bed. 'Stand up.'

'Why?'

'Just stand.'

I do as I am ordered. Francesca stands, rising up close to me, letting her sheet fall to the floor. She then tugs at my towel. I breathe in and let it drop. It catches between our knees. I shuffle back and kick it away. Francesca places her hands on my shoulders.

'I want to feel you. I want you to feel me. I want more than that, but you aren't ready, are you?'

I let my hands roam down her back and over her behind, then up again, tracing the length of her spine to her hair. Francesca copies me, going only where I go. I feel her shoulders, the tops of her arms, and then back to her behind; I am not sure which sensation is the most vivid: my hands on her or hers on me. I move my hands to her hips. I place my hands on her belly, full and relaxed; she does the same; we have to shuffle apart to accommodate the angle of our arms, the turn of our hands. Francesca looks up, brown eyes wide, patient and loving. I go to kiss her but she shakes her head. I move a hand down. She parts her legs slightly to allow me in. Her hand around my cock causes dizziness – small white lights before my eyes. My hand remains outside of her, just present on the moisture and warmth – the kiss of her. I feel her rise up, as if elevation will invite me in. She has stopped playing the game.

'I won't be able to resist much longer.'

'Why are you resisting at all?'

I cannot think of an answer; I don't know why myself.

'Daniel?'

I pull away, my cock bouncing out of her hands. I pick up my towel, wrap it tightly around my waist. Francesca sits down on the end of the bed, twisting the sheet about her, fastening it by her armpit.

'I'm sorry. You have to understand. I come from a "just fuck her" gender, a "just fuck her" generation, a "just fuck her" class. I just don't want to be so fucking predictable.'

Francesca looks irritated by this. 'You mean I'm not getting any on moral grounds?'

My laugh is wry – more a snort. 'I'm not even sure it's a moral thing. You have to know I want to. But if I do, that's it. Two things will be over. My marriage and . . .' I hesitate.

'What?'

'*This*. The beginning of this. Which somehow, in its madness, is keeping me sane.'

'How?'

'I don't know.'

'Please. Explain.' She forces a smile.

'I can't.'

'Try.'

What can I say – it is a feeling not a thought?

'Daniel?'

'If I fall in love with you . . .'

'What?'

'I don't know, sooner or later you'll cease to be warm, vulnerable, funny – the playful things you are. All the things she isn't, and then I'll be left with a choice.'

The meaning of my words hardens her expression. 'You have to be offered a choice to be left with one.'

'I'm sorry. You're right. Forgive me.'

I am leaning against the small desk, staring across the small room; Francesca is sitting on the end of her bed, looking into her lap, her long fingers curled up into little balls.

3

'The plan is simple. We arrive in Sant' Angelo. We book into a hotel. It's a very small town. The local *cosca* is small. The one thing you learn about Calabria, the *'ndrangheta* is built into the fabric of the community – there is no "them and us". The common myth about the Mafia is that it is representative of the Sicilian way of life. This is wrong – the Mafia is a distinct power base using violence to get what they want. A violent class. It's slightly different in Calabria – it's less well organized, and there is more connection to the centre of the community. There is also more denial, probably because of this. There is less big business, but they still get around. But be certain they are as violent and vengeful as any of their counterparts north or south.

'Anyway, the relationship between the community and the people I need to see means the whole thing should happen quickly. I say I've got a stolen painting. I write down what I want for it on a piece of Uffizi stationery. Someone will understand that the painting is not for sale, that I'm offering them something else – an "in" to the gallery. Then hopefully they'll come to me. I tell them who you are and that's how I can get access. I tell them you're in love with me (here I look across to Francesca sitting, as ever, angled inwards, watching me, listening) and that you'll help me because of that. I tell them we're not going to take anything from the gallery floors. That's the beauty: nothing will be missed. The painting I have is something from the vault, where there are a hundred like it collecting dust, each worth five hundred to a million euros, paintings for which there is a huge market all around the world. I promise them ten of them to start, more if they want. I use your personnel file merely as proof – you are who I say you are.'

'Are they going to wonder why you're approaching them?'

'I was here last year. I met their *capo di tutti capi*. They know I'm a copper. I'm going to tell them I was fired and now I'm looking for a big kill. Looking to retire early. If anyone asks, we're going – we're going to Malaysia, to build a palace in the jungle – say palace.'

'Why would they ask me?'

'They probably won't, but just in case.'

'I've been to Malaysia.'

'I know.'

'How do you know?'

'I found some photos when I was packing. I'm afraid I took some. You in front of some temples. By way of proof again.'

'And the Caravaggio?'

'If they're keen – and they will be – sooner or later they'll have to commit. I'll say it costs nothing to build a palace in the jungle and live in luxury. I'm looking for 500,000 euros for the first batch – less than 10 per cent, but in the meantime I'll take the Caravaggio. I'll say I saw it when I met the old man. One week, until we are given . . .'

'What's the money in the bag for?'

'That makes us look serious. I tell them it's the money I'm using to pay the people who are actually going to steal the paintings. That's why I want the Caravaggio. There's a moment between paying my people and them paying me after the sell-on when I've either got a whole load of paintings I can't get rid of or nothing – that's the key thing about the Caravaggio – that's what it bridges, the time when the middleman, the deal-maker, can get screwed. They've just got to decide whether it's worth it.'

'What do you think?'

'I don't know. I think so. My guess is that what-ever the symbolic value of the Caravaggio, they still don't care about it. Not compared to straight-forward cash. I've seen the way these people treat works of art. They're just interested in the money. The deal I'm offering is how the Caravaggio earns its keep. If they don't use it for a deal like this, it's worthless to them. As a piece of art – they really don't care. Don't care at all.'

'Why don't they just sell it to some rich private collector?'

'I think it works better for them this way – all the syndicates accept it as a deal marker: that's very useful. Plus, it's in terrible shape, so it would need to be restored; that leaves whoever buys it open.'

'So apart from telling people we want to build a palace in the jungle, what do you want me to do?'

'If you don't mind, I want you to be a little confused, not really understanding why we're there. If anyone asks, agree the paintings in the archive are worth what I said. It's important you sound confident that the one we've got with us is a masterpiece – they won't know it's not – and just . . . I don't know – the key thing is to look slightly brainwashed by me.'

Francesca laughs. 'Maybe I have been.'

I look over. 'I think it's the other way around.'

Francesca rubs her thumb down the inside of the seat belt. 'Do you really think it's going to be this easy?'

'I don't know. Maybe. On the one hand these people are like ordinary businessmen – if they're presented with an opportunity, they move quickly, efficiently. On the other hand, they are deeply paranoid and dangerous, so their first instinct is suspicion. These days it is usually the former. If they think they're getting a good deal, it should be quite straightforward. I've dealt with people like this for years now.'

'But what happens when they realize they've been double-crossed?'

I ease my foot off the accelerator. I haven't thought about this. Or rather I haven't thought about the implications for Francesca. In the original plan I'd be back in London, and relatively safe, as safe as I've ever been. But if she wants to go back to the Uffizi, she might become a target.

'It's OK. Depending on what happens, it'll look as though you've been used by me, so it'll be me they're after, and it's a risk I'm prepared to take.'

'Do you think they'll be suspicious with all the press about the picture?'

'They need to offer it to me. I can't ask for it. But yes, things would be easier without the publicity. Plus it's only a matter of time before Rome's art squad begin to narrow their search.'

'How come you know where it is and they don't?'

I pull over to the side of the road. The roots of olive trees have broken through the tarmac, the hard branch of one tree is bent across the passenger-side window. Beyond us there is a plain, olive groves, citrus groves, chestnut groves. There have been few organized enclosures. The patterns are random, erratic, merged.

'The dead man. That was the deal. I wanted a name. And in return I'd sell on his vases.'

She revisits the television pictures: Nenni and

Maria dead in their courtyard, thrown from the top of the building, a bullet in their guts, so the execution started with unbearable pain. Francesca is unlikely to know that fact. Or understand.

'Can he be trusted?' She tries to hide her fear.

'We'll see.' There is no point in being reassuring; I don't know the answer. I pull out on to the road, the tyres rolling over the hard ridges of olive-tree roots.

4

We approach Sant' Angelo from the east, from above, running down into it. It is a small town, low, adhering to the shape of the earth, the dip of two hills. The land around is harsh, unfinished, as if nature was tired of the making of it. The road is broken, subsiding, churned up by tough, dry shrubs. Francesca sits up, facing forward, looking around.

'I didn't think we'd be this remote. Where will we stay?'

'There'll be somewhere.'

We pass an old man sitting on a pony, no saddle; he is stationary – a kind of sentry. His clothes are thick, heavy – deep browns, greys. Camouflage. His cap is black. Francesca waves and smiles. The old man's face is fixed, brown eyes hard like hazelnut shells.

The town has a distinct start – a sharp line of dwellings made of crumbling and chipped grey stone. The road runs down steeply into a hairpin bend. Below, more dwellings, bigger houses. At the bottom of the hill an old woman crosses the street. I lower my window. Francesca leans over and asks for directions to a hotel. The woman looks down at her feet, speaks in a low broken voice. Francesca shakes her head. 'I think it's Greek. Or more Greek than Italian.' We both smile, thank the woman. I follow the road, stopping at every junction so we can decide on the most promising way. Francesca spots what looks like a piazza to our left, past a small white church, past the first shop we have seen. I stop at the corner. There is a table and three chairs on the pavement. There is a door and a shuttered window. Behind the shutters I can make out a sign: Moretti. It is a bar. I pull into the piazza. The centre of the little town. The place is empty, barren, a gravel square surrounded by bare trees. The buildings around it are nondescript, municipal, stucco crumbling, dirty. All shutters are closed. To the left a man sits on a bench. A young man, wearing thick glasses, jeans, smoking a thin cigar. I park; we climb out. Francesca asks the man for the nearest hotel. He points to a large building just off the piazza. She follows his finger to windows with balconies. It is the only hotel, we are told. For the tourists, Americans looking to visit their ancestors' birthplace. They only have a few visitors a month. Sant' Angelo is small; it was smaller one hundred years ago. Few Americans have ancestors here. We thank him and climb back in the car, pull out of the piazza and park in front of the hotel.

'Do I have to act in any way?'

'No. Just be yourself.'

'It's not how I imagined it.'

'It's just how I imagined it.'

We unpack our bags on to the street, the painting placed on the car roof. We are watched by a woman from a window opposite – old but ageless – fifty or seventy or ninety; she is talking on a mobile phone. Francesca waves. I clutch up all the bags and take them inside; Francesca slides the painting off the roof and follows.

The reception is modest: a long desk flanked by pigeon holes, backed by a board of room numbers and hanging keys. Ten rooms. There is a buzzer. Francesca rests the painting against her legs. I press the buzzer. The man from the piazza appears.

'It is my hotel. The only one, as I said.' He produces a clipboard with a registration card.

'We are not very busy so I sit in the piazza. Please. Fill this in. You are not Americans?'

Francesca points to me and says, '*Inglese*,' and then to herself and says, '*Italiano*, from the north'.

The man nods. 'My name is Carmine. I am from here. I went to university in Reggio. I studied politics. But there is no government in the south and in the north they think we're peasants. This was my father's. Why are you here?'

Francesca looks at me, leaning on the counter filling in the long form. Names, addresses, passport numbers, car registration. I say nothing. Francesca nudges me. I look up.

'We'll pay for four nights in advance. But we might not be here that long. How much is that?'

Carmine points to a small board. Thirty-five euros a night. I open my wallet, count out the money. Carmine folds it and presses it into the front pocket of his jeans. He points to the painting. 'What's in there?'

I smile. 'It is a present.'

'Do you know people in Sant' Angelo?'

I turn the clipboard around and push it towards Carmine. 'May we have a quiet room?'

'They are all quiet. Number ten is the best. We are empty. You can have that.'

'Thank you.'

He unhooks the key from the board and hands it to me. 'Would you like help?'

'No, thank you.'

Carmine points to the stairs. 'Right, at the top.'

The room is at the end of a long dark corridor. It is large and square. The furniture is heavy, dark, nineteenth century. The bed is big. There are two full-length windows with small balconies overlooking the piazza. Each balcony has two white plastic chairs mottled with brown cigarette burns. The en suite bathroom has a free-standing tub. I turn on the bath taps; they cough powerfully, loudly. The first water is rust coloured, but it quickly runs through. The hot tap is scalding. I cut off the water.

Francesca unpacks her clothes into the chest of drawers and wardrobe.

'I didn't think we'd find anywhere, but this is quite nice.'

I open a window, step out on to the balcony. 'Are you having second thoughts?'

'No.' She joins me for a moment, looks out over the dreary town. 'What are we going to do?'

'Tonight. Nothing. Have a drink. Eat. Have another drink. Sleep.'

'That's it?'

'If the opportunity arises, we talk to the locals.'

'What do we say?'

'Nothing. You're from Florence, from the Uffizi. I'm an ex-policeman. We're in love.'

'What if no one asks us?'

'They will.'

'What if we don't understand them?'

'We will.'

'How can you be so sure?'

'I've done this before. Not here, but close by.'

Francesca finishes unpacking. I open my bag and push my stuff into two drawers.

'What are we going to do with these?' Francesca points to the attaché case and the painting.

'We'll have to take the money and gun with us. Maybe Carmine will have a sneak around, find the painting. His first thought will be that it's stolen.'

Francesca sits on the end of the bed, hands pushed between her thighs. 'It's quite scary, isn't it?'

'Don't be scared. Think of it as a game.'

'Really?'

I nod. 'In a day or two it won't seem so strange. We're just playing a part.'

'Is this what you do all the time?'

'A lot of the time, yes.'

'And this was what you were doing when you first came to see me at the gallery?'

'Yes and no. I said I was someone I wasn't, but I was being myself, which is the best way.'

'You never quite believe people have jobs like this.'

I go back out on to the balcony. Dusk is falling – the colour of the sky is grey, a dying grey. The old stone of the surrounding buildings seems to darken even before daylight has receded. It is a hard, quick dusk; night will be dark, heavy. I shut the windows, the shutters, the curtains. Francesca stretches herself across the bed and turns on one of the two bedside lights.

'You didn't pack anything for me to read?'

'Maybe you could ask Carmine. I'm sure he'll have something.'

'What do you want me to say?'

I laugh. 'Do you have a book I can read?'

'You know what I mean. If he asks me.'

'Just say what we planned. You are who you are but we want to change our lives, move to

Malaysia. If he asks why we're here, don't say anything. I suppose, don't be too jolly. If you can, look suspicious. But you could just ask for a book and leave it at that.'

'I want to help.'

'You are helping.'

Francesca slides off the bed and leaves the room. I sit in the armchair in the corner. For a moment I wonder where I am. Outside seems vast, with interminable distances, a world unwrapped way beyond this town, the hills and mountains, Calabria and Italy, unwrapped beyond my knowledge of what is out there, my imagination to picture it. I feel far from the world, uprooted, lighter than I should be. I recognize the feeling. Adjustment to a new place, another new place, starting with doubts about the world, its existence, feeling it's little more than vibration, human hum and brown light, unmanageable and unreal, then developing into outright suspicion that these central elements – movement, sound, colour – are the material from which a world can be made. Everything around me is vibrating, in flux, without the substance of weight, embodiment. Nothing is embodied, least of all me. As a body, I am light enough to turn in my chair, to rise to the ceiling, to float away. It is profound homelessness. I am desperate to settle. I imagine myself standing by Sarah's full-length windows, looking beyond the spare trees, gently rocking on my heels. I push myself up from the chair and turn on the main light. I want brightness and objects to be present, which requires hard light and sharp shadows. I peer through the spyhole in the door. Francesca appears, distorted, shrunken, books in her hand. I open the door for her.

'He has quite a collection.'

'What did you get?'

Francesca fans out three slim paperbacks. 'Two thrillers and a romance.'

'A fitting ratio.'

Francesca leans up and kisses me. 'I hope not.'

I shut the door. 'Did he ask you anything?'

'He asked me what I did and I told him.'

'What about where you worked?'

'He didn't ask but I told him. He asked whether you worked there. I said you used to be a policeman. Not any more. And that was it.'

'Good.'

'It was strange. I can't think of the last time I really had to think before I spoke. I'm sure it made me seem suspicious.'

'How was he?'

'I think he's unhappy. Imagine being stuck here. You have all these ambitions and then . . .'

'Trust me, I know.'

'You're not running a small hotel in the middle of nowhere.'

'This is true.'

Francesca lies down on the bed, places two of

the books on the bedside table next to her and opens the other. I stay standing; inside I am still all vibration, human hum and brown light.

'I'm going for a walk. I won't be long.'

Francesca drops the book to her thighs. 'What time are we going out?'

I look at my watch. 'In an hour or so.'

'I'll be ready.'

Carmine is in the reception, leaning over a newspaper. He looks up; I ignore him. Another tactic – seem important. I stop in front of the hotel. To my right the street quickly dips into darkness; left is the piazza and a little light. I turn right. As my eyes become accustomed to the night, tiny lights appear in the distance, on the horizon; none are clustered. The town seems to end as abruptly as it started. Above my head a balcony glows, golden light spreads across the crumbling stone, out into the night. I can hear voices – the TV. The weather is mild, warm. I turn around and head back towards the piazza, now lit up by a string of coloured bulbs slung from tree to tree, soft dips of intermittent light marking out the hard lines of the square from the road. Bunting – green, white, red – is spun from the trees to the buildings. The bar is opening. A young woman, a girl, is setting out tables and chairs on the piazza itself, underneath the trees, the coloured lights. At the far corner of the piazza there is a small restaurant. I cut diagonally across the square, the dry gravel scraping and scratching under my shoes. I look in through the window. Two men – one young, in his twenties, one older, in his forties – are laying out the tablecloths. The seats of their black trousers are shiny and fallen; they have rolled their shirtsleeves up over their biceps. Their movements are expert: eight tables covered quickly with a simple flick and float. There is another restaurant two doors down. A middle-aged woman is decanting wine via a grey funnel from a small barrel into carafes. The wine is black. Neither restaurant has a menu outside. The middle-aged woman looks up at me. Her face is impassive, her hair seamed with silver. I wave. She nods back and continues with her work. The street rises steeply up the hill. I suspect that there are four roads in and out of this small town and all will be as uneven and subsiding as the one we entered by. I walk across the piazza to the bar. It is empty. I move a chair out of my way to make a sound, to announce myself. The girl appears. She is wearing tight black jeans, white shirt, black waistcoat; her only make-up is eyeliner, heavily applied. She has a leather wrist-band on one wrist, on the other, a leather cord wound around a number of times. There is a silver-studded black-leather choker around her neck. She wants to be fashionable, to make a statement, and finds the post-punk aesthetic does both. It is an unexpected look this far south, this remote. I am moved by her. The town around her must mock her day and night. I order an espresso and a packet of cigarettes. Not for me, I say – for my girlfriend. I ask which of the two restaurants is the best. I am told they are the same. I ask her name: Mariangela. She is sullen – like a teenager, but older. Maybe. It's hard to tell. A man walks in and around behind the bar. Mariangela is excused. Her father, I presume, and he is one of the men laying out tablecloths in the first restaurant. His biceps bulge artificially with his high, tightly rolled sleeves. I ask whether I need to book. He shakes his head. I order the espresso and cigarettes from him. I ask how many people live in the town. I am told five, maybe six thousand. The man is diffident, eyes narrow. What is the main work here? In the summer, fruit. In the winter, chestnuts. I nod. This is a nice place, I say. The man shrugs. I continue. The bar, the restaurant. The piazza. The hotel is nice. The man reluctantly acknowledges the basic truth of this. In the summer business must be good. Tourists. Americans. The man has ignored my order for espresso and pushes a glass of sparkling something across to me instead. It's dark, bitter, very alcoholic. I say it's good; it's not. I then say that I'd like a little place like this myself. Especially with a restaurant as well. Good cheap local produce. The man is proud of what he owns but shakes his head. I go on. The fat Americans coming here to look for their ancestors – eating, eating, eating. Big profits. The man leans down, arms flat on the bar, hands balled together, creating an extra bulge to his biceps. He looks through me. He's not going to talk. I speak for him. No profits? I suppose if I want good produce there's a premium. There is no reaction. Just the staring ahead, taking in the basic truth but unable to admit to it, confide in the tourist how his pride in his places is punished every time they come for their cut, after forcing him to pay over the odds for the produce in the first place. This is what I hear in his silence, in his refusal to acknowledge or disabuse me of these facts; it's the same all over the south. I tell him I know this. The man's eyes narrow, pull focus. He is now looking at me. The tourist on the other side of his bar. I explain: I was a cop once – Interpol. Tracking down stolen paintings. I worked this region. The man speaks for the second time. Then why would I want to have a little bar, a restaurant, if I know. I step back. I would do a deal, I say. With Lomazzo.

The bartender slides back off the bar, his face hardening, and looks out of the window on to the piazza.

I finish my drink and drop ten euros on the bar and back away. The owner looks at me. 'Lomazzo is waiting. When he takes over . . .' He shakes his head in disgust.

I thank him for the drink and leave. The piazza is busier. A few couples, young and old, walk around hand in hand, talking, smoking, laughing;

cars pull up and park. There is music from somewhere. A scratchy record or very old recording. A tenor voice. Mariangela is sitting on a bench next to the tables she set out earlier. She has a pad and a pencil; they droop from her fingertips into her lap. It is just warm enough to sit outside. She looks bored. I suspect she is happy there is no one to serve. I smile. Her eyes register me; the rest of her face does not. I walk back to the hotel.

Francesca is asleep, the pages of the book splayed by her thumb still resting inside. I whisper her name.

'How long have you been gone?'

'Not long. I've found a couple of restaurants.'

'There's more than one?'

She slides off the bed, collects underwear and clean clothes from the dresser and goes into the bathroom. She calls out. 'How cold is it?'

'Not cold.'

She reappears dressed just like she was when I first met her, except the Birkenstocks have been exchanged for Camper boots. She is wearing a little more make-up. Contacts in.

In the bathroom I unbutton my shirt, apply some deodorant and re-enter the bedroom looking down, concentrating on buttoning up.

'Have you decided what to do about . . . the things?'

'We leave the painting. We take this.' I pick up the attaché case. 'This is never left alone. The one thing which will end this deal is them getting fifty thousand euros for nothing.'

In reception we ring the buzzer at the desk and ask Carmine whether he wants the key. He says no. I ask of the two restaurants – I gesture in their general direction – which is the best. We are told they are the same. I leave the key on the counter.

Mariangela is still on the bench next to her tables. There are two couples with drinks. We take a table beneath the streetlamp. I slot the attaché case between my chair and the table. Francesca lights a cigarette. I produce the packet I bought earlier.

'I bought these for you.' I push them over the table.

Mariangela appears by us. Francesca orders a bottle of white wine – anything, she stipulates. Mariangela trails off into the bar. Her father comes to the door. I raise my hand, acknowledging him. He goes back in.

The wine is cold, the glasses small. I pour. The taste is fresh, strong, harsh. We sit quietly, Francesca tapping her boot against the side of the table leg. I stare down the street to the small white church, somehow luminous in the night, a glow coming off its white marble walls. I look up at the sky; it is cloudless, the stars bright, edges blurring with their blaze. It should be colder. High skies in January. Much colder.

'Are you warm enough?' I say in English.

'Yes,' Francesca responds in English.

We sip our wine. One glass is enough. Francesca calls Mariangela over. We are told her father says the wine is free. Francesca looks at me. I ignore her.

'Thank your father.'

Mariangela twists round and goes back to her bench.

We stroll across to the two restaurants. Francesca doesn't ask why we weren't required to pay for the wine; I don't offer an explanation. I choose the second restaurant because it is the busier. The woman I saw earlier funnelling the wine is taking orders. The customers are mostly middle-aged or older. There is a slight interruption in the conversation as we enter. We wait to be seated.

The woman directs us to a little table in the corner, by the window, as if we'd reserved it – wanting something cosy and romantic. The attaché case is slotted in by the wall. The woman lists the menu. *Primo piatti*. Pasta and sauces. I watch Francesca think hard – what does she feel like? I don't care; I'm not hungry. I want to taste the black wine, however.

Francesca chooses the *linguine e melanzane*, the steak. I signal the same. And ask for the wine I saw her with earlier. And water. When the waitress has gone I lean over the table, my hand reaching for Francesca's. 'Tell me about the man in the photographs.'

Francesca clasps my hand. 'His name is Francesco. Francesca and Francesco! He's a doctor. A researcher. Endocrinology. He moved to Boston. I didn't want to go.'

'You don't want to talk about it?'

'I don't mind. There's nothing to say. He loved me. I didn't love him.'

'How long were you together?'

'A year.' Francesca pulls her hand away. 'Daniel, I need to tell you something.' The waitress is back with the wine and glasses, adroitly placing them in the middle of the table while passing by.

'The reason I took so long the other night. I went to see Storaro.'

I take a drink of the black wine. It is better than I expected – spicy, peppery. I suspected this at the time.

'Why?'

Francesca sits up straight, then relaxes, crosses her arms on the table – she wants this to be a sensible disclosure.

'I needed to. I needed to tell him I was going away. With you.'

'No, you didn't.' I don't know why I'm being so obstructive, why I am so angry suddenly; I look around the small restaurant – a blind, arbitrary cast about. 'What did he say?'

'Nothing. Or rather nothing I could make sense of at the time. But then you . . . last night . . .'

'Why didn't you tell me this then?'

'Because you might have ditched me.'

'What did he say?'

'He was calm. He said just let him know where I was. And if he could do anything to help. I thought at the time he was just being sarcastic because he was hurt.'

'Have you spoken to him?'

'I called him when you went out.'

I disguise my fury. 'What did you say?'

'Nothing. That he should have said something about you to me.'

'What did he say?'

'He wants the painting. To let him know the moment I think you might fail. Not to tell you this.'

'But you're telling me.'

'Yes.'

'Then what happened?'

'That was it.'

'Don't call him again, OK? No matter what happens. Do you know how easy it is to trace mobile phone calls? It costs a hundred euros. He now knows where we are.'

My head is full of rage, my body straining with frustration, to control it. Who knows what Storaro will do with the information? This little town might be under siege within a day – some under-cover version of Team Storaro thinking they can make a deal with money. Spread enough cash around and Lomazzo will appear, looking to sell. A fundamental transaction: goods for money. Not how it works.

'Jesus, Francesca.'

She is embarrassed, hurt, tearful. How was she to know a simple call made such a difference?

'If you'd told me last night, it wouldn't have mattered. Your mistake was not telling me. Do you understand?'

We sit silently – a couple arguing and ruining their special evening.

Our food arrives: small bowls, forks already dug in. After her first mouthful, Francesca speaks.

'Do you want me to go?'

Yes, I think. Go. Now. Call Storaro from Catanzaro. Let them descend there.

'There is nowhere for you to go. Not tonight.'

She takes this well. Tomorrow she will be leaving. She shrugs away her disappointment.

'Why was the wine free?'

'Because I was in there earlier.'

'That's it.' She's not prepared to sit here all evening in silence.

I continue, 'I said I was an ex-policeman and would make a deal with Lomazzo if I owned a small bar and restaurant around here.'

'What did he say?'

'Nothing. But he didn't disagree with what I said, and I know how it works. The local *cosca* demands a skim off the takings. Usually every night to stop them hiding any.'

'That's terrible.'

'It's good.'

'Why?'

'I get to see the enemy.'

'Is that safe?' I can see a little adrenalin flush in her eyes – expectation, fear, excitement.

My response is flat. 'Don't worry. I won't put you in any danger, I promise.'

She nods, sucking in a thin ribbon of pasta. I have only had one mouthful of food. Even without Francesca's confession, this would be usual: stomach tense, mind focused elsewhere. My guess is that if the *cosca* is taking a skim from the bar and restaurants, Carmine is also paying up regularly. I need to talk to Carmine – chat, without Francesca around. Brag a bit – look at me, gorgeous woman from Florence, do anything for me, ex-cop, lots of connections. Be clear: I'm on the make down here.

The woman removes our bowls.

I reach for Francesca's hand. 'Forget about what just happened. I need to focus. We'll discuss it later. OK?'

Francesca swivels her hand so she's holding mine – palm to palm. 'Shall I just pretend we're on holiday?'

I'm not sure I don't detect a little sarcasm. I ignore it, smile weakly. 'Look around you. No one comes here on holiday. This is time travel. An entire century separates us. How much of the twentieth century do you think has affected these people?'

She cannot stay on the subject of holidays; she knows I'm thinking about something else – men coming tonight or tomorrow for other people's money.

'I don't think I could do your job. You're very brave.'

'You don't do things because you're brave. That's something you find out later.'

'Why do you do it?'

'I wanted a job like yours; no one would give me one. You take what you can get.'

Our steaks arrive, oily, bloody, a sprig of something on top, a mash of green vegetable on the side. I carve out a chunk. Most of the taste is olive oil; the texture is soft, stringy.

'You'd think between the perfectly simple food of Naples and the fabulously baroque food of Sicily, they'd have a good balance here. I think it was better in the summer. Fish, younger meat.'

'That's when you saw *The Nativity*?'

'Yes. It's in a terrible state. Cracked, split, frayed.'

'Beyond restoration?'

'I don't know. There's still a lot of Caravaggio there.'

'You'll be very famous in Italy.'

'There'll be a lot of angry people. I should have shared the intelligence.'

'Why haven't you?'

'Because *I* want to save it. Simple as that.'

The restaurant is thinning out. Departing diners say goodbye to seated diners, hands resting on shoulders as they pass, food interrupted for kisses and hugs. We are studied, I suspect talked about. I don't respond to any glances, just sip the black wine. I have managed half my steak, the green stuff. Something is making me feel slightly nauseous.

'Do we stay for *dolce*?'

'Do you want to?'

'I'd be interested in what they have.'

'Then we stay.'

Francesca stops the waitress and asks for something local, traditionally Calabrian; her smile is open, bright, forcing the waitress to smile back, after which, with a gentle stroke of Francesca's curls, the waitress says to me, '*Bella, Bella.*' I agree.

The dessert, a small smooth tower the same colour as the wine, is cold, hard, repelling the spoon unless the angle of entry is just right – sheer, oblique – and only then shaving off a thin crust. It tastes of nuts and pepper. Francesca manages to hack out a sizeable dent before giving up. A *digestivo* is then given to us, on the house, I suspect for no special reason other than that we are strangers. It is bitter, strong, cold, also tasting of pepper and nuts.

We are the last to leave. The waitress is friendly, kissing Francesca, saying they rarely get such elegant tourists. Why are we in Sant' Angelo? Francesca looks at me, anxious about playing her role in front of me. I smile. She says we are here for a number of reasons. Business, pleasure, romance. And laughs. The woman looks me up and down. She shakes her head. Francesca laughs nervously, not expecting such a clear negative judgement on her choice. I know word has spread already, from bar to restaurant to restaurant – my knowledge of their world, Lomazzo. They are suspicious of me. I lead Francesca to the door, smile charmingly at the waitress and wish her goodnight.

The piazza is empty. The bar is still open. I want to be around if there is a collection tonight. I give Francesca two options. She can stay with me, or she can go back to the hotel. She wants to stay. We walk down to the small church and sit on the steps. It is cold now. Colder. Nothing like Florence. Francesca tells me she doesn't believe Storaro loves her, not like he says; she saw it clearly when she went to see him two nights ago, seeing through her to the painting, even though she didn't realize it at the time. He's a man who wants many things, I say. He's quite something. She agrees. But still, you get used to thinking you're the centre of someone's desire. You can get to rely on it. I tell her Sarah could never get used to her desire for me. So she ditched the desire. Some people need to be emotionally aerodynamic. Francesca places her hand on my knee. I remain where I am for a moment and then stand. We wander back to the piazza. At the corner I hear the low roar of a car, gears shifting up. Within a second the sound is behind us. We are forced on to the pavement. It's a black BMW with black windows. It stops in front of the bar. The coloured lights above are reflected across the windscreen. I exert pressure on Francesca's hand – go with me, obey me. I position us between the bar and the BMW, Francesca facing the car. I ask her, in English, 'Do you want a last drink; we could go back or go in here – what do you think?' I have one hand on her hip, one on her shoulder, thumb stroking her neck. I hear the car doors open, a pause – there is no slam. I then say, 'Second thoughts let's just go back to the hotel.' Our turn – me taking her hand, guiding her round, is perfectly timed. We are immediately in a tangle with two men – young men – heading from the car to the bar. I apologize profusely, first in English, then Italian. I grip one by the upper arm to move round him. I don't recognize him; he's not one of my escorts from last year; it's a different BMW. The young men are hard, expressionless; one goes to push Francesca out of the way. I see this and quickly intervene, pressing the man's arm down, imposing my strength for a second, before ushering Francesca away. It's over in seconds, and I hear them mutter, '*Turisti*,' or a version of it, as they enter the bar. I check to see whether the bar owner has seen the tussle. He has, standing at the window, Mariangela next to him, leaning against him, fingers hooked in over her choker, pulling it down, away from her throat. I want something to be said. The soldiers to complain about the tourists; the owner to tell them, 'No, he's not a tourist. He's an ex-cop. He knows Lomazzo.'

We stop at the corner of the piazza, by the hotel, and wait in the shadow. The two men are in the bar for a minute only. They wheel-spin the car across the piazza, leaving zigzags of gravel, a hovering dust cloud, before stopping abruptly outside the restaurants. I turn towards the hotel. Francesca is shaking.

'You should have warned me.'

'There was no time. I'm sorry.'

'My heart's beating really quickly.' Instead of holding my hand to her heart, she folds her hand inside my jacket and over my heart. There is little to feel.

'I'm used to this – concentration slows the heart down.'

'I'm glad you were with me.'

'You wouldn't be here if it wasn't for me.'

Carmine appears as we enter the hotel, two fingers smoothing down an eyebrow; there is a little tomato sauce at the corner of his mouth. I flip the attaché case on to the counter, hold out my hand to receive the key. I watch Carmine wonder: who takes a case like that to dinner?

In the room I open one of the French windows and look across the piazza. The BMW is gone. Everything is dark. The shutters of the bar are closed. Nothing else is going to happen tonight.

I say this. Call it out to Francesca, in the bath-room, taking off her make-up.

'You mean in this room or out there?'

I shut the window, the shutters, the curtain. I undress, draping my clothes over one of the armchairs. I am tired. I rub my eyes, thinking of Sarah, probably just getting ready for bed herself.

Francesca turns off the bathroom light. She is wearing a T-shirt. I pat the bed. She sits on the side, pulls off two rings, her earrings, then shuffles in, and on to her side, facing me. I have also shuffled down and on to my side. Our hands, palms together, are pressed between face and pillow.

'How do you feel?'

'Tired.'

'Sleepy?'

'I don't want to sleep. I want to look at you.'

Francesca permits this, smiling, opening her eyes wide for examination, closing them, then moistening her lips, for a while content to be watched.

She whispers. 'How old are you?'

'Thirty-six.'

'Younger than me.'

'Younger than you.'

'Brothers and sisters?'

'No.'

'I have a brother. He has Down's syndrome. I don't see him as often as I should. My parents are very good with him, which is surprising given how self-obsessed they are. Maybe I'm the self-obsessed one.'

'What's his name?'

'Luca.'

I move a hand to Francesca's hip, pushing her T-shirt out of the way, resting it there.

'Do you mind?'

Her curls shake, drop across her cheek; she flicks them away. I stroke her, from hip to waist and back; the curve is gentle, smooth, inviting a continuous motion.

'I can see how tired you are.'

She leans forward and kisses me; our mouths open and bodies shift together. The kiss is long, uninterrupted, steady – a dedicated kiss, not hungry, tender or passionate. When it ends we both turn over, arms reaching for our respective bedside lights, switch them off.

The room is completely dark. I listen to Francesca settle, turned away from me. I sense she is going to sleep because this is what she thinks I want, what I need – an uncomplicated night, a full night of sleep. I reach behind me, blind to the part of her body I touch first – her lower back, her waist.

'Goodnight, Francesca.'

There is no response. She is falling asleep. Sleep often comes quickly when adrenalin has flowed. I turn on to my back. The shape of the room reveals itself – offering only depth, no form or colour. I stare at the ceiling. Can this really be done? Can I really pull this off? For the first time I admit I really don't know. What I need to do requires more than I know, something I cannot know. How they deal between themselves. So when I tell Francesca, don't worry, I've done this before, it's not true. None of it's true.

5

'You're not getting rid of me then?'

'Not yet.'

'I'm sorry.'

Francesca is in jeans, olive-green shirt, Camper boots, leaning on the balcony looking into the room, smoking. I am looking at the painting on the bed.

'It's hard to believe this is worthless. I mean it's dreadful, but it's so . . . so . . . I don't know – painted.'

'I don't think it's worthless – maybe a few thousand euros. He knew Titian. That's enough for someone to buy it.'

'What are we doing today?'

'We're going for a drive.'

'Where?'

'Around.'

'What for?'

'It's sightseeing time. Big houses. CCTV. BMWs. I don't believe these people live here.'

I join Francesca out on the balcony and look up

to the sky – brown, loamy, vast and low, with streaks of hard grey cloud. The piazza is deserted. Rain during the night has left dirty pools of water here and there; rain drips off trees, the bunting, the dull bulbs. It is cold. I say this.

'Do you think anything will happen, after last night?'

I turn and lean back on the balcony next to Francesca. 'I divide what I do when I am in places like this into two types of waiting: the soft wait and the hard wait. This is the soft wait. We're where we're supposed to be and we know something will happen but we don't know what and we don't know when. The hard wait, which will come sooner than you think, is when it all falls into place and you're just waiting for it to happen and be over. The trick: how to occupy these times? The soft wait – today: do stuff. Anything.'

Carmine is in good spirits, apologizing for being so diffident yesterday; he didn't expect guests – this is the first time in January in years. You want the business then you resent the work. I say it's the same whatever you do. This is why I want out – retire early. Francesca is leaning on the attaché case – flat on the counter – absently staring around the reception. I see Carmine sneak a glance at it. I sense Carmine's bonhomie has been ordered. We all say a cheery 'ciao'.

We leave the town by the east road, towards the coast, signposted Crotone. The road is worse than the one that brought us into town yesterday: two narrow lanes broken into three narrower lanes, collapsed, split by hard dry roots.

'Where are we going?' Francesca is sitting in her usual position, thumb under seat belt.

I am just happy to drive, concentrate on the road – the hairpins down, the long climbs, skirting each hill. Driving is a good way to wait. We follow the rim of a national park for an hour, passing through towns and villages with names like Arietta, Belcastro, Zagarise. At one point we pass through a piazza filled with police cars and vans, lights flashing, sirens off. I slow down. For a moment I expect to see a young man, handcuffed, led out of a building, followed by two cops bringing out the Caravaggio – removal men with a big rolled-up rug. We stop to watch. Others are watching. From windows, the street. Francesca listens in to conversations. It's a boss. An old man. A killer. She asks whether he's been arrested. No one responds. This drama is not for outsiders. We wait. Will I see the old man from last year? And if I do, what will it mean? Is the Italian strategy to arrest everyone who might have a connection to the painting and then plea-bargain? Probably a good one. I tense; my fingers drum the steering wheel; my feet tap the pedals. I am like Nenni waiting for me to decide whether or not to get into the Alfa Romeo. I tell Francesca to ask the people by the car: what is the name of the old man? Ask someone, and smile. She does, and the answer is: Camuccini. Not the old man. And not a name I recognize. We leave the town. The country is barren, spare, brown. Nothing is flat; it is all turned over, churned, unfinished. From the top of hills we can see vast black and grey forests, unbroken by roads. Thunderstorms, veils of thick grey rain break over the horizon as if the world ends there.

I think I recognize a hill village from last year – a tall cypress the village's central point. We stop. Look around. The village opposite is different, however. No church. Maybe that's the one? We drive across the valley. I cannot find the exact spot – the cypress, the house, the view. The villagers, when they do stray out of doors, ignore us. Francesca mooches about, finding broken walls to sit on, happy to stare out over precipices, across the vastness below, the low skimming sky. Occasionally she points something out to me – more storms, or sunlight breaking through the clouds above the plain, illuminating every detail, the stiff shapes of chestnut and olive trees. She never looks at her watch or checks her mobile or picks at her fingernails. I watch her walking across the small square, eyes raised, palm skyward, testing for rain – an aimless Egyptian.

It is not the place. We move on. Whichever direction we drive in we seem to miss the rain – always visible elsewhere, hard and dark, a destructive rain. We hit flooded valleys with runnels of water cascading along the road, forcing us to reverse and search for higher roads. We never find sunlight. There isn't a single person working the fields or feeding the goats; the chicken coops by the sides of the roads are empty. The buildings are little more than shacks. The grandest are small stone houses, with dilapidated wood shutters. There are no palazzos, country retreats, impressive houses with strong perimeter fences. The automobiles we meet – small vans, small cars, small trucks – are all local, old, earth-encrusted, rust-rimmed.

When we finally reach the coast road we have to drive for half an hour before we find a place open for lunch – a small restaurant, empty. There is no menu this time of year. We are brought grilled fish, grilled peppers. The terrace overlooks the Gulf of Squillace. The rough sea is a plane of churning flints. We watch an electric storm on this new horizon. For the first time today we experience rain, lightly hitting the opaque corrugated plastic roof directly above us.

I push my chair back. 'You've got to call Storaro.'

Francesca jerks up. 'What?'

'From here.'

'And say what?'

'That we've moved on. I've learned something. We're on the coast.'

'Like that?'

She is nervous, feels a little tricked; will she have to make the call in front of me?

'No. Just call him. But if he asks, tell him. We're

on the coast. Near Crotone. If he asks why, tell him what happened last night.'

'What if he asks where you are?'

'I've left you at a restaurant.'

Elbows on the table, staring out to sea, Francesca lights a cigarette. I go and lean on the iron balustrade at the end of the terrace. We are on a high clifftop. Gulls curl and swoop below, occasionally resting on a current of air, rising level with me, silver-black eyes spying, glinting.

I hear Francesca call Storaro. He's on her speed dial. She is deadpan. 'It's me. I said I'd call. I don't know. Fine. Fine. He's . . . I don't know. He dumped me in a restaurant without a menu. He met people last night. You'll have to ask him. No, I didn't. I'm not an informer; I've seen what happens to them, Storaro. Forget it. *Ciao.*'

Her voice hardly modulated. A call under duress. But not from me, from him – an old friendship. I give Francesca the thumbs up. Return to my seat, stretch out my legs, crossing them at the ankles.

'Thank you.'

'He didn't ask where I was. It seemed silly to tell him.'

'He doesn't need to ask. Now, no more calls. OK?'

She doesn't respond. We order *caffè*. There must be a way to speed this up. Whether or not the arrests we saw today were connected to the Caravaggio, irrespective of what Storaro thinks he can achieve, and how soon, this needs to happen fast. Momentum is the first principle in deal-making. It is like speed in movement – things becoming lighter, easier to manoeuvre. The impossible becomes possible. I need to be seen to be looking for a deal, not drawing them in – that will only make them unsettled. The thugs in the BMW. Their nightly visit is my opportunity. Tell them I want a meet with Lomazzo. Simple as that.

'Tonight. After dinner. I need you to go back to the hotel room and stay there.'

'What will you be doing?'

'Speeding things up.'

I can tell she wants to ask why have I decided to do this, what's changed from the original plan, whatever that was; but she decides against it and changes the subject instead.

'I can't imagine this place in the summer.'

'It's burning hot – forty-plus degrees. Wherever you look, the world is melting. Nothing is clear. There are no hard lines. Everything is about to turn from solid to liquid. The ground burns your feet through your shoes. The heat of the sun even suppresses the sounds around you. Only the scratching of insects and rattle of fridges cuts through. Cars pass by silently. It's the strangest thing.'

'I'd like to come here then. I like that kind of extreme. I like the desert.'

'I like the desert.'

'Maybe we should be telling people we're off to live in the desert.'

'Actually I'd prefer to live on the Upper West Side of New York City.'

'With me?'

'You want to live in the desert.'

'I could live in New York.'

'We'd have to sell the Caravaggio.'

'How much is it worth?'

'I think it's considered priceless. But I did read once – in restorable condition – about fifty million dollars. But that's on the open market. The black market would be a quarter of that. If anyone would take it.'

'You're not tempted?'

I laugh. 'I'm art's desperado, remember. Danger and glory, that's what I live for.'

'Right now my entire life seems lived by someone else.'

The afternoon and early evening is spent driving along the coast looking for a major road to take us inland, towards Sant' Angelo. The drive takes three hours, the car either pushing through floods and aquaplaning across the road or caught in mud, wheels churning for grip. Three times we have to reverse for miles after hitting impassable land-slides, lean-tos of mud from the edge of the road to the hillside. All the windows build up drifts of mud. There are long stretches of driving at five miles an hour – first gear, clutch half-depressed – over cracking road surfaces, the tarmac live under the tyres. We watch a tree break in front of us, the reason impossible to determine. This particular road has been long, it will be better to get to the other side of the falling tree than to find our way back. Its fall is slow – the cracking loud, the wood resistant to its splitting. I accelerate. The wheels spin. The branches scrape the back window. A real adventure, Francesca calls it. Later she says, as the road gives way on a corner and our rear wheel drops down, the car pulled back, 'We'll remember this.' Below us in umber darkness there is nothing but the promise of a further drop, the visible land miles away, low and flat. I try to get the car back on the road by jamming thin, spiny, inflexible olive branches under the wheel, digging them into the mud. It's a one-shot solution. It works, but I feel all the branches break hard, spin and shoot out. Francesca repeats herself: 'It's a real adventure. We'll remember this.'

It is night when we pull up by the hotel, both exhausted by the vigilance necessary to keep the car on the road. The rain has stopped. Carmine is behind the reception desk. I pass quickly; Francesca takes the keys from him without stopping. In our room I close the curtains and turn on the two bedside lamps. Francesca falls into the armchair, hangs a leg over one of the arms, swinging a booted foot.

'Right now I'd like room service and to watch TV in bed.'

I drop on to the bed, lying back, feet remaining

on the floor. 'I'm afraid we need to go back out there.'

'Really?'

I do not need to say anything; she heaves herself out of the chair. 'Give me five minutes.'

She shuts the bathroom door behind her. Will they even appear tonight – risk the BMW in such weather? I am irritated by the thought that they aren't going to turn up. I am impatient. I want this to be over and therefore I want things started by the end of the night. I have to believe they will be there. That's the point of them: always being present, taking your money, not giving you a chance ever, even when the rain kills your business. But then maybe they'll think with the rain there'll be nothing to take: who goes out to dinner on a night like this?

Francesca comes out of the bathroom, a little additional make-up for the evening, curls a little freer. I motion with my arms that I am going to need pulling up off the bed. Francesca is happy to assist. I change my shoes, socks, trousers.

Carmine is absent from the reception desk and doesn't respond to the bell. I hand the key to Francesca. 'You take it. You'll be first back.'

'Are you sure about this?'

'I do this all the time, remember.'

We choose the first restaurant. It is half-full and all heads turn. The bar owner – cuffs folded back at his wrists, the younger man still with the high, tight roll – seats us and we are served quickly, keenly, before others, already waiting. Is this deference due to my knowing who Lomazzo is, his power conferring status on us? Or is it more direct than that: in knowing Lomazzo we ourselves must be powerful and therefore dangerous in our own right? I look at Francesca chewing her bottom lip, spectacles resting on her eyebrows as she looks around the small room. Maybe it's just that as mysterious outsiders we are the closest thing the town has got to celebrities and this is how celebrities are treated. We are given a wine list. Francesca asks for the best local red – strong, like a Barolo. The younger man comes over to advise, his dark finger dragging down the list, explaining. I stare out of the window, the damp air softening the streetlamps, the coloured lights. It is a cosy night now – now we're inside the restaurant with the promise of food and well-chosen wine. My hand rests on the attaché case beside my chair. Francesca needs to take it back to the hotel with her.

The food is good. Basic produce better than the other place. I spot Mariangela in the kitchen, sitting on a worktop, hands on her knees, swinging her legs. The bar must be closed. I look across the piazza. No tables under the lights, the trees. The shutters are dark. I mention this to the owner. I am told Calabrians will come out to eat in this weather, but not to drink. He refills our glasses, backs away. I pick at my food, turning the fork absently, the pasta strips curling through the tines.

The tomato sauce is rich, spicy, oily. I am hungry but cannot eat. I try to concentrate on Francesca, animated, chatty, elbows on the table over her empty bowl, wine glass at her lips.

She says she will quit the Uffizi in the autumn, after the Titian exhibit. What she will then do, she isn't sure. Write, maybe. On galleries, museums, public spaces. Her passion. She could retrain – architecture, urban-planning. As a child she dreamed of building a city. She once read a survey: of the hundred most-successful people in various areas, businessmen, actors, politicians and so on, all – *all* – chose architecture as the work they'd most like to do.

'All?'

'All – really.'

'I was very impressed by Storaro's gallery, the collection, the hang.'

'He loves that place. It is the true extension of the good part of him.'

I remember him in his penthouse, sitting on a low chair, legs crossed, small hand holding fast to his short shin, keeping himself in that tight position, his chest swelling, shirt ruffled up between the lapels of his pinstriped suit. Daydreaming, bored, waiting, fantasizing – who knows?

The meal is finished with *grappa*. Francesca smokes. She watches my eyes shunting from her to the window – my vision passing through the glass to the piazza, beyond, to the BMW entering the town, slinking along the streets, windows darker than the night. I know she is now talking to avoid asking me: what are you looking for? What's happening? What do you expect to happen next? I reach for her hand, keeping my eyes fixed past her.

We leave the restaurant, Francesca tripping on the doorstep. I lunge forward to keep her upright, not letting go of the attaché case. As she is thanking me, I hear a car approach.

'If I hand you the case, take it and go straight back to the hotel. Don't worry about anything. I might be back in five minutes; I might be gone longer – all night. Don't do anything. Don't call anyone. Don't call Storaro. I know what I'm doing.'

A car appears. It's not the BMW. Francesca brushes her curls from her face.

'Understand?'

She shrugs. Of course. However, she doesn't want to take it in, absorb it, until she has to, until the moment when she won't be able to do anything about it.

We walk along the side of the piazza, underneath the trees, the coloured bulbs, the bunting. Everything is damp. The occasional raindrop falls from the branches, the cord, the wires.

'Remember. This is what we came for.'

'I'm just going to read until you're back.'

'Good.'

I stop at the corner of the piazza, ten metres from the hotel, not losing sight of the road I expect them to arrive by. I hand Francesca the attaché case.

'If you see Carmine and he asks where I am, just say I'll be back soon.'

Francesca rises up to kiss me but I hear another car, a more powerful engine, and move away, staring across the piazza, to the bar, to the church.

Francesca steps back, gently rubbing my arm. I hear her walk towards the hotel. My plan was to wait by the bar, but it's closed. I decide instead to wait in the centre of the piazza. To make a show of waiting.

6

It is clear that I am waiting. The bar owner knows, crossing with the young waiter – his son? – and Mariangela to the bar, a small brown sack of money in his hand. He knows because as the younger man goes to wave, to acknowledge me, his father grabs at his arm, holds it down, and their pace quickens across the piazza. Mariangela turns to look at me as her father opens the door of the bar. What does she think of this stranger standing in the centre of her world, standing between the serpentine pools of rain, beneath a grey night sky, the moonlight and starlight replacing the lamplight and the gritty glow of colour from the festival decorations? How much does she know about the men who come and take her father's money, her money – money which might buy her more accessories, more make-up, hair-dye, more music (she must be music mad), if they didn't have to give it away?

What about the son – the same age as the young men in the BMW: how does he feel, biceps like egg timers from the tight roll of his sleeves – is this some kind of unconscious symbol of his emasculated strength? I know his father is resigned; he understands this is the way it is. Has he explained it to them? Can he explain? Or does resignation come only from fighting a long unwinnable fight?

The lights of the bar go on, then a few moments later the lights go on in the apartment above the bar. No one looks down across the piazza to me. It has been explained. I know Lomazzo.

All the while I hear cars in the distance but nothing comes close to the piazza. What's Francesca doing now? Five minutes gone. If I turn around, I can see the balconies. She isn't there, smoking. Will she risk a look? What will she think? That choosing to stand in the middle of the piazza is procedural somehow. It isn't. I am doing it because I want them to know immediately that I am waiting for *them* – not strolling, not taking a breather on a bench, not waiting for a lover. Standing in the centre of the piazza, facing the bar, the place where yesterday we met – it will be clear. And with that, everything is equal, until we speak. And I want them to feel in control, in the first instance. This is why I'm standing here, I tell Francesca in my head. Will she really read until I get back? It's a nice image, her lying on the bed, sitting reading in the armchair, immersed as a waiting strategy, a strategy I recognize.

I hear another engine, a smooth low growl, no change in register as it winds around the narrow streets. Is this them? I picture only the car, the black windows, not the men inside – not yet. It doesn't approach from the direction I expected, but from the north side of the piazza, past the two restaurants. I don't look around – peripheral vision, instinct, is enough to know it's them. I hear an infinitesimal change in acceleration the moment the men inside notice me, a foot ever so slightly taken off the accelerator as they assemble the details. I hear the fractional speeding up, the adrenalin impression on the accelerator; they want to know why I am here – waiting for them.

The BMW draws to halt outside the bar. Tonight there are three of them. Three young men. They don't look at the bar. They line up against the car, staring at me. They are all wearing hooded tops, hoods down, tight, faded jeans, high-top trainers. They are in their mid twenties. There is something rehearsed about their manner – their pose. It has been practised. Copied from somewhere. American hip-hop culture. Gangsta rap. They are posing because they know what they look like – others have stood this way and looked a certain way, a way they like: legs apart, backs straight, hands together just below their bellies, heads jutting. It is smart to send boys like this – they are committed, ambitious. They want to be real gangsters, drive nice cars at night. They will also scare most people because the pose is intimidating

– it's designed to be, choreographed even. But it's not just a pose, it is also a code: we are dangerous, we are violent. They don't frighten me. Violence is only really deep in a few. Swift in fewer. One in five with these people. The rest do what they have to when it's necessary. So who do I have here? What is the spread? None immediately makes me wary.

I approach, letting them enjoy their pose a little longer. The first thing I say is in English, and it is enough to produce reflexive glances between them, pose interrupted. I keep on in English. 'I'm here to do a deal with Lomazzo.' (More reflexive looks – did they hear right?) 'I have a painting. Access to more. Tell him I want to meet him.' I then change to Italian, walking along the line of them – a military inspection. I must judge this right. I tell them, '*Sbirra*. Ex-*sbirra*.' I repeat the offer and what I want. Emphasizing 'Lomazzo'. Do they understand?

One breaks the line, stepping in front of me, hand disappearing around to his back and under his sweatshirt to his belt. A gun or knife. We both know there is no need to display which. It is my turn to show understanding. I back away.

I am told they don't know Lomazzo. Who's Lomazzo? They laugh. Their voices are low, breaking against the hard sounds of their dialect, throats roughed up by strong cigarettes, strong coffee, cheap wine. I wait for them to finish joking, laughing along with them, before saying in

English: 'Funny.' I then point to the hotel, directly to my window, and to Francesca on the balcony, leaning on the railing, smoking – watching. And for a moment I see myself – not from her vantage point but from somewhere else, higher – a point high in the night sky. I am part of a set of four singular humans and a car on a deserted piazza. I finish the conversation. 'You can contact me there.' And turn away. I am now a dark singular human crossing the deserted piazza. I look up to the window. Francesca is gone, the door left open, leaving a tall rectangle of dim gold light. I listen to the three young men crunch round the car and to the door of the bar. There is no need to knock. I hear the door open for them.

Francesca is waiting for me. She says, 'I saw you, I saw you.' Asks, 'What happened, what happened?' Leads me into the room, to the bed, sits me down, perches next to me, her hands in my lap. She elaborates, 'I needed a cigarette. You said don't worry. The moment I got in here, I thought – I don't know. So I went out there.' She points. Asks again, 'What happened?'

I am quiet, my shoulders are tense, my neck stiff. I ache from being tense and stiff in the damp air. I feel arthritic, ancient. Very tired suddenly. It's a tough thing to do at the end of the day, when you should be in bed. I picture the boys – they have become boys to me, despite being at that dangerous age: the age of fanaticism, implacable self-confidence, self-defining violence. I picture them watching me, the one with the weapon, the others keeping the pose. Did I impress them enough? They need to impress Lomazzo. Mythologize the moment, me. Hype me up because I was calm, insistent, unthreatened. A man waiting for them in the centre of the piazza.

Francesca tugs at my hand, wanting to know. 'What happened?'

'It's fine.'

She moves closer, pulling at my hand. 'I want to know, I want to know.'

She is on a curve of nerves – the upward slope. I can feel her breathing is shallow, excited. I sense a fast heart.

'Tell me!' She doesn't wait for an answer but awkwardly goes for a kiss, the nervous energy within her split between mind and body. She pushes me back on the bed and sits over me.

'Tell me.'

I stare up into her face: brown, brown eyes, dark, dark curls.

'There's nothing to tell.'

'I saw you. You and them, the men from last night.'

'Boys.'

'What did they say?'

'Nothing. I did all the talking.'

'What did *you* say?'

'That I wanted to meet their boss, that I had a painting, access to more, that I was staying here.'

'Was that when you turned around and pointed?'
'Yes.'
'Did you see me?'
'Yes.'
'I was having a cigarette.'
'I know, you told me.'
'How do you feel?'
'Tired.'
'I couldn't read.'
'You're excited.'
'Were you scared?' She doesn't want an answer. 'I couldn't believe it when I went out there.'

Her hands are on my chest, wrists together, hands opposed, as if about to give me compressions. Her hips roll. I feel her press down on me. She looks down at my face – a middle-distance stare. Am I going to respond? Her fear has turned into hyper-excitement, and she is desperate to fuck even if she doesn't quite know it yet; there is too much volatility in her to pin down what she is feeling, what will satisfy her, but her body is beginning it. My cock is hard, a ridge beneath her, something for her body to concentrate on. Her linen dress is bunched up and layered, like the mudslides along the roads. Her knees protrude, brown and shiny. I hold her knees and then run my hands up her thighs and under the layers of linen. She doesn't respond. Her thighs are tense, muscles tight as she rolls over the ridge and then back. Still the middle-distance stare. I am enjoying not being part of this – her taking what she wants because sensation has taken over. I also know I cannot give. All my energy must be contained, reserved. For tomorrow. The next day. The meet with Lomazzo when it comes. She slides back to my thighs, unbuttons my jeans, still not looking for permission or compliance. She frees my cock from my shorts, holds it – for a moment unable to decide what to do with it. She then pushes herself off the bed, the layers of her linen dress unfolding to her ankles. She turns out the lights. I hear her dress cast off, underwear detached and slipped out of. She is naked. She assumes her original position but this time sliding on to me and then levering forward, her hand searching behind for my cock and placing it correctly for a smooth rock back. She groans and quickly begins to rise and fall into a slow certain rhythm. A loving rhythm. I feel love from her – the gentle, full motion of her body above me, rising and falling. Her eyes are closed, face slightly upturned and to the side. Easing. She is coaxing away the excitement, the energy, releasing it with slow, controlled rocks forward and curls back. She is sexually graceful, lovingly erotic. I watch her body – round stomach, dark shoulders, arms straight and locked down. Her curls swaying. I think of Sarah, almost certainly asleep. Does this end it? Not the fuck, but the knowledge that my inner desperation is being smoothed away by this woman. Francesca retains her rhythm, but now she stays pressed to me, pushing back, dragging forward, and with increased pressure. She begins to come, top lip sucked in, thighs stiffening against me. Her orgasm is deep, a contraction of her stomach – the soft roundness quickly concave, a caught breath and then a letting-go of a long, long moan. She slides off me and rolls to my side. I feel conspicuous in my disarray, fully clothed, jeans and shorts pulled halfway down my thighs, my cock straining up. I want instruction. Are we finished? How does she want to finish this? I feel her hand around me, then her mouth, warm, smooth, tight, and my quick giving-in, my orgasm, numb, extended, muscular. All activity. I hear Francesca cope, staying with me, the long flow. She then lies back, shuffling up, to be fully next to me, close. It is my turn to end sex with sleep. Yet before I do I wonder what in all this would Caravaggio have painted? I am certain it would be this moment. Lovers almost fused together, yet their minds far, far apart, both stemming the return of fear with nudges closer. Could you capture that, maestro?

7

Francesca wakes me with coffee and hard bread, with butter and a chestnut paste. From Carmine's kitchen. She is in jeans and T-shirt, barefoot and braless. I am naked, having woken at dawn, stripped down and curled up behind her, face in her curls, without tickle, buried deep. Sleeping deeply in them. I didn't feel her separate, dress, leave. Didn't feel alone. I have noticed I have stopped dreaming. This has happened before. It allows work to be done. The mind to mend, or develop, or prepare. I have edge-of-sleep sensations, but nothing further in; there is no inhabiting of other realms. Maybe it would all be too much.

Francesca spreads the butter, the chestnut paste on to the dry, porous bread. Bites, chews, drinks the coffee. I sit up, back straight, sheets pulled around my waist. I feel good. Want some of that breakfast. I eat, brushing away the crumbs with each bite, leaning over to the table, drinking the coffee in a leaning position. Francesca is in the armchair, bread held in all five fingertips.

'Is today the hard wait?'

'Something like that.'

'Can we go out?'

'I won't.'

'You think something will happen?'

'It's not about that. It's just how I do it.'

'I should call work – check in.'

I don't want her to do this. For me, the world is currently suspended beyond this town, its few surrounding hills, the fallen trees and mudslides.

'Is that OK?'

I don't want to sanction or censure. I clear the sheet of crumbs and slide back into bed, facing the door, away from Francesca.

'OK. I'll wait.'

The message will come via Carmine, so it will be a knock at the door, unless Francesca goes out and it's delivered to her. I guess I'll be vetted first. Which means bullied in the back of the BMW, on the orders of someone more senior, watching from the front seat. But it will be the boys who do the work. Nothing much beyond a slap, a punch in the ribs, roomless, so without thrust, the power to really hurt. And then questions followed by threats: who do I think I am kidding coming here? How do I know Lomazzo? They're going to kill me. Feed me to the wolves. I can deal with all this, have done so before. After it all calms down they'll want to know the details of the deal. The journalistic details: what, when, where, who? After which I'll be kicked out, and depending on how I have impressed them, there will be some kind of a walk back to town.

I decide Francesca can't leave without me. What if they take her? Decide it'll be easier to get the information they want that way: a single slap, a single threat and they'll know everything. Why should she hold out? This was why it was a mistake to bring her, giving them access to a soft thing. I crane around. Francesca is still sitting in the armchair. She is reading a newspaper. Carmine must have given it to her. First thing then, I must prevent them from getting any kind of access to her.

We go out for twenty minutes around two p.m., with directions from Carmine, to a small shop for bread, cheese, salami. And then back for lunch on the balcony, under a white sky, sandwiches in cold hands. More coffee. We both have long baths, Francesca first, door open, curls tumbling over the back of the tub, relaxing in the heat. I watch as she washes her hair, curls transformed into long evenly stretched tresses.

I close the door when it is my turn. I need to relax entirely and not make a show of being relaxed in front of Francesca. I am happy she is not displaying impatience or fear and is letting this happen around her. I notice her occasionally looking up at me, searching for something in my face, in my eyes, keen to know what's going on in my mind, if she can read it for herself. I don't know what's readable there. I look into the mirror.

Some of the tiredness is gone; my eyes are clearer, my tongue pink. I check my hairline. Is it thinning? For a millimetre or so the trees are more distinct than the wood. Thirty-six – things shouldn't get too desperate until I am well into my forties.

In the bedroom we are both wrapped in towels, Francesca sitting on the end of the bed, spectacles on, pressing back and shaping the cuticles of her fingernails with her thumbnail; I am in the armchair, looking at my own cuticles. There is nothing much to see. Francesca unwraps and tightens the towel around her – a reflexive movement, her skin sensing the towel's give and both hands pulling it apart at the fold and rewrapping it. She continues the examination of her nails, now picking away loose skin. Her curls have jumped up, almost into ringlets, hanging high above her shoulders for the first time.

I am not surprised nothing has happened yet; they might wait until tomorrow or even the next day. But something tells me they won't. It will happen sooner. Tonight. Strangers don't come here often, not with deals. Not so brazenly. I watch Francesca; what is she thinking? Are her thoughts entirely concentrated on the job at hand – perfect nails? Neither of us mentioned last night: her loving fuck. Then me turning over into sleep. At least she didn't disappear moments afterwards. Francesca looks up.

'I'm scared.'

'Don't be.'

'What if something goes wrong?'

'It won't.'

'How do you know?'

'I just do.'

'I don't believe you.'

'They're just men. Men who want money. It is very simple.'

'But you're going to cheat them.'

'They don't know that.'

'I'm scared, Daniel.'

'Don't be. I know what I'm doing.'

8

The message comes at midnight. A knock on the door from Carmine. I say I'll be down. Francesca stands behind me. I shut the door and move her to the centre of the room, grip her by the shoulders.

'I will be gone a while. A few hours probably. But don't worry. Don't go downstairs. If Carmine comes back up, just say it's about the painting. Nothing more. Do you understand? Look at me. Do you understand?'

She nods.

'This is where it gets serious.'

She nods again. 'Are you taking the painting?'

'No.'

'The money?'

'No.'

'Not even the gun?'

I laugh. 'Definitely not the gun.'

She reaches up for a kiss. 'Be careful.'

She sees me to the door, watches me down the

hallway, closing the door as I disappear down the stairs.

The BMW is parked directly outside the hotel. I know the door will be opened, one of the young men from last night will climb out, making room for me, then slide back in. I guess, after the driver, there will be a fourth person, higher ranking, not just youth and muscle.

I am right. I greet them all in English, politely, smiling, then in Italian. The BMW leaves the hotel entrance with spinning wheels, into fourth, fifth gear before we have left the piazza. They know the roads, the bends and hills, the storm damage. The older guy, in his forties, looks over the seat at me. His face is dark, haggard, soft. He has big heavy eyes and smooth round lids. He is ghoulish. He wants to know who they have in the car.

'Daniel Wright.'

'Good evening, Signor Wright.'

I demonstrate my understanding of the game by not asking for his name.

We leave the town; the only lights are the full beams of the car pushing through the darkness.

'Where are you taking me? I want to see Lomazzo.' I say this to break the silence. To establish my Italian. I don't expect an answer and don't get one. I look at the driver, both hands on the wheel, arms locked, taking each bend with a roll of his shoulders. I am reminded of Nenni – all his crazy tics and spasms disappearing over a certain speed in the Alfa Romeo. It will have been men like this who killed him and Maria. This rank. I fold my arms. At least at night there is no need for a blindfold.

The drive lasts twenty minutes. It ends after a steep climb and a hump on to some kind of high plateau. I can make out constellations of light on the low distant horizon. The car's headlights are killed. All four doors open. I am pulled out; I tug away the hands holding my jacket. I hear a sliding sound. And an order I don't understand.

It is very dark. I cannot see the edges of where I am. I know they know the edges and can move freely. I cannot see any of the four men around me. I look up at the sky and feel for the car. I find it with outstretched arms and work my way round to the back, to reduce the angles of attack. A cigarette is lit just in front of me. It's not the ghoul. I hear the draw. It is the ghoul, however, who addresses me.

'American or English?'

'English.'

'Who are you? If I think you are lying, you will be pushed off the mountain. Below is a forest. You will never be found. The wolves will eat you.'

The wolves. No response is necessary.

'Why do you ask for Lomazzo?'

I pause before I say, 'I have reasons.'

'What are they?'

'I will explain them to him.'

From the darkness a fist drives into my stomach – fast in, fast out. I was expecting something; my

427

body was tense, deflective. The pain bursts through me. I am silent, concentrating on keeping my breathing steady. They need to understand that I can take this.

'Are you a cop?'

'Ex-cop.'

'Why?'

'That's my business.'

Fast into my right side, extra hard, just below my ribs, where there is little muscle to tense, to deflect. I have to hold the pain in, channel it somewhere – dispel it. I take a deep breath. It won't last much longer.

'Who's the girl?'

Speak. Clearly. Firmly. 'The girl is important.'

'Who is she?'

'She works for the Uffizi in Florence. She's the key.'

'What do you want?'

'I need to disappear.'

'Why?'

'That's my business.'

The crack is across my jawline, a fist hitting it, then sliding along it, misplaced, mistimed. It means I am able to grab the following arm, and straighten it by grabbing at the wrist and shoulder and turn the body to the ground. It exposes me for the next punch, again to my left side, deep into my kidneys. It's not a fist this time. The hand is flat, the fingers hard in: maximum penetration for maximum damage. The pain is extreme, fluid, up into my chest, my neck, my head, my eyes. I want to drop to my knees. I brace myself against the car. The sky is black, cloud-streaked, star-specked, close. A few hundred metres higher and we'd all be revealed by starlight.

'Why Lomazzo?'

I can't speak, the pain is too intense. *Why Lomazzo?* The words float inside my head. I can see them, but the answer . . . I hear Nenni telling me, warning me to forget it: go home, fix your marriage. Maria also. Straight advice. I search for a way to form words.

'The old man. He protected the old man. I met the old man. Last year. I trust a man who protected him.'

'Lomazzo is not *capo di tutti capi.*'

I pull in the pain. 'Then I have made a mistake.'

'Go home.'

Almost there. One more statement. Take one more hit to make it clear. 'If I go home, I take the deal somewhere else. Lorenzo Savarese. He will laugh at you.'

It is to the left side again, softened up, organ deep. My head is full of white. Of sky. Of snow. An empty gallery wall. I hear my cheekbone crack from a second punch to the face. I fall to the ground. There is no resistance left. I have to stay where I am.

After a moment I am picked up, warm breath on my face. The ghoul whispering, 'What is the deal?'

Blood flows from my mouth. So they've bitten. I explain, the words quiet, tight, barely audible. 'You tell Lomazzo. I can bring him paintings. No one will know they're gone. Each one worth five hundred thousand euros.'

'What do you want?'

'Ten per cent. Just ten per cent.'

'What else?'

'Nothing.'

I am pushed down, my head banged against the rear of the car. I roll to the ground. The car doors are opened, the engine started. The exhaust burns over my head. I roll away. The wheels are spun; grit and dirt spit across my face and hands. It's because I was a cop – punishment for that, before any business starts. I roll further away from the car, to the edge of the plateau. There is nothing beyond the edge. There is no slope. My left kidney burns. I want to vomit. Blood drips from my mouth, nose.

The car turns around. Lights on full beam shine on me. I sit up, shield my eyes. The car moves forward. The high beam is as blinding as the dark. I can't see where I might roll to, crawl to, if they are intent on pushing me off. The car stops just before me. The engine's din and heat has its own force, pushing me back. The doors open. I am picked up. Things are said I don't understand. I am dumped in the rear seat. I can't focus; my eyes retain the brightness of car headlights and all I can see is two columns of diffuse white crossed in front of me. The BMW speeds off.

My sight returns slowly. The beating is over – no death today. It's either to Lomazzo, now I've been softened up, or back to town, to wait. I'd prefer the latter. I need time. I am too weak, tired, broken by the pain to outline the deal again. To sell it. The ghoul looks at me. Smooth eyelids sliding over his big eyes. What's he learned? What will he say to Lomazzo? We drive on through the hard dark night. When we stop the headlights reveal a chipped and crumbling stone wall ahead. There is nothing outside the side windows. The left-hand door opens and I am pulled out and dumped on the hard ground. I can make out a few more buildings, the form of them in soft grey lines. The car reverses away. I've been left on the edge of the town. The first street is narrow, the only light from a single lamp above a front door. It is one-thirty-five a.m. My coat, my hands, my face, my neck are covered in thick sticky blood. My throat feels dry, despite the covering of blood; my teeth are coated, gritty. I need to drink. The ache in my side sends waves of pain through me. I can barely walk. I have to lean away from the pain, hold my body in a permanent stretch. A lucky punch. I should have protected myself better. I am at the end of another dark street. This town needs a little streetlighting. Not much, just on each corner. It also needs signposts. Not many, just to the piazza. To the centre of town. My mind rocks inside my head with every step, my brain a round thing rocking inside a shell. Light and signs and I'd be back at the hotel. No time at all. I fall forward, surprised by a surge of pain. My left knee collapses, collapsing inward, my body breaking in from the side, hip down. I just manage to stop myself hitting the ground, the hard, cold, cracked and split cobbles. Amazing what a few punches can do. Into the organs. The pain races. It has found channels in which to race. My mind is engulfed by it, rocking in it, inside its shell. I need to find out where I am. I look for the church, a spire above the rooftops, a crucifix amid aerials. There is nothing, just aerials. The town is bigger than I imagined. Bigger, more complex. I need to sit, to rest, rest and think and build up a little strength. I drop down on to the first doorstep. Maybe I should ask for help. Knock on the door. The way I look should be enough to signal: attention needed. Make it clear I am English, *turista* and not *'ndrangheta*. But I want to get back to the hotel, to Francesca. I massage my side, looking to ease away the pain. I know my kidney is damaged. A deep bruise, a rupture – something. A lucky punch. I try to stand but it's no good; the pain keeps me down. I need to assemble myself away from the pain, separate myself from the harsh glow in my side, the agony crushed in there. I focus on the long broad waves as they radiate out. Tell myself: take something from its shape, its rhythm; concentrate on its colour. A shadow of crimson. Make it something else. Music. I heave myself up, breathe out when the pain beats hardest. My eyes roll, roam the sky. I am up. I tell myself: keep to the widest streets; they must lead to the centre. I search for the church again. It is there. The white belfry, the gold crucifix. How far? Two, three rooftops. The road leads away; I take the first left. I am forced to slow down and let the pain take me over when it wants. No point denying it. Just move when I can. The church appears: a sharp white shining in the night. The piazza is ahead, dark, the coloured lights out and dull. I now need the support of a wall for each step. Sweat leaks out of me and is beginning to weigh me down; my clothes are stiffening with it. At the entrance to the piazza my eyes immediately go to the balcony. No one is there. Shutters closed. There is a faint light. A serrated glow. I quicken my pace, resist the pain for a few minutes, just to get me to the hotel. I pull in fast, sharp, energizing breaths. I can see myself from the mysterious vantage point above, crossing the piazza, a cripple dragging himself. Then the hotel steps, the door.

The lobby is dark. No Carmine, no night light. By the time I reach the stairs the pain is overwhelming. I climb slowly, one hand on the banister, other hand on the stair itself. I am bent over – a hunched thing – my legs barely lifting. I collapse at the top. There is a moment of delight, having made it, got so close. Calling close. I call. Press the bottom of my spine to the floor, then push myself up into an arch.

The bedroom door is open within seconds and

she is at my side, kneeling over me, hand on my chest, hand on my cheek. Her distress is silent. She just looks at my face, into my eyes. I whisper, 'Help me up.' She attempts to lift me but is defeated by the dead weight of my body. 'Wait,' I whisper. She sits back, hands on her thighs. I push myself on to my knees.

'Now.'

She hoists me up and guides me through the door, and lays me gently down on the bed, moving quickly for a pillow, tucking it under my head.

More delight, long waves of it, parallel to the pain, for a moment equal to it. Francesca leans over me, kisses my forehead. Warmth passes through me. My side is now numb – a hard block fixed in between ribs and hip.

'Run the bath.'

The sound of the water pleases me. Inside my head. It is clear, clean – purifying. Within a moment Francesca is back, standing, hands open, poised. What next?

I push off a shoe, tip of one pressing down on heel of other. Francesca pulls off the other and removes my socks.

'It was a lucky punch.'

'What happened?'

'Nothing. Questions. A display of ultra-violence. Help me out of my jacket.'

I lift one shoulder, then the other. We are quickly in a tangle, and I heave myself into a sitting position, lolling forward. Francesca takes the weight, then slides my shirt off my back. She gasps at the bruise. My whole side is purple. Raging with colour. There are hundreds of tiny pinpricks of blood-red dots just beneath the surface. There is something two-tone about the bruise; movement alters the colour: purple to red-pink.

'We should get you to hospital.'

'No. I'm fine.'

'Look at you. What kind of damage causes that?' She points.

'I just need a bath.' I lie back down, unbutton my jeans. Francesca helps slide them off.

'Are we going home?'

I swing my legs on to the floor. Francesca sits down next to me and places an arm around my waist, ready to steady me as I stand.

She holds me at the elbow as I walk slowly into the bathroom, keeps hold of me. I place a hand on her shoulder as I step into the bath and lower myself down. The hot water burns at the bruise. I grit my teeth. I remain rigid until the burning subsides. After about thirty seconds the hot water starts to work through my skin and my muscles begin to relax. My whole body has contracted with the pain. I begin to stretch out. I feel appreciably longer. I point my toes. Extend my neck. Roll my head. Francesca sits on the bathroom floor, arms hugging her knees. I look at her.

'You OK?'

'You didn't warn me.'

'I knew they'd rough me up a bit. But as I said, it was a lucky punch. Don't worry. I'll be fine.'

'I'm scared.'

'Don't be.'

'They could have killed you.'

'Possibly.'

'What happens now?'

'What do you think?'

She pauses. 'We wait.'

9

Sarah calls. I take it out on the balcony. There is a throb in my side, as if my kidney is bruised deeply and working hard to function. Walking is painful. Standing straight is impossible. A rib might be cracked. There is a sharp pain when I sit down or stand up. My jaw is swollen a little. My teeth ache. The back of my throat is still dry.

Sarah asks where I am. I say Amsterdam.

'With Tom?'

'He's not here.' What sort of conversation should I make this? 'Where are you?'

'At work.'

There is a long pause; I cannot think of anything further to say.

'Dan?'

'Yes.'

'Are you OK?'

'I'm fine. How are you?'

'I don't know. You just disappeared.'

'I thought it was for the best.'

Another pause. It is then my turn to say her name, make it into a question.

'Sarah?'

'Yes.'

'I'm pleased you called.' Does she stiffen at this? I hear hardness; she will not let this become an opportunity to start a longer discussion.

'I'm waiting to go into a meeting.'

I hate her for this. 'I'm standing on a balcony.'

'It's all right for some.' There is a dry, awkward laugh.

'Will you call again?'

'You can't just disappear, Dan.'

'You did.'

'I don't know what you mean.'

'Think about it.'

'This isn't the time for games.'

I am silent.

'I'll call you at the weekend. Will you still be in Amsterdam?'

'I don't know.'

I flip the phone closed. Look out over the piazza. 'It's all right for some.' I don't know what to think. To be heartbroken seems somehow impossible. Heartbreak requires a different kind of love – a love not formed by the extremes of feeling. It requires a vertical love, a central love, formed in the depths of ourselves, the heart of ourselves, not our mad edges. I know my love for Sarah comes from these mad edges, pulled in and amassed, and then thrust out. A centrifugal love, full of energy, somehow never content or calm. But then it doesn't feel stormy either. I picture my love as a snow drift gathering inside the shape of myself.

Francesca calls out, 'Is everything all right?' I don't respond. But I ask myself the question. I know I don't want to be in London, in that big house – there is no yearning for that. There is no yearning to be in an idealized home, full of imagined warmth, Sarah as lover, wife – idealized, loving. There is no yearning for something only Sarah can give me. And there is no desperation for Sarah to yield to me. Standing on the balcony only seconds after speaking to her I am not experiencing any of this, despite the frozen drifts of love that I know will never melt. And the pain. The layers of pain. Yes, it's all right for some.

I go back inside. Francesca is sitting in the armchair; she cares about the contents of the call, my reaction, what it might mean for her, so she's sitting nervously, waiting, unable to resist thinking through the possible outcomes. I say she was checking I was OK. She was her cool self. We might speak again, at the weekend. I am surprised by the lack of desperation, yearning I feel.

Francesca looks up at me. 'Daniel.'

I stop where I am. The pain is a pulse.

She continues, 'The things you feel for Sarah. I want you to feel them for me. I want to return those feelings. I feel those things for you.' Her eyes are serious, her smile is serious – a smile of doubt, concern, hope.

I shift to the bed, lower myself slowly, careful not to twist or bend between hip and ribs. The pain presents itself as a white light, a dizzy liquid. I stop midway. I need help and hold my hand out. Francesca is next to me.

'What is it?'

'Get me on to the bed.'

She tries to support me so my body remains straight as I lie down. I thank her, reach for her hand.

'Francesca.'

'Don't say anything.'

'I am glad you are here. That it is you.'

'I know.' She is pleased this is the case but understands it does not automatically lead to love. She changes the subject, her smile still serious. 'When do you think we'll be leaving?'

'I don't know.'

'I should call work. Tell them when . . .'

'What day is it?'

'Friday.'

I am a little surprised.

'What should I say?'

A burst of pain causes sharpness, impatience. 'Say you'll be back at work on Monday.'

'I want to stay as long as it takes.'

'Then say the middle of next week.'

She goes for her mobile. Now she has made herself clear to me, she wants to make contact with the outside world and let someone out there know where she is, let in a little northern normality to counter the southern insanity. But she's not sure – another part of her doesn't want the spell broken.

'I don't think I will call.'

'OK.'

'Are you tired?'

'Yes.'

'Then sleep.'

I don't need permission; my eyes are closing, my mind slipping away. Sleep is right. Better for mending myself. If they come back it might be tonight and I will need to be strong. Stronger. I hear Francesca run a bath, shut the door – the noise suppressed, distant, a choral hush. I gently turn myself on to my side, placing one hand between my thighs, the other under the pillow. My last thought before sleep invades me is to take the gun. Next time take the gun.

I sleep all day. Stir now and again. Sometimes aware of Francesca beside me, reading, or closer, dozing. I hear music – Bach. Dream it. A fugue. Light and long. The true soundtrack of flight. I have visions of myself running, running lightly over the hills of Calabria, hill to hill in single strides. I am happy to be running. Strong with big strides. I feel Francesca clasp my hand and wake momentarily. I quickly drift off again. I am no longer running. The fugue still sounds, four lines now so interwoven they are a single string climbing to the sky. I understand I can swing on this if I can reach it, and swing from hill to hill – on the move again. I grab at the music, yet despite a good reach and a strong grip it slips from my hand. There is something there to be held, I can see it, hear it, but somehow, whichever way I try to grab it, my hands are filled with nothing but ticklish air. I look up. There is a break in the clouds, like a hole in ice – round with hard sides. The music is pouring up. Music makes the heavens. When the end disappears I wake; the aching in my side is profound. My eyes stay closed. I hear Francesca on the phone. To Silvio. She will be back next week.

It is night when my eyes resist further sleep. Francesca is out on the balcony, smoking. I am hungry. Sleep has energized me into hunger. And I must eat. For strength. I join Francesca, placing my elbows on the wrought iron, cupping my face in my hands.

'We should go out and eat.'

'I thought we had to stay here?'

'We'll starve.'

'What if they come?'

'Then they wait.'

She grabs the railing, rocks back on her heels.

'I called work.'

I lean back on the railings myself, look into the bedroom.

'I heard.'

'I thought you were sleeping.'

'I was.'

I push myself off the railing, face her – she has turned, her arms now behind her back, gripping the railing that way and rocking back and forth.

'Nothing is real here, is it?'

'No.'

She looks up at me. 'I feel like nothing will ever be real again.'

'I know.'

'I don't like it.'

'It's horrible.'

'Hold me.'

She lets go of the railing, opens her arms to me. I cross my arms over her back and pull her in tightly. 'You've been very brave. Everything will be OK, I promise.'

She is crying. I pull her in. Move one hand to the back of her head, securing her. I want her to cry into me and feel safe in my arms. I want to transmit safety. Below, the red, white and green lights are turned on in the piazza. I rest my head in her hair. What does she really feel in all this unreality? What do *I* feel? I don't know. Big feelings felt subtly, precisely, then suddenly nothing. But mostly each moment is experienced too lightly to be fully comprehended, realized. Which is how I suspect she is experiencing things. It is why the embrace needs to be especially tight. To keep us from drifting off, drifting away. There is something fugitive in our existence.

I break us apart from the waist up, our arms
straightened and extended like brackets, allowing
for only a certain separation of ourselves as two
halves of one thing. Francesca sniffs, smiles, her
eyes a little watery, glistening. She is not embarrassed. I break a bracket to stroke a tear from her
cheek with my thumb, quickly returning to our
fixed position. I think to myself that if we had
more space we could turn like dancers – or is it
ice-skaters? – hips together, backs bent. Spinning.
Spinning away. It is a ridiculous image – laughable.
Yet it feels possible. From our general lightness on
this balcony, our general lightness in this town, this
landscape, we could just spin away.

'What are you smiling at?'

'Nothing.'

'Tell me.' She squeezes me with her elbows.

'I was imagining us dancing – like this. You know
– like ice-skaters.'

'That's very romantic.'

'I'm not sure I'd call it that.'

'What would you call it?'

'Sweetly absurd.'

'Is that how you'd describe us?'

'I'm the absurdity.'

She strokes my hair. 'You're very pretty, did you
know that?'

'Maybe once.'

She shakes her head. 'Still.'

I look over the piazza, to Mariangela setting out
the tables and chairs. 'We need to eat.'

Francesca lays her head on my chest. 'I'm not sure I want to go out there.'

'We have to.'

She drops her arms. 'Sorry. I know.' She turns, looks around – nowhere in particular. It is time to be practical. To be seen to be practical, and serious. To show me she remembers why we're here.

I grab her arm. 'Francesca. Relax. All we're doing is going for something to eat.'

There is the glistening promise of more tears – tears held back.

'Do you want to go home?'

She shakes her head. 'Please. Ignore me. I'll be all right.'

10

They are waiting. Music on. A crooner – Italian, super-sweet. The BMW vibrates. The front passenger door is pushed open. I need to make a quick decision: if I'd been given a moment to prepare, the gun, the painting, the personnel file would all be with me and Francesca told to stay where she is, but on the hotel steps it's the other way around – the only thing with me is Francesca, and, of course, the attaché case.

The ghoul invites me to get into the car. It is an order. I promised myself the gun; do I insist they wait? What about the other stuff? I try to imagine the conversation with Lomazzo. Suddenly the notion of taking these things seems ridiculous – I'll look like a salesman, picture propped up somewhere like a sample, Francesca's personnel file as some kind of certificate of credibility. But what about the gun? I should go back and get the gun. Then again, how long before I am searched? I turn to Francesca, hand her the attaché case, grip her upper arms, concentrate my look, speak in English.

'Go and get something to eat, then come back here. I promise I'll be back in one piece.'

Francesca remains with Italian. 'Don't go.'

'Francesca . . .'

'Please. Don't go. I'm . . .'

I interrupt her. 'In English; speak in English.'

'I'm scared. You don't need to do this. No one cares about this painting – not really.'

'I care. Now listen to me. I will be back in two hours, I promise. This bit's simple. They just want to find out what I'm really offering. It's a business meeting. Do you know how I know that?' She shakes her head. I nod to the car, to the open passenger-side door. 'Because I'm sitting in the front.'

Francesca drops her head, pulls away from me and runs back inside the hotel. I duck down into the car. The ghoul's slow lids drop over his big eyes. It's his greeting. I belt up. There is only one muscle guy in the back.

'I've got two hours if the girl's not going to get hysterical.'

The guy in the back laughs to himself. The ghoul just rolls his lids halfway down his eyes with a single nod.

I suspect homework has been done and they now know about my past life, my meeting with the old man, my reputation. Instructions will have been given not to harm me further.

We drive slowly through the town; the ghoul's handling of the car is less sure than the younger driver's from last night. He doesn't usually drive himself. Out in the countryside the muscle leans forward and drops a blindfold into my lap. Even at night – I must be going somewhere special! I pull at the elastic and secure it over my eyes. There is something relaxing about the total dark, the contoured blackness. I settle in my seat. I am aware of right turns, left turns, dips and inclines, but I don't bother to draw a mental map. The dull ache in my side is beginning to flare, to burn, to spread. The constant movement is aggravating the bruising, the damage – even a BMW's suspension cannot disguise the state of the roads. The pain doesn't worry me; my mind feels clear. I am ready for this. Adrenalin is working its way through my body. I am experiencing moments of synaesthesia: sounds as shapes mostly, but also movement as colour. I need this, extra-sensory information beyond others' capacity. Despite the blackness of the blindfold, the world is brown. Our movement through the night – a blur of brown; the guy in the back, fidgeting – movement and sound – a shifting brown. The night itself, above, beyond the dark windows – a vast brown. How far will I be taken? Why should Lomazzo live close to this little town and not the other side of Catanzaro or near Crotone? I promised Francesca two hours. That was a mistake; on these roads it could take two hours to get to wherever

I am being taken. We make a tight corner at speed; I am forced against the door, the handle digging into my side, pressing down on my kidney. I groan; I am momentarily light-headed. The muscle in the back laughs. Was he responsible?

We drive for another thirty minutes. It ends after a long incline with wide bends. The tyre tread turns on gravel; the wheels spin with a heavy crunch – brown heavy.

We stop. I don't move. Listen out for instructions. I am told that I can remove the blindfold. We are in front of a large house, classic twentieth-century southern European: geometric, ochre stucco, flat roofs, unadorned balconies and a loggia. A red Audi TT is parked in front of a double garage. The ghoul orders me to wait. The muscle stays in the back; he leans between the front seats and angles the rear-view mirror so he can see himself; he sits back and pulls his hood up. He is just a boy – twenty-two perhaps. He cleans his front teeth with his tongue; the sucking and smacking sound is white. I feel my side; the bruising feels live.

The ghoul comes out of the house and waves me in. I climb out of the car, followed by the muscle. He pushes me forward. At the door the ghoul raps the muscle guy on the back of the head.

The entrance hall is wide, bare – just a small table with keys on it. I am patted down by the ghoul. He is polite, patient, thorough. Legs, arms, armpits, groin, every inch of my chest. My mobile is pulled out of my pocket, checked, turned off, replaced. I stare ahead through an open door into a large open sitting room. The far wall is glass, giving on to a softly lit patio which overlooks a valley – there are distant lights, a dark scored line across the far horizon. Lomazzo – if it is Lomazzo who lives here – isn't around, waiting. When the ghoul is finished I am guided into the sitting room and invited to sit down on one of the two four-seater white leather sofas placed at right angles to each other. They face away from the French windows and are placed opposite a gas fire built into the wall. A big square frame of brass, big flames silently fluttering behind tinted glass. There is a lot of white leather in the room, including an Eames chair and stool placed in the far corner. I am not even sure they come in white leather. Persian rugs cover the terracotta floor. There are no pictures on the walls; there are no books, magazines, newspapers anywhere. Above the fireplace five Samurai swords are mounted. Hanging on the wall opposite there are a number of antique hunting rifles and pistols. The only other object in the room is a two-foot-tall model of the London Eye. There is a cord plugged into the wall. Does it turn? Light up and glow? I am tempted to ask the ghoul. I turn in my seat. Only the muscle is present, leaning in the doorway. The ghoul reappears from another door off the sitting room with a glass of whisky in his hand, a big, heavy square tumbler. He hands it to me without being interested in whether I want it or not. I thank him. I take a small sip and slide the glass on to the table in front of me. What does this place tell me about the man who lives here? What does it add to my internet profile? He's no aesthete. Which is probably a good thing. He's not pretentious. Which might have been useful. The room does tell me that he is inner-directed. Not flash or showy. Despite the white leather. He's unlikely to be a tracksuit, gold and Rolexes gangster. He won't be a silk gangster, either, a man who thinks the finer things in life are symbolized by sheer shirts. I like the glass I've been given. The whisky has structure.

A man I take for Pasquale Lomazzo comes in via the French doors. He is young – mid thirties. He is wearing designer jeans, belted tight, giving him a waist, a shape; a pastel-yellow shirt, sleeves turned back neatly, precisely halfway up his forearms; and bright white Nike trainers, laced with double knots. He has a square, flat face – sharply square, very flat. His features – eyes and mouth – seem cut in, his small nose stuck on. He is not unhandsome, but the squareness and the flatness of his face are disconcerting. His hair is black and very straight, side-parted, with a long fringe falling over his right eye, which he pushes away with the heel of his palm. There is an element of camp to the fall of the fringe and the manner in which it is palmed back, accompanied, as it is, by a little flick of the head. He is holding a glass of whisky in his other hand. He ignores the ghoul and orders the muscle out.

I stand, taking another sip of my whisky. Lomazzo places his glass on the table and offers me his hand.

'I am Pasquale Lomazzo.'

'I'm pleased you have agreed to see me.'

'Please.' He motions for me to retake my seat. We are at right angles to each other, both perched on the edges of the sofas, leaning forward, elbows on knees, hands together. I recognize this mirroring: of positions, of attitudes. It is for trust. For acceptance. Relationship-building. But who is mirroring who? I press a fist into my side. I need to find some way to accommodate the pain while I am seated.

'You are not well?' Lomazzo is immediately looking to take the advantage.

'I am fine.'

'Good. Why are you here?' He remains forward, looking directly at me. His manner is mock intimate, feigning concern: I am clearly mixing him up with someone else – an unfortunate mistake. His fringe rests across his right eyebrow.

I am used to this; I know to just ignore it. 'I have a proposal for you.'

Mock surprise. 'For me?'

I want to smile. Laugh even. This man is very predictable. I relax a little; this takes some of the edge off the pain.

'Don Lomazzo. Please. We both know you are who I think you are. I want to show you respect, but I also do not want to play games.'

Lomazzo's flat square face is immobile. His heavy fringe is beginning to fall across his eyes again. He is not yet ready to respond to this early show of candour. I continue, 'Let me explain. I will start with my situation. I have lost my job; my wife has left me. All this year. And it is only January. It has not been a good year.' I pause, smile wryly. 'I want money to leave my old life behind. Retire with the girl. I have come to you with a way to make the money I need.'

Lomazzo palms away his fringe. 'Men our age don't want to retire.'

I nod. 'Maybe. But I am tired. Very tired.'

'I am a businessman. My work is chestnuts, olive oil. I have a few restaurants and hotels on the coast. I don't understand how I might help you.'

'Last year I met the old man. Don Livi. I was told you protected him when . . .'

Lomazzo interrupts me; his fringe falls forward. 'As I say, you have made a mistake.' He goes to stand.

'Please wait, Don Lomazzo.' I know this is a critical moment; it could all end here. I sense that once Lomazzo has made up his mind there will be little I can do about it. I need to find some way of proving to him that I am serious about a deal and worth hearing out.

'I have come to you because I do not trust Lorenzo Savarese and this deal is not for Cosa Nostra.'

I watch as thoughts pass over his face – tiny muscles registering the names he doesn't want to hear, assessing my analysis; he knows this is about art. He remains seated.

'These are not people I know. Are they in chestnuts?' It's an attempt at mock obtuse. However, we both know that there was a slight narrowing of his eyes at the mention of Savarese, a man his own age, yet at the very top of his organization. I sit forward, mirroring again, and fix my eyes on Lomazzo's. For the first time I feel like I am leading the conversation.

'No, they are not in chestnuts. Let me explain. The girl. She is very senior at the Uffizi. The Uffizi has a vast archive of paintings – worth tens of millions to private collectors. No one sees them. Maybe the odd academic. I can get the paintings out. With my expertise, the girl's, we choose say thirty, forty – worth in total, sell-on price, ten to twelve million euros – more. I'm talking that kind of money with no one even knowing a crime has been committed. After taking my cut, you're left with eight, nine million euros.' I sit back.

Lomazzo doesn't respond immediately; he stays sitting forward, hands loosely clasped.

'I have been to the Uffizi. Long queues.'

I glance over at the fire, the gold and brown

flames shimmying behind the tinted glass – more burnt than burning. Lomazzo doesn't continue. The aroma of whisky is in the air. I notice that there is a chain around his neck, a small crucifix and a tiny Christ. Christ lies at an angle, caught in his chest hair. I feel an impulse to flick it free. Lomazzo moves his hands into the prayer position, fingertips at his lips.

'The girl is in love with you?'

I nod. 'Yes.'

This is considered. 'She is foolish. A position like that. A great institution. Why help you?'

'She is a young woman. Her job is dust and old things.'

'She is not so young – this is why, perhaps.'

We have been watched, studied. 'Perhaps.'

'You retire to Italy?'

'No.'

'London?'

'No. South-East Asia.'

'Where?'

'Malaysia. Build a house on the beach.'

Lomazzo looks unimpressed; it is not a world that interests him. He looks beyond me. 'I have been to London. I went on the London Eye.' He turns to look at his model. 'Have you been on it?'

'No.'

'Why not?'

I am not even sure I've been near it.

'It is very popular.'

'Yes.'

'The queues are longer than the Uffizi.'

'Possibly.'

'I think so. I queued for three hours.'

I sense he is proud of his patience, that his patience is an indicator of value. He stands, crosses to the model, pulls it forward and flicks a switch. The power illuminates the egg-shaped carriages, the wheel, and it begins to turn. There is a low whirring. Lomazzo then moves to the French windows.

'Calabria has no queues for anything.'

I turn in my seat. I can see Lomazzo's reflection in the window – the straight flat face softened and paradoxically given depth by the flat surface of the glass.

'It needs investment.'

He nods at this. He is curiously calm, distracted.

'Your project. Why don't you do it on your own – you become very rich?'

'I am one man. An ex-cop. That makes it difficult. Besides, this needs distribution. USA. Japan. As well as Europe.'

Lomazzo seems satisfied with this as an answer. We have bonded a little over our conversation about the London Eye.

'At which point do you make your money?'

'When the paintings are taken I will make a valuation based on black-market prices. I want ten per cent of this.'

'Before they are sold on?'

We both know this is a foolish expectation.

'There are other ways.'

Lomazzo turns from the window; his reflection recedes into the night. 'Other ways?'

'This is for later.'

'Later? I'd like to know now. I am intrigued now. Your risk is great. When the paintings have been removed, passed on, why pay you anything? I do not think you are serious.'

We are becoming too focused on details, on the structure of the deal. We need to talk principles first.

'I am very serious.'

'Then you know how to overcome this problem?'

I sit back; the ache in my side is increasing, arriving in harder and longer waves, forcing me to twist into a conspicuously contorted position to manage the pain. Lomazzo is clever – saying little, taking the energy out of the conversation, requiring me to work for everything. I need to gain some ground, make Lomazzo think about the deal – what's in it for him. A shift in the dynamic of the room is needed. I drink down the last of my whisky and push myself up from the sofa.

'It has been a pleasure meeting with you, Don Lomazzo. But now I must go. I promised the girl I would be gone only two hours. And I am in pain. I am sure once you have thought about it we will talk again.'

Lomazzo, shirtsleeves neatly folded back, jeans

neatly belted in, trainers blazing white and double-knotted, looks bemusedly at me standing without instruction.

'I am sorry. But I'd like you to stay longer.' There is no need for him to point out that I cannot leave without his permission.

I have lost ground rather than gained it. I look at my watch: over an hour has passed since I left the hotel. I feel my body is weakening. I have hardly eaten in the last twenty-four hours. The last hit of whisky was a mistake. I sit back down. My hands are shaking.

Lomazzo returns to the sofa, smiling, and again perches on the edge of the sofa, his knees almost touching mine. It is time to explain something to me, having established the correct and only dynamic in the room with the candour of his power.

'We are not a backward people. We do not have a Rome, a Florence, a Venice, but our history is long; it is noble. Our language is strong. But we are not respected. The north – they think we're animals. Further south – Sicily – they think they are different altogether. I have been to the Uffizi. For us, your deal is a good one. Yet there are things I don't understand.' He pauses. 'But I think you are hungry.'

I can barely concentrate, the pain seems to have taken me over, yet I know that Lomazzo has revealed his first weakness. He wants the deal because of its prestige: stealing from the Uffizi is penetration of the establishment, and in the wider world of organized crime, among their more international rivals, they will no longer be thought of as unambitious local brigands. This is why I was shown the Caravaggio last year – the old man wanted the world to know who had it.

Lomazzo calls out. The ghoul appears. They speak in deep strong Calabrian. Within a minute bread, olives, a hard cheese, salami are brought in. A bottle of olive oil. There is no cutlery. I am told to eat. Lomazzo waves his hand over the food.

I roll up a slice of salami, pull at it with my teeth, chew slowly. I break the cheese apart, press it into the bread, tug at the crust with my teeth. The flavours are strong and raw. I apologize for my hunger. Lomazzo shrugs, sits back, palming away his fringe, content it seems in watching me eat. I try to relax; I have been in the company of men like this before many times. Senior *mafiosi*. Career killers. Ambitious killers. I have eaten with them, drunk their whisky, their wine. They are not of a kind. There is nothing instantly recognizable in them. They do not give off coldness; they are not visibly brutal. They do not delight in all pain and search for its possibility in all things. My assessment of Lomazzo is that he is a practical killer. Not particularly vicious, or showy, or self-mythologizing. But he is content with its need in his world – its rightness as a legitimate business tool.

He sits up and places his hand on my knee. 'It is good that you eat in my home.'

I swallow. 'You are very generous.'

He removes his hand. 'It is bread, meat, cheese. You bring me masterpieces.'

With this I understand the deal in principle has been accepted. For a moment the ache vanishes. I look up. Engage him directly. 'Not yet.'

Lomazzo pats me on the knee again. 'Soon, I am sure.'

'I hope.'

He checks his precisely rolled shirtsleeves, pulling a little at a fold, to create extra sharpness. 'You know, you are the first policeman in my home.'

I don't bother to correct him – ex-policeman – understanding that for him there is no distinction.

'It is important for you to understand what this means.' He rests back, unfurls his arms along the top of the sofa and crosses his legs.

I finish the food, popping the last olive into my mouth. 'I understand. But it is a good deal. A good plan.' I have to adjust my position – sitting forward to eat has compacted my ribs and hips together, locking them. The stiffness, the aching has returned. 'As I'm sure you've worked out, if it goes wrong, it happens before you are involved.'

Lomazzo nods slowly. 'This is true.' For no apparent reason he looks down towards his chest and, straining to see below his chin, blindly arranges the necklace into a neat V; he holds the tiny crucifix, the tiny Christ, between his thumb and forefinger.

'So when can we expect a first delivery?'

'If things proceed as planned – and I have a guarantee of your good faith – a couple of weeks.'

Lomazzo drops the crucifix into his chest hair and replaces his arm along the top of the sofa, legs crossed.

'A guarantee?'

I concentrate all my energy away from the pain and on to Lomazzo: this moment must be full of confidence, a moment of singularity. I picture the Caravaggio newly restored hanging against a bright white wall.

'Yes. A marker. That I will get my money. It is only fair.'

Lomazzo tenses; his limp hands ball into fists; the muscles in his square flat face spasm. 'You speak of guarantees. Of markers. I don't understand.'

I expected this. He wants to be trusted. He wants to be trusted for many reasons. It is a sign of respect. Perversely it is a sign of legitimization – he is a businessman like any other. He also wants the freedom to break the deal without a thought. And finally, and most likely, he wants me to do the work, deliver the paintings, and then not to honour the deal. It is this fourth reason which will lead to the Caravaggio. However, I need to find a way of taking Lomazzo there without being seen to offend him as a legitimate businessman. In chestnuts and olive oil.

'Don Lomazzo. As I'm sure you appreciate, there is a need to spend money up front. What little money I have is for this. At the moment everything I do is an expense for me. At the same time, this is your world down here. A guarantee is needed that my cut is safe.'

The hands fall limp. 'You come to me with this deal, not the other way round.'

'I understand that. But this is something we must think about.'

Lomazzo is amused. 'You do not need to think. What is it you want?' He stares at me, his eyes searching for any flicker on my face which might tell him what I have in mind. I allow this, confident there is nothing to read. Lomazzo breaks his stare, palms away his fringe. 'My car? Would you like my car?'

I guess it is a joke and laugh. 'As I said, we should think about it.' I look at my watch. 'We don't have to make any decision now. I am late. I must go.' I stand slowly, careful to pick any crumbs from my clothes and brush them from my hands on to the plate.

'Please. Sit.' Lomazzo nods at the vacated place.

I hesitate, bent over and stiff, my side hard, unforgiving, not allowing for any free movement. I feel ridiculous, vulnerable.

'Please. Sit.' The repeat is firmer, Lomazzo's eyes fixed on where he wants me to be.

I do as I am asked. Again. I am losing control of the situation – the pain constantly diverting my attention, my focus, my strength. I don't seem able to produce enough adrenalin to allow me to concentrate on the games being played. I picture Francesca waiting, trusting me, believing that I know what I am doing. How long did I say I'd be, two hours? That's almost up. I didn't anticipate that the deal might be concluded in one session. I imagined I would outline the details, sell it to them, then be sent away for a couple of days while they do their own checking, their own calculations, assess the risk – think themselves halfway to the Caravaggio without me. It would then be up to me to keep sweetening the deal until the Caravaggio was the obvious, the only choice. Lomazzo watches as I press up at my ribs, then down on my hip, looking to create some space for my kidney to breathe, relax, repair.

'Would you like another drink? It might help.'

I shake my head, teeth clenched, jaw tight. The pain is getting steadily worse and I am getting weaker. I need to go. But Lomazzo wants to take advantage of this and make me work harder. The thugs have softened me up and now I am really being tested. A test I would certainly have passed if I'd been in better shape, my energy fired up, mind focused.

'Let me make a phone call first.' I dig inside my jacket pocket for my mobile, flip open the lid and turn it on.

Lomazzo, arms still across the back of the sofa, hands limp, relaxed once again, flicks the fingers of his right hand. 'Please. Wait.'

I place the phone on the table. I am too tired to argue.

'Just a few more questions. Where does the money you have come from? Do you have other partners?'

An easy question. 'The money is stolen.'

Lomazzo is surprised; he smoothes his right eyebrow with the heel of his palm. 'From?'

'A dead man and his wife.'

He nods; I sense the details do not interest him. 'Is anyone looking for this money?'

'No one knows it exists.'

'How much?'

'Fifty thousand euros.'

'Where is it?'

'Some is here, some in Florence, some in London.'

A smile. 'Do not worry. This is a lot of money in Calabria, but not for me.'

I pick up the phone. 'Forgive me, I must call . . .'

'One more question.'

'Yes?'

'Do you love this woman?'

My finger is poised on my phonebook key when I realize I don't even have Francesca's number, a stupid oversight. I flip the phone closed and place it back in my pocket.

'I love my wife.'

'Please answer my question.'

'She is very beautiful, very intelligent, sexy. She is very sweet.'

'But do you love her?'

'For the purposes of the deal the important thing is that she loves me.'

'I am not so sure. Women like to be loved.'

'Then she feels loved.'

'It is important. You must be sure.'

'Don't worry.'

'I am not worried. These are things for you to be concerned with.'

'I am not concerned.'

'Good. In business . . .' he waves his hand behind his head at the window, indicating, I assume, business elsewhere in the world, 'you can insure against risk. But here, in the south, business is less formal. We use different methods. We do not take risks – not outside of our world. To make it clear for you – failure is punished. There is no need for a loss adjuster. It is an effective insurance. With your deal, as you rightly understand, it is you who are taking the risks, and you are also right that in doing so you deserve security – a guarantee you called it – that you will receive what is yours. Which means I must think of a way to make you feel secure. The difficulty here is that to do that, I must take a risk, which as I've explained, is not how we do business.' He pauses, shifts forward on the sofa and places his hand on my shoulder.

'So as you can see, this deal is not as good as you think.'

I stand, slipping away from Lomazzo's hand. 'I will think about what I need.'

Lomazzo sits back, fringe falling forward. 'Please. Sit.'

There is no way to relieve the pain; it's not muscular any more, it is inside my kidney – a malfunction of the organ, affecting my metabolism. Sweat is beginning to creep out of my skin, the back of my neck; my hairline is damp. I ignore Lomazzo, cross to the French windows, press my forehead against the cold glass and close my eyes. I need to think clearly for a moment and get myself out of here. If I was stronger, I'd just insist – close down. Brave out whatever they offer up for being intractable. But I'm not strong. I open my eyes and look out through the window. There are fewer lights on the horizon. The sky is cloudless, high, black. The night feels very warm. However, I don't trust my senses any more; my body is no longer my own. It is a slave to the damage – damage ordered by the man sitting behind me. Damage from a lucky punch. But then it wasn't so lucky – flat hand, fingers extended to the kidneys. A martial arts attack. Maximum damage.

I push myself away from the window. OK. Where are we? Francesca won't panic, so forget her; Lomazzo is hooked, so just hold out. He'll tire soon. I turn back to the centre of the room.

'Don Lomazzo. What do you do on other

466

occasions? I am not the first person to approach you with this kind of deal.'

From behind, Lomazzo's head is sculpted black stone, a marble block, edges severe.

'Please. Sit.'

He refuses to talk unless I am exactly where he wants me. I return to the sofa.

'There are ways. But first, you see, we are not a powerful people. So I have to ask myself: why are you here? It's a question that won't go away.'

'I have told you. I met the old man. He seemed . . . honourable.'

'Yes. But still. There are other people.'

'There are.'

'Who else have you seen?'

I thought I had made it clear: I don't want to go to Savarese and it's not a deal for Cosa Nostra. So he's displaying another weakness. Lomazzo wants this to be his deal, his glory, and not have others – Savarese, Cosa Nostra – saying they were offered it first. This would reflect badly on his status.

'No one.'

There is a nod; he is pleased, satisfied. 'It is important.' He nods again to himself; this is a good rule he has set himself. It is a foolish rule, I think.

'So what will it take to make you feel secure?'

Lomazzo must be led there. It must be his idea.

'That must be your decision. My risk is fifty thousand euros, my cut around one million.'

Lomazzo crosses to the window. 'You must tell me. This is your deal.'

I stand again, this time determined to stay standing. 'As I've said. It must be your decision. I suggest you think about it.'

Lomazzo looks around, amused. 'You suggest I think about it?' For the first time this evening there is impatience in his voice. He palms away his fringe, palm remaining against the side of his head. His thoughts are unclear. He doesn't like this.

I must gauge this perfectly; I can't take another beating.

'Don Lomazzo. I need rest. My pain was caused by one of your men. I have come to you with a good deal. We both know that. Forgive me, but if I go to Savarese, he will not care that you turned it down. He will understand: it is easy money; I am not an amateur.'

Lomazzo rolls his head – a prism turning. My lack of an answer is now irritating him. He doesn't want explanations or ultimatums, his competitors invoked. He wants to be told what I have in mind.

I now accept that the deal, for the most part, will be concluded tonight. He wants clarity and certainty – it is a testament to the attractiveness of the deal I'm offering. I just have to wait until Lomazzo is happy that it will work – it will happen. In the meantime I need to offer him something, tempt him in the right direction; he is not used to being worked, coerced. I remember a similar deal in New York. Some big Brooklyn mob family looking to secure a large amount of heroin from a new importer: the Russian mafia. An important relationship. Both ambitious and murderous. One protecting ground, the other looking to embed themselves in new territory. A middleman was chosen to hold the marker. And what was the marker? No one could believe it. Three violins. Stradivarius. Worth over a million dollars each. Stolen from a bank years before. Thought to have been destroyed. The deal worked like this: if the Americans didn't take the shipment, the Russians got the violins; if the deal was completed, the violins were returned to the Americans. A perfect example, even down to the marker being created by an Italian. I tell the story. Adding myself in. A peripheral figure. Looking to get back the violins. But making it clear – the marker we are looking for might take an act of imagination.

Lomazzo passes me, drops a hand on my shoulder, patting it. 'I understand.'

I am allowed to remain by the window; Lomazzo stands a few feet behind me. Our reflections are so clear that our expressions are each as visible to the other man as if we were standing opposite one another.

I am not sure what Lomazzo has taken from the story. To my right, the London Eye turns slowly. There is something about myself I don't recognize in the window. I ignore the slight rocking of my body, looking to control the pain. It is more than that – more profound. I look light, insubstantial, spectral. As if not entirely present. It has something to do with the simple fact that I can do nothing but wait for Lomazzo to say something decisive and then permit me to go. I have no more to give, and with no more to give there must be less of me. But it's also because for the first time I am beginning to realize this might fail – I am no longer bulked out with certainty. If anything, I am bulked out with pain – the hard transparency of pain – and that is what is giving me this spectral appearance in the reflection of the night-dark glass.

I look at Lomazzo in the window, standing behind me. He is not insubstantial. He is bulked out with power, with certainty. He understands that the man before him is his captive until he says otherwise, until the deal is done – the details finessed to his satisfaction. And in addition I sense, having taken away all my strength, my options, any capacity to operate outside of his sway, he is also full of me. A double man now. And then beyond that there is also his happiness. He likes the deal; it is good for his organization, for others' perceptions of their ambition, their power, their sway.

And it is at this moment I realize: I will never be offered the Caravaggio. It is there to read in Lomazzo's reflection. For him the deal has been done and the Caravaggio has not been offered.

As an option it is as far from his mind as paying my cut up front before even a painting has been stolen.

And I know why. I am an outsider. And no matter what I offer – whatever the brilliance of the deal – the painting is on the inside. I have made a straightforward category error. It was never going to be offered. My plan was madness – hubris. Just like Nenni thinking he could work on the outside, work with me, a man from the outside. This is not a world with two-way traffic. I was never going to be allowed in, not even for a day, an hour. Not for the briefest moment. If it was possible, right now as I turn into a transparency in front of this dark glass, as I sweat and rock back and forth, the Caravaggio would be mine – because the deal is a good one, we are both agreed. But it is a good deal between an outsider and an insider and the structure will be arranged accordingly.

I am shaking. My reflection vibrates. Shivers in the glass. My skin, although covered in sweat, feels dry and papery. My eyes, full of tears – tears of stupidity, absurdity, tears of shame, embarrassment, desperation – cannot see clearly, yet they also feel dry and papery. I am also aware of rage, of anger, but again, dry rage, paper anger. I want to will a reversal, a new beginning, to start again strong, knowing what I know. But my will is little more than a residual hope for a miracle. That Lomazzo will be moved by my foolishness, my broken heart, and give me a second chance, a little time to toughen up and then come for the painting – with real strength, real force, an over-coming certitude. Aspects I do not possess. Not now, maybe not ever. Is my trembling visible? What is Lomazzo thinking watching this – seeing all of me, a rocking back and forth, a dry and papery face, eyes fixed neither inward nor outward but on the absence of action, my inability to do anything but stand here and know that it is over. I hear myself saying, 'This isn't happening, can't be happening.' My voice sounds ridiculous, a pointless yelp inside a small, betraying body.

I hear Lomazzo say something. A quiet voice – a spun echo. I don't understand. He repeats himself.

'You want to go home to the girl?'

I look at him via the window. The pastel shirt is the brightest thing in the room, brighter than the white sofa, brighter than the revolving lights of the London Eye. Do I? Yes.

'I can understand that. You are hurt, scared. She is beautiful.'

I turn. Am I scared? No. I don't know what I feel. I am dizzy. Thin. Light. A vapour. I search for the back of the sofa, to lean; it is too low. 'It was a lucky punch.'

Lomazzo nods his head. Possibly, possibly.

'We do not have violins here. I think you bring us the paintings and then we see. I must explain. It is I that need a guarantee, not you. And for me, it might be the girl. I take her and I know you are coming back. It is very simple: what you want, what you think, is irrelevant to me.'

I go to vomit – a contraction in my stomach, my chest, my throat, retching hard. But there is nothing, dry nothing, just the back of my throat thrown forward, my chest lurching, stomach pulling in, breathlessness. I hold up my hand, signalling: wait, wait, please wait.

Lomazzo is still. Waits.

'OK. I was wrong. Work the deal any way you want. But we leave her out of it.'

I hear a snort, self-satisfied and ringing with ridicule. Lomazzo wanted complete capitulation and he's got it. He approaches me, fringe forward, hanging over his eyes, and places a hand on my shoulder. I tense. But he does nothing, says nothing. No whisper, no punch. He just palms away his fringe and leaves. I hear the French windows slide open, slide shut.

OK – think this through: nothing can be done without Francesca. He knows that. So it was just a threat, a further explanation, display of power – the candour of power. There is no reason to think Lomazzo doesn't still want the deal, and as long as that is the case they won't touch her. The person they don't need is me. If they wanted, they could scare her into working for them. And showing her my dead body would probably do the trick. Is that what is going to happen? I'll be killed in the next hour or so as the most efficient way of getting to her, now that I have made the scam seem so simple, the structure so clear, the profits so attractive. Is the robbery of the Uffizi, the thing I came to Italy to investigate, going to stem from me? I should laugh. But I need to get out of here.

The front door is locked. The French windows are locked. Walking causes white sheets of light to cut across my vision. I try the door off the sitting room. A kitchen. The ghoul is sitting on a stool at a counter, reading a newspaper, a glass of water in his hand. He looks up; his big eyes are tired, bloodshot. He takes a sip of water. There is a gun on the counter. A revolver. He stands and slots it into his belt. He smiles, open-mouthed; his teeth are big and overcrowded.

We go out to the BMW. We are alone. I guess if I were being taken somewhere to be shot or pushed over a ledge into a forest, to the wolves, there would be others. Maybe not. Right now one man could do it. I have no reserves. Not even for self-preservation. I am invited to get into the car by the ghoul; he adjusts the gun in his belt. My body is seizing up. It is a slow manoeuvre. The ghoul waits patiently. Once I am in I rest my head back and close my eyes. I hear – it is a distant soft sound – the ghoul belt up and start the engine. He then taps me on my arm. I open my eyes. The ghoul is dangling the blindfold. Is there any point, I wonder. I take it anyway. I secure it over my eyes with weak fingers. You don't hide your location from a man being taken to his death. But that doesn't concern me; while I'm being taken back to the hotel, I fear Francesca is being taken from it.

11

I am told nothing as the ghoul pulls up by the hotel. Nothing is said as he leans, pulls at the door handle and pushes open the door for me. Despite his features – big eyes, slow lids, olive pallor and teeth-filled mouth – his face doesn't lack kindness. I cannot tell what he knows, what I will find or not find when I go into the room. I have an impulse to confide in him. This was only ever about the Caravaggio. Tell Lomazzo there was never a deal. Sorry. But I say little. What is said is said weakly. The soul in collapse is not talkative. Or polite. And there is still much to be done. If Francesca is waiting for me. To get us out of here. The ghoul waits patiently while I unfold myself from the car. He waits while I climb the few hotel steps. He doesn't pull away, even when I'm inside. How long has he been ordered to remain there?

There is a single light on in reception. Carmine is reading a newspaper. He glances up; his face is impassive, hard. I must look like a junkie, pale, sweating, stumbling. Does he know why I look like this? He will know everything. Has he let them take Francesca? If that's what they wanted. Perspiration builds up on my top lip. I wipe it away with the back of my hand.

The stairs are easier than last night, but I am sicker now. There is a strip of light below the bedroom door. Even if Francesca is in the room, there is no guarantee that she will be alone. Is that why the ghoul is waiting? To drive the thugs home after the deal has been explained to us. To Francesca. I will be beaten again to show her; they understand bruises themselves are not convincing enough. She must see the impact and pain. Will they beat her? Yes, probably. Across her beautiful, playful, bright face. And threaten rape with hands on her, so she experiences just a little of that invasion. I turn the handle of the door. It is not locked.

Francesca is sitting on the end of the bed, hands in her lap. There is no one else in the bedroom. She turns to me, her body twisting, knee coming up on to the bed. She looks pale. The movement of her body reveals she is not alone. Behind her, sitting in one of the armchairs, is Storaro. I am too weak for visible surprise, for rage, to demand explanations.

Francesca stands, the top button of her jeans open, her stomach, full and brown, cradled out. Her hair is pushed back, forced back by constant handling, fretting hands.

Storaro is in one of his pinstriped suits. Has he been told vertical lines will give him the appearance of extra height? As usual the suit is buttoned up, his shirt crisp white, collar open. He is sitting with his hands on his thighs. He has been waiting for me. He has insisted on waiting. It is the attitude of waiting.

So there is a further audience for my defeat, my failure. I will not explain. Let them look, work it out – the transparencies caused by pain should show it all.

I sit on the bed. Where is the big black and chrome Range Rover Vogue? Where is Luca?

Storaro looks uncomfortable. This is a very different country from the north. He understands why he is here but also knows he himself is not understood here. This part of the country is not used to him – his type. Not used to legitimate riches. The demands of this kind of rich. And the attention it expects. He is aware his money will buy him only hard land. He is unprotected by finer things – elegance, luxury, extravagance, solid barricades in the north.

I stare at Francesca. 'Why is he here?'

Her eyes are red. Her brown stomach heaves above her jeans. Was she resting when he arrived? Reading? Learning how to wait? The bed has a single impression on her side. A book is open upturned on the table.

Storaro speaks. 'Do you have the painting?'

I glance over at him. He remains seated,

478

although in expectation his hands have moved from his thighs to his knees. He repeats himself.

The answer – the truth – pulls hard at my stomach, refusing to be spoken, and I buckle up, almost tumbling to the floor. Francesca bends down, a hand on my shoulder, massaging it, and whispers, 'What happened?'

I brush her hand off my shoulder and push at her to step away from me. I need air, space, clear sightlines. Her and him. The door.

'Get me the gun.' My peripheral vision senses Storaro's hands flex at his knees.

Francesca stands over me. She needs to explain. Justify.

Storaro does it for her. 'Francesca called me. She was worried about you. It is sensible she came to me. She could have gone to the police.'

Francesca adds, 'I didn't know what to do.' It is said pleadingly. It doesn't add much.

I watch a bead of sweat fall from my forehead and on to the carpet. A slow, silver, transparent drop. It revolves in the air. It lands dully and becomes a small grey-black spot. I am too weak to stand, to sit up even. I have to speak to the floor.

'What are you doing here, Storaro?'

'To help. I want the painting. But I also want to help.'

I twist my neck, to face him. A small man in my sideways vision sitting patiently in an armchair, hands on knees.

'Fuck you.'

The meaning of my English is not lost. He gets up off the chair and crouches by me, legs apart, elbows on his knees, hands dangling between his thighs. The position is tight, compact. He bounces; his toes flex in soft shoes.

'We had a deal. You came to me. I kept away. It's what you wanted.'

Another deal. Another simple straightforward deal. With Storaro as certain of its viability as Nenni and his vases. I shouldn't make deals; I don't understand people well enough. One push from me and Storaro topples over.

'Francesca?'

She moves in close.

'Help me up. Help me change.'

Storaro bounces up, a boxer in his corner, preparing for the first round, his body, unlike mine, pain-free, vigorous, agile. I watch him as my shirt comes off, peeled down my back, and the full extent of my injury is obvious; the bruising is raised on the skin, purple, red and brown, pink. His jaw tightens and he reaches for one of his hard curls. Francesca works around me, towelling off the sweat. It is all I can do to stand, arms raised like a compliant child. The strain causes me to shake. There is fresh sweat. Francesca drags down my trousers, leaving them around my ankles while she pulls off my shoes, my socks. Storaro is back in the armchair, perched on its edge, hands further over his knees, creeping to his shins – nerves, impatience.

'Do you have the painting?' He just wants to know. His impatience is boring him. The suspense is boring him. Watching me is boring him. My beaten body challenges him. Might his will fail at such punishment? The question bores him. He continues, 'If you do not have the painting, Francesca is coming with me.' He lifts his chin imperiously. 'It will be too dangerous with you.'

Francesca qualifies, 'We're all leaving. Together.'

I am standing in boxer shorts. My right leg twitches despite seeming numb. I press my foot into the carpet to judge the amount of sensation in my leg; I cannot tell what I can feel. Francesca helps me on with a T-shirt, trousers. She guides me back to the bed. I lie back and close my eyes. Francesca pulls on fresh socks; she has to jam on my shoes, the heat of my body causing my feet to swell. How must she feel attending to me like this in front of Storaro? Does she feel humiliated being reduced to my dresser? She is the image of subservience: doing much with limited command. I thank her. Gaze into her eyes, past the redness, into her deep warmth. Is this scene ever played out in her romances? I assume so; they are not usually gender progressive.

Storaro is up again. On to his small feet. He flicks open the button on his suit jacket. He has a round belly. It is pulled in and then hidden with the quick buttoning up of his jacket.

'Daniel, do you have the painting?'

I am aware that I am fighting a new battle.

Solely with myself. The denial of failure. I cannot admit defeat. Not to this man. I cannot watch his face dismiss me and instantly formulate new plans.

'Go home, Storaro, and take Francesca with you.'

To Francesca I say, 'You were right to be scared. It was OK to call. Now you must go.'

Storaro is waiting for an answer, hands thrust into his pockets.

'Pack, Francesca,' I say wearily.

'I'm staying with you.' It is said boldly, crossly even, also with some pride in what we have achieved together.

What *is* that, I wonder. I repeat, 'You're going with Storaro.'

She is now openly cross: too many orders, decisions about her. And crossness fights tears. She makes Storaro's confession for him. 'He doesn't care about you. He doesn't care about me! He just wants the painting.'

Storaro reiterates, 'I just want the painting.' It is beautifully, wondrously straight in his mind.

It is my turn to make myself clear. '*I* just want the painting.'

It is only now that Francesca notices that the top button of her jeans is undone. She breathes in and fastens it up and pulls her T-shirt down, a full stretch, the fabric exposing its weave, its sheen, its elastic limit. She looks at me. Do I mean it, she is thinking, or am I matching Storaro's clarity of desire as the only way I can think to get rid of her.

Storaro speaks, misinterpreting me, thinking my confession means we're still in this together. 'I can get a medical team down within an hour. I can get you money. Anything else you need.'

He is as foolish as me. Medical teams, money, promises of anything. None of it will make any difference.

'Help me up, Storaro.'

He is happy to handle me if it's going to help me focus, prepare for whatever it is I have planned. He pulls at my elbows first, then grabs at my upper arms. He is strong, as I imagined. I lean against him, my whole weight pressing down, my head on his shoulder. I whisper, 'One more day. That's all it will take.'

Francesca steps towards us. 'Don't promise anything, Daniel. You need help.'

I am silent. Storaro is unsure what to do with me. I am too weak to move; I clutch at him, head still resting on his shoulder. He calls to Francesca. She settles me back on to the bed. Can Storaro really believe I will ever be battle-ready again?

'But you must take Francesca with you,' I add. It is a late clause. Unbusinesslike. I watch him pull at his obstinate curls. He knows Francesca is almost as inflexible as himself.

'I'm not leaving you.' She could hardly be more different from the heroines in her novels. She is standing in jeans, T-shirt, Birkenstocks, spectacles, her curls greasy with activity, her hands pressed flat into her pockets. She is attacking this situation like the moving of an awkward piece of furniture; after hours of hard work, it remains something to be solved. Emotion is irrelevant.

Storaro wants only compliance. In business things rush forward with compliance.

I try to sit up. 'Go, Francesca. I'll see you in Florence.'

'No. You need me.'

Nothing is said for a moment. Francesca remains where she is. Storaro looks down at me. He knows she won't leave with him on his instruction. He needs more effort from me, or me to relent and let her stay.

Has the ghoul gone? Can we even leave if she does stay? I glance over at the gun.

'Get me the gun, Storaro.'

He follows my sightline to the attaché case; his opening of the locks has the quick precision of a man who is used to opening up cases like this – a reflexive flick to reveal documents, contracts. He pulls the gun free of its mould of money. It is big in his small hand, an unwieldy weight, an absurd shape in his awkward grip. I motion that he should place it on the bed beside me.

'I could shoot you. You're small but I'm a good shot.' I laugh. I hear Francesca laugh.

Storaro recognizes his vulnerability to guns and bullets. He pulls his fat little stomach in. I like that he's frightened. I reach for the gun. It is not awkward in my hand, despite my weakness and the exertion involved in pointing it straight at this man.

Francesca steps back. I feel like drifting the barrel, the sights, to her – displaying a mad moment. But I rest the gun down. Storaro's stomach pushes out at the button of his jacket.

'The painting is yours, Storaro. Now leave.'

He is a man of fast transitions. His chest swells. The onrush of pleasure. There is a release of boredom, of being in this scruffy room, in this dirty little town, with resistant, contrary people. He sees the painting hanging in his gallery. Himself alone with it. It is a bright image despite the picture's darkness, his own, deeper darkness.

There is no final appeal to Francesca to go with him. His long eyes blink quickly for a few moments, his thoughts calculating what has been said, promised. And other things – my punishment, my gun: things to forget. I sense his mind is fizzing with thought.

We watch him leave, troubled only by the fact that he is leaving behind the unknown and the uncontrollable. A tremor of his body is visible under his tight suit.

I am still on the end of the bed, the hand of one arm flopped in my lap, the other an untrustworthy prop. Francesca, hands still in her pockets, is leaning forward on the balls of her feet. What next? What do we do?

I call her down. To my level. So I am not talking to the floor, my lap.

She kneels, looks up. 'What is it?'

'We have to get out of here.'

'Why?'

'Please, Francesca.'

'Tell me what happened?'

'We've got to leave. They could come for you.'

I'm not sure she hears. Nothing in her expression tells me that she has heard me.

'You need rest.'

'Forget me. They threatened to take you.'

This time she hears. Her curls vibrate with the tiniest shake of her head caused by the slimmest shiver of fear passing through her body. She has taken in the threat and projected it forward, and for a moment she is experiencing fear as a real thing and not as an act of the imagination.

'Please, Francesca. Pack what you need and let's get out of here.'

She is on her knees, rocked back, hand at her mouth – yes, pack, she is thinking. Pack.

I drape my good arm around her waist, pull her to me. Whisper.

'I'll be all right. We just need to get out now.'

It is enough. She breaks away from me, scans the room, and then starts to pull everything – mine, hers – out of the drawers and dump it on the bed. I hear her swipe everything in the bathroom off the shelf and into her washbag.

My mouth is dry. Sticky dry. What does that mean? Fucking Lomazzo. I should have come back for the gun. But then I'd never have got past the hallway, the ghoul. No point thinking I could have shot Lomazzo, rescued the painting Wild West style.

Francesca stops what she's doing for a moment, thinking, then returns to her quick, unfussy, stuffing of everything into the two bags. She leans the painting up against the bed. The attaché case is placed on the bed. Everything we brought with us is assembled – a metre square.

Are they really going to come for her or am I concerned over nothing? Or is this part of what Lomazzo wants, for his influence, his sway to abide even when he's ceased thinking about me and the deal. He wants the Englishman to be broken down further, broken into acts of fear.

What would I do, I wonder, if Francesca had gone with Storaro? I'd go to bed now and sleep, gun next to me. Hope there will be a moment of strength in the morning to get me out of here.

I stand. Francesca helps me on with my over-coat. I place the gun in the right-hand pocket – it is heavy, a full weight. I pick up the attaché case, the larger of the two bags.

'Can you manage the painting, your bag?'

Francesca collects them up, heaving the painting under her arm, gripping it at the bottom of the ornate frame; a little of the gold leaf flakes away. I transfer the attaché case to the hand holding the bag and open the door, wait while Francesca goes ahead of me. The reception is dark. I check outside. The ghoul is gone. There is no sign of the big black and chrome Vogue. Did the ghoul follow Storaro? It's just past midnight. Maybe it was time to do the rounds. Concentrating on core business. Is Lomazzo's *cosca* so small? Just himself, the ghoul, three thugs and a beamer? I hope so.

We dump the stuff in the boot of the car. Francesca climbs in the driver's side; I lower myself in the passenger side.

'Do you know how to get out of the town?'

'What happens if they try to stop us?'

'We don't stop.' I lean back in my seat, almost to full length, pull the gun from my pocket, fix my fingers around the handle, over the trigger, lay it in my lap.

Francesca stares at the gun.

'I could say, don't worry, but we're past that point.'

'Couldn't we just go to the police?'

'What police?'

She starts the engine, pulls away from the hotel and out into the piazza, cutting across and down the street by the bar and towards the church. At the bottom of the street, we turn right, tracing in reverse my slow route from the edge of the town to the hotel two nights ago, when all this started. The town is quiet, dark, empty. The wheels bounce over the cobbles, the engine echoes off the walls, the headlights, on full beam, open up the darkness.

'I'm guessing if they didn't want us to leave, they'd have waited outside the hotel.' It is neither a question nor a statement, just a thought articulated, sent out for input, a different perspective.

Francesca is sitting up straight, body forward, concentrating; she rolls the steering wheel to take a sharp bend, changing down the gears, anticipating an incline. We approach the edge of the town. The road slopes away to a final bend before the crumbling stone houses become hard, ancient land. I am tempted to kill the lights, the engine, and coast down in darkness. If the BMW is waiting, maybe the boys are asleep and we can slip past.

There is no one there. No black mass, sudden lights, sudden roar.

We leave the town behind; Francesca driving cautiously, remembering the subsidence, mudslides, hard-ridging roots. I settle back, adjusting the seat, trying to make as much room for myself as possible. When we hit a main road and I am certain we are heading north, I will climb into the back, try to stretch out.

I turn to Francesca. 'I'm sorry.' Francesca stays front-facing. 'I got it so wrong. So, so wrong.'

She snatches a look at me. 'Tell me later.'

There is nothing more to tell – you either get it right or wrong.

'I'm sorry about Storaro. I didn't tell him to come. He just . . . you were right. He just sat in that chair and said where were you? What had you found out? Did *I* know where the painting was? He said your life wasn't worth sparing if it came to it – you're just a mercenary. Only interested in glory, money. He'd save me. I think he was going a bit mad, just sitting there, talking, imagining all kinds of scenarios in his head. Himself as a kind of hero. He said he'd save me. It was said so calmly, just letting me know.'

I am not really listening. There are headlights in the rear-view mirror. A mile or so back, swooping along the dipping road. They joined us from the left, suddenly. At a junction. Francesca is still speaking.

'He went quiet only moments before you arrived.'

I ask, while concentrating on the two fixed beams, starry and snaking, behind us, 'Was he alone?'

'No, his people went to eat.'

I nod. 'Can you slow down?'

'Why?' Francesca's eyes go to the rear-view mirror. 'Do you think it's them? What do we do?'

'Slow down.'

Francesca eases off the accelerator. The car makes ground. The lights are high. The shape has little speed. Francesca looks across at me. She is waiting for instructions.

'Pull over. And cut the lights.'

'Really?' She wants eye contact with me, to interpret my decision. But my focus stays in the rear-view mirror, following the lights, the black form drawing closer.

'Do it now.'

We are tight to the edge of the road, just past a bend. The following car will not pick anything reflective until the last moment, if at all. In thirty seconds the car passes. High, loud, unsteady over the uneven road. The black and chrome Vogue. Storaro. Were they lost? Are they lost? The big car heaves and humps in the blackness. They didn't see us. We are alone.

'Do we follow them?'

'Wait.'

'Maybe they know the way out of here.'

'No.'

We pull away after a couple of minutes. I don't want Storaro knowing I've failed and am fleeing. Lomazzo has already had that privilege. I turn my face to the window. The ground is dark with the hard silhouettes of olive trees. Old shadows. The night sky is black, a vast scoop of hard black shellac curving to the earth. The horizon seems fixed. I look left, right, ahead. We are in a valley, a wide, dipping plain, hills all around. I can see the car from way up – a wedge of light in front of us, vacuuming the ground.

The sweat building up on my forehead, soaking my eyebrows, dripping down my cheek, forces me to mimic Lomazzo and palm away at the side of my head. It's not enough. I pull up the bottom of my T-shirt and wipe my face.

Francesca turns to me. 'I don't know where we're going. There isn't anything here. Nothing.' This is also neither a statement nor a question, but this time input, extra perspective, is irrelevant – there is only forward.

I watch a hilltop, its peak almost a crescent. If there were decisions to be made, roads to choose from, I'd think: keep that to our left; but there is only forward.

'We'll hit a major road sooner or later.'

'How do you know that?'

'I'm sure all we need to do is get over the hills ahead and then it's the A3 or the coast. Either way, we just turn left.'

'Are you sure?'

I think: no. I return to the window, to the olive trees, the crescent-topped hill, the shellac sky. I rest my head against the glass; it is cold, smooth. I press myself there, against the vibration of the car. I have given everything. Lomazzo, Storaro, getting us out of here. Surges of adrenalin allowing small bursts of movement, thought, planning. But that's it. My brain rocks in my head, my muscles are falling off my bones, my senses only able to take in broad dull heavy stimulus. My head slides forward, half sleep, half delirium. I try to keep my head back, poised on the headrest, but it requires too much effort.

'I need to lie down, Francesca. I'm sorry.'

She stops the car. I push open the door, climb out, hand clasping the roof, levering myself up from the seat. My last effort. I steady myself on the road before folding forward the front seat and tucking my body into the rear of the car. Francesca leans over, pushes the seat forward, pulls the door shut.

'Try to get some rest.'

We set off again. I try to get comfortable, back and bottom on the seat, legs bent to the floor, hands clasped over my stomach. The few breaths of night air have emptied me of sleep. I can roll my eyes back and see the night sky, but I mainly focus on the night inside the car, the red glow of the dash seeping into the back. Sweat rolls down my neck and drops on to the seat. The worst it can be is renal failure, and if that is what is happening to me I'd feel a whole lot worse. But I'm guessing. My instinct tells me it's a minor infection caused by the punch, aggravated by not enough water, too much adrenalin, stress, failure. Antibiotics should be enough. Even just water. I call out.

'When we can we need to stop for water.'

I try to turn on my side, face the back of the seat, legs curled up. I am too tall, falling between front and rear seats; even the other way around – facing forward – I tip between them. There is only my first position. With upwards to stare at. At least it doesn't cause me further pain. Slowly my eyes begin to close. I think of the ghoul. What satisfaction that must be: those big, heavy lids tiredly sliding over those big, bulging eyes. How nice to shut out all that light.

I am aware of travelling, of motion forward, of rocking and jolts upwards. And time – I know sleep is lasting only minutes. And the night. It remains night. I am not being driven into day. My dreams, broken into by waking, are all of Nenni and Maria. They are in a narrow street. Brushing themselves down from death – black grit, petals, ash. There is so much detritus it begins to trap them, forming a cone around their legs, up to their waists. They are stuck. Only able to swivel their upper bodies. They try to reach out to each other. They call out to me, but I am watching them from behind a bright light, a bright orange fizzing light. It is dawn. Nenni and Maria are lying on a street, face down. They look comfortable, as if alone in a big bed, making use of all the space. Maria's hand seeks Nenni's. Their fingers flick when they touch. All else is still. I watch as Maria's hand, high on fingertips, scurries towards me. I want to kick it away. It is too spidery for a hand. My foot hovers, following its scurrying, my arms are wide for balance. I'm going to give it a good stamp. I drive my foot down but it is resisted by an upward stream of air. There is a waking moment – a jolt, and the sky, the red glow of the inside of the car – and then . . . the three of us are sitting on wide steps, elbows on knees, hands clasped, chatting. I am in the middle. Nenni and Maria, relaxed, sometimes leaning back to chat behind me, are sharing a joke. In Neapolitan. I am stressed, wringing my hands, wringing out water, forming a puddle between my feet in which I can see myself – fretting. Just tell them, I say, and wring my hands hard, palms and fingers twisting pink and white. Nenni and Maria are suddenly tiny. Sitting on the edge of the step, swinging their legs, heels tapping the marble. I call down to them, 'Get out of here. Get out of here.' They can't hear me. They curl their hands behind their ears. I try Italian, English. Husband and wife look at one another and laugh. A pantomime laugh: hands on stomachs, rocking back and forth. I want to swipe them off the step. Swipe them into the sharp point of a blowtorch pointing towards them. A single-flame inferno. A sun. A pointed sun. Conical. A dart. Blazing. Aimed at the roof of a building. We are all there. All. Francesca is somewhere, I am sure. And Lorenzo Savarese. I am sitting on the edge, swinging my legs, heels tapping. Nenni and Maria are next to me, standing, hand in hand, barefoot, toes curled over the edge – bodies swaying forward, billowing. I am looking up at them, shielding my eyes from the light. Savarese is close. He has a very long fringe – Lomazzo's fringe – and palms it away, smashing the heel of his palm into his eye. He is furious. Why did I go to Lomazzo? I ignore him and laugh at Nenni and Maria tempting each other to lean further over the edge, using only their feet and toes to keep them upright. I don't see them fall; I am looking at my side, my hand sunk into my flesh, wrist deep. My skin is open like a slash pocket on the side of a jacket. I can draw my hand in and out as I please. As Nenni and Maria hit the street I look over and nod. Savarese also looks over, fringe hanging down to his feet. I reach over to grab it. One pull and he'd be over. My hand disappears into the hard strands of hair. It is not hair, but thin stiff marble threads. Fixed to the roof. Columns. Hundreds of them, but with space enough to slip between if I thin myself, arms wrapping around them and pushing hard. If I have enough left in me, I can find Savarese and kill him.

I wake under washes of light. I grip the top of the rear seats, reach for the top of the passenger seat and lever my body up.

'Where are we?'

'On the *autostrada*.'

'How long have I been asleep?'

'Not long. An hour. How do you feel?'

'I don't know.'

'We're about an hour and a half, maybe two hours, from Naples.'

'Do you want to stop? I think we should.'

'When we get to Naples.'

I lean on the passenger seat; Francesca is settled into her usual driving position.

'You look awful,' she says.

'It's my kidney. I need to drink a lot of water.'

'You look a bit yellow.'

I reach over and flip down the sunshield and look into the vanity mirror. There are too many lights – white, yellow, red – striking my face to tell what colour I am. My skin is pallid, though, pores open, the sweat evident; my eyes are watery and red. It is not the exultant face of success. I am not travelling north to glory, adjusting myself to a new existence, my presence producing awe and projecting back humility. There is nothing. There is the same. Less. If I make it at all. I flip up the sunshield, fall back. My saliva is metallic-tasting and I know that's a sign of something. I swallow. The saliva is like tin in my throat. The back of my tongue is numb. I look at my hands. There is nothing to see. A young man's hands, hair-flecked, solid. They are not evidence of profound disintegration. I am simply sick.

I wake again as the car hits the off-ramp, pulls through a car park and stops outside a motel. The pain I feel is dull, throbbing, coming in waves, but it has somehow disconnected itself from me, as if sleep has distanced it and it needs to be reintegrated with my body before I can actually experience it as pain.

Francesca opens the door, pushes the seat back. I need help to get out, to unfold myself and keep me on my feet. She guides me to the kerb and lowers me down. We do this without instructions, without a single word being spoken. I sense Francesca is finally allowing her fear and exhaustion to hit her, now we are safe, far from the town, in the anonymity of a chain motel. She goes to register.

The car park is empty, flooded with light – the air suffuse with a smoky sodium glow. What does

Francesca think, now we are free? Have the last few hours retained the feeling of unreality she spoke about only a day ago? I hope so. There is no reason for her to experience this directly, beyond the mad notion of being part of a romance, a thriller, which I assume was her real motivation for coming along. I shake my head at the absurdity. The concrete between my feet is split. If I had any power over her memory, I'd like her to remember only our drive to the coast, watching the storms over the hills, over the plains, out at sea. The lightning always veering to the horizon. And the frantic drive back – the elemental roller-coaster of nature. That's it. The rest I hope she forgets or at least regards as part of a dream, a nightmare – an unreality.

She is back, hooking my arm over her shoulder, her arm around my waist. I am not sure I can make five steps alone. My balance feels off. What's that a sign of?

We push through the glass doors. There is a drinks machine by the elevator. Francesca shouts, whispers, I cannot tell: she will come back for water. 'We're on the fourth floor,' she adds. 'No guests and we're on the fourth floor.' The elevator is bright, the mirrors on the walls reflecting the light, further mirrored by steel panels.

'I'm getting you to a doctor in the morning.'

I nod. As a plan there seems no reason to contradict it.

She keeps hold of me, propping me up with her

hip, while she drops the card key into its slot. She then shuffles me through the tight hallway and sits me on the bed.

'I'm going to get water.'

Two beds. A bathroom directly opposite. White tiles. White towels. Water will give me some strength back. Strength not to leave it like this. If I'd thought about it, this was also a thing to do. After I'd recovered . . . but my mind was on other things – the wrong things. It all happened because my mind was on the wrong things. Myself. And the painting.

But first I need to flush out the infection. If only temporarily. For a few hours. A day. For strength and for a little of the pain to be taken away. Water. I've never had good kidneys. Too much strong alcohol always made them ache. My annual physicals always revealed minor infections, remedied by drinking water. So this is not new and I know what to do. A couple of litres to rehydrate, then that again – more, double – to flush out the poison.

Francesca returns with four half-litre bottles. Unscrews one of the caps. Hands it to me. The water is cold, with high sodium content. The first mouthful makes me retch, my dry throat, tight stomach rejecting it. I wait a whole minute before the next sip. The water intensifies the metallic taste in my mouth; it does nothing to rid me of the dryness, my thirst. Francesca is standing over me, hand poised over the next bottle cap. I look up at her and say, 'What must you think?'

She doesn't respond. I sense her thoughts are as distant to her as they are to me. I don't have long-distance relationships, isn't that what she said? The distance between us now is incalculable. What is she thinking? Looking forward to the reality back in Florence, at her job, of dust and old things. Even if she isn't thinking about it, deep down she must wish it. It was probably being wished last night when I disappeared, only a few miles away, only thirty minutes away, playing with gangsters for mythological paintings. Realizing distance isn't only measured in mileage. Travel time. It's measured in the fact of the other, their world making sense, in its totality. Being able to inhabit their world even when not present.

I keep drinking – my stomach now contracting, wanting more. I take a fresh bottle from Francesca, dropping the empty one, hearing the bounce on the tiled floor.

A fresh layer of sweat breaks out. A reaction to the water. My metabolism needing to adjust. I drink on, take the third bottle. No amount of water relieves the dryness, my thirst. I look up at Francesca.

'It's not what you signed up for, is it?'

She has the fourth bottle ready.

'Francesca?'

'I'm here.'

'Please say something.' I search her face. I wonder after all this whether she doesn't look a bit like Sarah.

'I don't know what to say.'

Is that possible? They look alike and I've missed it all this time?

'How are you feeling?'

I think they might have similar eyes – the glint cold, flinty. No, surely Francesca's are warm, with the glint of gold. That's her spark – gold dashed against gold. Sarah's were always more silvery – cool.

Francesca is saying that she just wants to get back, she's tired. Tired.

She looks tired. Unfolding before me. And she wants to sleep folded in – safe. That's true tiredness for you, the unfolding of yourself. Not having the energy to collect yourself up, in bundled arms, to deposit yourself in sleep, where reassembly can take place. She is scared she is past the point where she will ever be whole again, everything folded back in. She will be fine. I have been where she is many times. I am somewhere different, however. I am leaving myself and the folds are disconnecting, separating, leaving a trail behind me.

'You will be fine.'

She takes the fourth bottle from me – empty.

'You look a little better.'

I feel some strength returning. I manage to shuffle back on the bed and sit up. Francesca goes into the bathroom, turns on the shower. She closes the door. I hear her shower, brush her teeth; I hear the toilet flush. I lie down just before she opens the door. Pretend I am sleeping. I hear her

– a reach away – pull down the top sheet of the next bed. The light goes off. I open my eyes. Is she all folded in? Probably. I hope so. She prepared well. My clothes are damp, stiff from sweat. I am not bothered. I look at my watch: 3.45 a.m. exactly. Second hand climbing in springing jerks to the top.

NAPLES

There is the sensation of turning, of my body – a quarter missing – somehow a circle, turning. A sensation of lightness, of being airborne. There is numbness also, beneath my ribs, from ribs to groin, down my left leg. My leg still behaves as I want it to, taking me out of the room to the elevator and to the car, but there is little to feel as I massage it – all the sensation is in my fingers. Every few steps, I need a wall to stop and rest against. And I need the gun to be in my right pocket for balance. Adjustments, considerations, must be made. But I am working. Functioning well enough. I feel myself curling my toes as I walk; I am not sure why. I don't like the sweat on my body, dried, stiffening my skin. I would like to be clean, but cleaning up, showering, would have disturbed Francesca, curled up, folded in, her thumb in her mouth. How many nights have I seen her sleep and not seen that? She must be scared. Thinking to herself: when will this all end? When will I get home? Saying to herself: all I want to do is get home. To her cosy apartment – real fire, warm shadows, big bed. And Storaro. A man she knows. Knows and can anticipate. Exercising his power, his limited love. An abundance of presence. Not like me – a man thinning out. Whose edges are now sketchy. Disappearing.

The dawn is brown. The drive is simple. I sit like Francesca, more slumped, less energetically, less elegantly, but still like her, wedged in the corner, with one hand on the steering wheel, the other – a full extension of my arm – resting lightly on the gear stick. I can't see in the rear-view mirror. The gun is on the passenger seat; streetlights run along the barrel. I am not thinking about its purpose, my purpose. My mind is too concentrated on the road, the gear shifts, the brown dawn revealing Naples, the rain, its slow fall dropping on the dark road, a blur beyond the windscreen. And getting there. I am concentrating on getting there.

I am turning again, in my seat, my body pulling upward, the numbness a lightness, yet there is a weight keeping me earthbound, but not from turning. There are two parts of me: one dead, turning, one heading forward.

There are two parts of my mind. And a third – a narrow blank between desire and sadness, the other two parts. I feel if I flick out my tongue a tear will be gathered up from my cheek – it is this that proves the sadness. As for the desperation, it is my dull fingers drumming on the steering wheel, eyes shunting left and right, determined to make the quickest time, to be there in the quickest time.

Naples is brown. In the dawn. My twin mind. It must be good not to be a grey city, ever. To be bright, to be dark, to be blue, to be brown.

The barrel of this gun, its handle, are black. One part of me is black. The other is pushing forward. What is the colour of movement? Is that green?

The traffic is light, fast; I have to make decisions, light and fast like the traffic.

I do not want to do this bent over, desperate and sad. I must be straight and integrated. There are momentary visions. I expect it to happen in a doorway. To happen fast and for there to be calm and panic, and white noise, low, high, soundless even – the sound of sound at the height of the mind.

And then the saying of dead names, married names: Italo and Maria Nenni. It is their deaths for which you are dying. I can be bent over for that part. The whisper. I can show my vulnerability then – what it has cost me. After which Savarese will stir. And with an upward reach of his arm, a holding-out of his hand, he will pull me down to hear what I am whispering – it's important to know why he is dying. But then I am neither pulled down nor pushed back, only entered into. A blade – making space inside of me, a place of division, desperation, sadness. The two sides of dying.

I see this happening in the heavy shadows of the black walls in the brown light of a long, long dawn, in an old Naples.

I met Savarese two years ago. In a doorway. Passing by. We were introduced. I was a man doing a deal with his people. He was polite, diplomatic, politic. In jeans, a navy T-shirt, with flip-flops on his feet – youthful, handsome, casual. His face was a little fleshy, but with strong big bones. His eyes looked elsewhere, to decisions, appointments, power.

I leave the car off Piazza Garibaldi, a man in an overcoat, a lame leg, a heavy object clutched in his pocket. You see the body first, nothing second. The handsome face is missed. With the shuffle of a classic cripple, a dragged limb, leading by the shoulder, you expect a distorted face, crooked mouth and desperate eyes.

I draw in air. It is damp, clings to my throat. I have to pull it down hard into my lungs. My chest tightens. I feel better for fresh, morning air, for its glittering inside of me. My thoughts become sharper. I pull myself straighter. I am going to kill a man, and I am going to do it because it will make me stronger and understand better this world, and it means next time I won't fail, won't make such a foolish mistake – I won't be on the outside, not after killing Lorenzo Savarese. I stop, arm reaching for a black wall. No, that's not why I am going to do this. It's because there is nothing left to do but make right the deaths of Nenni and his wife, deaths that could have been avoided if only I hadn't been thinking about myself, the grand plan – the Caravaggio.

I remain where I am, squinting, eyes inward, assessing. I'm killing Savarese because . . . The reason is there. I look further inward. Because he . . . I nod my head. *Think*. Because . . .

I don't know why, not really. I need to rest and think it through.

I am on the edge of Forcella. The dark edge of the heart of the city. Empty at this hour. Political posters, pop posters, cheap advertising ripped off black railings. Cigarettes, gum, smudged between paving stones. Syringes line the gutter.

I slump slowly, a dead weight, on to a stone step, a shallow step, exposed to the street. I rest my head against the black brick, the iron door. Dawn is almost gone; it is now about my feet, a darkness different from shadow – smoky.

Kill Savarese. Shoot him. I've got a gun, bullets – my right hand is good and steady. I want to. Want a showdown. Bang, bang – you're dead. 'Wanna know why?'

But it is this that defeats me.

I push myself up, head further into Forcella, towards Via San Gennaro. I feel half of my body has disappeared and it is now just an absence under my overcoat. It's disconcerting and I hit the left side of my chest – there is nothing there, although my fist is repelled. The metallic taste is back. It is as though my tongue, the inside of my mouth, my throat, have all been plated with mercury – everything is slippery, smooth, numb. I grab at the handle of the gun – I can still feel it and grip it well.

There are images of Francesca's apartment. Of lounging around in front of the small fire in the big stone hearth. I tense when I see this, when I see myself recovering from all this. Francesca at work, fending off Storaro until he gets used to . . . me and her. The days are long.

I move on. Air in my lungs, my body turning, with every step a new reach to the wall. I am slowing down. Francesca will be awake and . . . I don't know: heading home. Calling Storaro. Telling him the story in full. Bursting full of detail. Rightfully leaving me behind. There are two images: the top button of her jeans open, her full brown stomach cradled, and her thumb in her mouth. Sarah.

Sarah. Look at me. At me now. The look of me.

It is time to sit down again. I need to find somewhere to rest for longer than a moment. I scan the street. Eyes running along the floor, halting, moving on, thinking to myself: just a place with shadow. To sit. And take stock.

All the doors give directly on to the street. I make my way, hand never leaving the wall, to the next street. The first Vespas are out and alive, curling their quickest way along the empty streets – the racing line – not expecting to meet a man moving so slowly. Every street takes all my energy, every street reduces me further.

I think: taking the life of a man is not going to make me well. There will be no transference of strength.

I find a deep step – a long step disappearing, with corners of true darkness. A place to be invisible. I slide down the wall, into the dark, pull the gun from my pocket and lay it in my lap.

The gun is heavy, pushing my legs apart, settling between them – metal, cloth, stone. It is a weight, inert, holding me down. I rock my head to the side, to the wall, to rest it. I look down at the gun, the dense shape sitting between my splayed, useless legs.

I have an image of myself in this corner, slumped. It is at the back of my eyes. I can see it as if I am looking in, searching my own eyes. For the image. It's there, I know. I know because I am in this corner, slumped. But I can't quite make it out.

If my body is two halves, my mind also two, then I am now fully two. One sitting, eyes open, one kneeling, staring in. I feel sure I am both men. Something tells me, at this point, two of me is possible. I nod. The sitting man nods. The kneeling man is looking in, concentrating on finding himself in the backs of the eyes of the sitting man. There is nothing.

The sun is high – a blazing white disc. A tall cypress sways. The very tip sways. A green tuning fork. The painting has been unrolled on the hard dusty ground, for a moment buoyed up on dust dispersing. There is a table and chairs. A car. But I am alone. The painting's cracks, the webs of cracks and fissures, are gone. It is now dark, glistening. Freshly painted perhaps. I kneel over it, the entire work in the backs of my eyes. I dab a finger into the paint.

I wish I could stand – here, there; doorway, hilltop; the sitting one, the kneeling one. But I know it's no good. My weakness is one, less than one. It is a point at the centre of me. There is now another image in the backs of the eyes of the sitting man. It is of a man in a corner, dying.

I summon the last of my strength and lift my hand. I stretch out my index finger, extend my thumb. A hand as the shape of a gun. No need to mime. I have the real thing here. Ready to shoot a man. But I cannot think why. Oh, yes. The reason – that funny man and his wife. Killed by him. Jinxing the whole thing from that moment. Reason enough. I stare at my hand in the shape of a gun. I could kill him. Making this the real thing. It's no good. A hand in the shape of a gun is not for killing. I curl the stretched finger over my nose and turn my extended thumb into my mouth. This is what it's for. A long while since I've done this. I am certain it is not an image. If I searched the backs of my eyes, there would not be two of me sucking two thumbs.

The sensation is too singular. As is the clarity of my last thought: Believe me when I tell you, maestro, please believe me. It was never for the glory. It was always for love.

ACKNOWLEDGEMENTS

This novel was written during the first two years of the life of my twins, Wilder and Macleod. It should perhaps be dedicated to them, but in my view it is too dark a work to be connected with such loveliness. Even so, their presence may be felt in the one too many references to the need for sleep.

Many people have supported me through the writing of this book, so here is a list: all at BLINC (for my two sabbaticals); Jim Poyser (for the Calabrian road trip! and being the strongest of readers); Simon Trewin and Sarah Ballard at PFD (for the long view); Luke Meddings (my *consigliere*); Keith Baverstock (the indefatigable Naples connection); Valarie Smith and Brian Libby (my mavens of Portland); Mum, Dad (love); Thomas Harding (a tireless friend is a rare thing indeed); Richard Macauley (for being the acutest of readers of *BIN*); Paul Tyrrell (for the title – extra thanks for that); Neil Marengo (suits by Mark Stephen Marengo); Emma Horton (copy-editing is a bright art); Tessa Balshaw-Jones (for help with the Italian); Leo Hollis (for energy and selflessness); Kate Barker at Viking (for her inimitable candour); and WS and SB (for their quiet guidance across the waters of influence).